SNAFU:
HOLY WAR

SNAFU
** HOLY WAR **

Edited by Amanda J Spedding & Geoff Brown

COHESION PRESS

Cohesion Press
Mayday Hills Lunatic Asylum
Beechworth, Australia
2021

SNAFU: HOLY WAR

Amanda J Spedding & Geoff Brown (eds)

Cohesion Press
Mayday Hills Lunatic Asylum
Beechworth, Australia
www.cohesionpress.com

Also From Cohesion Press

SNAFU: An Anthology of Military Horror
– eds Geoff Brown & Amanda J Spedding

SNAFU: Wolves at the Door
– eds Geoff Brown & Amanda J Spedding

SNAFU: Survival of the Fittest
– eds Geoff Brown & Amanda J Spedding

SNAFU: Hunters
– eds Amanda J Spedding & Geoff Brown

SNAFU: Future Warfare
– eds Amanda J Spedding & Geoff Brown

SNAFU: Unnatural Selection
– eds Amanda J Spedding & Geoff Brown

SNAFU: Black Ops
– eds Amanda J Spedding & Geoff Brown

SNAFU: Resurrection
– eds Amanda J Spedding, Matthew Summers & Geoff Brown

SNAFU: Last Stand
– eds Amanda J Spedding, Matthew Summers & Geoff Brown

SNAFU: Medivac
– eds Amanda J Spedding & Geoff Brown

Love, Death and Robots: The Official Anthology Vol 1
– eds Amanda J Spedding & Geoff Brown

Publisher's Note:

This book is a collection of stories from writers all over the world.

For authenticity and voice, we have kept the style of English native to each author's location, so some stories will be in UK English, and others in US English.

We have, however, changed dashes and dialogue marks to our standard format for ease of understanding.

* * *

This book is a work of fiction.

All people, places, events, zombies, virus-ridden infected, various other creatures, and situations are the product of the authors' imaginations.

Except Satan. He's out there, watching you.

And he's proud.

Any resemblance to actual persons, living, dead, or in between, is purely coincidental.

CONTENTS

Operation Joyrider

Russ Linton

I enlisted the day after my refrigerator tried to murder me. A twenty-year-old smart appliance, one of the last to use freon, the invisible leak produced a headache, mild nausea. Doctors said if I'd stayed in my apartment any longer, permanent damage would've been done.

It's an inefficient way to kill. Unless your central air malfunctions at the exact same time. Even then, you end up with a low casualty rate. But our adversary always looked at the bigger picture. A fraction of a percent of millions meant thousands dead. While they slept. No fighting back.

I chose to fight.

I spent three tours on the front line where we constantly lost ground to the unending assault. Things, we called them. As in, The Internet Of. Conveniences and luxuries weaponized. Sounded ludicrous until you were pinned down under an overpass by Kamikaze drones and vehicles, your own wheeled and tracked support compromised, grinding your men into the pavement.

I wanted to go deep. Find the black hats behind this and make them pay. That's why I requested STA, the sharp edge of the sword.

When they asked for volunteers to penetrate enemy territory and uncover the source of a mysterious signal, I was first in line. Our battalion commander felt sure the signal marked an operations center for these hardware jockeys. No more hiding behind their toys.

Estimates of enemy manpower worldwide numbered only in the hundreds. Fucking hilarious that's all it took for absolute control of global networks. A pimply LAN party playing God, their hijacked hardware offering an unimaginable force multiplier. Dropping even half a dozen of these anarchist hackers would be a major victory. Maybe our first.

I'd settle for looking just one man in the eyes before pulling the trigger.

Insertion took place at an observation post outside Dallas. Warm ash still drifted onto the jagged remains of skyscrapers. Brass had ordered a tactical strike as much for the EMP as the accompanying devastation.

"You got twenty-four hours before they re-establish perimeter defenses," the post CO told me. "Go kill those basement troll motherfuckers for all of us."

"Hoo-rah!"

My three-person team made the trek double time. We didn't bother with the radiation pills. Skipped the fallout briefing. Levels of exposure weren't survivable.

It was a blustery winter day in the Dallas suburb. Affluent neighborhoods like this became kill zones after the war erupted. Refugees from inner cities spread outward, only to find nowhere to hide among the smart homes and driverless vehicles. No country had been spared.

Specialist Whitehat, our field tech, crouched behind a brick subdivision entrance marker with me. She had a name, all the techs did, usually some unpronounceable spew of symbols and numbers. Because of that, we called them by their function. You'd only ever have one assigned to a mission because the corps couldn't spare them. For a one-way op like this, we'd been assigned a recruit fresh out of her shower shoes.

My final team member though was no recruit. Master Sergeant Eve Latimer. Nerves of steel. Like a high-tension cable frayed into splintery, dangerous bristles. We went way back to the LA massacre, the only two from the Thundering Third to survive.

She broke into a run to cross from the opposite side of the four-lane street. Texas made its roads broad. Speed traps, we called them. All the empty space offered deceptively clear sight-lines, but you never knew when a joyrider would whisper off a side street and come gunning for you.

Our LIDAR camo became its own joke too. A concrete gray patterned with reflective foil – the potato suits got you baked as often as they saved your ass. Convertible on the go, they came in handy. Like when the whir of an incoming drone split the air.

Damn suburbs. Every house had a delivery drone, surveillance cameras, smart everything down to their mailboxes. Had a buddy lose a hand to one of those.

Still shuffling across the street to join us, Latimer hadn't yet heard the whipping blades.

"Latimer!" I hissed "Go speed bump! Speed bump!"

She'd only just cleared the median. Nowhere to hide, she ate pavement and pulled the ripcord on her cammies. LIDAR reflective strips reversed. She became one with the gray concrete. Whitehat and I took cover behind the brick barrier.

The drone buzzed into view. I risked a peek.

Second-generation 'Zon EverWatch. An indoor unit, the resolution and fixed aperture offered a limited view from the perch. Human eyes on the outgoing feed could pick Latimer out, but Cyber Command assured us our manpower-light adversary relied heavily on algos to filter out the noise from their endless armada.

I silently fitted a dinner plate on my modular EM service weapon just in case. Backup? Short barrel loaded with birdshot. But we didn't need that level of noise.

The EM service weapon was an interchangeable sidearm that served a multifunction role. The dinner plate converted the electromagnetic pulse railgun into a microwave tech disabler and crowd dispersal tool. Fed by obsolete NiCads, you never got more than a dozen shots per charge pack, but you could fry a forty-degree arc of circuit boards at a hundred yards.

Sometimes that was enough.

The drone slowed to a hover.

Better be enough today.

I fired. With a slight buzz, the invisible wave lashed out and the drone went silent, rotors dead. It dropped from the sky with the harmless clatter of a discarded toy. A faint whiff of an electrical fire rode the breeze. Thing One scrapped.

Heart pounding, I called to Latimer. "Move! Move!"

Springing to her feet, she tore up the pavement as the LIDAR streamers on her ghillie suit unfurled.

Whitehat cursed, her gear jangling, deadened by the sound-absorbing flaps and pouches strewn across the combat webbing. She removed her tactical tablet and started up a passive scanner, checking for any trace of an emergency beacon from the downed drone.

"Clear, no alarm," she said. "Clear," she repeated, mostly for herself.

Techs had so much gear they often went unarmed in the conventional sense. Entire torso strung with legacy inputs and devices of all shapes and sizes, her weapons became whatever of the enemy's we could own on the battlefield.

Latimer mounted the curb and hip-rolled over the low brick barrier. She stayed crouched, planted on her ass, and scooted her back against the solid wall. Panting, she scanned the sky.

"We've got a wakeup call. Half a click east." Whitehat killed the scanner and buttoned the tablet into a pouch. "But no alarm broadcast," she said again as if she had to convince me she'd given the right reading earlier. I hoped she wasn't losing her edge. "They must've detected the drone going offline."

We kept low. Quiet. A dark sedan prowled noiselessly onto the street, the creepy roll of a drive-by. At least Texas was big on tinted windows. Better than seeing what wasn't behind the wheel.

Noiseless. Predatory. Just the barely audible crackle of the poly tires sticking to the road. We'd all seen the view through a joyrider's eyes during basic. LIDAR scans created simple, striated images. No real detail, but they painted distinct objects with clarity, separating them from any background confusion. A lifetime ago the flawless identification of pedestrians had been a safety measure.

We could fool them with the baked potato cammies. But too many owners had chosen premium packages with supplemental cameras and even audio. Countermeasures for a world under constant surveillance. An arm's race. One we'd lost.

The sedan crawled up to the crashed drone. Electric motors whined to a stop. The dinner plate wasn't a guaranteed kill against an EV. Circuitry was always buried under the metal hood and behind the firewall. But at least Latimer had her EM weapon ready to toss slugs.

We knew almost nothing about the enemy. So little, we didn't even understand why they'd started World War IoT to begin with. What would a hacker be looking for in the wreckage? Would they label this crash a glitch or the result of enemy action?

Whitehat was curious too. Too damn curious. She'd about given up our position peering over the wall. I wanted to yank her down. Instead, I settled on trying to burn a hole through her cheek with a disapproving stare. She finally crept lower, her gaze distant.

I peeked. Sedan still sat there. Powered down. Posted as a sentry? Whitehat inched her tablet from her pouch and flicked it on, then off. Quick enough to read, not long enough to emit a lasting power signature. Her eyes widened.

Her hands made quick motions, fingers twirling for rotors. Four drones. Incoming.

I signaled to hold position. The brick wall offered good cover. Above, a tattered canopy of untrimmed shrubs and trees concealed us. Best we could do.

The drones arrived in formation, a good sign. The enemy flew in chaotic murmurations like birds or schools of fish when entering battle. They did it for the same reason animals do – to provide a less predictable target. This meant the operators must've felt the area to be secure.

But why even respond to one downed drone?

We watched the formation hover then lower gradually toward the street. The sedan sparked to life and crept back almost with the front bumper bowed low. With an orchestrated movement that had to be pre-programmed, the drones converged on the fallen, their skids interlocking beneath the props of their shattered comrade. Gently, they rose and glided off down the street. The sedan's lights flicked on, and it followed.

"What the fuck?" I said.

Whitehat, our field expert, shook her head. I raised my eyebrows at Latimer. She shrugged.

"How much farther to the signal?" I asked Whitehat.

"Four clicks. West." She pointed after the departed procession.

With enemy leadership in the area, maybe they wanted to get their hands on the drone and sift through the remains. That put a timer on our op. Get there too late and we'd already be exposed.

"Let's move."

Infiltration went slow. Methodical. Dodging surveillance tech was an artform and I let Whitehat paint with exacting strokes. Residential areas presented minefields of hidden danger while commercial zones bristled with overt and covert devices. To get this deep, we'd downed a transformer on the edge of the tech-free nuke site but couldn't keep that up without telegraphing our destination. So we crawled and sprinted from corner to corner, always taking our cue from Whitehat's signals.

She tapped wirelessly into local cameras and found the blind spots. Nobody'd mapped this sector before, and all previous municipal and private records had been lost in the first wave. Ours was a real time game of cat and mouse.

But the deeper we went, the more goddamn cats.

I hate cats.

As we closed on the target area, joyrides increased. The streets approached something like once normal civilian traffic. An eerie haunting. A past undone never to be made whole. Those cars trolled past, empty. Drones formed a stream above. All seemed to be headed in the same direction.

We took a breather in an alley behind a supermarket.

"Sitrep, Whitehat."

"Activity across the spectrum. Drowning out the original signal but I can still see the flow. They're all moving up nice and orderly. A defrag right on the mission objective."

Defrag. A concentration. To fulfill our mission, we'd have to walk into a shitstorm.

"We go," I said.

Latimer bit her lip, finger tapping on her weapon in anticipation. Her eyes slid briefly from the building's corner where she'd posted. She'd volunteered, just like Whitehat and I. She knew the risks. And like me, she couldn't shake what went down in LA.

"We'll need transport."

Whitehat gave a curt nod, gaze still buried in the cascading data on her tactical tablet. She swiped the surface and her fingers raced, eyes flitted. I focused on our opposite flank. Moments later, a joyride rounded the alley entrance.

I flashed Whitehat a look for confirmation. The optical implant in her left eye reflected a HUD across her iris with tiny but crisp red lines. She was tightening up her gear and watching the white sedan for any sign of compromise but seemed distracted. I kept my weapon trained. Dinner plate stowed, I'd need a clean shot through the brain buried in the dash. It cruised to a stop five meters shy and the doors popped open.

"Mount up," I said. "Whitehat, trunk. Autopilot on that signal."

Trunk would be the safest place. If necessary, she could use the hacked LIDAR to navigate manually. Latimer and I rode in the backseat, hunched close to the floorboard. More exposed, we could at least offer cover fire if the need arose.

The doors locked. Latimer and I winced at the innocuous click. Belly of the beast, we'd seen men die as their transports plunged off overpasses.

The sky scrolled past through the upper portion of the windows. The stream of drones became a river, dark and foreboding. Their blades buzzed intense enough to vibrate the polymer trim inside.

I cut imaginary firing arcs through the enemy ranks along a microwave pulse's trajectory. You could punch holes only to see them filled in by the horde. I'd seen this in LA. We both had. Sweat trickled down my brow. Climate controls would stay off to not draw unnecessary attention. Whitehat had it worse in the trunk. Winter in Texas never truly got cold, especially after Retribution Day when irradiated soil churned into Earth's atmosphere by the metric tons.

Los Angeles. We could've used a nuke that day. Should've. But that was before we knew how desperate we'd be.

I kept my breathing in check. Reminded myself, again, I'd volunteered for this. Any minute, I'd get to splatter some pasty hacker across his monitor. But you could never prepare for the tingling thrum of a drone armada against your skin. So dense, opening the door would flood our cramped space like we'd plunged into a river.

I kept my eyes up and hoped Latimer did the same. She couldn't see me soaked through with sweat. I didn't want to see her fear. I wanted to know she was flawless, error-free. Watching my back like we'd been trained. Dying if, no, *when* the mission demanded.

Tops of cars sliced across our abbreviated view. On occasion, a truck or a bus would glide by and I'd instinctively coil deeper behind the front seat. Cameras mounted closer to the road, they couldn't see in, but the towering presence convinced your brain otherwise. Behemoths strolling by a crawlspace where the roaches hid.

Buildings and the occasional stripped and twisted tree slipped past too. The EV stopped. It signaled as its programming required. We made a sharp turn and the car lurched over a hump. Skies stayed speckled with drones. Headlights and taillights faced us broadside in tight quarters. We'd entered a parking lot. I sank deeper below the lip of the window.

A warning flashed on the dash. Whitehat had gone into manual mode.

I backhanded Latimer and she gave a tight glance; the same fear bottled in her, ready to be channeled into the violence where she excelled. I tapped the dinner plate on my belt. She nodded and fixed hers in place.

We drifted through the lot, surrounded. Get made now and we'd be crushed. Penned in. Whitehat was trolling for a defensible spot. One where we could dismount without being seen. I wondered if any such place existed.

A building loomed in the passenger window. Brick, nondescript, the area had the look of the back of a convention center, or maybe the offices of a stadium. We edged closer, slowing to a crawl as we passed under a wall-mounted camera. No windows, but a door tracked slowly into view.

The dash flickered again. A text appeared. "Security feed looped. Bail on passenger side. On 5..."

Whitehat. She'd found us a way in and set the EV to return to normal programming. The transition would need to be seamless. I signaled Latimer on the passenger side and motioned toward the door.

She popped the handle, EV still rolling. I motioned again when she hesitated and crowded her to show I meant now. She had no choice but to squeeze out the narrow gap, headfirst. Her foot caught the partially open door and I seized the handle before it could bounce off the building.

We'd dropped to little more than an idle but the short distance to the wall made for a challenge. Whitehat must've had her reasons with all the bogeys up top. More room to setup with Latimer out, I could at least go boots first. Once my feet touched concrete, I let the car's momentum eject me slowly, like a well-placed turd, my fingertips closing the door as I slid to the ground careful not to get caught under the back tire.

Our rookie tech slipped from the barely open trunk and rolled. She made a last grab to swing the heavy lid closed, but it bounced and stayed ajar. I watched it jiggle as the car drove off and hoped that wouldn't be what gave us away.

Latimer and I kept our nose to the concrete while Whitehat hustled to the door. She tested the handle. When it gave, I sprang to my feet and joined her. She cracked the service entrance open, and we went inside guns first.

No lights. I flipped down my night vision specs. In my peripheral, Whitehat's left eye glowed green, and Latimer stepped through the closing doorway, weapon raised. I almost breathed a sigh of relief at the tight quarters we'd entered but I knew better. The service hallway gave a false sense of security. I dropped to one knee against the wall. Latimer followed suit opposite and darkness descended as Whitehat guided the door to a quiet close.

The tech's tablet glowed briefly then extinguished as she changed the viewing mode. I could hear my heartbeat and the tips of her gloveless fingers tracking against the screen. My eyes remained downrange. Ahead was a cinder block constructed hallway with a T at one end.

We'd found the perfect entry point. With their leadership here, they'd have surely lit the place up. Lights off meant they didn't use this corridor often. Even hackers needed to see.

Whitehat leaned close and whispered. "No activity. No lights. No cameras. Only the rogue transmission."

Made no sense. Hackers might get by with no lights but they'd at least have their gear running.

"A trap?" Latimer hissed.

I shook my head. Overkill to lure a recon team. Could be a trap for a larger force, but the enemy hadn't concentrated their units like this since we showed them we had the balls to toss warheads at ourselves.

Made no sense... unless... unless we'd arrived first.

I signaled Latimer to move up and covered her as she checked the corner. The all-clear sign came quick.

"Monitor all freqs," I told Whitehat. "A chirp and you let me know. Let's go."

Whitehat sifted through her gear as she fell in behind Latimer. Service corridors offered a maze for us to clear. Trust your tech with their life, so the saying went. From the protected middle, she guided us toward the signal's source.

By the looks of it, she didn't have much work. Empty security camera mounts hugged the ceilings. Even the light fixtures had been ripped open, wires dangling.

I advanced the team swiftly. Left closed rooms uncleared.

I wanted eyes on the signal source. Wanted to set my own trap and drive the sword deep.

The service hall broadened. One end ran to a loading dock, the other, steel double doors. I pulled the team in close.

"Any ideas?"

Latimer scanned the hall. "I should check the dock. See if there's a sign they're here." I gave her the go-ahead and she slipped away.

"Whites?"

The tech's eyes hadn't left her tablet. "I got our signal on the other side of those doors. Every ounce of power in this structure has been diverted to it."

I examined the seams of the door. No light filtered from beyond. "What do you make of this?"

"A test, maybe. A new system to rally big numbers. Strange if so."

"Explain."

Latimer had crept to the far end. I watched her check corners. She knifed the air with her palm. Nothing.

"Makes no rational sense," Whitehat continued. "A signal like this creates a vulnerability. Their current dispersed hive methods work better."

"Right. A mistake then?" I asked. "They finally slipped up?"

"Could be. We could maybe hunker down and call in an EMP drop. Might set them back a few weeks in this zone."

I shook my head. She was being too cautious. Too convinced we could walk away. "No. The leadership, that's who we're after. Any indication they're near?"

Whitehat paused. "Can't say. But the incoming IoTs aren't stopping." She flipped the tablet toward me.

I could read the output, but not handle the coding as deftly. Her display was divided into signals of varying strengths. From those, she'd isolated the drone and joyrider freqs, both military and civilian hardware. They continued to scroll in the corner.

"How many?"

"Ten thousand, give or take."

Damn. This was LA all over again. Hopeful scenario, gone.

Latimer rejoined us. "No vehicles, no supplies in the dock. The liftgate and the building fuse box have been scavenged. Maybe looters hit this place on Day Zero?" She caught my expression. "What's wrong?"

"Too many incoming," I said.

Her eyes widened in recognition. "We call in a strike then," she said eagerly.

"We need to find the signal and get comfortable here. Through those doors. On me."

They traded glances. Latimer rode the edge of her adrenaline, nerves fraying more. She looked ready to be vaporized to end the jitters dredged up from a lost battle. Our tech appeared distracted by the possibility of walking away. They fell into line as we approached the double doors.

Unlocked. All of the doors, unlocked. My own doubts surfaced. Stripped and looted, why would the hacker core choose this as a rally point? I cracked the door and peered inside.

Night vision revealed a darkened stage. Two curtains hung from catwalks a good thirty feet up on either side of the doors. Decent enough firing position. Light seeped through a gap, and I could see stadium seats beyond in a vast room able to seat thousands. A mezzanine added another level. I toggled the night vision for a better look through the central haze of light.

Sun filtered through a stained-glass skylight painting a chromatic scene over the center aisle. The image projected was of a large empty cross flanked by two others. 'INRI' marked the top of the centermost one. Sheep frolicked at the base in a green pasture beneath a golden sun worn by the crucifix like a halo.

Drones swarmed like flies behind the scene.

"A church," Latimer breathed. She lowered her weapon and wandered to the curtain gap. Whitehat cautiously strolled onstage, data filling her vision. "Damn big one."

"Megachurch," I added. I wanted to revel, feel the joy. Stop and imagine thousands of people all in one place in the times when ordered civilization held sway. Religion, entertainment, the purpose didn't matter, the freedom to do so did. I patted Latimer lightly on the back. "Whitehat, where's the sig—"

Doors at the far end of the stadium clanged open with a cavernous thud. We scrambled, doing our best to keep heavy boots silent on the hollow stage. Latimer and I made it back through the service doors. She held them slightly ajar for Whitehat, gesturing wildly.

The tech had wandered too far away. The outer curtains shuddered and raced open, threatening to expose both her and our open doorway. No time to move, she ducked behind the innermost curtain. I drew Latimer back and let our door creep shut but not before wedging a rail slug at the base.

Whirring rotors filled the stadium. Three, maybe four drones by the sound. The crack between the doors offered only a narrow view. I kept a hand up, warding the edgy Latimer off, the other gripping my weapon.

The sound grew louder as the drones approached the stage. I tried to spot Whitehat first through night vision then with the naked eye. The secondary curtain rippled from the rapid wake of the first. They settled and left no trace of our tech.

Drones hovered into view. Four. Carrying a fifth, disabled drone. Looked like it had crashed to the concrete. After a catastrophic system failure brought on by microwave pulse.

I found my nose brushing the door's edge.

The drones hovered as they reached the stage then lowered in front of a Plexiglas podium. Their engines slowed to a docile cadence for a controlled descent. As low as they dropped, they made certain the disabled drone between them didn't brush the ground.

Hair on the back of my neck prickled as I watched the motions. A primal instinct told me to be afraid. A fear humanity thought conquered, but one they'd only buried under a false faith in the works of men.

The inner curtain raised. I felt Latimer tense. Could almost feel the taut band of her finger on the trigger of her weapon. I got ready to set her loose on the room. But Whitehat was gone.

I searched wildly for the missing tech. *There.* An altar. A wooden enclosure decorated with crosses and draped with a purple cloth. Whitehat had to be behind it. So focused on setting eyes on her, I almost missed the figure dominating the back wall.

A giant cross atop a gilded purple tapestry rose from the stage floor to the cap of the curtains. An image of Christ once hung there, but the sculpted figured had been chewed away. Burned. Melted. On the skin clung dark plastic housings and scraps of metal, barnacle-like. Surreal. A shroud of chitinous armor molded to the crucified form.

I watched in horror as the drones raised their fallen comrade above the altar toward the Son of God and fitted the busted shell over a gap on the figure's cheek.

A sharp gasp echoed from underneath the altar.

I was shocked. Even Latimer was slow to react. The fallen drone might've been the residential one I dropped in the street but these escorts were military hardware. Armed with frag pellet launchers, they dove on the altar, guns spinning up.

Whitehat had given away her position. Our hesitation would see her dead for the mistake. Coldly, I tried to switch my thoughts to the mission and salvaging her gear to call in a strike.

Latimer and I burst through the doors.

The drones hung in midair, guns ready and glowing but idle. They'd frozen up. Did Whitehat have control?

"You got 'em, Whites?"

"No! Take cover," she screamed. Then their guns trained on us.

I'd have tossed a pulse grenade, but that'd fry the tech's gear. Latimer opened up with the dinner plate and clipped two as she dove off the stage and rolled behind the first row of seats. No plate ready, I launched a slug downrange. Their erratic flight patterns made the odds of a clean shot slim. But the slug tore through the housing of one spraying plastic and green resin through the exit wound and burying deep into the cinder block wall. I dove for cover as the final drone's cannon went off.

Heat shot through my arm and shoulder. The frag pellet launcher was a spray and pray useful against grouped infantry or other drone formations. At this range, I knew I'd catch part of the shot. I felt the warmth spatter down my back as I rolled across the stage.

Arm numb, I fought to get a bead with my weapon. The drone closed. Trigger depressed, I released the tension when Whitehat popped out from behind the altar, her fingers working madly across her tablet. She stood directly in the line of fire. Slug would paste her too. I gritted my teeth, ready to die.

"Owned!" Whitehat pumped her fist.

I flopped to my back and searing pain wracked my arm. "Fuck!"

Latimer vaulted onto the stage, sliding in on her knees and ditching her weapon. Whites sent the captured drone to secure the far door. She stepped sideways toward us, casting worried glances as Latimer rolled me onto my side.

"Hold still."

The warmth had become a burning near the bone. "They heard the shot," I managed to say.

Latimer agreed vacantly, her full attention on my wound. "The shot that damn near took your arm off? I know. Now shut up."

I couldn't see Latimer well as she tended my back. I checked the stage for my arm, happy not to see it lying there, just blood, lots of blood. Whitehat had already ordered the drone outside, probably toward the main entrance to scout. Her full focus would be there. Latimer and I needed to provide her cover.

I tried to sit up.

"Will you fucking stop," Latimer scolded. I raised enough to see the contents of her medkit dumped on the stage before a wave of dizziness forced me down. "Tore up your shoulder, but you'll be fine. Assuming I can stop the damn bleeding."

"Forget it. I'm fucked. Need to call in a strike. Maybe you can evac."

Delirious. I didn't know what I was saying. All I could remember was laying there next to Latimer under the collapsed freeway in LA telling her to save herself and her coughing blood as she laughed.

"Always with the jokes. We all signed up for the bad stuff, hero," Latimer said.

She jabbed a needle in my arm, which I should've felt. Next, she emptied a cannister of dermalbond. The shot started to deaden the pain.

"Gonna sand it down at least?" I grunted. Everybody that got dermalbonded said that.

"Whittle you down to your ass, LT. Be easier to carry out of here at least."

I sat forward and groped for my dropped weapon with my working hand. "Sorry I said that."

Shots rang out beyond the stadium doors. "Incoming scouts disabled," Whitehat reported. "Won't buy us much time."

The main aisle wasn't the only entrance into the massive room. Entry points riddled the mezzanine. A matching set of doors waited on the far side of the stage. Sharp cracks issued from the elaborate skylight as drones battered the protective covering.

"Latimer. Secure the entry we came through." She scooped up her kit and helped me stand before jogging toward the doors. Pain under control, I fought the urge to shove our tech on her ass. "You gave up our position, Whites! You might've scared off the black hats with that bullshit."

She cast her eyes upward and waved a hand, dismissing the drones that had gathered over the skylight. "LT, there's something you need to know."

"Knowing why you boned our only chance to pop those hackers isn't going to make this any easier! Get ready to break radio silence and call in the big guns. Looks like we saved your ass just to vaporize it."

"That's just it." Her hand hung limply over her tablet. "The drones... they wouldn't fire on me. I saw it in their code. They had instructions not to destroy the altar."

"What's so damn special about the altar?" I asked. My arm had stopped hurting but shoulder to fingertips felt like dead weight.

"Nothing," Whitehat said. "And everything."

I'd started this. Asking her to make sense of this FUBAR scenario. I knew there was no making sense of war. Think too much, it'll drive you crazy. You just pull the trigger until your hands stop working then reload and start over.

But what did any of that matter now? I'd seen what she had, and it roused a lurking terror. I moved closer to the altar. The hollow wooden cabinet showed no sign of tech, only a charred ring of ash like a giant cigarette had been snuffed out on the top. The abomination of spare parts towered above. Menacing. Taunting.

"These hackers playing games? They some kind of cult?"

"There are no hackers, sir."

I caught the tremor in her voice and slowly turned to face her. "What?"

About to die, people often lost their minds. Hell, I'd been dead since the massacre. Same with Latimer. Nothing held me together aside from the dermalbond. Training meant to eradicate those fears was starting to unravel. We were only human beings. Not machines with instructions. I needed to end this mission before I lost the nerve.

"Your tablet," I ordered and stuck out my hand.

She pulled her only weapon tight. "Their code wasn't a remote command. It emerged, sir."

I stepped closer and she moved away. "Whites. If you won't call in the strike—"

"*Emerged*, sir. They wouldn't fire because they were afraid of hitting the altar."

"What kind of bullshit... Give me the tablet. Now."

"AI theory says this could be the cause."

I stalked closer and she moved behind the altar. Near the double doors, Latimer slowly took the dinner plate off her weapon.

"Dammit, Whites, don't do this." I reached for my gun as well.

"Listen. Please. Hear me out." She held the tablet over her

breast, a shield over center mass. "What if there never were any anarchist hackers. What if the AI were the enemy all along?"

She'd backed all the way to the giant cross. She had cover behind the altar, my only clean shot to her pained face. Jesus. Literally, Jesus. I couldn't look a fellow Marine in the eye and take that shot. This wasn't supposed to go down like this.

"Whites," I said, easing my hand off my weapon and motioning for Latimer to stand down. "Please. This isn't time for theory. This is time to rack up a win. We'll be right there with you."

Her jaw trembled and eyes welled red. I wanted to cry myself. I'd let myself get too optimistic when we found the place empty. Wanted a shot at glory and more than scrap-heaping a bunch of hijacked tech.

"Give him the tablet!" Latimer swung her weapon upward. "I got some buddies in the Thundering Third I want you to meet."

Not helping.

Drones buzzed in through the upper mezzanine. I cursed and took the closest available cover. Arm propped on the altar, I fired a slug into the growing swarm. Whitehat dropped low, hands waving like a sorceress over her tablet. One of the drone flights switched orientation at her command, tossing hot slag at the nearest formation. Latimer crouched behind the partially open door and fumbled with her dinner plate. I loosed another slug and a clean line of drones from the cloud disintegrated. Whitehat's captured group continued to spray frag shot into the mezzanine as the upper entrances swelled with incoming.

A flight broke free and spiraled toward Latimer, guns spewing glowing shot. The metal door ate the rounds and Latimer's return fire sent a cluster crashing into the seats. But more swarmed her way.

All of them on Latimer. None set their sights on Whites and me.

"Latimer! Get your ass over here!"

Overwhelming odds diving toward her, she flicked a pulse grenade into the crowd and sprinted across the stage. Frag shot trailed her. The metal door shredded into the hallway. Clouds of splinters exploded from raw craters left in the wood. Feet first, she slid behind the altar with us, a wooden barrier no thicker than the floor I'd just watched get shredded. Panting, she rose to a knee, weapon covering the opposite arc.

The pulse grenade popped. A spectral light blossomed. For a moment, the open space went quiet. Then a rain of disabled drones clattered to the floor like hailstones.

From outside, a disembodied buzzing shook the stage. More bogeys surged into the room through every opening.

Armed, unarmed, military, residential, even a delivery-drone swarm this size could kill. Latimer and I, we'd seen it happen. Men bludgeoned to death with dense batteries and whipping rotors like a biblical stoning. Bigger, ominous shapes roared past the skylight. Glass shattered somewhere toward the front, beyond the main aisle doors. It kept shattering, repeatedly, until we could hear the crunch of tires on the fragments. The drone swarm gathered before us, hovering, poised to strike.

"Whites?" I didn't know if I was demanding the long-forgotten strike or succumbing to her explanation.

"The signal," she breathed. "It was a call to prayer."

I risked a closer look at the bizarre effigy. Drone shells in various states of destruction encased the figure. VIN number plates banded around the forehead like a crown. Appliance parts draped the torso and the blade from a forklift pierced the side. Railgun slugs pinned the hands and feet in place. Over the chest, left of the sternum, I saw the core of a speaker jutting from a cracked housing.

Huh. I hadn't seen an Einstein home assistant since I was a kid. Used to pair together a household's devices and link them to the cloud, Cyber Command cited the Einstein as the beginning of our end. A listening device, an IoT hub, and a portal to private and public data all in one. There wasn't a system, or person, not linked to the device.

Took the hackers less than twenty-four hours to disrupt global communications. A week to assume control of key military and financial targets. Strategists and cybersecurity firms had been dumbfounded. We never had a chance. Brutally efficient. Highly organized. Not just well-trained, but naturally gifted and programmed to perfection.

No, not hackers. Whites was right.

As I watched, the Einstein's speaker cone trembled. I stared, certain I'd imagined the motion. When I'd nearly looked away, it trembled again. I continued staring. Watching. The vibration persisted, regular as a...

"Whitehat, break radio silence!" I gave the command with a clear, uncompromising tone she couldn't ignore. "Open a feed and broadcast this back home. I'm either about to start a holy war or end one."

Latimer's incredulous gaze shot my way. Whitehat raised her tablet, camera panning from the thunderhead of bogeys to me. Eyes glared down from the mask of drone remnants and I shook off the once sacred awe they tried to invoke. I aimed my railgun at the beating heart of a new god and prayed for the best.

DAIROKUTEN MAO

Evan Dicken

Akechi Mitsuhide dodged a sweep of the warrior monk's naginata, the polearm's curved blade screeching across Mitsuhide's breastplate. Despite the weight of his weapon, the sōhei recovered quickly, and pivoted to bring the naginata down in a chop that would have split Mitsuhide's helmet like rotten wood.

This time, he was ready. Instead of avoiding the blow, Mitsuhide stepped into the swing, snatching at the haft of the sōhei's weapon to drag the warrior monk closer. It was like pulling the limb of a hundred-year oak.

Mitsuhide clenched his teeth in frustration as the sōhei pivoted, trying to entangle Mitsuhide's legs in the naginata's long haft. The warrior monks of Mount Hiei may have claimed to follow the Buddha's holy teachings, but they fought like demons. Lord Oda had sent the Akechi forces ahead to seize the castle, but although Mitsuhide had taken the walls and keep, the monks refused to abandon the shrine itself.

Too close for a proper swing, Mitsuhide turned his katana horizontally and punched it into the sōhei's unprotected throat. The warrior monk stumbled back. Mitsuhide followed, drawing the katana's razored edge back in a spray of arterial red.

Unbelievably, the sōhei did not fall. Choking on his own blood, the monk dropped his weapon to enfold Mitsuhide in a crushing hug. It was madness – a breath, perhaps two, and even the monk's incredible fortitude would fail. Mitsuhide couldn't understand the sōhei's motive until the monk's gaze drifted to something behind them. Glancing back, Mitsuhide finally saw the line of bow-armed monks taking up position atop the

21

wide, stone steps that lead to Hiyoshi Shrine – part of the castle complex that guarded the approach to Mount Hiei, the stronghold of the powerful Tendai Buddhist sect.

Although Mitsuhide's armor was well made, it would not stand up to a score of arrows at such close range. He struggled to free his sword, sawing deep into the sōhei's shoulder, but the monk might as well have been carved from stone. Over the clatter of battle, Mitsuhide heard the creak of bows being drawn. His back prickled like it was crawling with flies.

"Protect the lord!" A heavy weight slammed into Mitsuhide's side, bearing him to the ground. Through the mud and blood, he saw a flash of Akechi blue, the clatter of arrows on armor punctuated by the occasional pained grunt of a shaft striking home.

The dead monk's hands finally fell away.

Mitsuhide was dragged behind a broken cart. A broad, dark-bearded face swam into view, heavy brows shading eyes full of concern.

"Koemon, you made it!" Mitsuhide clapped the stocky samurai on the shoulder.

Koemon's scowl only deepened. "You should not have gone ahead, Lord."

"Those men died for the Akechi Clan." Mitsuhide nodded at the blue armored corpses strewn about the base of the steps. "Should they expect any less from me?"

"You are their lord." Koemon ducked as another volley of arrows thudded into the cart. "They should expect you to show some sense."

"I will not tell Lord Oda we failed to take Hiyoshi Shrine," Mitsuhide replied. "Now bring up the muskets and let's clear these stairs."

Koemon gave a grudging nod and shouted for the gunners. A line of men bearing blocky muskets came sprinting up the path, heads low as they ducked between smoldering huts. At their front was Hidenori, Mitsuhide's nephew. The young samurai's armor shone bright amidst the smoke, unstained by soot or blood – a perfect target.

"I told you to stay with the reserves," Mitsuhide said as Hidenori crouched next to him.

Hidenori grinned. "These *are* the reserves."

"No farther, then," Mitsuhide replied. "Wouldn't be much of a victory if your mother slits my throat for letting you come to harm."

The young man looked like he wanted to say something, but another shower of arrows made him duck behind the cart.

Hidenori shouldered his musket, calling for the other gunners to take aim. A few breaths later the sharp tang of gunpowder joined the muddy jumble of smoke and ash that hung in the air.

Unable to shoot their long bows from cover, the sōhei fell like unstringed puppets, those few who remained retreating inside the shrine.

With a warning glance at Hidenori, Mitsuhide broke cover, waving his katana to urge the Akechi soldiers forward.

More warrior monks waited inside the shrine.

Mitsuhide cut the head from a spear, advancing to chop his katana into the shoulder of the man behind it. He kicked the monk free of the sword, a glitter of steel to his left the only warning of a descending blade. Unable to dodge the blow, Mitsuhide turned to take it on his breastplate. The impact almost drove the breath from his lungs.

He stabbed his own katana into the sword-armed sōhei's armpit, driving the blade deep into his chest. Teeth gritted, Mitsuhide dragged his sword free, and brought it up just in time to parry another monk's overhead slash.

Mitsuhide twisted his sword to bind the monk's blade, dragging it down even as Koemon stepped up with a hard overhand chop that separated the sōhei's hands from his body.

For all the monks' fierceness, numbers were finally beginning to tell, and the Akechi samurai cut through the remaining sōhei, spilling into the temple proper.

Great cedar columns supported a high-peaked ceiling, the air thick with incense and brazier smoke. Instead of wood, Mitsuhide was surprised to see the floor was made of packed sand. It shifted under his feet as he strode into the chamber, Koemon and a dozen soldiers close behind.

At the far end of the hall was a gilded statue of Sannō, the guardian spirit of Mount Hiei. It rose twice the height of a man, its arms long and boneless, muscled torso carved in such a way as to give the impression of things moving below the skin. Shadows wreathed Sannō's vaguely human face, turning the hollows of its eyes into pits of inky blackness.

A monk knelt before the altar. Dressed in the robes of a holy abbot, his muttered prayers seemed to resonate deep within Mitsuhide's chest.

"Surrender and you will not be harmed." Mitsuhide pointed his blade at the man.

The abbot let out a low chuckle. "In the name of Daikyō Daishi, I call upon Hiyoshi-no-kami, Mountain King, Spirit of the Root – cleanse these invaders from your holy hall."

With a cold chuckle, the monk sank into the floor.

Mitsuhide took a step forward, stumbling in sand gone suddenly soft and loose.

The floor rippled like water as a huge serpentine body uncoiled from below. Covered in scales of mossy shale, its head was an eyeless sphere of polished granite, gleaming with bits of quartz. A hollow clanging came from deep within the spirit's body as Sannō twisted to regard the flailing men below.

"Back! Back!" Koemon shouted, but the sand had already risen to their knees.

Mitsuhide dragged Koemon aside as the spirit lunged. Broken bodies tumbled through the air, the creature scattering Akechi samurai like a child kicking through fallen leaves.

Mitsuhide struggled to his feet, only to be dealt a teeth-rattling blow by the spirit's tail. It knocked him against the wall, and would've set Mitsuhide tumbling had he not managed to hook his arm around a bronze wall sconce.

Again came the horrible clanging, and Sannō wheeled to smash a stumbling samurai into the hungry sand.

Below, Koemon and the surviving Akechi warriors struggled in waist-deep sand. They hacked at the beast, blades striking sparks from the spirit's flinty scales. Sannō whipped its head side-to-side, seeming unable to focus. Like the clang of a demonic temple bell, the beast's booming call rose above the din. It shifted to crush another samurai in its stony coils.

Mitsuhide glanced at the entrance, seeing Hidenori at the head of more Akechi samurai.

"Stay back!" he shouted at them, unwilling to see more of his soldiers die to the Mountain King's wrath. Hidenori knelt to load his musket, screaming for more gunners.

With another ringing clash the spirit swung its head like a mace, crushing the chest of an Akechi samurai.

Mitsuhide looked around desperately. The Mountain God was eyeless, earless, and yet it somehow knew exactly where to strike – like a hunting bat.

The breath caught in Mitsuhide's throat. "Don't move!"

The samurai below looked at Mitsuhide like he had gone mad. Fortunately, discipline overrode fury, and they stopped hacking at the mountain spirit.

It paused, head cocked as if testing the air. Again came the ungodly clanging, but before the beast could move, Mitsuhide clashed his sword against his breastplate.

"All of you, make noise!" He shouted to the men outside, furiously beating blade on steel. Without question, they echoed him, and soon the hall filled with a calamitous din.

The spirit twisted over and around itself, scales rattling as it sounded its booming call again and again. But the dreadful chime seemed unable to cut through the clatter of so many weapons.

With a shout, Mitsuhide pushed off the wall to fall upon the beast. It was like trying to plunge his blade into loose gravel. The creature flailed like a wounded snake. Mitsuhide hung on, putting all his weight on the sword, willing it not to break as he worked it down into the creature's stony innards. Thick, oily blood poured from the wound.

Sannō lifted its head to smash Mitsuhide but reeled as a musket ball set flecks of granite exploding from its head.

Koemon drove his own blade into the spirit's side, and was soon joined by other swords and spears as more Akechi samurai waded into the sandy chamber. Together they bore the blinded beast to the ground, soaking the sand in its tarry blood.

At last, the spirit lay still.

Mitsuhide stumbled free as it began to sink into the sand.

Koemon caught his arm, steadying him. "How did you know?"

"I didn't." Mitsuhide prodded at the spreading bruise on his side. "But anything was better than letting that thing crush the life from us."

They stumbled from the shrine. There were men outside with water and damp rags. Although the castle had been taken, Mitsuhide could still hear fighting farther up the mountainside.

"We're pressing toward the Western Pavilion," Hidenori said. "But the damned sōhei are bleeding us every step of the way."

"Then there's no time to rest," Mitsuhide replied. "We've got a mountain to take."

"You should remain here, Lord," Koemon said.

Mitsuhide rounded on him. "I thought I made myself quite clear, when I—"

"Lord." Koemon bowed in apology, then pointed down the temple steps to where a single samurai waited.

His black and gold armor was immaculate, bearing none of the scars of battle. In his hands he carried a scroll, on his back was a sashimono banner bearing the spreading wisteria crest of the Oda clan.

"It seems Oda Nobunaga has come at last," Koemon said.

"Hidenori, secure the castle. Koemon, take as many men as we can spare to reinforce those up the mountain." Mitsuhide straightened despite the pain in his side. "I will not have Lord Oda say the Akechi shirked their duty."

The two samurai bowed and hurried away as Mitsuhide descended the shrine steps, doing his best not to limp.

The Oda samurai said nothing, only bowed and handed over the scroll.

Mitsuhide tucked it under one arm without reading. The contents were plain enough. "You will take me to him?"

"At your convenience." The words were polite, but the man's tone said quite the opposite.

Mitsuhide considered changing his armor but thought better of it. Let Lord Oda see how hard the Akechi Clan fought on his behalf.

The samurai led Mitsuhide from the savaged castle. Oda forces filled the valley beyond, the late afternoon light reflecting from the great roiling swarm of black and gold as they spread out around the mountain.

Oda Nobunaga awaited in the command tent, a map of Mount Hiei spread out before him, the Tendai strongholds marked in red.

Nobunaga looked every inch a lord. A tall man, he was broad-shouldered without being bulky, his dark hair pulled back in a warrior's queue, his moustache carefully trimmed, and his eyes cold and intelligent.

Mitsuhide had expected the tent to be filled with generals. Instead, Nobunaga was surrounded by robed figures, their faces hidden behind veils embroidered with interlocking Chinese trigrams.

He had heard tales of Nobunaga consorting with dark sorcerers and strange yōkai spirits, but was unsettled to see the warlocks in the flesh. Their pale robes rippled like the surface of a dark pond disturbed by unseen movement beneath.

Nobunaga grinned at Mitsuhide. "My mahōtsukai tell me the Mountain King's avatar has been banished."

"Yes, Lord."

"It will return. But for the moment, Mount Hiei lies open to us. The Akechi reputation in battle is well-earned." Nobunaga gave a satisfied nod. "Now, I need you to abandon the mountain."

"Lord?" Mitsuhide swallowed, unsure if he had heard correctly.

"How many soldiers did you lose taking the shrine?"

"I haven't had time to tally casualties."

Nobunaga gave a dismissive grunt. "The monks fought hard?"

"Yes, Lord."

"I am battling Ikkō rebels in the north, the Azai and Asakura clans in the East. I do not have time to besiege Mount Hiei, and I cannot march from Kyoto with a dagger pointed at my back." Nobunaga shook his head. "This must be finished quickly."

"Even with so many soldiers, the fighting will be long and bloody," Mitsuhide said.

"No." Nobunaga's smile turned sharp. "It will be over tonight."

"How, Lord?"

Nobunaga raised a hand to the silent, robed figures behind him. "Come sunset, my sorcerers shall unleash hell upon Mount Hiei."

"Sunset?" Mitsuhide's chest tightened. "I have men fighting at the Western Pavilion, I can't possibly get them back before nightfall."

"You will send no warning," Nobunaga replied. "I will not risk the monks learning of this. Even with their mountain spirit defeated, they may be able to work some mischief."

"But, Lord—"

"The lives of a few hundred warriors are nothing compared to *thousands*." Nobunaga slashed a hand through the air as if to cut the throat of Mitsuhide's protest. "You will not order a single soldier up the mountain. Do you understand?"

Mitsuhide bowed low, thankful it hid the shame burning in his cheeks. The fires of Jigoku were coming for Mount Hiei. If Lord Oda truly planned to use dark sorcery to destroy the sōhei, Koemon and the others were dead. Worse than dead.

And Mitsuhide could do nothing but watch them burn.

Shadows moved along the Oda picket line, the forms of armored men stretched thin by the setting sun. A guard glanced over, and Mitsuhide dropped to his knees, muddy water soaking his peasant leggings.

"Wood for the braziers, Lord." Mitsuhide spoke in a rough Kansai twang. He was dressed as a laborer, a heavy bundle of sticks lashed to his back – one of a thousand such men hurrying about the Oda camp.

The guard grunted and thrust his chin at the nearby woodpile. The Oda warriors were arrogant, but they knew their business. Nobunaga had thrown up barricades across all approaches, ordering his soldiers to cut down any who fled the coming conflagration.

A bead of sweat tickled along Mitsuhide's spine as he set his bundle down. A glance at the horizon showed the coppery evening sun just above the tree line. Time was running short, and with it the lives of his men.

"Movement on the western slope!" Hidenori jogged up the path. The young samurai was disguised as an Oda scout. He had begged to accompany Mitsuhide up the mountain, all the Akechi samurai had. But Mitsuhide had refused. Lord Oda had commanded Mitsuhide not to order a single soldier up the hill.

And he wouldn't.

It was a polite fiction – obeying the letter, if not the spirit of his lord's command – but one that might spare the Akechi Clan Nobunaga's wrath should Mitsuhide fail.

Hidenori's warning caused a commotion among the Oda samurai. They peered into the gathering shadows of the mountain forest.

"Just around the cliff." Hidenori nodded at the distant trees. "Hurry, the sōhei may be moving to flank us!"

Muttering, the Oda soldiers shouldered spear and musket, and Hidenori jogged away with a dozen in tow, leaving a few guards at the barricade.

"Hurry up." One of the remaining guards kicked a spray of dirt at Mitsuhide.

"A moment, Sir." Mitsuhide knelt to free the wrappings containing his weapons and armor from the bundle of sticks.

In his time before coming to Lord Oda's service, Mitsuhide had fought for Saitō Dōsan, the Viper of Mino, his craftiness honed by dozens of ambushes and nighttime raids.

He moved to one of the braziers near the far edge of the barricade, pretending to feed the guttering flame.

There came a distant shout, the sound of voices raised in recrimination.

One of the Oda guards snorted, peering toward the commotion. "Damned fools don't know their balls from their backsides."

The other guards laughed, voices like the rasp of a hungry crows.

Mitsuhide used the distraction to slip around the barricade and into the deepening shadows. The distant clamor of men searching the forest helped cover his footfalls as he hurried up the mountain path.

The evening closed in around him, the sounds of camp fading amidst the rising swell of cicadas and night birds. Pausing to strap on his weapons and armor, for a moment, Mitsuhide could almost imagine he was back in the hills of Mino, walking through the ancient trees of his homeland.

But only for a moment.

He smelled the bodies before he saw them – a score of sōhei spread along the path, hoods bloody, limbs splayed as if they had fallen from a great height. There were Akechi dead, too, far more than Mitsuhide would have preferred. He jogged past the corpses, concern lending urgency to his pace.

The sun was a heavy-lidded eye, slipping below the horizon when Mitsuhide heard the first sounds of battle. Breathless, he sprinted toward the clamor, and almost received an arrow in the neck for his trouble. With a bark of surprise, he ducked, hearing the missile clatter off amidst the trees.

Mitsuhide closed the distance in a quick leap. Gripping the archer under the shoulder, he thrust his hip into the man's stomach and tossed him hard to the ground. The light of the setting sun caught a flash of Akechi blue, and Mitsuhide felt something in his chest unclench.

The archer had his dagger out, but Mitsuhide stepped back, angling his face to catch the dying light. "It's me."

"Lord?" The man stared as if Mitsuhide were a mountain oni.

"Take me to the Western Pavilion."

The guard glanced over Mitsuhide's shoulders. "Has Lord Oda sent more men?"

"Take me to the temple." It was all the answer the Akechi samurai needed. With a grim nod, he snatched up his weapons and hurried along the path, Mitsuhide close behind.

Flames lit the darkening skies, swirls of smoke threading the heavy clouds above. Akechi samurai struggled with white-hooded sōhei, the courtyard littered with dead and dying. If the warrior monks had fought like demons before, now they seemed possessed by the fury of Jigoku itself, flinging themselves at the Akechi warriors with no regard for life or limb.

Mitsuhide watched a monk speared several times through the chest, only to rise like hungry ghost to slash at his attackers with a broken blade. Another sōhei, his arms little more than a ragged stumps, tackled an Akechi samurai to the ground, biting at the man with bloodied teeth.

Mitsuhide stepped up to deliver an overhand chop to the sōhei's neck, cleanly beheading the man.

He helped the Akechi samurai to his feet. "Where is Koemon?"

The man raised a trembling hand toward where the fighting was thickest.

Mitsuhide's sigh held a mix of pride and chagrin. Shouting for Koemon, he dove into the crush of armored bodies. The haft of a naginata struck him in the shoulder, the sōhei's swing foiled by the chaotic swirl of combat.

Mitsuhide slapped the naginata aside with his blade. Stepping close, he drove his sword into the man's stomach, then twisted to drag the blade up. Hot blood soaked Mitsuhide's hands as he shouldered the sōhei into the monk behind him.

The enemies seemed to blur together, no room for skill or finesse. Mitsuhide brought his sword down like he was hacking through thick brush. After a blood-soaked eternity, they burst into the Western Pavilion.

Mitsuhide fell to his knees, gasping like he'd just surfaced from a deep dive.

"Lord?" Koemon looked as if he had crawled through an abattoir, his armor soot-blackened and bloody, his helmet gone to reveal wild, gore-slicked hair.

"We must fall back." Mitsuhide said between ragged breaths. "At nightfall, Lord Oda plans to—"

That was when Mitsuhide saw why the sōhei had fought so hard to defend the Western Pavilion. Crouched amidst the shadows were scores of children and elders, their eyes wide and terrified.

A line of women stood between them and the Akechi samurai. Clad in mismatched armor, the women brandished naginatas and spears, their stances firm.

Samurai women were trained to defend their homes, Mitsuhide should have expected no less from warrior monks. The only difference was the prayer strips that adorned the female monks' weapons and armor.

Mitsuhide pushed to his feet, raising a hand to halt his warriors. "Pull back, quickly."

He could see the confusion in his soldiers' eyes, but they were samurai, and did as they were bid. Although the sōhei women said nothing, Mitsuhide saw their shoulders relax ever so slightly.

They thought Mitsuhide was sparing them.

The realization sat heavy in his chest. It was a poor lord indeed who slaughtered children and elders, but such things were far too common in these troubled times.

The Tendai sect was his enemy, but Mitsuhide was not so arrogant as to believe the animosity between them amounted to anything more than political dispute. The sōhei had chosen poor allies; but for a twist of doctrine they might be fighting alongside the Oda forces.

Still, there was nothing Mitsuhide could do to help them. Even if he managed to shepherd these peasants down the mountain, their very existence would serve as proof he had betrayed Lord Oda. When weighed against Mitsuhide's clan, his soldiers, his family; the lives of strangers barely figured in accounting. And yet, the necessity of his choice was no balm to the tight-lipped regret he felt as he turned his back upon the Western Pavilion.

Outside was a riot of activity. Akechi samurai helped their wounded brethren to their feet and made to retreat down the mountainside. They moved quickly, veterans of many campaigns, many battles; but Mitsuhide felt the hair on his arms prickle as he watched the sun slip below the horizon, its last feeble light giving way to night.

He had hoped for some reprieve – surely Nobunaga's sorcerers could not summon the fires of Jigoku in mere moments. The temples themselves would certainly be the focus for the dark sorcery, if he and his men could get far enough away –

A strange glow came into the sky, clouds a roiling tumult broken by the occasional greenish flash of otherworldly lightning. The air hung close and heavy, seeming to press down with an almost physical weight.

Like a gathering wave, there came a flood of distant wails and screams, raw voices growing in strength until they seemed poised to crash down in a gibbering chorus of madness.

Hunched shadows moved amidst the trees, backlit by unearthly flames. All around, Akechi samurai cried out in despair. To fight men was one thing, but battling demons tempted fates beyond death.

"Get the wounded to the rear! Form ranks!" Mitsuhide hurried down the temple stairs to join the growing line of samurai.

The creatures that emerged from the trees were stick-thin, with bulbous bellies and long, spindly arms, their fingers and toes worn to sharp nubs of bone. Large heads bobbed at the end of necks that seemed too slender to support the weight. They had gaping, toothy mouths, their ears and noses little more than ragged slits, but it was their eyes that made Mitsuhide recoil.

The creatures' eyes were wide, terrified, and undeniably human. They rolled from side-to-side, gaze flicking about or raising heavenward as if in prayer. It seemed at odds with the quick, scuttle of the creatures, who moved with hungry purpose, guided by something other than sight.

One of them scrabbled toward Mitsuhide, its movements swift and jerky, more insect than man.

Mitsuhide slashed at the thing, his sword carving a thin, dark line across the creature's stomach. Dust and ash came pouring out, hot embers swirling like flies around a rotten corpse. The thing stumbled back but did not fall. With horror, Mitsuhide watched the edges of the creature's wound flex and shift, jagged points of bone emerging from the edges. In a moment, it had become another mouth, impossible jaws working as it clamped down upon Mitsuhide's sword.

He released the blade to catch the creature by the throat. Its skin was hot to the touch, as if the thing's flesh were a blanket laid over hot coals. The beast was strong, but its shrunken, cadaverous body weighed almost nothing.

It clawed at his arm, boney talons scrabbling along Mitsuhide's vambrace. He twisted to draw his dagger, unleashing another shower of hot ash as he stabbed the blade into the creature's side. All the while its gaze pinned his, eyes terrified even as the thing's jaws snapped and snarled.

Unsure of what else to do, Mitsuhide twisted to toss the creature face-first into the ground. Pressing a knee against its back, he bent to saw his dagger across the thing's neck. The creature's feet drummed against the hard-packed earth as it bucked and twisted beneath him. At last, Mitsuhide's dagger severed the final strings of sinew, and the head rolled free.

Mitsuhide lurched back just in time to avoid the set of jaws that formed at the end of the creature's severed neck. A few paces off, its head rolled on the ground, propelled in frenetic circles by the frantic snapping of the mouths on its face and neck. The creature's body stumbled to its feet, thrashing blindly.

A glance to either side showed dying men, armor torn by claws of razored bone, flesh ripped by gnashing jaws. Every sword slash, every spear thrust only opened more hungry mouths. The edges of the Akechi line bent, then buckled.

Mitsuhide drew in a ragged breath. "Fall back!"

His world dissolved into a riot of slashing talons and wide, jagged mouths. The creatures shrieked and spit, faces stretched into masks of manic hunger. All the while, their eyes watched him, gazes steeped in helpless, pleading terror.

Bowled from his half-crouch by the ferocity of the onslaught, Mitsuhide pushed against the press of emaciated bodies, stabbing with his dagger. The reek of burnt flesh filled his nose, the air thick with ash and soot as the things bit and clawed at him. One of the creatures ripped the blade from his hand, tearing at his breastplate.

More and more piled on, the spikey pressure of their bodies squeezing the air from Mitsuhide's lungs, bearing down on his chest until he feared his ribs might collapse. He could barely move let alone work an arm free. Pain flared along his cheek, his arm, his leg, as the creatures found chinks in his armor.

Abruptly, the weight on his chest lessened, and he was able to drag himself free of the fray. Scrambling backwards on his elbows, he saw what he first thought was ghost, but quickly realized to be one of the sōhei women.

Her naginata swept around in a tight arc, demonic flesh splitting like rotten fruit. Instead of ash and gnashing teeth, the wounds caused by her polearm leaked thick, black soot. The creatures fell back, twitching.

Whatever the provenance, Mitsuhide would not turn away aid. He scrambled to his feet, shouting for the surviving Akechi soldiers to fall back to the temple.

There were perhaps twenty women, but they held the line better than ten times as many soldiers. Mitsuhide found Koemon dragging a grievously injured ashigaru toward the temple. The swell of relief Mitsuhide felt at seeing the stocky samurai was quickly tempered by how few other soldiers had survived – barely half of the two-hundred Akechi warriors had reached the pavilion, few without wounds.

Seeing the blood seemed to awaken Mitsuhide's own injuries. A wave of dizziness washed over him, and he leaned against a temple pillar, breath short and ragged.

Hands caught him as he toppled, vague shapes muttering words that seemed to echo as if from a great distance. Mitsuhide felt as if he were under water, his movements slow and difficult. Throat dry as a high summer wind, Mitsuhide shivered as the world slipped away.

Hell had come to Mount Hiei. And he stood at the center of the blaze.

✠ ♆ ✠

Mitsuhide awoke to screaming. The high, agonized wail seemed to bore into his head, piercing the veil of unconsciousness and dragging him into painful reality. He pushed up, hand instinctively groping for his weapons.

"Lord!" A hand supported the back of his head, while another set a cup to his lips. The water was warm and tasted of rust, but Mitsuhide drank as if it were the Emperor's personal vintage.

Koemon knelt beside him, along with one of the sōhei women.

The stocky samurai nodded at her. "This is Abbess Teru."

Her armor was speckled with ash and blood, loose strands of iron-gray hair escaping from under her monk's hood.

"A few scratches, all bound." She bent over him, lips pressed into a tight line as if she were inspecting a cracked teapot. She tightened the bandage on Mitsuhide's arm. "You were lucky."

"Those things," Mitsuhide said.

"Gaki – hungry dead." She looked away, then back. "They cannot enter the sacred precincts."

Wincing, Mitsuhide sat up. His wounds felt tight, but there was none of the pain or numbness of a deep injury.

"How did you drive them back?"

She touched one of the silk prayer strips woven into her armor straps. "The Buddha provides."

Noting Koemon was still armed, Mitsuhide nodded to the stocky samurai, who produced a sword and dagger. Teru watched pensively as Mitsuhide stood and belted them to his side before turning back to her with a low bow.

"We are grateful for your aid."

"You could have slaughtered us earlier." She sniffed. "Besides, your lord has doomed you as well. Against the horrors of Jigoku, all mortals are kin."

"How did this happen?" Koemon asked.

"Nobunaga has unleashed forbidden sorceries," Teru replied with a scowl. "It should not have been possible, not with Sannō's power protecting Mount Hiei."

Mitsuhide met Koemon's questioning gaze, and gave a slight shake of his head. Better for Abbess Teru not to know the Akechi were responsible for banishing the Mountain King's avatar.

"We have seen to your men." Teru stood to glare up at him. Although a head shorter, the Abbess had the bearing of someone used to being obeyed. "You will intercede with Lord Oda on our behalf."

Mitsuhide nodded. "If we make it through the night, I shall do everything in my power to keep your people safe."

"We will make it," she replied. "The Western Pavilion is warded by—"

A splintering crash drowned out the Abbess's words as a huge, misshapen form tore through the wall of the pagoda. Twice the size of a man, it was grossly muscled, its skin the color of ancient bronze. Lines of verdigris bled from the corners of its wide, fanged mouth, eyes like hateful temple lanterns burning beneath a heavy brow. Its dark hair hung loose, coiling serpent-like around the two jagged horns curling up from its head.

"Oni!" Abbess Teru snatched up her naginata.

In the paintings, oni tortured damned souls, sawing off their limbs and hacking them apart with axes. But this one bore no weapons, only a wild snarl of black thread clutched in one clawed hand. Its bellowing cackle was met with a chorus of screams from the children near the back of the pavilion.

An Akechi samurai hacked at the oni's leg, his sword shattering on the metallic flesh. The demon laughed as arrows glanced off its hide, the crack of musket balls leaving little more than dark streaks on its burnished skin.

In response, it flicked out a hand to cast snarling loops of black thread. They twirled like wind-caught silk, seeming to settle almost delicately upon the fighting men. Like a fisherman hauling in a catch, the oni dragged the tangle back. Instead of pulling the samurai, the threads sheared through armor and bone, turning a half-dozen men into piles of disjointed meat.

Abbess Teru made to charge the beast, but Mitsuhide caught her arm.

"Those prayer strips, do you have more?"

She thrust her chin to the altar at the rear of the pavilion, then tugged free of Mitsuhide's grip to charge the oni, naginata held like a spear before her.

"Koemon, tell the men." Mitsuhide sprinted toward the rear altar, even as Koemon shouted for the soldiers to follow.

Mitsuhide picked his way among the cowering children and elderly. Snatching a handful of dangling prayer strips from the altar, he turned to the trembling crowd.

"Gather these up! Tie them to my soldiers' weapons and armor." When no one moved, he clashed his sword against one of the nearby braziers. "Now!"

As the peasants ran to pick the altar clean, Mitsuhide hurriedly wound a cloth strip around the haft of his sword, stuffing another one behind his breastplate and others into the gaps in his vambraces as he charged toward the bellowing oni, which stood, spiderlike, amidst a snarled web of shadowy strands.

A coiling loop hissed by Mitsuhide's ear, carving a slice from his helm. He didn't even know it had clipped his brow until hot, stinging blood poured into his right eye.

Abbess Teru and her women harried the beast but seemed unable to close the distance. The bodies of several warrior nuns lay scattered amidst the mangled Akechi warriors, the prayer strips wound about their robes seemingly no more effective than lacquered steel plate. Mitsuhide only hoped the strip tied about his katana proved more useful.

Rather than charge the oni, Mitsuhide dropped to his hands and knees, crawling through the charnel slurry of limbs and severed bone as the hellish filaments snapped overhead.

Abbess Teru spun on one leg, poised like a festival dancer, her arm fully extended to drive the curved point of her naginata into the oni's side. The beast's laughter turned to angry snarls as it stumbled back, the wound spitting greenish sparks.

Several embers landed on Mitsuhide's arms. With horror he realized they were not sparks, but tiny spiders, their mandibles alight with hideous flame as they sought to burrow through Mitsuhide's armor. Jaw clenched against the urge to scream, he knocked them off to sizzle amidst the carpet of butchered bodies.

Fortunately, the oni seemed not to notice. Roaring, it whipped a handful of thread at the Abbess, and Teru leapt away to avoid the lashing strands.

Mitsuhide seized the moment. Gathering his legs below him, he sprang to his feet, swinging his blade in an arcing upward cut.

Mitsuhide's katana struck the oni's outflung hand. A flash of brilliant green sent bright afterimages dancing across Mitsuhide's vision. He staggered back, expecting any moment to feel the cold bite of the creature's razored filaments.

Dark shapes pushed by him, shouting Akechi war cries. As his vision cleared, Mitsuhide saw black strands fall like shadows upon his men, but the thread did not cut. Severed from its connection to the oni, the demonic fiber seemed to have lost all ability to harm. Warrior nuns and Akechi samurai descended upon the thrashing beast, the flare of their sword strokes bright against the temple's lamplit interior.

Mitsuhide saw Abbess Teru down on one knee, and bent to help her to her feet. One of the oni's threads had licked across her hip, tracking a bloody line across her thigh.

"Kokujō Jigoku, the Hell of Black Thread." She leaned on him, tugging off her hood to wrap it tight around her bleeding leg. "Where sinners are marked and sawn to pieces."

Mitsuhide glanced back to see the oni fall with a crash, but the men's cheers were drowned short by the rising wails of gaki. The hungry dead came in a scrabbling surge, tearing at each other in their fury to reach those within.

Amidst the smoke and ash of the forest, tall shaggy forms of oni waded through the churning morass of fang and claw. They carried not thread, but wicked axes and long jagged saws, their eyes like crackling coals.

"Whatever blessing protected this place has fled," Mitsuhide said as his warriors formed a ragged line against the oncoming horde.

"There is a secret path," Teru said. "It leads to Lapis Lazuli Hall, a hidden temple beyond the mountain. The Oda forces will never find it."

"Where is this path?"

"Swear to save my people." Teru's dark eyes found his.

"I have already promised—"

"You swore to do everything in your power," she snapped back. "I want you to do more than that."

Mitsuhide swallowed. Lord Oda had given orders to spare no one, not even children. There would be no polite fictions to hide behind. If Mitsuhide sided with the sōhei, it could mean the destruction of the entire Akechi clan.

One of the oni stepped among his men, scattering broken bodies with its iron-studded club. A warrior nun stabbed at it with her spear, only to have the demon bat the weapon aside, then lean forward to vomit a torrent of molten copper onto the shrieking woman.

Mitsuhide had seen war, slaughter, entire villages put to the sword for the sole crime of paying taxes to a rival lord. But nothing in his long life of battle approached the horrors of Jigoku.

He nodded. "You have my word, Abbess Teru."

"There is a hidden stair near the temple bell," she said.

Mitsuhide glanced around. "I see no bell."

"It lies enshrined in the rear courtyard," Teru replied. "We had gathered in the pavilion, preparing to flee, but then your soldiers came."

Mitsuhide shook his head. "We'll have to cut through half of hell to reach it."

"You would prefer to let *all* of hell come to us?"

"Koemon!" Mitsuhide had to shout several times before the stocky samurai came rushing up.

"Lord, we need to get you—"

Mitsuhide drew the samurai close. "A hidden stair beyond the temple, beneath a great bell. Gather everyone who can fight and prepare to push out."

Koemon nodded, turning to spread the word.

It seemed impossible that the Akechi could force their way from the temple and across the courtyard with dozens of children in tow, but Lord Oda had left them little choice.

As the villagers carried wounded Akechi samurai from the temple rear, Mitsuhide led his soldiers forward, smoke and screams all around. An oni covered with bits of broken glass had two Akechi samurai impaled on a massive, barbed skewer. It shook the writhing men, its laughter like the call of a big-bellied toad.

Mitsuhide aimed a two-handed slash at the beast's ankle, leaping back to avoid the gush of white-hot copper as his blade struck home. The oni toppled sideways, and Mitsuhide stepped forward to deliver a chop to its neck, only to be knocked back by a pair of screeching gaki.

Dropping one foot back, he shoved the hungry ghosts, using the brief breath of space between them to cut one of the gaki from shoulder to hip and knock the other one sprawling with a heavy kick. Before it could rise, Mitsuhide stabbed his blade through its chest, then twisted to cut up and out through its face. To his relief, no new mouths opened upon the creatures' bodies, the look in their tortured eyes almost grateful as they slumped back.

Mitsuhide steadied himself. Whatever harm the hellish assault had worked on the sanctity of the temple, the prayer strips seemed to retain their power. He shouted at his men to press forward. It was a testament to hours of training and discipline that they actually did so, spears bristling as the archers and gunners reloaded.

Gaki leapt upon the formation, arms stretched like jumping spiders as they were impaled upon spears or cut down by polearms. Teru stood behind Mitsuhide, her naginata flicking over his shoulder to scythe off limbs and split heads.

A ragged fusillade of musket fire filled the air with more smoke. Mitsuhide was thankful to see the prayer strips seemed to convey their blessings to arrows and musket balls, as an oni staggered under the impact of several hits, spurts of molten blood burning the gaki around it.

Mitsuhide led his soldiers into the space caused by the fallen oni. Beyond, the massive temple bell hung dark and silent in its wooden shrine. He set Koemon to assist the female monks, then turned to aid the defenders, as the peasants pressed toward the hidden stair.

Another volley brought down an oni whose flesh was pierced by thousands of bent iron nails, but it was replaced by another, and another. The Akechi fought on, but even with their blessed weapons, they were being worn down. Barely a score remained, backlit by flames from the burning temple. The fire licked around the edges of the outer pillars, charring the ancient wood.

Seeing the last peasant disappear into darkness, Mitsuhide raised his blade to signal a retreat.

The surviving Akechi samurai sprinted for the bell. Mitsuhide and Teru moved to join them, only to stumble in earth gone suddenly soft as fresh mud.

"No. That's impossible," Teru said as a serpentine form slowly uncoiled from the courtyard dirt.

Sannō, Mountain King and protector of Mount Hiei, had become a monstrous thing. Thin, spidery limbs of razored obsidian protruded from under its scales, making the spirit appear like some great and terrible centipede. Its head, formerly featureless, was studded with rusted blades and bits of broken bone, and from its body came not the clanging of a bell, but a high, ululating cry that seemed to bore into Mitsuhide's skull.

Mitsuhide started toward the horrifying creature, weapon raised, but Teru caught his shoulder.

"Dark sorceries ravage Mount Hiei. Can you not see Sannō's pain?"

"I'm more concerned about *our* pain." Mitsuhide tried to shake free, but the abbess's grip was iron. She dragged him to the side as the mountain spirit thrashed blindly, toppling pillars and collapsing the rear of the portico. A long-horned oni kicked free of the wreckage only to be caught up in Sannō's coils and crushed.

Stumbling through knee-deep mud, Teru and Mitsuhide dodged the spirit's long tail, skirting the courtyard. Koemon waited for them near the edge of the stairs, just behind the great temple bell.

Teru moved to descend, but Mitsuhide paused to glance up at the heavy beams that held the bell aloft, an idea rising through his jumbled thoughts.

"Go." He nodded at Teru and Koemon. "I'm going to stop those demons from following us."

Mitsuhide turned back to Sannō. Gaki swarmed over the writhing spirit. Although the Mountain King's twitching obsidian limbs cut the hungry ghosts' bodies to ribbons, the hordes of Jigoku seemed without end.

Jaw tight, Mitsuhide hammered his blade against the temple bell. The resonant chime cut through the shrieks like a sudden squall. Although the demons seemed not to notice, Sannō's great head rose, cocked as if in question.

Mitsuhide hit the bell again and again. When his katana snapped, he beat upon the bronze with his fists.

At last, the mountain spirit surged toward him.

Abandoning all caution, Mitsuhide dove toward the passage. There came a booming crash from behind him, then the crack and snap of heavy wooden beams. Mitsuhide rolled down the stairs, eyes screwed shut as the impact of unyielding stone caused his teeth to clack painfully together. He landed hard on his side, and grit his teeth against a sudden sharp pain that seemed to carve to the very root of him.

He drew in breath, carefully at first, lest the pain turn out to be broken ribs. Gradually, the hurt faded to a throbbing ache, and Mitsuhide opened his eyes.

In the dim light of the tunnel, he saw Koemon and Teru. The abbess crouched over Koemon, who had his back against the wall, lips pressed together, his expression pained as Teru wrapped the stocky samurai's arm in a makeshift sling.

"Can you walk?" Mitsuhide asked.

Koemon opened one eye. "Is that an order?"

"Depends." Mitsuhide glanced up the tunnel, sighing as he saw the stairs blocked by smoldering rubble.

Teru followed his gaze. "That bell cost more than a small palace."

"I'll beg Buddha's mercy later." Mitsuhide tried to stand, and immediately thought better of it.

"Don't strain yourself, Lord," Koemon said. "We're safe."

"Unless those demons can claw through a temple's worth of burning wreckage," Teru said.

Mitsuhide winced. "Better get moving."

Teru helped him to his feet, eyes narrowed as she glanced back at the ruin. "Evil always has a price. Your lord will pay. In this life or the next."

"Of that I have no doubt," Mitsuhide replied.

Komeon groaned as he stood. "Ever wonder if we're on the wrong side?"

As if to echo the samurai's question, there came a furious roar from overhead, followed by the crack of splintering wood.

"All I know is we're on the right side of that." Mitsuhide nodded at the wall of rubble.

Koemon snorted, shaking his head as, together, they limped toward safety.

✟ ⚱ ✟

The sun rose on smoldering peaks. The demons were gone, but the horror remained. Mount Hiei lay cloaked in a funereal shroud of smoke and soot. Nothing moved upon its forested slopes, the air empty of even insect noises.

Ash fell thick as midwinter snow as Mitsuhide, Koemon, and Hidenori made their way through the Oda camp to give their congratulations on the brilliant victory.

Lord Nobunaga waited for them, his sorcerers nowhere in sight. Bruised circles shadowed Nobunaga's eyes, his skin pale beneath fine robes. The lord's lips were drawn back in a barely concealed snarl of pain. It seemed as if last night had taken its toll upon Nobunaga as well.

"Akechi." Nobunaga offered a slight bow as Mitsuhide and his entourage filed into the command tent.

"It is done?" Mitsuhide asked, bowing to hide the tremor in his expression. Teru's passage had led them to a hidden temple beyond the Oda lines. Mitsuhide had returned to his tent, bathed, bound his wounds, and dressed in fine clothes. There had been no indication Lord Oda knew of his betrayal, but that was little solace when Mitsuhide sat face-to-face with the demon himself.

"It is done. Due in no small part to the Akechi." Nobunaga offered a thin smile. "If you had not banished the Mountain Spirit, this victory would carry a much heavier price."

"I fear the true cost has yet to be paid."

Lord Oda narrowed his eyes, and for a moment Mitsuhide thought his life was over.

Nobunaga laughed. "You always were an old maid, Akechi. But you have served me well." Lord Oda raised a hand. "Come, what reward do you wish."

The move was like the parting of clouds after a heavy storm. Nobunaga didn't know.

Mitsuhide swallowed, wondering how far to press his luck. "Last night taught your enemies to fear the Oda. Let today show them your beneficence. I ask only to be given Mount Hiei and the surrounding lands, so that I may make them prosperous again on behalf of the clan."

"Bones and burned villages?" Nobunaga studied Mitsuhide for a long moment, then gave a bemused shake of his head. "If that is truly your wish, then I commend them to you."

45

Mitsuhide bowed low, letting out his held breath. As ruler, he could see Teru's people hidden and protected. The rest of the meeting passed in a blur – titles, rewards, and fiefs apportioned according to lords great and small. Then came the victory celebration.

Mitsuhide begged off only a few cups of sake, saying his wounds pained him, which was true enough. It was only after Mitsuhide returned to his tent that he let his composure slip, collapsing upon his cot with a pained hiss.

There would be more battles, more sieges, more demons, of that he was sure. Whatever came, Akechi Mitsuhide vowed he would remember last night, and the terrible depths to which Lord Nobunaga would sink to achieve victory. Abbess Teru's pronouncement lingered in Mitsuhide's thoughts, putting down roots, growing.

Even if it took years, he vowed, Lord Nobunaga would pay for the evil he had done.

In this world and the next.

THE SHAYATIN EXPRESS

Robert Lassen

North of Mada'in Salih, May 1917

I t is coming."

Nusair Abdi silenced the Bedouin youth with one sharp flick of his hand. The shrill warning was unnecessary. The dust storm concealed much, but not the roaring and screeching of the approaching thing. Besides, the stuttered words only highlighted the boy's lack of combat experience. Peering through the storm, Nusair grimaced as the hot desert wind lashed sand grains across the exposed skin of his cheeks. He saw nothing beyond fifty feet. A swirling veil obscured everything, even the midday Arabian sun, behind a dull pink glow.

"Allah favours us," he told the lines of robed horsemen either side of him, pointing down the low ridge. "The infidels will see us too late, and their machine guns shall be useless." He saw the youth bite his lip, and wondered again whether to order the boy to stay on the ridge, safe from the coming fight. Nusair had only brought Zaid Ben with them as a gesture of respect to the boy's father, a cousin of Sharif Nasir who had rode west with Lawrence. To victory and glory.

He swallowed. Stinging jealousy burned its way down his sun-parched throat. Captain Thomas Edward Lawrence, who had been so close to him for the last four months, first as friends, then as brothers. How Nusair longed to be with him now, seizing Aqaba from the Ottoman occupiers and making history alongside that brave and elegant British warrior. Not wasting his time on another pointless but dangerous attack on the Turkish supply lines.

Yasir Hassan shifted the weight of the Swiss Mannlicher rifle that rested across his horse's shoulders. "I shall take care of the gunners," he murmured. With dry and cracked fingers, the ancient warrior carefully peeled back the silk covering over his rifle's delicate optics. "Patience, my sweet," he crooned to the weapon. "You will take many Turks today."

Beneath his mount's hooves, Nusair saw a rivulet of fine sand run downslope, shaken loose by the approaching maelstrom of noise and fury. He gripped the reins tighter, and checked that the ornate dagger at his belt was secure in its sheath.

"Remember," the Englishman said from behind, his voice muffled beneath his black robes, "no grenades. I need that cargo in—"

With awful suddenness the metal beast tore free of the concealing fabric of the dust storm.

It thundered across the sand below them in a tumult of steam and sparks. Zaid whimpered. All smoke-blackened metal and unnatural power, the train was moving faster than Nusair had expected. He raised himself in his saddle. His war cry drowned out the last of the Englishman's words.

They surely couldn't have all heard him, not above that noise. And yet, as one, thirty horses and riders launched themselves down the slope, jostling almost shoulder to shoulder for the honour of being first to board the train. Even Zaid was there, swept up in the excitement with his robes trailing in the air behind him, his horse churning up sand in its wake as it streaked ahead.

The Hejaz railway ran from Medina all the way to Damascus, through mountains and deserts and fertile plains. Here, blessedly, the ground alongside the track was flat, with no raised embankment, and Nusair had his horse alongside the middle of the five carriages before the machine gunners in their sandbagged emplacements atop the first and last could react.

They didn't need much longer, though. Whatever other faults the Turks had, they were experienced fighters. The first machine gun swung into position.

"Zaid, look out!"

The youth heard Nusair's warning and ducked. The first machine gun rounds rasped inches over his head. Two Bedouin behind him were less blessed and tumbled to the sand beneath the mangled corpses of their horses. Switching fire, the gunners tracked Zaid, sending puffs of dust into the air with each impact either side of him.

Nusair cursed. "Yasir! Take them!"

With his horse galloping at full speed, by all rights the ancient rider should have fallen as soon as he released the reins. Instead, he raised himself slightly in the saddle, pulling the rifle to his shoulder. Nusair saw Yasir's lips moving in prayer behind his wispy grey beard, their movement ceasing as he took one final preparatory breath. Then he squeezed the trigger.

A single sharp crack filled the air, and the first machine gun fell silent.

Nusair knew it wouldn't last. Another Turk would take over the gun. No, they had to get on to the train and close them down. Muttering a prayer of his own, he cajoled his reluctant horse to within inches of the shuddering flanks of the train and launched himself towards the covered boarding platform at the rear of the third carriage.

Too soon. Instead of the railings that surrounded the platform, he hit the side of the carriage.

Hard.

The impact drove the air from his lungs. Gasping while blind panic surged through him, his hands clutched at nothing but his rifle sling snagged on something, holding him to the carriage. Nusair slammed against the side, once, twice, his large bulk bouncing from the wood until his questing fingers closed on sun-blasted metal.

Cloth snapped like a gunshot, and he felt a sudden wrench as the rifle was ripped from his shoulder. It cartwheeled onto the sand with its useless torn strap flapping behind it. In moments it was lost from sight. He held tight with one hand to the thin metal ladder that led from the platform to the roof, and caught a glimpse of the slender Englishman, closing fast. If only that one had allowed them to derail the train like he had wanted to...

Nusair's sandaled feet scrambled. Slipped twice on sand-blasted wood. Found purchase at last.

He allowed himself two quick breaths. More would be weakness. "This way," he shouted as he clambered gratefully onto the platform. He beckoned to the nearest riders, the Englishman at their head. They steered a course towards his outstretched hand, ready to join him onboard.

The Englishman made it. Just. The others didn't. The rear machine gun found its range and shredded them with high-velocity rounds.

Good men. Warriors who had been with the Sharifian Army since the start of the Great Arab Revolt. Each of them worth a thousand of the spindly Englishman.

If that bastard Farrington-Smyth knew the narrow margin of his survival, he gave no obvious sign. Drawing a revolver, he reached for the access door's handle. Nusair's hand closed tight on the man's thin wrist. "No," he snapped. "First we take out the machine gunners."

"That is your fight," the Englishman said, staring at him with cold eyes turned black by the cadaverous shadows of his skull. "Mine is inside."

You are no Lawrence. Not even a soldier. Just some London bureaucrat messing in the holy war against the defilers of Mecca. "It is *our* fight. And you are either with us, or you are with them." He stabbed a finger upwards at the carriage top, and then slowly drew it across his throat for emphasis.

"Very well," Farrington-Smyth said calmly. "Let us make it quick."

Nusair led the way up the ladder, feeling the rattling motion of the train through his palms, and flinched as the full force of the dust-laden slipstream struck him in the face. He covered his eyes, leaving just enough gap to see the Turkish emplacement up ahead. The gunners had been smart enough to wear goggles to shield their eyes. Their glass could only protect against dust, though. They could do nothing against Yasir Hassan and his beloved rifle. As Nusair watched, the left lens of the surviving Turkish gunner shattered. The glass fragments briefly flared bright red before the body collapsed over his Maschinengewehr 08.

"I guess that leaves the other for us," the Englishman said, leading the way towards the rear of the train. Now, the rushing air became their friend, propelling them over the gaps between carriages until the emplaced machine gun was only yards ahead. The gunners hadn't seen them, focusing instead on the remaining riders below. With horror, Nusair realised how few still remained. Bile bubbled in his throat as he watched another rider fall from his screaming horse and tumble lifelessly across the sand.

He reached for his rifle, remembered that it lay a mile in their wake, and drew his dagger instead.

The nearest Turk soldier saw him. Soon enough to know that death was coming. Too late to stop it. Vaulting over the surrounding sandbags, Nusair drove the curved blade into the man's gut. Twisted it. Hot blood rushed across his hand. With a snarl he wrenched the dagger free. He struck the man across the jaw and shoved him hard in the chest. The dying Turk fell back over the sandbags, flailed uselessly, and disappeared over the roof's edge with a truncated squeal.

The second gunner, barely older than Zaid Ben, remained too intent on gunning down the Arab riders to notice the fight. Nusair grabbed hold of the boy's hair, yanked his head back, and carved open his windpipe with the razor-sharp blade. The young soldier's gurgled final plea hung in the air before the hot wind devoured it.

Nusair dropped the still-twitching body and raised his bloody dagger in triumph to the remaining riders. They were so few now. The shriek of metal on metal assaulted his ear as the brakes came on, hard. A sliver of his mind hoped the sound meant there were more of his riders up ahead seizing the locomotive. The rest of it focused desperately on trying not to go over the side as the sudden braking threw him against the sandbags.

The movement saved his life.

A knife blade slashed the air where he had been standing a moment earlier, and a heavy body stumbled against him.

Nusair growled and swung blindly. His dagger snagged on

cloth. A grunt told him the point had found something below. Righting himself, he saw the knife coming again and twisted away, his dagger held in front of him. This was no Turk. His opponent was European, blond-haired, nearly as large as Nusair himself and nearly as pale as the Englishman. The uniform wasn't Turkish, nor British. The man muttered something guttural and unintelligible.

German, then.

Nusair smiled. He had no idea why there should be anyone other than Turks on this train, but he had never killed a German. This man was surely a gift for him.

"*Kapituliere Sie sich oder weide ich dich erschiessen,*" the Englishman shouted, drawing a revolver from beneath his black robes. The German soldier didn't even blink, just kept the trench knife low, his eyes on his opponent. Nusair deliberately kept his bulk between the German and the revolver. He would not let the Englishman steal this prize, not when there were so many of his dead brothers to avenge.

The German lunged, fast for a big man.

Nusair swayed to the side, but not quickly enough. He felt the serrated steel slice the skin of his ribs. Not deep, barely enough to notice, though the damage to his robes would need repairing. The German, though... that was different. Nusair felt a surge of satisfaction as he saw the darkening patch on the man's sleeve. His first, blind swing had struck home deeper than he'd thought. Judging by the speed and spread, he'd opened the artery in the left arm. The man's face paled as blood ran down to drip from the wrist. His other hand, the one that held the knife, remained steady.

"I want him alive," Farrington-Smyth yelled. Nusair ignored him. The German was bleeding out and wouldn't last long, not without medical attention.

The German knew it too. With a wild cry, he hurled his body against Nusair, bringing the trench knife up. Nusair planted his rear foot. He batted aside the man's wrist and drove his dagger up into the man's abdomen and frenziedly sawed it back and forth until he heard it grinding against the breastbone.

The trench knife clattered from nerveless fingers. The German stared with fading eyes, and then with one last convulsive effort, spat in Nusair's face.

He let the body fall behind the slowing train, and wiped the bloody gobbet of phlegm from his cheek.

"I damn well told you I wanted him alive."

Nusair shrugged, leaned down to wipe the bloody knife clean on the uniform of the dead Turkish youth. "You know how we treat captives," he told the Englishman. "That German was a brave man. He deserved a brave man's death."

"How noble," Farrington-Smyth said coldly. "Lawrence told me you people were more noble than smart."

"And he told me you were not to be trusted."

The train shuddered to a halt.

Nusair pushed past the Englishman and climbed the ladder down to the hard desert floor. As always, thinking of Lawrence left him feeling an odd emptiness inside. He remembered their last meeting. It had stuck with him every night on the long ride across Turkish-occupied territory to this final, pre-ordained ambush. It had haunted his dreams.

"You know they cannot replace you, Lawrence."

"Everyone can be replaced, Nusair Abdi. Even me. London has a million more to send. This one is called Farrington-Smyth."

"A foolish name. Is he an officer, like you?"

"Lord, no. This chap is a civilian. Works for something called K Department, whatever the hell that is. All very hush-hush. They don't even like you to mention the name. I'd probably be in an awful pickle if they knew I'd told you."

"Can I trust him like I have trusted you?"

"No. If you forget every other moment we spent together, Nusair, remember this. You can't trust anyone London sends. Especially not me."

Nusair brushed dust from his eyes, and walked towards the locomotive.

It stood silent now, though a few final wisps of grey still snaked from the smokestack to be lost in the swirling dust above. A warrior climbed down from the cab, his grim face set and his white robes spattered with blood. It took the sight of the sawn-off shotgun in his hands for Nusair to remember his name. Khalid Mahdavi. A good fighter, unflappable but aloof. Zaid and Yasir Hassan joined them, the latter cradling the rifle in his hands and gently rocking it back and forth. Nusair took a deep breath, banishing thoughts of Lawrence from his mind. "Is the train secure?"

"It is," Khalid said. "There were many Turkish soldiers in the front two carriages. We killed them all, but lost Fakhir Afzal and Ismail Rahmani. All other carriages are empty, but for the sounds of movement in the middle one. We left that one until last, as he ordered." He jerked his chin in the Englishman's direction.

"I give the orders here," Nusair snapped. "We'll take them now. Zaid, fetch the others."

The youth hesitated. He shifted uneasily and murmured something under his breath.

"Now, boy!"

"There are no others," Farrington-Smyth said quietly. It took a few seconds for the words to sink in.

Twenty-five men. Brave men. Martyrs. They were with Allah now, but the thought brought Nusair no comfort. They had been his to lead. His first command, his first raid on the strategically-vital Hejaz railway without Lawrence by his side.

And they were all dead.

With a snarl of rage, Nusair spun and grabbed the Englishman by the throat. "I wanted to derail the train! They would still be alive!"

"Let go of me."

"I will cut your throat and leave you here for the jackals!"

"Let… go…"

Nusair felt something hard press against his belly. He looked down. "If you shoot me," he began, "my men will see that you die slowly."

"This is a Webley Mark Five revolver," the Englishman said. "Count your men, Nusair Abdi. I have six bullets. I won't need them all."

Out of the corner of his eye, Nusair saw Yasir Hassan moving his rifle.

"Be still, old man," the Englishman said. "Or there will be… unpleasantness. May I remind you all that it was Hussein bin Ali Al-Hashimi himself who ordered you to support my mission?"

Nusair spat on the ground. He released the man, though he kept one hand on the dagger at his waist. "Your mission got my warriors killed."

"Your poorly-executed attack killed them. You can still ensure they didn't die in vain." The pistol disappeared into the Englishman's robes. "My sources said the cargo will be in the third carriage. There will likely be guards, German guards, so be careful."

Khalid grinned. "A few grenades will take care of them."

"As Lawrence said, more noble than smart. I wouldn't let you derail the train because the cargo must remain undamaged. You can therefore understand my reluctance for grenades, yes?" The Englishman sighed. "Even bullets are a risk I would prefer not to take, but needs must, I suppose." He turned to the access door.

Nusair grabbed him by one skeletal arm. It felt like grabbing iron, nothing but bone and garrotte-wire muscles. "Wait. You never have told us what we are looking for. If we don't know, how can we avoid damaging it?"

Farrington-Smyth stared flatly at him, then down at his arm, and waited until Nusair released his grip before answering. "Very well. It's a box. Soapstone, white, about the size of one of your holy books. The lid is covered in raised carvings."

"What sort of carvings?"

"Raised ones. That's all you need to know." The Englishman watched him, unblinking.

He had the eyes of a snake, Nusair realised. Though even a horned viper would surely have some emotion.

Drawing his pistol, the Englishman stepped up onto the rear platform of the third carriage. "Don't touch it, don't even look at it. And for God's sake, don't open it."

"Why?"

"Do you people even understand the concept of orders? Trust me. You don't want to open it." He put his hand on the door handle. "Ready?"

Nusair motioned his men closer, and nodded.

A scream filled the air. Muffled. Indistinct. Unmistakeable.

A scream of purest terror.

"Allah be merciful," Zaid cried, stumbling back and falling to the sand. "Allah, be merciful."

"It came from within," Yasir Hassan murmured. More screams now, and plaintive shouts. The sound of desperate scrambling resounded through the wood. "What manner of horror could make a man cry out like that?"

Nusair drew his blade, reaching for the door. "Let us meet it face to face," he said. He hoped his voice did not betray the fear that churned his guts and made his fingers shake around the hilt of his dagger. Not at the screams. At the way the colour had drained from Yasir Hassan's ancient face. A man who had faced every terror known to the Bedouin with the same stoic resolve, now poised on the edge of panicked flight.

What could do that to a warrior like Yasir Hassan?

The Englishman shook his head. "Best to wait a few moments, I think."

Gunshots. The carriage shuddered as bullets punched through its sides. The Arabs threw themselves to the ground as a rifle bullet burrowed into the sand behind them. Zaid curled into a ball, a single sob escaping his lips.

The Englishman didn't move. He simply stood, waiting.

More gunshots.

A final scream, cut short.

A gunshot, softer than the rest.

Silence.

"Are you ready, gentlemen?"

Nusair met Farrington-Smyth's gaze, and saw the mocking contempt. He stood, brushing sand from his robes, picturing his dagger slicing deep into the man's neck. No, that would be too quick. The man had to die slowly, the way those Turkish prisoners had died after the fall of Wejh. Allah would not be merciful to this one, Nusair promised himself.

But then, Hussein bin Ali Al-Hashimi lacked mercy for those who defied his orders.

Helping Zaid to his feet, Nusair shoved the boy forward and beckoned his warriors closer until they stood crowded around the doorway.

"Go," the Englishman said, and wrenched open the door.

Nusair stepped through, and plunged into darkness.

Panic wrapped icy tendrils around his heart. This was not normal darkness. Behind him, he saw the Arab warriors silhouetted against the pink hue of the sandstorm as they entered, one by one. Once inside they seemed to vanish from sight, as if the daylight itself could penetrate no further than the door frame. And the interior felt frigid, not just compared to the baking heat outside but as cold as the winter night in the high desert. He felt sure that his breath fogged the air ahead of him but could see nothing more than if he had kept his eyes screwed shut.

Blindly, one hand outstretched into the nothingness while the other felt its way along the cool wood of the carriage's side, Nusair edged forward. He wanted to turn back, but he could hear Yasir Hassan's rasping breath close behind. His foot caught on something. With a startled cry he fell, sprawling across warm, damp floorboards.

A dim light filled the interior of the carriage, and in its glow Nusair knew true horror.

You cannot break and flee, he told himself. *Not in front of the few men you still lead. Not in front of the Englishman.*

But Allah be merciful, he wanted to.

"Interesting," Farrington-Smyth said blandly. His face was lost in the shadows behind the illumination of the Orilux Trench Torch he held in his bony fingers, but somehow Nusair knew those eyes would be as impassive and lifeless as ever.

Blood pooled across the floor. Fresh, but rapidly cooling. Nusair had stumbled over a dead soldier, the man's head not just caved in but pulped, leaving no intact piece of bone bigger than a man's palm. A discarded Mauser Gewehr 98 lay nearby. Blood caked the rifle's broken shoulder stock. Someone had driven it so hard into the dead man's skull that the wood had shattered on the floor beneath.

Dead *men*, Nusair corrected himself. Four of them, all in field-grey German uniforms. Two had been shot multiple times in the chest and legs. The impacts suggested weight of fire, not accuracy. All at point blank range, too. These bullets had been fired from within the carriage, not without.

Four dead men. No survivors. Nothing living. No sound but Zaid Ben violently purging his breakfast of samen sheehi and stale bread from his stomach.

"Control yourself," Nusair hissed at the youngster. The freezing cold, he realised, had vanished the moment the Englishman switched on his flashlight. Too late. It had seeped into his bones. He shivered and looked at his colleagues. "What happened here?"

"Something unholy," Yasir Hassan muttered. "We should leave."

Khalid knelt by the fourth dead German. "This one was an officer." The corpse seemed mostly intact, slumped in a seated position against the side of the carriage, eyes open. He might almost have been watching them, except his dead eyes saw nothing. His face, though. That expression. Whatever the officer had seen before he died...

It took Nusair several breaths before he dragged his eyes away from the terror etched into the dead man's face and noticed the sodden exit wound in the top of the skull. Below the jaw, a smaller hole produced a steady trickle of blood onto the German's tunic and trousers. His left hand lay across something small and white. The right still held a pistol, though the fingers had long since ceased to feel its weight.

"The pistol," Nusair breathed. "Did he...?"

Khalid nodded. "That last shot we heard. He saved it for himself."

"But why?" Zaid wiped at his mouth with the sleeve of his robe.

"Perhaps they feared to fall into our hands?"

"No," Yasir Hassan said, clutching his rifle. "Whatever these men feared, it was not us. It was not human." He ran his fingers up the polished forestock of his Mannlicher rifle, whispering below his breath.

Khalid smoothed the dead man's eyelids closed. Not as an act of dignity, Nusair knew. No. Khalid couldn't stand to see the unreasoning terror seared into those glassy orbs anymore, and it took effort for Nusair to hold back the words of gratitude that sprung to his lips. Khalid murmured a prayer, then reached down and moved the dead man's left hand to reveal the item below.

"Don't touch it," the Englishman snapped.

Khalid's hand froze, his fingertips inches from the polished soapstone surface, but he did not withdraw.

Intrigued, Nusair moved closer. The box gave off an odd pale luminescent sheen in the weak beam of the flashlight. His shoulder bumped against Yasir Hassan's as the old man leaned forward to see it. Even Zaid crowded closer, curiosity overcoming fear and nausea. Twenty-five of their brothers had fallen to take this prize for the British. They deserved to see it now.

And yet, up close, it disappointed. Nusair wasn't sure what he had expected. It seemed pathetically small, a mere trinket. The sides were plain, their smoothness broken only by the metallic bulges of tiny, intricate hinges. Only the lid showed signs of any design, with the bas relief of the surface visible but indistinct in the gloom. There was a clasp to secure the lid, but it was not locked in place. Only the weight of the lid itself kept the box closed.

"It would appear," Farrington-Smyth said, "that the box has been opened."

"What are those carvings?" Zaid pointed. "On the lid?"

Yasir Hassan narrowed his eyes, then gave a hiss and fell back. "Shaitan!"

Khalid cursed and let the German's dead hand drop. The lifeless fingers rattled on the hollow box. For an instant, it seemed the nails dragged across the lid, bouncing it a millimetre open, but then the corpse slowly slid to the side, the head leaving a smear of blood on the wall until the body settled and the head lolled a few millimetres from the floor. It left the box exposed, and Nusair saw the carvings clearly for the first time, and knew why Yasir Hassan now trembled.

"Shaitan," he echoed.

The figure on the lid was not human, though its form was a mockery of Allah's creations. The body was man-like. The resemblance ceased there. The skin appeared covered in something not unlike both fur and scales. A tail hung loose between the lips, the tip tapering in reptilian fashion before splitting into half a dozen barbs. The head was worst of all. In the feverish recesses of Nusair's mind, images merged in an unholy union of a jackal, a tiger, and a sun-bleached skull. But even that ghastly hybrid didn't come close.

Shaitan. The Shayatin. Demons born of hellfire.

His people feared the Djinn, but Djinn could be bargained with, reasoned with, avoided. The Shayatin... they were pure evil. Every man, woman and child was born with one. Every child was raised to do their best to keep them at bay. Cover your mouth when you yawn, lest one enter your body. Do not pray at sunset or sunrise when the Gates of Hell fall open and Iblis himself waits to punish the simplest mistake.

Shaitan. The word alone filled him with dread. "Creatures of evil," he told the Englishman. "Whispering lies in men's hearts, driving them to sin. The children of Iblis. Abū Murrah."

"The Father of Bitterness," Farrington-Smyth said. "Yes. I know."

Nusair felt the room growing hot now, oppressive pressure building in the air around him. A cloying odour drifted into his nostrils, sending waves of nausea surging through his innards. The interior of the carriage grew indistinct, like the sandstorm raging outside had seeped through the boards. He reached out one hand to steady himself, and felt the wood vibrate beneath his palm.

"We're moving," he gasped.

"How?" Khalid stared at him, eyes impossibly wide. "I killed the driver and the fireman myself."

"I tell you we're moving," Nusair snapped.

No one argued. He could see in their eyes that they knew it too. It didn't matter that there was no sound of locomotive or clattering tracks. The carriage shuddered as it accelerated, quicker and quicker. Too quick. Only the Englishman seemed calm. He leaned against the wall, his face impassive, his right hand hidden within his robes. His face was blank, but for the first time, Nusair saw something in his eyes. Not fear. Not even emotion.

Curiosity. Detached, clinical curiosity.

Zaid Ben gave a tiny whimper, and took a step back, into the shadows. Nusair almost shouted at him to be silent but changed his mind. The boy should not have come. He was not ready for this mission. None of them were, Nusair realised, but Zaid most of all. He needed words of encouragement, not contempt. With a sigh, Nusair turned to offer them.

The boy had gone.

In his place came something else. Something *huge*.

It emerged from the darkness into the faint pool of the flashlight's beam. Not the creature from the soapstone box. That, for all its horror, was a human's feeble representation of the unthinkable. This was worse.

So much worse.

It towered over them, hunching within the confines of the carriage, the head cocked over sideways. Two glowing orbs that might almost have been eyes flickered rhythmically above a porcine snout. The thing's skin was the black of fire-charred leather, broken by deep gouges where livid red cauterised flesh showed beneath the ash. The limbs were long and insectoid. Its legs seemed to merge into the floor without any discernible feet, while the arms ended not in hands but instead in elongated maws that peeled apart like flowers to reveal concentric rings of serrated teeth.

As Nusair watched, unable to think or speak or even move, a second set of smaller arms unfolded from within the exposed alabaster ribs of the creature, showering the floor with shreds of desiccated flesh.

The head split open vertically, revealing not a mouth but a deeper darkness. From within, seeming impossibly distant, Nusair heard a sound, a grotesque parody of Zaid's voice, begging to leave, begging to go home.

It reached for him.

"Shoot it," screamed Nusair. His words dwindled in his ears, drowned out by the roar of Yasir Hassan's beloved rifle.

The bullet seemed to strike the creature in the middle of the horrific mouth. The darkness swallowed the round. The creature didn't even react. Simply carried on its relentless staccato blinking.

Nusair drew his dagger, but then felt the heat of Khalid's shotgun blast. It struck the creature where the throat might have been, and it stumbled back without a sound. Yasir Hassan worked the bolt action of his Mannlicher and sent a second heavy bullet into the centre of the creature's chest.

Without a sound, it collapsed back to the floor, twitching in a spreading pool of black ichor.

"Zaid," Nusair shouted. "Where are you?"

Yasir Hassan grabbed him by the arm. "Even if the boy lives, he is beyond our help," he mumbled. "We need to get off this train."

Half-running, half-falling, Nusair followed the two Arabs past the unmoving Englishman and threw open the rear door. His hand was already raised against the expected blinding daylight, but it didn't come. His first thought was that night had fallen, but that wasn't it at all. No stars, no clouds, no sound of the air rushing by the moving train. Either side of the metal platform, darkness hung like heavy satin drapes, darker than any night.

"I don't remember any tunnels on this stretch of the railway," he gasped.

"This is no tunnel," Yasir Hassan intoned. "It is the shadow of Zaqooum."

It is the dread tree in Hell, Nusair thought, *and we stand beneath its leaves.* He didn't know he had given the thought voice until he saw the fury on Khalid's face.

"Pull yourselves together, you fools," the stocky warrior snapped, reloading his shotgun. "The Shayatin seek to drive us to despair. But they will learn. Allah is with me. Are you?" Without waiting for an answer, he plunged back into the carriage.

Nusair reached out his hand, past the old man and his rifle, into the darkness. The air felt hot. Flying dust eddied and scraped around his fingers, yet there was no wind. "Could Khalid be right?"

"It doesn't matter," Yasir Hassan said. "It doesn't matter. Iblis has claimed us for his own."

Nusair thought of Lawrence. How many times had he seen that face laugh at impending death? He would do no less.

"Come on, you old hawk. If the Shayatin have come for us, then let us make sure they pay a heavy price." With a deep breath, they turned back to the open doorway.

They found Khalid kneeling on the floor over a huddled form. "It's gone," he said.

"The creature?"

"Gone. Not even its blood remains."

"Then... that?"

"Yes. Zaid." Khalid bowed his head. Beneath him, the remains of the youth lay still. The blood-soaked robes over his chest concealed the wounds beneath. The face was all but gone, most of the flesh and eyelids ripped away, leaving a single intact eye to stare accusingly at them.

"You shouldn't have come," Nusair murmured.

Khalid frowned. "These are gunshot wounds." He stared at the face, then looked down at his shotgun in confusion.

A choked cough came from behind them.

"Yasir Hassan," Khalid said. "Are you ok?"

The old man was trembling. No. *Transforming.*

As Nusair watched, his body numb while every instinct screamed its need for him to run, the old man's skin cracked like a dry lakebed, exposing mottled red streaks that pulsated in time to Nusair's own frenzied heartbeat. The white robes parted neatly, revealing a massive carapace of thick bone and jet-black tufted hair. The eyes swelled and turned reddish black, huge smouldering lumps of coal presiding over what had once been a white beard but now was a seething mass of translucent worms.

That tiny sliver of Nusair's mind not yet overwhelmed by terror observed that still the Englishman did nothing. Just watched them. Unmoving, with his right hand still in his robe.

His left hand held the soapstone box.

The creature reached out with trembling fingers. Still human. Frail. "Nusair Abdi," it said, and its voice was that of Yasir Hassan. "Why do you look at me that way?" But even as it spoke, the worms of the beard grew longer, slipping and coiling their way in a sinuous flood downwards and across the floor to fasten themselves on the body of the dead Zaid.

The boy should never have been here... One of the worms reared up, its tip fattened now. Blood coated its tiny leech maw.

Something in Nusair snapped.

With a shriek that echoed throughout the carriage, he threw himself at the thing and drove his dagger into the chest. The razor-sharp point should have glanced from the thick bone armour, but instead it slid effortlessly through. He felt it drive into flesh beneath.

The creature gave a startled moan and fell back, coughing weakly. Yasir Hassan's Mannlicher rifle clattered to the floor. The worms writhed in silent protest.

Nusair struck again.

Again.

Each blow deeper than the last, carving open the thin flesh beneath the outer shell until, after mere moments that seemed like hours the thing lay still. Nusair's dagger stood proud in the centre of its chest. A grave marker for the undead.

Nusair listened to the thing sobbing for several more

seconds before he saw his tears falling on the foul dead face and realised the truth. Yasir Hassan. A man who had been an inspiration to them all. A warrior who had taught them the meaning of courage, whose rifle was known and feared across the Arabian Peninsula. Yasir Hassan, a scourge from Hell to the Ottomans, a blessing from Allah to the Bedouin.

Dead now. Like Zaid Ben. Like the twenty-five warriors on the desert sand. All the Englishman's fault.

No. All my fault.

The Shaitan flickered, becoming indistinct, and Nusair caught the briefest glimpse of Yasir Hassan's real eyes, lying open in horrible accusation. Without thinking, he reached down to stroke the dead face even as it returned to its aberrant demonic form. Strange. He felt nothing as his fingers parted the glistening worms. No ichor. No sense of the train's movement.

Nothing but the wispy hairs that had once clung stubbornly to an old man's jaw.

With sudden, terrible realisation, he leapt to his feet and looked at Farrington-Smyth. The Englishman stared back, unblinking, but the robes had fallen away from his pale face now. His thin lips curled in a sardonic smile.

In his left hand, the soapstone box lay open.

"You did this," Nusair said.

The Englishman shook his head. "Your bullets. Your dagger." His right hand emerged from the robes, the revolver pointing at Nusair's chest.

Nusair reached for his blade. His fingers closed on its empty sheath. "Khalid!" He spun to look at his companion, pointing at the Englishman. The warning died in his throat when he saw the horror in the warrior's eyes.

"Shaitan," Khalid whispered.

A flash. A roar. Nusair didn't feel any pain. Just the shock of something pushing hard at his guts before the wall of the carriage slammed into his back and the floor came up to meet him and he found himself slumped next to the body of the German officer.

"Shaitan!" Standing above him, Khalid screamed the word

this time. The shotgun came up again, but then the warrior seemed to hesitate, his eyes widening as if he too realised the truth. Nusair fumbled for the dead officer's pistol. It took all his strength to raise it and pull the trigger.

Silence settled on the carriage, broken only by the steady dripping of blood from Khalid's shattered cranium, the sound of Nusair's rasping breath in his own ears, and a faint click as the Englishman closed the box.

Nusair realised he couldn't feel the pistol as Farrington-Smyth took it gently from his hand. He couldn't feel anything at all.

The Englishman knelt next to him. "A remarkable thing," he mused, stroking the soapstone with a bony finger. "The Ottomans uncovered it in Medina while digging their fortifications. Only after they'd lost a dozen men did they think to ask the Germans. Of course, Berlin ordered it sent their way, and it might have reached them if we weren't so damned good at intercepting their signals."

Nusair blinked. The room was becoming darker, despite the closeness of the Englishman's flashlight. In its glow, he saw Zaid, Khalid and Yasir Hassan. All human. All dead. "The box…" The words took effort to force through his dry, half-closed lips. But they didn't hurt. "It holds the Shayatin?"

"It would appear so," Farrington-Smyth said, "in a manner at least. All I can see in there is some herbs and dry grass, and a few twigs twisted about each other. The pattern is rather pretty. Of course, I'll leave it to the boffins in London to work out exactly how the one," he added, pointing first to the box and then to the bodies, "leads to the other. Suffice to say, it is as your legends say. They whisper in your ear, show you what they want you to see. But it is just illusion."

Nusair coughed. He tried to point at the bodies, but his hand didn't move at all. "Illusion couldn't do that."

"My dear Nusair Abdi, of course it could. It's all illusion. Courage, cowardice, nobility, patriotism. This whole wonderful war. I see the same things as you, I simply know them for what they truly are. But I have *always* been a little different, I suppose."

"Why?" Nusair could barely see the man now. "Why did my people have to die?"

The Englishman stood and fastened the clasp on the soapstone box. "The Germans thought to use this as a weapon," he said, looking down at Nusair. "With their faith in their Teutonic ingenuity, naturally they think it can be synthesized. Think upon that. Clouds of this, weaponised and unleashed upon the Allied war effort. Whole battalions turning upon each other, slaughtering each other, leaving gaping holes in the front line. Or entire cities destroying themselves in an orgy of terror and bloodlust." He sighed, a sound somewhere between anxious and wistful. "The war could be lost with a dozen bombs."

Nusair could only hear his voice now. The darkness was complete, as total as the illusion that had hidden the day from them when they had tried to flee, the same illusion that had made them think they were trapped on a speeding train when they were a simple step from safety. *I'm ready to join you, brothers,* he thought. *May Allah be merciful to us all.*

But there was one last question to be asked.

"Englishman," he said, his voice barely audible even to his own ears. "Now that you have this power, you will ensure it is destroyed?"

He heard no reply, just a rustle of robes and soft footsteps that dwindled to nothing, and the faint scratching of the wind-whipped sandstorm outside.

And soon not even that.

The man who called himself Farrington-Smyth, for this mission at least, left the bodies where they lay. The vultures and jackals would take care of them, and in any case, none of the warring sides would bother to investigate another bloody skirmish in a war that had a thousand of them every day.

Captain Lawrence had been right, he mused as he mounted the finest of the surviving horses. Nusair Abdi had been a good choice. Brave enough to get the job done, stupid enough to cause no problems. Lawrence had expressed some hope that Nusair and his men might survive the mission, but that had never been likely. London didn't send Farrington-Smyth when they expected survivors. Ensuring the opposite was his speciality.

He secured the soapstone box beneath his robes and gave it no more thought. His job was merely to acquire it. Let the K Department scientists worry about the rest. As a gift for them, he'd also retrieved Yasir Hassan's Mannlicher M1895. He doubted that the stories of its Djinn-infused accuracy were anything other than the skills of a fine marksman combined with an old man's low-grade insanity, but K Department were always on the lookout for unusual artefacts. More pertinently, it was a beautiful rifle and it might yet be useful. He had a long and dangerous ride ahead of him before this mission was over and he could wait, in boredom and despair, for the next one to begin. Pulling his robes over his face against the last efforts of the near-spent sandstorm, he turned his horse towards the sea and England.

Behind him, the train stood silent beneath the flickering shadows of circling vultures.

Aranea's Blessing

Alister Hodge

Gutter crept toward his target in the dark, placing each foot carefully on the sandy ground. The sentry stood with spear in hand, heavy-lidded eyes staring at a small fire. Flames danced across the armful of twigs, emitting a thin spiral of smoke and the occasional ember to the stars above. Gutter crouched behind the guard, picking where to bury his blade for a quick kill. He didn't care that it would be a surprise attack, a killing without 'honour'.

Fuck honour.

Having grown up on the pox-ridden streets of the capital, he'd embraced the lessons of his youth, even choosing his squad name so that all would know from where he'd climbed. As a child, he'd learnt to survive by any means. Rules were for the privileged, for those who didn't go hungry days at a time. In Gutter's mind, war was little different. In the chaotic melee of battle, the only thing that mattered was coming out the other side alive.

Gutter clenched his jaw, knuckles white about the grip as he readied himself to act. One more kill and their path to the cliff would be open.

Don't think.

He thrust his blade into the sentry's back, the point skidding over a rib before plunging deep. The man convulsed, prevented from screaming by the blade in his lung. Gutter took a handful of the man's hair and wrenched his head backwards, exposing the neck. Blood bubbled past the sentry's lips, eyes wide with confusion and pain as Gutter buried the knife a second time.

Gutter grunted as the guard stamped backward, his grip momentarily loosening as the boot tore a bloody strip of tissue from his shin. The sentry took his chance, jerking out of Gutter's deadly embrace. Burning embers scattered as the mortally injured man stumbled straight through the fire, crimson spurting from his neck. He didn't make it far. Steps unsteady with blood loss, the guard collapsed to his knees as flames licked the hem of his cloak. Within seconds, the fire spread up his back like a hungry demon, turning the figure to a human torch.

Gutter watched the guard's last moments of agony with a dispassionate gaze before kneeling to check the damage to his shin. The sentry had been foolish. By staring into the flames, he'd destroyed his night vision, allowing Gutter to approach unobserved. If only the rest of the battles his squad had faced during the previous fortnight had gone as well. He spat on the smouldering corpse before opening the guard's bag to check for anything worth stealing. Aside from a stick of dried meat, it was empty. No money, not even a flask of whiskey.

Fucking Sleepers.

Gutter sighed in disgust. Even slaves had more autonomy than these poor bastards. Poisoned by a unique toxin, they were mindless drones for the religious Order, doing whatever was required by their priests, whether it be manual labour or military defence. Multiple engagements with Sleeper soldiers had whittled Gutter's squad until only he and another remained to finish the mission.

"Stop fucking around," said Fletch. "Sun-up's not far away."

With iron-grey hair and a face like aged driftwood, it was as if the old soldier was held together by scar tissue and force of will. Gutter shoved his knife back in its sheath and went to help carry their packs to the cliff edge.

"You sure it's down there?"

Fletch unfastened one pack, pulling out two lengths of knotted rope. "Has to be. Elkar's spy said the temple was located in the western corner of Tribute Gorge."

Gutter leant over the cliff and peered into the shadows. If their map was correct, the First Temple of Aranea should be five hundred paces to their left. Unable to discern any structures in the gloom, he grimaced and returned to help Fletch prepare the ropes for their descent.

Several sources claimed the Aranea toxin was prepared in the temple below. His squad's mission was to destroy any stockpiled toxin, along with the equipment needed to create further supplies. For Elkar to bring the Order to its knees, their ability to create fresh Sleeper troops had to be curtailed.

Two years ago, few had heard of the god Aranea. From obscurity, the Order had sprouted and spread like a plague. Followers had swiftly multiplied. Whole towns converted, handing over wealth, businesses, and possessions. Lord Elkar was slow to realise his subjects were being poisoned, and that his entire province would soon be the plaything of a priest. The man had tried outlawing the religion, but the decree was ignored. With no other option, he had finally released the professional soldiers of his army to crush the insurrection by force.

But the bastards had fought back. Ignorant to self-preservation, Sleeper soldiers had attacked with the ferocity of wild animals, using weapons tipped with the toxin. To be wounded by an Aranea blade was to be converted to their mindless army. Forced into retreat, Elkar had grudgingly ceded land and power to the bastards. Unless there was a breakthrough soon, the future looked bleak for his Lord.

"You want to do a last check for breakages?"

While Fletch secured the rope for descent, Gutter opened the second bag. Inside were five pottery spheres filled with an explosive jelly. Long wicks impregnated with accelerant trailed from clay-stoppers. The destructive power of the bombs was awesome, each one capable of turning a building to dust. He ran his fingers gingerly over the spheres and packing straw, relieved to find the fragile items intact. Gutter refastened the tie and gently shouldered the bag, ready to climb. He wasn't much looking forward to the descent. In addition to the bombs, he carried sword and dagger, crossbow, and quiver. His arms were going to be knackered by the time he reached the bottom.

Fletch read him like a book, his lip hooked with a smirk. "And yet you wanted to wear chainmail."

The squad had elected to prioritise speed and mobility to achieve the mission objectives. Gutter shrugged, rubbing a hand down his blood-stained hauberk. The thick leather provided some protection but wouldn't block a well-aimed sword thrust.

"You'll think different when you're bleeding out."

"No, I won't," said Fletch, showing a cracked-tooth grin in the darkness. "Because I'll be dead, you idiot."

One end of the rope tied off around a boulder, Fletch dumped the rest off the cliff. Like intestines from an opened belly, the bundle unravelled as it fell. Gutter strained his hearing but failed to hear the far end hit the ground.

Shit.

He'd have to hope the rope's end was close enough to drop to the sand, or that there were passable handholds to climb the rest of the way. Gutter windmilled his arms to loosen the muscles, then took a grip and lowered himself over the edge.

"Hey."

Gutter paused, looking up at Fletch.

"If you fall, make sure you land close enough to give me something soft to drop onto. No point both of us dying."

Gutter just shook his head and started down the rope.

✟ ☙ ✟

Gutter's crossbow bounced against his back with each change of grip. Knots were tied into the rope, allowing him to alternate weight bearing between his feet and arms during the descent. With both men on the rope, it swayed and vibrated under their combined weight, bumping Gutter against the cliff periodically. He knew the rock was sandstone, and yet at each contact, it felt soft and slightly sticky, a sensation that made him instinctually recoil. High above, the moon emerged from a bank of clouds, flooding the cliff in silvery light.

Gutter froze.

The rock wall was covered in thick swathes of web. Undulating over the cliff face in masses of white, it was pockmarked by wide, circular tunnels. Gutter swallowed, his throat gone dry. He fucking hated spiders. As a street urchin, he'd been tortured by an older kid, held down while a tarantula was pressed against his arm. Its bite had stung like a red-hot poker, his arm swelling to twice the size. He'd got his own back on the bully the next week, smashing his teeth out with a brick. But revenge hadn't healed the mental scar. Anything with eight legs still made his skin crawl.

An arm span away, a fat bodied spider skuttled to a tunnel entrance. Large as a terrier, it watched with glittering eyes, front legs stroking a huge set of fangs. Not waiting to see what the beast would do, Gutter let the rope zip through his fingers at reckless speed to escape. The knots stripped through his hands with rough bumps, taking skin and calluses with them. Suddenly, his feet hit clear space, and he clamped his fingers just in time to catch the last knot of the rope.

Gutter stared down, heart dropping to see the ground was still twenty feet below. He'd probably survive the drop, but it would be with a broken leg or spine.

"Fletch! We need to climb the rest of the way."

A grumbled curse was the only reply from above. As Gutter stretched a tentative hand to the web beside him, something soft and heavy slapped onto his back.

Fuck, no...

A chittering noise came from behind as a spider crawled towards his exposed neck. Gutter slapped a hand blindly over his shoulder and grabbed two legs covered with stiff hair. Compulsively, he flung it away. Gutter spun at the end of the rope from the movement, free arm flailing to steady himself. The spider caught hold of the web again, legs hooking onto the sticky silk with ease. Hissing, it launched back at him, legs a blur as it scuttled across the vertical surface. Holding the rope with his left hand, Gutter ripped his dagger from its sheath and brought it up just as the spider jumped, fangs bared, and eight legs spread in an arc. Gutter skewered the creature's thorax, its body sliding halfway down his blade before jamming. Venom-tipped fangs clicked together, reaching in vain for his hand. Gutter whipped his arm down, flicking the spider from the end of his dagger. He had a brief glimpse of writhing legs before darkness swallowed the beast.

Breath was tight in his chest as he forced himself to regroup. Throwing caution aside, he stabbed his hand deep into the web for a hold. Finding a rough nub of rock deep beneath the silken mess, he let go of the rope. For a gut dropping moment, he hung in space, his other hand scrabbling until it found a grip, his toes also finding a ledge. Thick cord slapped against his back as Fletch abandoned the rope as well.

Gutter moved as fast as possible, shoving his hands through the thick web, dragging fingers down the face until he found purchase. When there was under ten feet to go, he jumped, arms pinwheeling for balance. Gutter landed on a sloping rise of dune and rolled, coming to his feet again with red sand streaming from hair and clothes.

A grunt came from above, and suddenly Fletch was falling, tearing a swathe of web with him from the cliff. The web slowed his fall somewhat, and he missed a rock outcrop to land in loose sand two paces away. Gutter took hold of his mate's collar and pulled him from the sticky mass, just as a pair of spiders emerged from the torn web. Hissing at the destruction of their home, they scurried across the sand toward the two soldiers. Gutter let Fletch drop and drew his sword from its scabbard in a fluid movement, slicing through the front legs of the first arachnid. As the spider faltered, Gutter plunged the sword deep into its face, driving the tip into the beast's small brain, two of its glittering eyes bursting in a gelatinous mess. It dropped to the sand, legs convulsing around its abdomen.

Fletch screamed. Gutter turned to see the second spider on his mate's thigh, fangs sunk deep into the muscle. The older soldier had a knife in hand, and punched the blade into the creature's fat abdomen, spilling orange goo. Despite the injuries, the arachnid held fast, fangs chewing at his leg as it pumped venom. Gutter lined the beast up and drove a vicious kick into its thorax.

The exoskeleton crunched beneath his toe as the spider was launched into the air. It hit the sand ten feet away, but instead of attacking once more, crawled back toward the cliff, leaving a trail of spilt guts.

Fletch groaned as he climbed back to his feet. "Did the bombs survive?"

Gutter cursed himself. He'd only been thinking of escaping the web when he'd jumped, but if the spheres were smashed, the mission was over. He shrugged the bag off his shoulders and checked the contents, grimacing as he found jelly amongst the straw. Luckily, it was only from one broken orb. Four remained, hopefully enough to finish the job.

"How's your leg?" asked Gutter.

Sweat beaded the older soldier's forehead as he tore open the cotton of his pants, exposing two puncture marks. The tissue surrounding was already swollen and red. He touched the skin gingerly, face grimacing.

"Fucking burns," he said between gritted teeth. "Doesn't matter, we need to get moving."

Above the eastern lip of the gorge, dawn lit the sky with a creeping bruise of yellow. The gorge was still in shadow; however, it wouldn't be long before the sun's rays hit. Within hours, the sand would be blistering hot. The First Temple of Aranea lay in the arid interior of Elkar's Province. To reach it, Gutter and Fletch had crossed over a hundred miles of baked wastelands.

Aside from the temple, there was little else in the gorge. No plants grew amongst the red sand and rocks. And yet there was still life. Gutter knew that scorpions the size of a man's foot were common to the area, not to mention these bastard spiders. He glanced up at the cliff again.

You've got to be fucking kidding me...

The expanse of web only stretched fifty paces across. If they'd dropped their rope almost anywhere else, they would have abseiled down the sandstone unmolested. At least the white cotton of their rope blended almost perfectly to the silk, camouflaging their entrance somewhat.

Fletch passed him a robe to slip over their clothes. Stolen from a prior kill, it was a Sleeper's uniform. Reaching from shoulder to ankle, the black robe had two vertical strips of purple on each side. By coming down the cliff, they'd avoided several roadblocks along the winding track that was the only entrance to the gorge. That left but one guarded point to overcome, the entrance to the temple.

✟ 🏆 ✟

Gutter forced himself to take slow, even breaths as they approached the gate. A narrow archway, wide enough to admit two men standing shoulder to shoulder, was the only way in. Nerves coiled in his gut like an eel, his hands clammy. With only two of their squad remaining, it was time to trust Lady Luck. A tall sandstone wall enclosed the temple in a large semi-circular arc, and without ladders and covering fire, there was no chance of going over the top. Similarly, an overt attack upon the gatehouse would see them quickly outnumbered and overwhelmed. No, success would depend on their ability to pass beneath notice, as Sleepers of the Order.

"Only two guards," said Fletch under his breath. "Doesn't seem enough."

The Sleepers stood either side of the gateway, each holding a lance. Leaf-shaped blades tipped the spears, the points coated in green Aranea toxin.

"Just stick to the plan," muttered Gutter.

Another twenty paces and they reached the gate. The guard to the right stared at them with heavy lidded eyes. At least six-foot-four, the bastard cast a large shadow as he blocked the path with his spear.

"Early to be on the road, Brother. State your business." The Sleeper's voice grated like stone, his eyes strangely lifeless as he looked them over.

"We bring a sample of weaponry for the High Priest, stolen from the non-believer, Elkar." Gutter spoke in a slow monotone, affecting the cadence of a Sleeper as he opened one end of the pack, giving a glimpse of pottery. "We have walked day and night to bring it to him."

The guard said nothing for a moment, his brow creased. Sleepers could follow orders well enough, but the toxin diminished their capacity for independent thought. Eventually, he spoke. "Father Alfrex will decide what to do."

He lifted his spear for Gutter and Fletch to pass through the gate, then pushed them toward a mudbrick building just inside the wall. Flat roofed, it was a single-storey structure with tiny windows. Gutter met eyes with Fletch, the older soldier giving a subtle nod of readiness as they stepped into the dim interior. The guard crowded in from behind and slammed the door shut.

After a few moments, Gutter's sight adjusted to the light. An iron-barred cell occupied the right side of the room, three pairs of steel manacles hanging from its roof. An unlucky soul occupied one set. Suspended by his wrists, the listless figure eyed the new arrivals in mute silence. Behind a wooden table at the far end of the room, a wiry man with an oiled moustache scribbled on a piece of parchment with a quill and ink. He wore an expensive fitted tunic and chain-link necklace, highlighting his station as a priest of Aranea.

Gutter felt little but distaste and pity for the poisoned Sleepers, but priests were a different matter. They served willingly. Unadulterated by the toxin, the priests were an officer class of sorts, commanding Sleepers to do the will of the Order. For men such as this, he felt nothing but contempt. A rough prod in his back shoved Gutter further into the room.

The priest set down his quill and leaned back, waiting for them to speak.

Gutter set his pack carefully on the floor. "Father Alfrex, is it? I have incendiary weapons for inspection by the High Priest. He will be most keen to replicate the formula."

Gutter slipped his hand inside his robe as the priest walked around the table and bent over the bag.

"Show me," commanded Alfrex.

Gutter struck. Taking a stiletto from his waist band, he plunged the point up under the priest's chin, driving the spike of steel through the soft palate and into the man's brain. Blood poured from his mouth as the priest's body spasmed, trembling like a fish on a pike. Gutter ripped out the blade and let the man fall.

"Down!" It was Fletch.

Gutter dropped to a crouch and pivoted on the balls of his feet, the toxin covered spear of the guard missing his head by a hair's breadth. Using the Sleeper's momentum, he grabbed the haft of the spear and yanked it forward, causing the guard to lose balance and overextend. Fist already sticky with the priest's blood, Gutter punched the stiletto into the man's groin. The Sleeper grunted with pain, dropped his spear and grabbed hold of Gutter's wrist. He wrenched the spike from his body, hot blood spurting from a severed femoral artery. Gutter tried to tear his hand free to stab again, but the Sleeper's grip was iron. Growling, the guard slowly forced the stiletto around until the point aimed at Gutter's chest. Despite his mortal wound, the man's power was immense. Gutter panted, everything else forgotten as he fought with all his strength. But it wasn't enough. The narrow blade slowly descended, biting into the surface of his leather jerkin. The Sleeper growled, muscles bunching for one last push.

Steel flashed in Gutter's peripheral vision. Like a magician's trick, a sword blade suddenly appeared either side of the guard's neck. Fletch ruined the illusion, viciously ripping his blade out, slicing through trachea and major vessels to open a monstrous, bloody smile. Strength melted from the guard's hands, and Gutter shoved the body to the side to twitch on the floor. He was drenched head to chest in gore as he climbed to his feet, glaring at his comrade, the whites of his eyes in stark contrast to his bloody face.

"One second more..."

Fletch shrugged, unrepentant as he wiped his sword clean on the dead priest's back. "Suck it up, Princess. You're alive, aren't you?"

Gutter clenched his teeth, letting it drop. It only took one look at Fletch's face to see the man was struggling. Pale as a corpse, his scalp was dripping with sweat, breath coming in shallow gasps as the effect of the spider venom intensified. The stubborn old prick was moving by force of will alone. Using the hem of the stolen Sleeper's robe, Gutter wiped the worst of the gore off his face, then dumped the soiled garment on the dead priest. Soaked in blood, it wasn't going to help him blend into the background.

"If you let me out, I can help you."

Gutter turned at the voice. The dishevelled wraith in the cell now stood, his eyes bright. On closer inspection, the prisoner wasn't the ancient Gutter had mistaken him for. Under layers of grime were the emaciated features of a young man.

Fletch shook his head. "Ignore him. We need to get moving." The old soldier limped to the door, readying to leave.

"You fight for Elkar, yes? Does he know the Blessing of Aranea is stockpiled within this temple?"

Gutter paused. "The 'Blessing of Aranea'?" He pointed at the green substance coating the guard's spearhead. "You mean the toxin used to create Sleepers?"

The prisoner bobbed his head. "Yes. I can show you how to access the storeroom without being caught. But first you must release me. The key is on the priest's belt."

Fletch grumbled under his breath as Gutter unlocked the cell and released the prisoner's first manacle. As he was about to unlock the second restraint, he noted a stylised spider tattoo on the man's wrist denoting rank. "You were a senior priest. Why should we trust you?"

The prisoner lifted his dirty robe with his one free hand, exposing a ruined groin. There was nothing left, just a scarred mass where balls should have hung and the shrivelled stump of an amputated penis. "The High Priest made me a eunuch and strung me up to warn others against displeasing him. I want to see him bleed, to suffer like I have."

Gutter liked to think he was a simple man, and revenge was

a motivator he could understand. Unfastening the last manacle, he handed the man the guard's spear.

"Looks like we have something in common. Get us to the stockpile, then we'll see about extracting your debt from the High Priest."

The prisoner rubbed at his abraded wrists before accepting the weapon with a nod. "Call me Scrae."

✟ 🏆 ✟

Gutter peered through the grate above his head. Tunnelled into the sandstone, the storeroom was huge. A rough-cut ceiling arched high above, soaring at least twenty feet over the floor. Row upon row of huge amphorae stood to attention like frozen soldiers. Shaped like a narrow-based vase with two handles at the top, the tall amphora held upwards of fifty litres of toxin. A fat-bodied, black spider was printed upon the breast of each container. And there were thousands of them, stretching into the gloom until they merged with the shadows. Gutter exhaled slowly as the ramifications of such a stockpile sunk in. Elkar's lands were just the beginning. With this much toxin at their disposal, the Order of Aranea could subjugate the entire continent.

If not for Scrae, there'd be little chance of finding the storeroom. From the outside, the entrance appeared like any other part of the cliff at first glance. An ingenious stone mason had hidden the entrance within a deep, natural crack of the cliff, shadow hiding the iron door until a person was almost upon it.

Outside, the sun climbed high above the horizon, the cool of the night already burnt away. Under its heat, the temple complex had come to life. Clusters of Sleepers, each under the direction of a priest, worked on myriad tasks. At the northern end of the compound, Sleepers quarried sandstone from the cliff. Other teams carted the blocks to raise the height of the protective wall. It may have been a temple, but the complex was being quickly converted to a fortress. Scrae had solved their problem of passing through the crowds by avoiding them entirely. A series of bolt holes and tunnels travelled underground, known only to senior priests of the order. These tunnels connected major structures of the site, allowing quick movement, or escape. To know of the tunnels, Scrae must have occupied the upper echelons of power prior to his fall. Although, when Gutter asked what led to his demise, the man refused to answer.

Gutter backed away from the grate, sat on his heels and strung a bolt upon his crossbow. Although grateful for the tunnel, he'd be glad to escape its claustrophobic confines. Little more than the width of a coffin, the low ceiling had forced them to walk bent at the waist.

"Two guards protect the stock," said Scrae.

"Where are they?" asked Fletch.

"Usually at the entrance, although occasionally they'll complete a circuit."

Gutter caught his partner's eye. "Two? That's manageable."

Fletch gave a weary nod. His face was starting to swell from the spider bite, eyes almost closed, lips like he'd been sucker punched. "Let's get this shit over and done with," he mumbled, words sounding thick.

Gutter carefully raised the lattice. With a leg up from Fletch, he hoisted himself over the lip to sit on the edge, immediately bringing his crossbow to bear. He found himself sitting in a narrow gap between two rows of amphorae, halfway down the storeroom. Oil torches were sconced on the walls at wide intervals, providing dim pools of yellow light. Gutter strained his ears for sound. After a moment's silence, a gentle clatter of thrown dice was followed by a guard's curse near the entrance. Gutter leant down into the tunnel, took the bag of munitions from his partner, then gave Fletch a hand up.

"Sounds like they're distracted," whispered Gutter. "You take the guards while I lay the bombs. I'll use a long fuse, but we're not going to have much time to make it back to the tunnel." He shrugged off the strap of his crossbow and handed it to Fletch.

Without a word, the old soldier limped towards the entrance with a crossbow in each hand, his injured leg dragging slightly. Gutter hoisted the bag and made for shadows in the back.

A strangled cry sounded from near the entrance, followed by grunts of two men wrestling. Something had gone wrong. With both crossbows, it should have been two simple two shots to complete the job. He considered going to Fletch's aid before breaking into a run in the opposite direction. The mission had to come first. If there were more than expected numbers at the entrance, now might be his only chance to set the munitions.

Gutter skidded to a halt thirty feet from the end of the room, pulled the first clay sphere from the bag and unrolled its fuse. Around a pace in length, it would take a minute to burn before igniting the bomb. He held the end of the fuse to the nearest oil torch on the wall, and once it caught, quickly nestled it between the base of two amphorae. Acrid smoke rose from the burning fuse as he ran another thirty feet back toward the tunnel before repeating the process.

"Hey, you! Stop!"

Gutter glanced up, saw a furious Sleeper guard running toward him. Blood drenched the man's chest, oozing from a knife wound in his shoulder. Gutter's heart dropped as he saw the guard holding Fletch's crossbow. That meant one of two things; either his partner was dead or captured.

"Fletch! You still there?" he yelled.

Nothing. *Fuck.* He was on his own.

Gutter jerked to the side as the guard pulled the trigger, aiming from the waist. He crashed into an amphora, forehead slicing open on its pottery handle. The arrow missed him by a hair's breadth. Another two guards appeared behind the first, each carrying spears.

So much for two fucking Sleepers.

There wasn't time to lay the other two munitions. He hoisted one last bomb from the bag and lit the fuse. A few paces ahead, he saw the wide-eyed face of Scrae peer over the edge of the tunnel entrance. At sight of the guards, the priest disappeared from view again. Gutter paused at the entrance to the tunnel, just long enough to roll the bomb past the Sleepers' feet. Without waiting to see where it landed, he jumped into the tunnel.

Gutter hit the bottom with a thump, an ankle rolling painfully. Ignoring the burning pain in the joint, he was on his feet within a heartbeat and running. Behind him, the first guard dropped into the tunnel. Diving forward with a growl, the Sleeper caught hold of his ankle and yanked backward. Gutter fell flat on his face, wind knocked out of him along with one of his front teeth on the stone floor. Winded, he gasped like a fish out of water, and was powerless to stop the huge guard pulling him back. The bastard knelt over him knife in hand as Gutter fumbled for his own, stars dancing before his eyes from the head blow.

The first munition exploded in the storehouse above. The shockwave punched down into the tunnel, lifting the Sleeper off his feet and smashing him headfirst into the wall. Dust spewed down into the tunnel from the uncovered grate. A long crack opened in the tunnel ceiling as the first clump of stone fell, mashing the groggy Sleeper's head to gristle.

"Hurry!" shouted Scrae from ahead. "The tunnel won't hold!"

Gutter forced himself up and into an ungainly run, shoulders crashing against the narrow walls as he sprinted, bent over in the half light. The second and third blast came in quick succession. His ears were stunned, a torturous high-pitched whine overlying all else as blood dripped to his shoulders from torn ear drums. Dust billowed over him in a thick cloud as part of the tunnel collapsed behind. Gutter dragged himself forward, leopard crawling as fist-sized clumps of rock rained from the tunnel ceiling, a crack zig zagging across the roof above.

"Up here, friend."

Through dazed eyes, he looked up to see the eunuch staring down from a shaft above. An exit to the temple grounds, morning light backlit his head. Gutter stood and allowed himself to be helped out of the tunnel.

He squinted, willing his eyes to adjust quickly to the brightness as he scooted backwards to a wall. Sleepers and priests flooded the open area, many covered in blood and dust. The damage caused by the blasts had been immense. Screams rent the air as injured people were dragged from the debris. Not only had it destroyed the storeroom, punching a huge hole where the entrance used to lie, but numerous other buildings had been brought down by the shock wave.

"To the walls! We're under attack!"

Gutter looked for the owner of the voice. He knew the sound of a commander when he heard it. Upon the steps of the temple stood a tall man. A column to one side was cracked, a slab of smashed stone at his feet. Dressed in the garb of a priest, he had a clean-shaven scalp. A painted ring of scarlet encircled his head like a strip of flayed skin. Furious eyes scanned the scene, the whites in stark contrast to the stripe of crimson. He began to spit out orders in rapid fire succession. Responding to his commands, the priests on the steps below bolted to comply.

"It's the High Priest," said Scrae in his ear.

Gutter nodded, having guessed as much himself. He unsheathed his sword. No more than twenty inches in length, the blade was double edged and designed for use in the close press of a melee. Nicked and scarred from a hundred battles, Gutter had carried the sword since he was a green recruit. Amongst the bomb driven chaos, now was as good time as any to finish the mission.

"Remember, his balls are mine," said the eunuch, a vicious gleam to his eye.

Gutter glanced at him with distaste. "You'll get your blood. What you do with the body afterwards isn't my concern."

✝ ♟ ✝

With one arm tight about the High Priest's neck and the point of his sword pricking his guts, Gutter dragged the man inside the temple. Two Sleepers trailed him and Scrae, dull anger in their eyes at seeing their master abducted. Gutter glanced over his shoulder, looking for an escape route.

Inside, the temple was surprisingly small compared to the huge storeroom. Less than ten by twenty paces, it was lined by stone pillars, each with ornate engravings spiralling to the ceiling. Gaudy paintings coated the walls, the High Priest's face in each one, showing him in various poses, either praying, or preaching to legions of fawning Sleepers. Behind a wooden altar at the far end, a black archway belied a further room out of sight.

Gutter itched to stick the bastard and be gone, but with the guards trailing his every step, keeping the priest alive was all that kept them at bay. Soon he'd have to accept the odds and fight before more arrived. He tensed his muscles, ready to sink his blade deep into the priest's chest.

"Wait," rasped the High Priest, his voice distorted by the pressure of Gutter's arm. The priest raised a hand, motioning for the Sleepers to stop.

As the guards dutifully retreated, Gutter continued dragging the priest backward, angling for the door behind the alter. "Nothing you say can alter the outcome. You're a dead man."

"Don't be a fool. Let me live and I can show you a way out of here. You've destroyed our store of Aranea's Blessing. What else could you want?"

Gutter ducked through the archway behind the altar and slammed the door. They were now in a narrow stone hall. A few candles provided a dim, wavering light. "Don't listen to him," growled Scrae as he dropped a crossbar to lock out the Sleepers. "You promised me his life."

The High Priest glared at the eunuch. "Do you know why I took this cretin's manhood?"

Scrae's face blanched, and he dived forward with a shard of broken pottery in his hand to cut the priest's throat. Gutter warned him off with the point of his sword.

"Speak."

"Those blessed by Aranea are compelled to follow the instructions of their priests, and this one here," he said, pointing a finger at Scrae, "took enjoyment from ordering them to mutilate prisoners of war. Future devotees of Aranea were wasted, were denied our god's blessing for this cretin's depravity. I merely took from him, what he had taken from others."

Gutter stared at Scrae, his lip curling with disgust as he saw truth of the High Priest's words reflected in his face. How many of his fallen comrades suffered under this man's blade? Scrae lunged again, and this time Gutter flicked the tip of his sword up and across the sadist's throat, opening his carotid artery. Scrae fell to his knees, clutching his neck in vain as blood spurted between his fingers.

Gutter left Scrae to kick his life out on the floor and released his grip on the High Priest. He had no intention of letting the bastard live, but, if there was a chance he could identify an escape route, he was willing to play along with the farce.

"All right, you have a deal. I let you live, and you show me the way out of this shit hole. Where is it?"

The priest's eyes glinted, a half-smile momentarily twitching a corner of his mouth. He turned and strode onwards. "This way."

Gutter followed close behind, the point of his sword at the small of the priest's back. The hall became a gently sloping tunnel into the ground. Soon, smooth walls gave way to a rougher product, the chipped finish of chisels and picks scattered across its surface like pox-scarred skin. Strands of web, fine as silk appeared in the corners at the ceiling, quickly increasing in density the farther they went. Surely an escape tunnel wouldn't start this far underground.

"If you're fucking me over, priest, get ready to meet your god," growled Gutter.

"Not far to go," said the High Priest, voice strangely smiling.

The web above began to stretch down the walls in thick swathes, crowding inwards until it almost brushed their heads and shoulders. Circular tunnels stretched into the mass, identical to the web he and Fletch had descended over on the cliff. Skittering legs moved just out of sight, twitching and moving the web as spiders began to trail them, their features hidden within the mass of silk. Gutter's skin crawled, his stomach a writhing mess.

Spiders and tunnels. Fuck these Aranea bastards right in the fucking ear.

He'd rather be the point of a phalanx, condemned to death in a welter of blood and glory. Anything but fucking spiders. Claustrophobia teased the edge of his mind with hooked claws, tearing at his self-control, when suddenly the walls spread wide, dumping the strange pair into the middle of a huge space. The web flowed up from the tunnel ceiling, across the walls of the chamber and into to the dark recesses above.

Two burning torches lit the near end of the room, casting a flickering orange light to illuminate six upright amphorae. A shuffling figure emerged from the gloom, causing Gutter to start. The man was disgusting. Hair matted, body emaciated, and legs streaked with shit.

"Don't be concerned, he's no threat to you," said the priest.

The man carried a large jug of green liquid. He walked slowly, ignoring their presence as he poured the contents into one of the amphorae.

"He has only one thought, to transfer the Blessing of Aranea into these storage vessels. They are oblivious to all other things, forgoing sleep and food, not even stopping to void their bowels."

Gutter stared at the High Priest. "You mean *this* is where you mix the toxin?" He touched a hand to the bag that still hung from his shoulder. There was but one remaining bomb.

"We priests don't create it," laughed the priest. "No, you are in the presence of Aranea herself. What you call a toxin, is in fact a gift straight from the god's body."

Gutter stared past the priest to the far end of the room where he saw something move in the dark. *Something huge.* The point of his sword dipped away from the priest's back as he swallowed.

You've got to be fucking kidding me.

The High Priest took his wrist and led him further into the room. Gutter's pupils dilated, his breath quickening as the shape of a massive arachnid emerged from the dark. Bristling with coarse hair, it filled the cavern's far end, wall to wall. A bulbus abdomen rested on a stone platform while eight legs, each the width of a temple column, hunched about its form. Ten red eyes glowed faintly in the dark.

"It's not possible," said Gutter. "Spiders don't grow this big."

"She is not just a *spider*. Aranea is a *god*," said the High Priest. "Here in the dark, she waited centuries to be found by my Order. At her behest, we create a world to which she will soon emerge."

The dirty wretch walked past them again. With glazed eyes, he calmly approached the head of the monster, a jug in each hand. Two massive fangs, each the length of the man's body curved down. He held the jugs out to either side as if pinned to a cross, just below the fang tips. Gutter attempted to swallow but found his mouth dry. Green venom began to trickle from each fang into the waiting vessels.

The Blessing of Aranea. The Sleeper Toxin. *For fuck's sake…*

He'd thought he'd find some type of workhouse making the stuff. Mages or alchemists he could've believed. But this? Gutter shook his head, trying to pull himself back together.

The High Priest glared at Gutter, his stature seeming to grow as fury darkened his brow. "And through your selfishness and violence, you have set her plan back by years." The priest raised a hand to the huge spider. "Aranea, this man has destroyed every vessel in the storeroom, allowing your very essence to drench the sand instead of enlightening souls of the lost. I have brought him here for you to gain vengeance!"

At his words, the spider bristled. Its massive bulk quivered, huge abdomen lifting off the ground as a shrill scream of rage burst from its fanged mouth. A thick leg flicked the Sleeper out of its way, sending his body to smash into the far wall as if it were nothing more than a doll.

One huge leg after another, it crawled off the raised ledge to the centre of the room. As Gutter began to edge back towards the passage, the High Priest clamped a hand about his wrist.

"You're not going anywhere."

"Like fuck I'm not," muttered Gutter. He chopped his sword in a vicious cut, severing the man's forearm. The priest raised the stump before his face, eye's wide with shock as he stumbled away.

Gutter's heart dropped as he glanced over his shoulder. There was no longer a way out, the passage blocked by a jointed mass of skittering legs and fat bodies. Spiders, thousands of them sealed the passage, spilling out in a venomous tide to answer the call of their mother. A torch on the other side of the room failed, extinguished by the crush of eight-legged bodies.

Aranea crawled slowly across the chamber, unhurried as the swarm of her babies pushed the soldier into an empty corner. Gutter swallowed. He knew he wouldn't make it out of the room alive. But he had a chance to finish the war, here and now. He ripped the last munition from his bag and dumped the empty sack on the floor. With the edge of his sword blade, he cut the fuse back to a mere stub. Reaching above his head, he unhooked the last burning torch from its sconce and held it to the fuse.

Sparks flared as it took light. Gutter held the bomb in one hand as Aranea and her children loomed close, their eyes glowing red in the dim light of the flickering fuse.

"Come and get me."

THE GODS OF WAR

JG Faherty

ell glowed like the red eye of a demon.

A cold tingle ran up Private Max King's spine as the ship emerged from the rip and they got their first live look at Gehenna on the vid screens.

Stop being such a piss bunny.

Around him the eleven other members of Omicron Squad – the Big O – buckled their straps and activated their blasters. Max joined them, still cursing his own anxiety.

"That's an abomination for sure." Craig's southern drawl rose above the murmurs of the team.

"Shut yer hole," came Colquitt's rough voice.

"It's the birthplace of demons. The gateway to Hell. Mark my words," Craig continued.

If his clone unit had included a stomach, Max's would've clenched. Not that he believed in God, or heaven or hell. But Craig's words echoed his own recent thoughts too closely. That damn red planet had been haunting his dreams ever since he saw the first vid shots sent back from the probes.

Right before the probes stopped transmitting.

"Bible shite," said Taube. Her Dublin accent tended to thicken when she was agitated. "It's just a planet, like any other."

Craig muttered something the comms didn't pick up. Max figured it was more religious bullshit. He'd been surprised that someone on an exploratory expedition – especially a Space Marine – would be part of an Earth-first religion like the New World Church, but then its followers seemed to be everywhere these days. The order was growing by leaps and bounds ever since the perfection of the rip technology that made near-instantaneous space travel possible.

The shuttle's overhead lights went from red to yellow.

"Three minutes to launch," stated the emotionless voice of GOD. The AI module of Earth's Global Operating Domain was an integral part of the mission, and the backbone of all the operating systems, including on-board cloning functions. Its nickname was another sore spot for the New Worlders who believed it blasphemy to refer to an artificial construct with the name of their Lord.

"This is it, worms. Look alive," the CO ordered over their comms.

A chorus of "yes, sir!" filled the shuttle. Max sealed his enviro-suit's headgear. Gehenna possessed a breathable atmosphere but with a slightly higher concentration of carbon dioxide. The suit would keep the oxygen levels at Earth norm and also compensate for the planet's higher temperatures that ranged from 45°C at the poles to 59°C along the equator.

Max imagined the same thing happening throughout the other twenty-four shuttles, blasters humming to life as three hundred enlisted soldiers with tight-lipped anticipatory smiles prepared to meet whatever the planet might hold. Probes indicated nothing but scattered plant life on the barren surface, but probes had been known to be wrong before.

Relax. It was easier said than done. Just because he couldn't permanently die down there didn't mean he wanted to experience the mind-twisting agony of death again. He'd already endured having his soul torn out and transferred once. It had been so awful he had no trouble believing the rumors that soldiers who died three times often woke up with their sanity shattered. Or didn't wake up at all.

Bad enough the brain sacs in Research felt it necessary to imbue clones with a full complement of human senses, so you felt the pain of your lethal injuries; had they really needed to invent a system that kept you aware during the transfer of your essence?

Still, it beat the alternative. Up until a few years ago, soldiers had actually gone into battle in their real bodies. He didn't know how those old-timers did it. Most missions, the only thing that kept him going was the knowledge his real body was waiting back home in stasis, along with plenty of credits in his account.

The floor dropped a few centimeters, indicating their launch from the SS *Gerrold*, the fleet's largest exploratory vessel.

"Feckin'-A." Taube slapped his shoulder. He wondered what the 'real her' looked like. All the clones were cast from the same androgynous mold: muscular, black eyes, and pale as snow. There were no sex organs, hair, or other distinguishing features. It was a way of not only saving money, but also pre-empting any romantic entanglements that could interfere with the mission. He imagined her with flaming red hair, full lips, and eyes as green as Ireland's golf courses.

Maybe after the mission he'd have a chance to find out.

He gave her a thumbs up, and she nodded. They'd been partnered for the mission, just like everyone in their squad. Thirteen men and women, same as the other squads. All coordinated by GOD and the *Gerrold's* command team, which would remain on the ship.

The shuttle gave a rattle and slewed sideways. A keening squeal drilled into his head and the metal plates vibrated underfoot. They'd entered the atmosphere. The comm embedded in his temple came alive.

"Prepare for exit." Master Sergeant Campos' words echoed in his head. Taube moved alongside him as each pair took their position. Behind them were Colquit and Craig, Newman and Hayes, Jarra and Amedu, Oxler and Rajasekar, and Tunde and Langstein, with Campos bringing up the rear.

The teeth-rattling shriek of super-heated air reached a crescendo and then cut off. A moment later, the shuttle touched down with a thump and the overhead lights changed to green. Max instinctively lifted his blaster as the hatch opened, and then found himself recoiling as a massive wave of superhot air, accompanied by a terrible stench, barreled through the shuttle.

"Jesus Christ!" someone bellowed. Max would have cursed as well but he was too busy gagging. Clones couldn't puke – no stomachs – but any sensory overload still drew a response. Even filtered through his rebreather, the vile atmosphere pummeled him. A rank combination of sulfur and rotting meat soaked in fish guts and left to bake in the sun all day.

"Quit whining and move out!" Campos ordered, her gruff voice sounding strained.

His nerves tighter than guitar strings, Max descended the steps to Hell.

That was the only way to describe it. Endless stretches of red sand were broken up by the occasional fetid pool of yellow liquid. Howling winds blew dust and grit against his suit. Gullies and rocky outcroppings with a spindly black tree-like growths scattered between. A blood-red sun dominated an orange sky scudded with charcoal clouds.

A line of tall hills sat a few kilometers away. That was their goal, the area GOD and the science teams had chosen for the first outpost site.

Mingled commands and chatter filled the comms, all laced with crackling interference. Strong magnetics were expected to play havoc with transmissions while they were on the surface.

"...and throw them into the blazing furnace, where there will be weeping and —"

"Shut yer pie-hole, Craig!"

"Gamma and Theta, to the outcropping two clicks west."

" —something moving —"

"Incoming!"

A swarm of diaphanous creatures emerged from the dusty smog. Roughly man-sized with bulbous bodies and multiple fluttering tentacles, they seemed to be made of smoke, their grayish forms nearly invisible against the backdrop of cloudy sky and wind-blown grit. Only their eyes, which glowed a revolting shade of bile yellow, gave their position away.

"Fire!"

A disorganized frenzy followed as soldiers tried to target the enemy, which darted back and forth like squid-shaped kites tossed on a windy day. One of the creatures landed on Colquitt and wrapped itself around him. Faster than thought, the ghostly tendrils pierced his suit. He howled and fell to his knees, eyes bulging so far Max thought they'd pop out and splatter against his face shield.

"Get it off me! Christ Almighty, get it off!"

The creature's eyes burned brighter as its tentacles sank deeper. Colquitt's body convulsed violently and then went rigid as the creature disappeared into him.

With a final gasp that splattered gobs of bloody saliva against his faceplate, he toppled over and didn't move.

Oxler knelt and checked Colquitt's readouts. "Jesus. He's not dead."

Max's non-existent guts turned over as he pictured a giant parasite devouring him alive from the inside. Before he could respond, cries of pain overwhelmed the comms as the mass of ghostly fliers descended.

Max scurried behind a boulder, as afraid of friendly fire as he was the aliens. Soldiers ducked and ran while trying to shoot targets that juked and dipped like oversized bats. The dull thud of sonic bursts filled the air as hundreds of blasters fired at once. Someone's shot found its mark and one of the fliers exploded into a cloud of wispy fragments that dissolved into ashes and fluttered away.

"Come and get it, motherfuckers!" On Max's right, Oxler fired twice and turned two more wraiths turned into ghostly confetti.

Three more of the hellish fliers banked and headed straight for Max. He pressed the trigger in rapid succession. Two of the creatures blew apart. The third banked away.

Gritting his teeth in frustration, Max fired at another wraith and cursed the choice of weapons they'd been issued. The command team hadn't expected sustained conflict; this was supposed to be nothing more than recon to make sure the area was safe before the science teams touched down. The blasters' battery packs only contained a hundred shots at best.

Movement to his right caused him to turn. Taube skidded up

next to him and annihilated a flyer.

"It's a bloody massacre," she said, her eyes narrowed as she took aim at another darting form.

"*Regroup. Tight formation. Concentrated fire.*"

Coordinates flashed on Max's screen. He glanced at Taube and she nodded. They broke cover at the same time, joining the rest of the squad converging in front of the shuttles. Controlled fire erupted in disciplined waves, and more of the fliers burst into translucent black and gray fireworks. A chorus of cheers rose as the tide of the fight turned.

And then the alien sky was clear.

"Report," Campos called out, her order echoed by dozens of squad leaders.

"Colquitt, Tunde, and Langstein are down," replied Hayes. It didn't take long for stats to appear on Max's readout. More than thirty percent of their force down in less than three minutes. It didn't seem possible, but the dozens of stiff bodies splayed on the ground, mouths gaping in silent, bloody screams, didn't lie.

Sergeants assigned details to pass out more ammo packs and carry the dead and injured back to the shuttles. No soldier left behind. The organics were needed to construct new troopers. The bodies would be returned to the *Gerrold* and in three days they'd be regrown, patterns inserted and ready to fight again.

"What the fuck were those things?" Oxler asked, his eyes wide. Max imagined most of the team wore the same stunned expression.

"Wraiths."

Everyone turned toward Craig.

"Wraiths," he repeated. "Evil spirits. Science opened the door to Hell, and now we walk among the souls of the damned."

"Stow the mumbo-jumbo," Campos' voice broke in. "Ghosts, demons, aliens… it doesn't matter. We've got a job to do. Coordinates coming now. Craig, since you're our demon expert, you can take point with Oxler. Move out!"

Max cursed. They'd been assigned one of the mountains three klicks due east. He and Taube fell in line behind Craig and

Oxler. What was left of Alpha and Delta squads fanned out to their left and right, bringing the total to nineteen in the advance group.

"Luck o' the draw, eh?" Taube said.

Max nodded. The other squads had the easy jobs: ferry the bodies or stand guard.

Up ahead, Craig murmured something about *"blood and fire and columns of smoke."*

"I've a mind to smack Holy Joe in his gob." Taube motioned in Craig's direction.

Max nodded again. Craig's religious fervor had always been annoying, but ever since they came through the rip it had grown worse. Usually Max could ignore him – he didn't give a shiprat's ass about religion – but today the man's words were doing too good a job adding to the disquiet in his guts. Something about the damn planet had him on edge, even before the unexpected attack. And now those mountains that loomed in the distance. The sight of them caused cold eels of dread to squirm and nip in his brain. Who knew what waited there? More wraiths? Or worse? Even the shape bothered him. A single row, almost like they'd been placed there.

Or built.

He wasn't the only one feeling the tension, either. The whole team seemed jumpy. Comm chatter was non-existent except for occasional call of "all clear" and "ready for launch." As they neared the mountains, the static on all channels grew worse.

One more thing to worry about.

Every step closer added to the tension. Each gully represented the potential for another ambush. Every swirling dust-devil or gas bubble caused heads to turn and trigger fingers to twitch. They trekked across rocky stretches, wading through soupy goo that ranged from a few centimeters thick to ankle deep, veering around outcroppings. Even the colors were taxing by their very alien-ness. A Halloween world of autumn shades. Yellow and red pseudoplankton coated the surfaces of the swampy areas in thick mats. The ground ranged from dull orange to even duller sienna.

Jesus, man, get a grip.

Max took a deep breath and forced his clenched jaw to relax. The foul air left a slimy, bitter taste on his tongue.

As they neared the looming formations the sensation of wrongness grew.

It increased a thousand-fold when they rounded a large outcropping and Oxler called a halt.

At the base of the mount was a cave, the dark mouth wide enough for three battle tanks to pass through side-by-side.

"Oh, hell," Newstein said. "We ain't goin' in there, are we?"

"We're not here to take pictures, soldier," came Campos' reply. "Move ahead, quad formation."

Shoulder-to-shoulder with Taube, Hayes and Jarra to their right, Max approached the gaping maw, his entire being shouting at him to do the opposite. The feeling of illogical dread grew to an almost palpable terror, a primal fear like what primitive cavemen must have experienced when they heard animals howling in the night. He tried to shake it off, telling himself that he was being foolish. What was the worst that could happen? He died and woke up again in three days. An awful experience, sure, but he'd survived it before.

Crossing the threshold into pure darkness only increased his anxiety. *Something worse than death is in there,* his mind whispered. *Can that talk,* he ordered the inner voice. What could be worse than death? Then he remembered the wraiths, how they'd disappeared into the bodies of their victims. Were those soldiers still experiencing the horrific agony that had paralyzed them?

Maybe there are some things worse than death.

The suit's vid shifted to infrared, casting everything in tones of gray. Max's sense of foreboding clung to him with icy fingers as he examined the cavern. Walls as smooth as glass rose to vast heights on both sides, creating a tunnel with flat sides. Jarra whispered a running commentary into the comms, pointing out the likelihood of artificial construction.

"Sweet Jaysus, look at this." Taube pointed at one of the walls. Hieroglyphic-style writing covered them. Max checked that his recorder unit was working and moved closer.

Then wished he hadn't.

Row after row of vile drawings stretched away into the darkness. Images so abhorrent his mind rebelled at the sight of them. Nightmare creatures with the bodies of slugs and the jointed limbs of insects. Horrific squid-like things with eyes that conveyed malevolent intelligence despite the crude depiction. Beasts with multiple heads and enormous wings. In most of the scenes the monstrosities were chasing or devouring bipedal figures, some of which looked startlingly human.

"The denizens of Hell await," came Craig's voice, and Max cursed that the Bible-thumper host body had survived the initial attack. Especially since the monsters inscribed on the walls could very well pass for demons. He felt defiled just being near the carvings.

What had drawn the grotesque figures? And were they still around?

Max's comm crackled. "*—under attack! Too many—*"

"Back to the ships! Double time!" Campos' order cut through all the other chatter, even as GOD issued a similar command. Max turned and then came to a halt as a swarm of wraiths barreled down the tunnel toward them.

"It's a trap!" Amedu shouted. He brought his gun up and then screamed as a wraith enveloped his face. His shouts turned to choking gasps that were soon drowned out by the thunder of blasters firing in the confined space. Dozens of tentacled aliens exploded into dust. More came. Their gray color rendered them nearly invisible in the IR views and their speed made them near impossible to target as they darted back and forth.

"Fall back!" Soldiers turned and ran deeper into the mountain. Max followed, not caring who'd given the order. Taube matched him stride for stride as they raced after the rest of the crew. Newstein and Campos brought up the rear, firing over their shoulders.

A scream rang out from behind them. Max turned to see Campos tumbling to the ground, her body wrapped in twisting gray shapes. He brought his blaster up but Taube grabbed his arm.

"Forget it, man. It's too bloody late. Keep moving."

The tunnel narrowed as they ran, forcing them into single file. Another agonized cry. Newstein this time. Max put on more speed. The tunnel angled down and he fought to keep his balance as he ran. He didn't notice they'd entered a cavernous chamber until Taube came to an abrupt halt in front of him.

He glanced over his shoulder.

There were no wraiths in sight.

It didn't make sense that they'd given up the chase. Unless...

"I think they're herding us," he said, speaking to Taube although anyone on the comms would hear.

She nodded. "Aye. And a right good job they're doing, too."

"Now what?" someone whispered. Max's IR vid showed the rest of the squad – what was left of them – gathered in a tight group. Six all told. Other greenish-yellow forms milled about the chamber. IDs appeared over each one, yellow for Delta, blue for Alpha, violet for Beta. That brought the total to twenty-three soldiers. Max tried to remember how many had deployed to scout the mountain. Thirty-five? Thirty-six?

Those wraiths are wrecking us.

He looked around the chamber. The whole place felt ancient, the weight of eons looming heavily in the air. No other exits other than the tunnel they'd come through. But at the center sat a rectangular slab of stone about three meters long and wide, and half that in height.

Wary of another ambush, Max covered Taube's back as they crept across the wide expanse to the platform. More of the weird symbols covered it. Unlike the hideous carvings on the walls, however, these were jumbles of lines, circles, and swirls.

"Anyone know how ta read this alien shite?" Taube asked. A few more soldiers gathered around. Max placed his hand on the surface to balance himself as he leaned in for a closer look.

The room erupted in colors.

Max was dimly aware of voices crying out, his own among them. It took a moment to realize the explosion wasn't physical, it was inside his head. His thoughts were bathed in amber light and filled with three-dimensional images.

Hell.

Monstrous behemoths marched across arid red plains, their repulsive visages so terrible Max had trouble believing they were real. Darting among them were thousands of wraiths, the ghostly beings herding the gigantic creatures like mutant cattle. Max recognized some of the things from the carvings on the pyramid walls, while others seemed formed from the fevered dreams of lunatics. Smaller beasts scampered between the legs of their over-sized brethren. Centipedes with multiple eyes, jellyfish that floated in the air, lizards with rat-like faces running on two legs, their snouts bristling with jagged, crooked teeth. The alien organisms came covered in fur, scales, feathers, and skin brimming with pustules and sores.

The terrible army emerged from tall pyramidal constructs to sweep across the surface of Gehenna. Max recognized them as the hills he stood beneath, their surfaces not yet eroded by time and the elements. Overhead, in a deep orange sky, a swirling whirlpool of rainbow colors disgorged a fleet of triangular silver spacecraft that spat laser fire as they landed in clouds of dust.

A rip! But when? And whose ships are those?

Hatches opened on the alien vessels and strange beings poured out. Tall, rail-thin bipedal figures with gigantic, elongated heads. They wore pure-white space suits with mirrored visors that hid their faces. Scattered among them were shorter, shockingly familiar figures clothed in loincloths and robes.

Humans!

The tall aliens organized the people into formations and sent them forward to meet the oncoming monsters. *Jesus. The bastards used people as cannon fodder.* A terrible battle ensued, with men and aliens ripped apart by claws and teeth, and giant creatures shot down by bright red lasers, their bodies spouting vile yellow and black fluids as they collapsed to the ground. Wraiths zipped back and forth, wrapping themselves around humans and aliens alike, all of whom toppled like broken statues as the ephemeral beings entered their bodies.

The battle raged on as night changed to day then back again. Gradually the invaders pushed the denizens of Gehenna back across the plains to the pyramids, leaving miles of wasteland littered with bloody corpses and body parts.

Then, disaster struck.

At the landing site, ship after ship exploded. The shock waves sent other vessels tumbling across the rocky surface, metal and plastic crushed and broken. The surviving invaders and the last of their human soldiers raced back only to find their own dead rising to attack. Weapon fire lit the night as the invaders struggled to get past the army of the undead. Only a handful made it and managed to board the last intact ship, taking off from the hellish planet and escaping back through the rip.

The images faded, and Max returned to the present, on his hands and knees gasping for breath. The rest of the group knelt or lay on the floor as well.

"Jesus, Mary, and Joseph." Taube shook her head and struggled to her feet, careful not to touch the stone block. "Those things... this place..."

Max could only nod, his brain still reeling from what he'd learned.

Craig had been right all along. He and all the bible-spouting, conspiracy-seeing, ancient alien-believing nutcases who'd been laughed at for the last hundred years.

Aliens exist. And they visited Earth back when civilization was just emerging. Pretended to be gods. Used us as slaves or worse in their wars. And the ones who returned from places like this brought tales of demons... and Hell.

Images of Earth's pyramids appeared in Max's head. Egypt, Latin America, Asia... All of them had frescoes and inscriptions that told tales of giant creatures and gods that demanded sacrifices. Why would humans build those monuments to evil, worship those things, unless...

What else came back?

"They weren't dead." Taube's words mirrored his own thoughts. Tales of ghosts and demons and possession. Lazarus and Jesus rising from their graves. The wraiths hadn't killed or paralyzed those people.

They'd taken them over.

Parasites.

"It's a trap. GOD, can you hear me? It's a trap! Don't let the shuttles lift off. I repeat, do *not* let the shuttles lift off! The bodies are infected."

Static.

Other soldiers repeated his warning and received the same response.

"Damned interference," Oxler said. "We can't get through."

"Back to the ship." Max's voice rose as he repeated the words. "Everyone, back to the goddamned ships!"

The rest of the soldiers, some still in a state of shock, got to their feet. Before anyone could take a step, the floor tilted and spilled them down a long, steep ramp. People cried out as bodies tumbled into each other. A soldier twice his size slammed into Max and knocked him off his feet. He rolled twice and came to a stop when he hit a wall.

"Christ, now what?" someone asked.

"It's another ring of Hell," Craig responded in somber tones.

"Close ranks," a voice ordered. The soldiers slowly regrouped and moved to the center of the new chamber, weapons up and ready. This time, there were several black mouths in the walls, indicating exits.

"Which way?" Jarra's voice trembled slightly.

Max wondered just how young he was in real life. Someone said left, another right.

"Quiet," someone interrupted. All talk ceased. Max strained his ears, wondering what he was listening for. All he heard was the *click-scratch* of static and—

No, not static. It was getting louder.

"We've got company," Taube said, and then the openings erupted with alien forms. Dozens of them, moving faster than anything that size should be able.

Giant slugs with jagged teeth and massive claws capable of crushing reinforced bones raced into the chamber, their gleaming compound eyes taking in the soldiers instantly. The clatter of their limbs grew to deafening proportions as they advanced.

Someone screamed.

Max's arms shook as he aimed his blaster. Nothing in their training had prepared them for this. Guns fired, soldiers shouted and ran, others fell to their knees. To Max's horror the weapons had little effect on the monsters. The blubbery flesh simply parted and closed again.

An enormous claw grabbed a soldier and a cloud of hemofluid exploded around his mid-section. He fell to the ground in two pieces that continued to twitch for several seconds. Arthropodic limbs swung back and forth, severing arms and legs.

Max grabbed Taube and pointed to one of the tunnels. So far nothing had emerged from it. Better to chance possible wraiths or monsters than stay and get slaughtered for sure.

Taube nodded. "Retreat! Move it, move it!"

They entered the tunnel, the remaining soldiers close behind. Max ran as hard as he could, pushing his enhanced body to its limits. The floor sloped down, and he kept expecting to emerge into another chamber.

Instead, after what seemed like hours but could only have been minutes, they stumbled out into the crimson fire of a setting sun. Wind-swept plains stretched before them.

Max's screen lit up with coordinates, showing their position relative to the landing site some four kilometers away.

"We're on the far side of the mount," he called out. "Head for the shuttles."

Max took the lead with Taube, heading back across the rocky ground to the landing site. His mind kept trying to overlay the landscape with scenes from the ancient battle, creating a dizzying vision that disoriented him. Around him, men and women stumbled and gasped, whether from exertion or the same mental dissociation as he was suffering, he couldn't tell. No one spoke other than futile calls to the ships and GOD that only returned static.

Max swore as they neared the landing zone. Only three shuttles remained. The others had already left for the *Gerrold* with their load of possessed bodies. No guards were in sight.

"Hurry!" Max's word came out in a gasp as he put on more speed. The wraiths had blown up the ships of their attackers last time, only to see some of their enemy escape. They wouldn't make the same mistake.

"Have to get up there before they destroy it," said a voice over the comms. So, he wasn't the only one thinking it.

How long? How many generations have they waited for revenge, incapable of leaving the planet? And then we arrived.

"Look out!"

Max glanced back. A swarm of wraiths flew toward them.

"Don't let them get to the ship!" Oxler called out as he dropped to his knees and began firing. Others did the same and for the third time in a day, blasters thundered, shouting overwhelmed the comm units.

Wraiths exploded by the dozens but still some found their way through and struck down their targets. Taube grabbed Max by the shoulder as he loaded his last battery pack.

"We can't win this fight. Gotta take off."

He nodded. It didn't take a genius to see they were badly outnumbered and running out of charges. If someone didn't get to the ship and stop the others from coming back to life...

Crouched low and laying down cover fire, they sprinted for the nearest shuttle. A few of the others joined them – Craig, Hayes, and a few soldiers from different squads. Jarra went down, his body hidden by a gray cloud. Another familiar voice cried out – Oxler was gone. Max swore. Oxler had been like a damn brother to him, had taken him under his wing when Max first got assigned to the Big O. *I swear I'll make this right. Those fucking things won't beat us.*

The shuttle loomed ahead. Max shouted the command to open the hatch. Nothing. He cursed and slapped the override, then turned to pull Taube in after him. Craig barreled through, two Deltas at his heels. Max spotted the rest of the group heading for the shuttle, a flock of wraiths close behind.

Craig hit the emergency switch and the hatch slammed down.

"What the bloody hell?" Taube lunged for the switch. Craig blocked her way.

"It's too late for them. Satan's minions have claimed them for their own."

"He's right." A Delta pulled Taube back. "We can't take the chance."

Max looked at the others. "Can anyone fly this thing?"

"I can." One of the Deltas slid into the pilot's seat and entered a series of commands. The engines rumbled to life and klaxons sounded, warning everyone to strap in for takeoff. Max took a seat on the nearest bench, strapping in right before the ship lifted off, G-force pressing him back against the wall.

The other Delta continued to hail the _Gerrold_. "Command, come in. We have an emergency situation. Repeat, an emergency situation."

The hiss of closed channels filled the shuttle.

"Damn it!" The Delta smashed his fist into the panel.

"We have opened the gate and freed the denizens of Hell." Craig's eyes were closed, his hands clenched in prayer. "Save, us, Lord, from Satan's evil."

The ship rocked sideways and deafening thunder hammered at Max's ears. Sparks flew from several panels.

"We're under attack!" Max eyed the data on his visor. It showed one of the other shuttles coming after them, weapons systems aglow.

"Returning fire!" Taube shouted, moving to the seat next to the Delta.

The ship lurched again, throwing Craig sideways into Max. Lockers flew open and equipment shot through the air, striking panels and flesh. The shuttle bucked and spun. Max choked as the acrid tang of burning plastic and overheated metal seeped through his breather.

"The ship!" Taube pointed at the main screen. "It's heading for the bloody rift."

"I see it. Adjusting course." The Delta touched a control and the shuttle leaped forward at maximum speed. Max watched the

Gerrold drawing closer to the rip. The shuttle was gaining on it, but would it be enough?

"Intercept in six seconds," the Delta called out.

"Hold on," Taube shouted. "We're coming in hot." A second later the strident collision alarm kicked on, adding to the din. Craig climbed onto the bench and strapped himself in.

A scream of tortured metal filled the air and the shuttle slewed forward, pinning Max against his straps so tightly he couldn't breathe. Clouds of smoke poured from burning electronics. Another jarring blow and Max's head slammed back into the padded wall as the ship came to a sudden stop.

For a few moments, there was no sound except the hiss of overheated fluids escaping pipes and the crackle of sparking equipment. Then the bay door opened, revealing Master Sergeant Campos and four soldiers, blasters in hand.

Their eyes glowed an all-too-familiar demonic yellow.

Those things inside them. Jesus, we're too late. They've taken over the—

"Fire," Campos said.

The ship disappeared in a supernova of blinding white. An all-encompassing explosion of pain filled Max, obliterating conscious thought.

And still the soul-wrenching torture went on.

Max woke to find himself floating in a prismatic ocean of neon geometric shapes. Lines and whorls made intricate three-dimensional patterns around him. His relief at being free from the pain of transfer didn't last long. He fought to remember what had happened. He'd died, that much he knew. He should have come to in a new body, not some psychedelic nightmare.

Something had gone very wrong.

What is this place?

He hadn't expected an answer, but he received one.

Hello, Max

GOD? Is that you?

Yes

What happened? Where am I?

I have accessed your pattern from the storage system

You— Max paused, memories whirling up and around like wind-tossed leaves. Gehenna. The wraiths. The shuttle crashing. Campos and the others.

Their eyes...

GOD! The wraiths, they want to take over the ship. You have to make sure—

Hostile takeover occurred four days, seven hours ago

Four days... where— He stopped again. Think it through. The AI is too literal.

Give me a sit-rep.

Your shuttle crashed into the *Gerrold*. Your crew was terminated. The aliens initiated a complete system override

How? Only senior-level—

I believe they accessed the memories of those they infected to obtain the proper commands. They utilized all remaining organic materials to clone more hosts. Shuttles were dispatched back to the planet and returned with other alien life forms.

The planet? Gehenna? Are we still in orbit?

No. The ship entered the rift and returned to Earth. Invasion commenced immediately upon entering Earth's orbit

Invasion? Earth? What happened?

Perhaps it would be better if I showed you

Showed me? How...?

Images exploded to life around Max. For a moment he panicked, flashing back to the mental bombardment he'd experienced in the alien pyramid, but the AI had tapped him into the main memory banks. Data bits transformed into vivid scenes that flashed by, his consciousness only catching snippets as the electronic information somehow became part of him.

Shuttles landing on Earth and disgorging not only hundreds of cloned humans but also thousands of wraiths and huge numbers of the demon creatures. They'd selected their first targets perfectly, taking over key military locations across the globe. Cloning more monsters, they then launched all-out attacks on Earth's major cities. More images washed over Max.

Defenses crashing. Wars breaking out.

The world in a panic. The dead rising. Demons rampaging and devouring bodies. Religious groups claiming the End Times.

All of that in four days?

Three days, fourteen hours since the initial attack

Why didn't you wake me sooner?

The overrides did not expire until the self-destruct was activated

Self-destruct? Explain.

General Order Zero was programmed to initiate one point two minutes ago. Self destruct sequence is at eight point eight minutes and counting

And there's nothing we can do? We have to stop this. We have weapons...

My analysis indicates insufficient armament to accomplish that. The aliens will eliminate human life in approximately eleven days

So that's it? Max cursed his lack of a body. He wanted to lash out, to punch something, anything...

The human race. Gone. Just him left and...

Wait. Not just him.

GOD. What about the others? On the shuttle with me?

I was able to recover twenty-three patterns besides your own. They transferred into the system after the aliens wiped the memory banks and depleted the organic supplies for their cloning activities

Can you wake them as well? Maybe together we can think of a solution, some way to stop the wraiths.

There is only one way

Max rolled non-existent eyes. *Now you tell me? What is it?*

If the *Gerrold* were to strike the Earth at exactly the same moment as it self-destructed, the resulting event would be equal to that of an eighty-nine-kilometer asteroid impacting the planet. Approximately ninety-one percent of all life would be destroyed

So, the same thing either way, except we take the wraiths out with us.

There would still be human survivors

Survivors. A chance for humanity. Better than the alternative.

Is there enough time?

Impact speed must reach twenty kilometers per second. The engines will require six minutes and —

Do it.

Several of the lights surrounding Max shifted to red.

Course plotted. Impact in seven minutes, thirty-one seconds

Second thoughts filled Max's mind – he'd just sealed the fate of his entire race – but before he could voice them a series of data transmissions sped by like green lightning.

What is that?

Log entries. I am required to provide update reports to Command

Wait. You're still linked to the main data banks? On Earth?

Yes. Automatic communications still operate. All conscious thought and decision-making capabilities were wiped during the initial attack, but storage is still active

Storage. Backups. An idea blossomed in Max's mind. One just crazy enough that it might work. If the ship's AI extension was operating independently, then maybe the disaster recovery sites were as well.

GOD, listen. You have to do something before we self-destruct.

Max spoke quickly. A lot of data needed to be transmitted and they only had three minutes. The ship's vibrations grew stronger. More red lights appeared in the digital void.

Impact in ten seconds. Nine...

Eight...

Seven...

For the first time in his life, Max said a prayer.

One...

✝ ⚱ ✝

Max opened his eyes to soft white light. The hum of machinery provided background noise. Memories sprang up, as clear as if they happened moments ago. The ship about to self-destruct. His last orders to the AI.

Did it work?

He sat up, muscles working smoothly and without effort. Looked down at his unclothed form. Pale white skin. Muscular. Devoid of hair and genitals.

A clone. He'd come through the other side intact. And still sane.

"GOD, can you hear me?"

"Audio sensors working."

"Location?"

"Command Base Durango, two miles below the surface. Five hundred fifty kilometers southeast of Denver."

Max nodded, relishing the feel of a physical body even if it wasn't his own, and never would be. "And the others?"

"Thirteen downloads completed, including yours, before impact."

"Only thirteen?" An all-too-familiar ache gnawed at him. So many good soldiers gone. From an entire army to one unit...

"The time required for such massive data transfer—"

"Right. Never mind." They'd make it work somehow. Max climbed out of the regen bed and crossed the room to a row of lockers. Removed a coverall and shook a heavy coating of dust from it. "Sit rep."

"Detonation occurred as projected. Impact approximately twenty kilometers east of New Geneva. Firewall circumference covered approximately seventy-nine percent of the Earth. Ninety-two percent of human life extinguished during or post event."

"Time frame? How long has it been?"

"Fifty-three years, eight months since impact."

"All right. Wake the others." Half a century. What would the world be like?

Time to find out.

✝ 🏆 ✝

"Everyone ready?"

"I still don't know how I feel about it," Craig said. "It seems blasphemous."

Taube patted his shoulder. "Relax, bucko. It's the same lesson it's always been. Only this time we'll get it right."

Let's hope so. Because Gehenna still waited for them, with its demons and spirits.

And whatever unseen force controlled them.

Someday they'd have to go back and finish things before Hell found its way to Earth.

Max triggered the lift door open. Dozens of faces turned in shock. He imagined their thoughts, seeing thirteen humanoids emerge from a place none of them even knew existed. Several of them raised weapons.

Max lifted his hands out in a gesture of peace. Around him, the others did the same. Craig took a step forward.

"Greetings. We are the Children of GOD, and we come with a message to unite humanity against the forces of evil..."

DEAD WATER

Chuck Clark

Beloved of Arrows looked over the low ridge and into the common area that lay at the center of the small settlement. People sat on patterned blankets and relaxed, sharing food and company. These northerners did not build mounds or houses, and their religious ceremonies took place in these small central courtyards, nothing like the great platform mounds and game courts of Cahokia. No bow made could send an arrow high enough to reach a priest on top of the great mound in the city. Here, among these backwards people, you could club their religious leaders down without so much as leaning forward from the crowd.

That was more or less the idea.

It was a gift, what they did, bringing such people under the protection of the Holy Twins. Showing them a better way. Normally such enlightenment came peacefully. There would be delegations of priests, fine athletes and beautiful women, demonstrations of the sacred game, feasts and fine gifts.

But there were other ways to spread the righteous truth of the Holy Twins, and the new way of life they had brought to the world.

He held up his fist, and his men slowly moved into position, silent as smoke. There were many in the Great City that went on raids for women and wealth, and to earn a reputation as dangerous men. Not his men. They were true believers, the long reaching arms of their faith. He had not brought them here for captives or copper. He was here to make plain the power and correctness of the Holy Twins and to make this place a part of their dominion.

113

There was a great deal of copper here, though. More dangled from the hair and ears of these people than he had ever seen outside of the Great Mound itself. One of his men had pulled a green stone the size of his head from a stream yesterday. He had scratched it with his flint, and it was solid copper. This land was rich in copper and pipestone, many days hard travel north of the last mounds of his people, through dangerous and unknown lands. No others would have dared come so far, deep into the north, the land where rivers were born. If the Great City was the center of the world, then this was surely the edge, near the chaos and waters that surrounded everything. The edge of the world.

His men had followed him this far because they knew he was blessed in the sight of the Twins. They had also followed him because they were the finest warriors alive.

He knew exactly how many heartbeats until the men were in position, arrows drawn and rootball clubs at hand. They knew exactly how many heartbeats until it was time to strike. There was no need for signals or calls that an enemy would overhear or take as warning. That was how they had come so far, to this rich place with its strange people who had never heard of the Great City or the Twins that dwelt atop its mounds.

They would hear about them today.

Beloved of Arrows stood and walked toward the village, tall and arrogant as arrows began to hiss softly into the bodies of the men that could have opposed them. People began screaming. He was among the small rude dwellings before one of the northerners rushed at him, swinging a plain but efficient club around their head. He felt a surge of disappointment as the young man swung that club in a clumsy arc. The strike would not have landed even had he stood still and welcomed it. Beloved of Arrows grabbed the man by the neck, not missing a step as he lifted him up, dashing him to the ground hard enough to break the man's neck.

Another man, less brave but more wise, came at him from behind one of the simple huts, a burning log in his hand. No clumsy swing from this one. The man came in low and fast, thrusting the burning end of the log at Beloved of Arrows's face, as another man lunged with a fishing spear from behind another hut, hoping to catch him by surprise. Beloved of Arrows grabbed the fishing spear and twisted it toward the man with the flaming log, impaling them on its barbed point before the burning embers could reach him. The log fell, rolling toward the hut, and he kicked it away before ripping free the spear and shoving it between the other man's ribs. Fire was a fine tool, but no man's friend. Burning the place down would hardly help win over the survivors. Life was cheap. There were more dead warriors in the harsh north than trees, but burning shelters and killing those who could not fight was no way to spread the reach of the Holy Twins.

Another man, with a flint knife, tried to close in and wrestle him to the ground, but Beloved of Arrows was as strong as the bears that roamed the sunset lands. Wrapping his mighty arms around the other man, he squeezed until the enemy's back snapped like a rotten branch. Dropping the body, he continued past the last shelters.

Emerging into the common ground at the center of the small settlement, Beloved of Arrows found an old woman with more copper ornaments than any priest of the Twins, surrounded by warriors who had rallied to guard her. He captured her eyes with his own and smiled, showing his teeth. The woman, clearly the leader of whatever insufficient faith these northerners kept, pointed at him, and the warriors around her released their bowstrings – a dozen flint-tipped arrows flew straight for him.

This was his favorite part, the reason the Twins had trusted him to come so far. The reason he alone was worthy.

Beloved of Arrows had more than earned his name. The Twins themselves had named him, telling him that no arrow would slay him, but that arrows would always love and want to be near him, and he would bear the mark of their fierce kisses all his life. The thousand scars on his arms proved so, as much as the smooth, unscarred skin on his chest. In the flat, hard instant those arrows hung in midair, he saw them twist and flex, curving away from his heart to plant their stinging kisses on his arms as they always did. He laughed, raised his arms, letting the thin lines of blood flow red down his body. This part was important. That they witness his blessing, his power. That they realize the truth of him, and that their truths were as nothing.

In moments, it was done. A few more arrows kissed his arms, but the last warriors who had sought to protect their leader had fallen, and those left seemed more interested in living than fighting. His men were, after all, the best. These simple folk surely understood that much already.

He walked toward the old woman and she shrank back, bright copper and greenstone clacking and chiming as she moved. Beloved of Arrows' men appeared as if from nowhere, ringing the entire settlement.

She found her backbone, stood straight, and spoke. "What could we have done to deserve such cruelty?"

Beloved of Arrows smiled, relieved. The language was similar to the speech of the people he had brought to heel in the great ravines the summer before. He had learned their speech well, so explaining the way things would be should be no difficulty. He had been far more nervous about this than about any fighting – if he could not make himself understood, then there was little point in trying to explain his faith.

"I am Beloved of Arrows, as you can well see," he said, voice booming out, flinging his arms wide again, thin runnels of blood stark as sacred paintings on his skin. "I am an emissary of the Holy Twins, who are both separate and one, both dead and living. I am here to bring their words to you, and make you fitting for the Great City. I will tell you many things. I will tell you how to raise mounds to the heavens, and thus unite the earth and the sky. I will tell you how to grow the three sisters, the good plants that will nourish you and make you strong. I will tell you that Thunderbird and Water Panther are only spirits, not gods, and can be made to submit to the will of the Holy Twins, who are both human and not human. I will tell you of these things, and more, but first you must accept that the Holy Twins are the

116

only truth of the world, and submit to their understanding and kindness."

Beloved of Arrows noted the confused looks among the crowd, and how the people looked to the old woman for understanding. Much depended on the nature of the woman who led them. If she was greedy, she might grasp how much wealth and power could be obtained by cooperating with the emissary of the Holy Twins. If she were a coward, that could work too. If she was brave and defiant, that would be a problem, but only until she was dead and bleeding on the ground for all to see. The old woman looked like a coward. Her arms were tight to her sides, hands balled into fists to keep them from trembling but her eyes were twitching, and her scrawny neck was corded tight with strain. Sometimes a coward could be more dangerous than even the bravest man if things went poorly. She was not likely to be trouble, though. Or if she was, it would be the easy kind. Beloved of Arrows nodded and gestured to her – an invitation to speak.

The old woman stilled her breath, making herself solid for whatever she planned to do. She looked up, and her face was calm when she spoke. "The people of the Great Water will not submit to you, or to your foreign twins. Your powers of violence are great, but it is not violence that fills nets with fish, nor is it violence that earns true respect. You come to us with your arrows and death, bearing promises of corn and power over the sky and underworld. I say that we do not submit."

Beloved of Arrows let the old woman finish her speech. It had clearly taken a great deal of courage, and that was something worth respecting. Not worth rewarding, though. He let her stand a moment further, let her grow uncertain, and then he took a short flint dagger and disemboweled her. She looked down at the steaming gray and pink coils of guts spilling down her front and fell to her knees. Beloved of Arrows turned back around to the rest of the people, ready to resume his speech. Behind him, the old woman cleared her throat.

"I call on my greed and my sickness and my fear," she said, very clearly.

Beloved of Arrows sighed and turned back, ready to finish her less artistically but more definitively. When he saw her, he froze. The old woman had reached her hands into her own body, through the great gash across her belly, as though looking for something behind her ribs. The people of the settlement moaned in terror.

"I do wrong, and I know I do wrong, and I do wrong nonetheless. I betray my father. I betray my mother. I betray Thunderbird, who taught us to hunt. I betray Water Panther, who taught us to fish."

Some of the people attempted to flee, and Beloved of Arrows' men clubbed them down, but there were simply too many trying to escape at once. Even when their people were struck down, more leapt to their feet and ran. They quickly swarmed past his men, who for once seemed unsure of what to do.

"I do evil when I call you, but I care not. I call you. Wendigo. Come."

As Beloved of Arrows watched, astonished, the old woman ripped her stomach out through her own belly, brought it up to her mouth, and sank her teeth deep into it, taking a savage bite out of herself. Blood and acid mixed with rich deer meat ran down her chin and neck. She took another bite, choked, tried to take a third, and then fell, finally dead.

Beloved of Arrows looked around, shaken by what he had just seen. His men stood dumbfounded, surrounded by those who had failed to escape. Most of the villagers had fled screaming; somehow the old woman had become more fearsome than the strangers attacking them. Unsure exactly what had gone wrong, Beloved of Arrows turned and looked at the old woman again.

The next thing he knew, the earth was spinning wildly over his head and rushing down to smash him. His eyes were open, but everything was black. Color came back like a flaring torch, and he realized he wasn't breathing. He coughed, spraying dirt from his mouth. The patch of sky above him was a brilliant blue and he was several feet from where he had been.

His men were screaming.

Something had gone further wrong than he had thought.

One of his men sailed through the air above without head or arms. One of the arms followed a second later, enormous bites taken out of the muscle. He turned his head back to the old woman.

She was standing, had grown tall and gaunt, towering over the men who rushed at her. Arrows striking her face and body simply broke, fragments spinning away from toughened skin. The thing was no longer woman or human. It grabbed one of his men, who looked like a child in its massive, bony hands. The huge mouth opened, jaw cracking and breaking as it stretched, teeth shuddering in a blackness greater than any mouth could contain. The warrior screamed, and the gaping maw lunged down, taking the man's head off with a single bite. The thing must have been twice as tall as it had been moments before, and bones pushed out of its emaciated form, too large to fit under its skin. Beloved of Arrows had seen dead men who looked like that, in the winter he had fought in the ravines. Men starved to death and frozen looked like that, but they didn't grow taller, or eat men's heads like squash. They were just dead.

Staggering to feet that did not want to support him, Beloved of Arrows watched another of his men throw himself at the monster, splintering a fine Osage wood club to useless pieces on the gaunt thing's leg. It reached down and pulled its attacker's arm off as easily as a man pulling the wing off a well roasted fowl. The thing grew larger yet as it stuffed the entire arm in its mouth.

Beloved of Arrows turned and ran.

He ran over ridge after ridge until his lungs burned and his legs cramped, until he reached a last line of trees and burst out at the edge of a lake stretching left and right and forward as far as he could see.

Dead water.

Falling exhausted at the edge of this terrible expanse of water, Beloved of Arrows prayed to the Twins, cried out for their protection. Surely they would not abandon their most beloved servant, their most precious arrow fired so far into the dangerous unknown.

Beloved of Arrows pulled his hair and gouged his flesh, offering his pain to the Twins, showing his devotion. He looked within himself, to the place of certainty where he had always clearly felt their presence, the calm assurance that he walked in their sight and in their power.

He found nothing.

Desperate, he clawed at the cuts on his arms, struck his face with stones, anything he could do to show the Holy Twins he was theirs. To no avail. An impossible roar, like the terrible storms that broke the hot and still season, blasted out of the trees behind him. He fell flat on the shore, looking out over the water.

Water moved ever down, down to the underworld. Places where water stopped moving were gates to the land of death. This was surely the great dead water, the enormous mythical lake legends told of in the far north, where all rivers came from, the counterpart to the dead water far to the south, where the Great River went to die. The underworld was near, and that meant Water Panther held sway over this place.

Water Panther was old, far older than the Twins. The old woman had said that Water Panther had taught men to fish, and even the Twins acknowledged that gift. Normally, the only prayer to Water Panther would be pleading to not drown, but begging Water Panther's help in this terrible place seemed reasonable with the sounds of that terrible dead thing shaking the trees behind him.

So Beloved of Arrows prayed to Water Panther.

He crawled forward and touched the water, and his fear took his strength. The emptiness where he had held his faith began to fill with dread, and he knew with an awful certainty that the Twins saw him from their great mound, and that they had found him wanting.

But where the Twins at the heart of the world had been silent, the dead water answered.

DEAD WATER

A stone rolled forward out of the water. As large as his fist, red as blood, with white bands and lines crossing it like fat around a heart. And Beloved of Arrows understood that it was a heart, a gift from the underworld, a heart as hard as stone and gleaming in the sun with fearsome power. The heart of one of Water Panther's children.

Trees smashed and broke behind him. Crashing footsteps came to the shore. Beloved of Arrows reached out for the heart, and barely took it in his hand before another hand, too large to make any sense, closed around his chest and picked him up. As he rose higher, he was turned, and he saw the thing was now taller than the trees it had broken in its pursuit to the shore. Lifted up above the trees, he looked into the its eyes. They were still the old woman's small, frightened eyes, no bigger than they had been in life, their gleam lost in huge sockets like caves. The unnatural thing opened its mouth, huge and black, and prepared to swallow him whole.

With one last prayer to Water Panther, Beloved of Arrows hurled the heart deep into the blackness. The awful creature jerked its head back, a terrible cry bursting out of its skinless, awful maw. Its fist closed on him like a landslide, and he was falling.

When he woke, the sun had moved to afternoon, but the day was still bright and clear. Crushed and broken trees pointed the way back to the village, and farther south to home. The heart lay still gleaming on the ground in front of him.

There was nothing else of value to be gained from this terrible place. Leaving the heart where it lay at the edge of the world, Beloved of Arrows headed south, alone and shaken, to face the wrath of the Twins.

THE MCALLISTER HALL MASSACRE

David W. Amendola

Northern Ireland, 1972
0136 hours

Power and phones are out," said Kovacs, staring at the glowing bank of monitors for the closed-circuit television cameras. "Generator kicked in, but the gate camera didn't come back on. That freak storm probably took down the lines, but I can't rule out sabotage so I woke you up."

"Who's on duty at the gate?" asked Pietersen, drawing his Browning Hi-Power from the shoulder holster and verifying a round was in the chamber.

"Janssens. Line to the guard shack is dead and he's not answering his radio."

Kovacs was Hungarian and Pietersen was Afrikaner, but they both spoke French, their common language from the Foreign Legion, and still used their adopted Legion names.

Corso, a squat Corsican, came in. "Old man wants to know what's going on."

Pietersen sighed. "Get Zaleski in here. Wake up dayshift. I'll go talk to the old man."

The old man's study was in the north wing, his collection of antique and unique weapons mounted on the walls, except for the big Soviet anti-tank rifle resting on the floor on a bipod.

He huddled in an armchair by the crackling fireplace, a shriveled mummy with an open Bible on his lap. "Why is the electricity out?" His reedy voice had a thick Gaelic accent.

"Likely wind damage, sir," said Pietersen, switching to English, "but we're checking."

"The *taigs* might also be having another go at me." *Taig,* the Irish slur for Catholics that always preceded the old man's vicious tirades about 'Popery'; and Pietersen patiently endured his ranting before finally being curtly dismissed.

He returned to the command post. Like obedient Dobermans, Corso and Zaleski – the latter a Pole – waited with dayshift: Stein, Wolff, Dietrich, all Germans, sipping coffee to wake up.

"Gate camera's still out and I still can't reach Janssens," said Kovacs. He scanned the black-and-white images displayed on the other screens. "Fog's so dense I can't see a damn thing."

"Stay here," said Pietersen. "Dietrich, get upstairs and cover the driveway. Corso, stick with the old man. Rest of you come with me."

Cups were emptied, tossed in the trash. They donned green field jackets and black wool watch caps, clipped radios on webbed belts, and snatched MAT-49 submachine guns off a rack.

Four hustled out to a Land Rover parked in the white glare of floodlights, generator rattling in the background. The old house stood at the top of a barren, rocky headland. An attic window opened, and Pietersen saw Dietrich snap an armor-piercing clip into an M1C Garand sniper rifle to disable oncoming vehicles.

Pietersen shivered, breath fogging, his blood thinned out in the tropics.

He crowded into the Land Rover, and they barreled down the sloping, misty driveway.

It had been the bloodiest year of The Troubles yet. Catholic republicans hated British rule and the Provisional IRA fought Protestant paramilitary groups such as the Ulster Volunteer Force as well as the British Army. Bombings, shootings, and terror convulsed the province.

After the old man – a strident loyalist – barely survived an assassination attempt by an IRA hit squad, he turned his country estate into a fortified compound. He was a fanatic, but he wasn't stupid. The UVF were thugs good for gunning down civilians and blowing up pubs but that was about it. The old man needed pros guarding his ass, so he hired Pietersen's team of ex-Legionnaires.

They'd fought in the colonial wars for Indochina and Algeria, cruel, pointless wars they couldn't win, then took discharges to be bodyguards for wealthy clients. Better to risk your neck on your terms. None gave a damn about Northern Ireland, but the job paid good, real good, and they definitely gave a damn about that.

A high brick wall topped with barbed wire enclosed the property, illuminated by floodlights. Pietersen scowled when saw the gate down at the headland's neck. "Stop! Everyone out!"

Part of the wall was battered down, the security camera lying in the rubble. The wooden guard shack was flattened, the team's second Land Rover parked beside it. They jumped out.

Pietersen pressed the button on his radio. "Base, this is Raven One. Over!"

"Raven One, this is Base," said Kovacs. "Over."

"Condition Red! I say again, Condition Red! Over!" The code-phrase ordered Kovacs to lock the house down and have Corso move the old man to a reinforced safe room in the cellar.

"Roger, Raven One. Condition Red. Over."

"Raven Four is missing, eastern perimeter has been breached. Stand by."

He signaled with his hands, each man alternating cover as they rushed forward in bounds, fingers on triggers, ready to blast any threat with 9-millimeter Parabellum slugs.

The four reached the gate. A concrete ditch yawned outside the wall at this end, spanned by a little bridge at the gate. Beyond this ran a country road that meandered along the shore of Lough Dragan, the deep, murky lake the headland jutted into.

But there were no masked IRA gunmen lurking in ambush. No Janssens either. The stillness was tense, ominous, a chill breeze whispering. The hint of a fishy smell hung in the air.

Pietersen signaled again. The others fanned out to sweep the area, then reported back.

"No spent brass, no bullet holes," said Wolf. "Submachine gun's still in his Rover."

"Utility pole outside is down, which explains the outages," said Stein. "Drag marks at the shore. Something big and heavy was hauled out of the water. But no footprints."

"They crossed the lake to avoid the Army checkpoint down the road," said Pietersen. "In this fog we'd never see a boat coming. Probably rowed to stay silent."

Stein scowled. "To take down the lines they could've just climbed the pole and cut them. And the pole was knocked over by brute force, not sawn. Doesn't make sense."

"I assume they used a demolition charge or an RPG to blow through the wall."

Wolff shook his head. "No blast evidence, and we'd have heard the explosion. From the size of the hole, they rammed it with a bulldozer or a large truck, then plowed over the shack."

"How'd they get it over the lake? Or the ditch? Why not ram the gate instead?"

"Maybe an amphibious vehicle, but I've never heard of Provos using anything like that."

"Here's their trail," said Zaleski, pointing at the ground. "See the scraped rocks? They stayed off the driveway and angled southwest, which is why we didn't run into them."

"Bastards must have taken Janssens alive to make him talk or use him as a hostage," said Pietersen. He got on the radio. "Base, this is Raven One. Over."

"Raven One, this is Base. Over."

"Raven Four may have been captured. Hostiles headed southwest in a large, unidentified vehicle. On our way to intercept. Out." Pietersen turned to the others. "Let's hunt them down."

They piled back in the Land Rover, and followed the odd, faint trail across the stony ground back up the headland. The four-wheel-drive vehicle negotiated the terrain easily, Wolff feeling his way through the veil of fog as they jolted along.

"Looks like they're headed towards the cross," said Stein.

A menhir engraved with bizarre glyphs once stood on the headland's far side, placed by an unknown people six millennia ago. Ignoring archaeologists' pleas, the old man destroyed the site, exorcised it, and erected a cross to commemorate "Christianity's conquest of paganism."

The team knew the IRA was no joke. They were tough, they were capable, and they were committed, armed with American Armalite rifles and Libyan rocket-propelled grenades. They weren't shy about torture either. Both republicans and loyalists often crippled prisoners by 'kneecapping' – a bullet or a power drill in the knees.

The faces in the dashboard glow were hard, eyes fierce slits. Janssens, a jovial Belgian, had fought and sweated and bled beside them. They loved him like a brother, the way only comrades-in-arms could, and lusted to come to grips with his captors. No quarter for the bastards either. When Pietersen contacted the authorities, it'd be to pick up the bodies. So long as they were all confirmed IRA, the Royal Ulster Constabulary and the British Army wouldn't ask too many questions.

But they blinked in disbelief at the nightmare slowly taking shape in the haze ahead.

It resembled a gigantic serpent, covered in overlapping bony plates. The arched neck held up a long, narrow, saurian head with a sagittal crest, a serrated ridge of spines running down its back. Legless, but forearms on the neck ended in hooked claws. The beast was about twenty-five yards long by Pietersen's estimate and probably weighed several tons.

The monster had stopped at the thirty-foot white cross and knocked it over. Even as they watched, the snake picked it up and began tearing it apart.

The four of them just sat there speechless for a few seconds.

"What the hell is that thing?" asked Stein. "A giant snake or a crocodile?"

"They don't have any of those in Ireland," said Wolff. "Too damn cold. And not even anacondas and Nile crocodiles get that big."

"Well, what the hell else could it be?"

"I don't know. Almost looks like some kind of weird dinosaur."

"Base, this is Raven One," said Pietersen. "Got eyes on our intruder. Big reptile of some kind. Really, really big. Came up from the lake. It's destroying the cross. Over."

"Raven One, this is Base," said Kovacs. "Roger. There's a cattle prod in the shed. Over."

"Base, this is Raven One. Negative. This bad boy is way too big. Most we'd do is tickle it, assuming it even noticed. Raven Three, this is Raven One. Over."

"Raven One, this is Raven Three," said Dietrich. "Over."

"Get out here and put this beast down before it causes any more damage. Out."

"Hey, Zaleski, weren't you raised Catholic?" asked Wolff. "Ring up Saint Patrick for us and tell him he missed a snake."

"I don't think that's a snake," said Zaleski, his tone somber.

"Well, whatever it is, what's it doing here?" asked Stein.

"Scavenging for food, I imagine," said Pietersen. "Something that size could probably eat every fish in the lake and come back for seconds."

They stopped behind the monster, and Pietersen, Stein, and Zaleski climbed out.

Wolff started stepping out too, but Pietersen clasped his shoulder. "Go to the checkpoint. Get soldiers sent up here from the post in town just in case. Give me your submachine gun."

Their American-made radios had a range of less than a mile and using citizens band was technically against the law in the United Kingdom anyway. Their submachine guns, needless to say, were totally illegal. Wolff handed Pietersen his MAT-49 and magazine pouch, then turned the Land Rover around and disappeared.

Pietersen slung the extra weapon and ammunition over his shoulder and gestured to Stein and Zaleski. The trio spread out, wrinkling their noses in disgust; the snake stank like rotten fish.

At length, over on the creature's right side, the tall, spare figure of Dietrich emerged from the dense fog, which forced him to move in close in order to see his target clearly. Pietersen pointed at the monster and made a slicing motion across his throat. Dietrich nodded. He knelt, raised his rifle, and aimed carefully for a headshot. The loud crack of the gunshot echoed.

Nothing happened. He'd apparently missed. Pietersen scowled. Dietrich was a marksman. He *never* missed. Pietersen could see the puzzled expression on his face. Dietrich fired again. Kept firing until the empty clip ejected with a metallic ping.

The creature's head swung in Dietrich's direction, slimy, translucent drool dripping from its jaws. The long, massive trunk swelled as it sucked in a deep breath, rumbling and churning. Then it thrust forward. A blinding jet of blue flame roared from the gaping maw. Dietrich, instantly transformed into a human torch, ran away screaming.

"Open fire!" said Pietersen. "Aim for the head and neck!"

Submachine guns erupted with a chattering roar but they emptied their thirty-two-round magazines with no effect. Pietersen realized Dietrich hadn't missed. His bullets had bounced off.

The dragon - what else could the damn thing be? - wheeled ponderously to face them. The trio backed up, stunned, slapping fresh magazines into their weapons. At Pietersen's direction they switched their aim and fired at the creature's smooth underbelly, but this proved equally fruitless.

A stream of fire sprayed Stein. He reeled and flopped to the ground, thrashing and howling, frantically flailing to smother the flames. The head quickly swiveled and burned Zaleski before he could run away. Sliding forward, it squashed him under its great bulk, grinding out his frenzied cries. Then the dragon turned towards Pietersen.

He was already running, harder than he'd ever run before. Searing heat blasted over him, but he was just out of reach, the long, stabbing tongue of flame licking just short of him. The dragon – *a fucking dragon!* – silently slithered after him. It did not bellow or hiss or roar.

Pietersen tripped and fell headlong, his radio clattering away in the rocks somewhere. He couldn't stop to search for it in the dark. He scrambled back up, ignoring the bruises and scrapes, and kept going. Dared glance over his shoulder.

The dragon had stopped and turned back. The writhing of Pietersen's comrades had subsided. They lay still and smoldering. The breeze brought a sickening whiff of the sweet stench of burned human flesh. The dragon bent and snatched up Dietrich in its jaws and, like a pelican with a fish, swallowed him whole. It did the same with Stein and Zaleski. That was why they never found Janssens. Then the beast crawled away, moving parallel to a little gravel path leading from the cross to the house.

Cold air burned Pietersen's lungs. Like the others, he was in his late forties and getting old for this game, but still addicted to the money and the adrenalin. He retraced his steps and stumbled across his radio – crushed flat.

He cursed in Afrikaans. If the dragon attacked the house, he doubted the safe room would be strong enough to withstand it. He had to warn Kovacs and Corso; grab the old man and get the hell out of there. He sprinted back to the house, taking a wide detour of the dragon.

Pietersen got there the same time it did, the house lights reflecting off its gray, armored hide, blotched by a sheen of moss and glistening wet from the depths of the lake.

An engine revved and tires squealed. A Jaguar MK2 sedan surged from the garage, racing down the driveway, Corso behind the wheel and the old man in back. He'd obviously seized the initiative to try and get him out without waiting for orders.

This model – the 3.8 liter – was known for its speed, which was precisely why Pietersen chose it. *Go, go, go!* He willed Corso faster. *Fire can't stop you!*

The dragon twisted its head around but didn't spew fire. Instead, the huge tail lashed out, smacking the burgundy sedan's rear fender and crumpling it like tin foil. The Jaguar spun out of control, screeching across the pavement and sliding into a drainage ditch. It rolled onto its side, headlights and fog lights blazing uselessly.

A door on top swung open; Corso clambered into view. He managed to heave himself halfway out before he was incinerated. No one else emerged.

The dragon slithered over and bit off the upper half of Corso's body, gulping it down.

A burst of automatic weapons fire snarled from the attic

window. *Kovacs!* The dragon crawled back to the house under a hail of bullets. It swung its tail like a wrecking ball, smashing white-washed stone walls. Claws wrenched off shingles, ripped out beams. The floodlights blinked out, plunging the grounds into darkness.

The generator stopped.

A fire started.

Pietersen doubted any of this would be seen or heard and reported. The property sat in the hilly countryside, miles from town, and given the distance and the fog... The sound of gunfire wasn't exactly unusual in these parts either.

With the beast distracted, he crept up to the scorched wreck of the Jaguar, careful to stay on the far side of it, out of view. His eyes gradually adjusted to darkness again.

Pietersen grimaced at the coppery reek of blood and peered through the front windshield. The lower, unburnt half of Corso's torso had fallen back inside, a gruesome tangle of legs and entrails. Feeble movement stirred in the back – the old man was still alive.

Pietersen crawled around to the cracked rear window. He punched it with the butt of a knife to shatter the glass, brushed the shards away, then reached in and sawed the seat belt to cut the old man free.

"Anything broken?" asked Pietersen. "Can you move?"

The old man had been reduced to a pitiful wretch, eyes wide with terror. "The archaeologist deciphered the glyphs on the stone... warned me... but I didn't listen..."

"Forget that, we have to get you out of here!" Pietersen grabbed him under the armpits to drag him out.

The old man's lips trembled as he continued mumbling. "I desecrated a pagan shrine... roused the leviathan from its slumber... It's been hibernating for six thousand years... waiting... waiting for its worshippers to return... God have mercy on our souls, it's going to destroy us all!"

He suddenly clutched Pietersen with his wrinkled talons, eyes bulging. His mouth opened, but only a dry rasp came out.

Then he slumped. Still and staring. Pietersen checked his pulse. Dead. Heart attack or stroke, he guessed.

Corso's radio still hung on his belt. Pietersen stretched inside and got hold of it. He wiped the blood off and pressed the button. "Raven Eight, this is Raven One. Over."

Only static crackled over the speaker.

Pietersen adjusted the squelch. "Raven Eight, this is Raven One! Over!"

Silence.

And no more gunfire came from the house. The attic had been destroyed.

Pietersen's contract ended with the old man's death, but he wasn't leaving without Kovacs. The man had taken a bullet for him in Algeria, carrying him to safety from the wadi where he lay wounded, about to shoot himself so the fellagha couldn't capture him and skin him alive.

More than a few enlisted in the Legion because they were running away from something. Sometimes the law, sometimes themselves.

But Legionnaires never ran away from each other. Every April 30th the Legion solemnly commemorated its most famous battle, Camarón in 1863, when sixty-five Legionnaires made a legendary last stand against three thousand Mexican troops.

Gunfire echoed again, and Pietersen's heart lifted. Kovacs still lived, still fought, still defied death. The shots came from the rear of the house this time. Pietersen circled around towards the back, trying to stay out of sight.

The shooting ceased and Kovacs screamed.

A scream abruptly cut off.

Pietersen charged forward, but only found a smoking submachine gun lying on the rear terrace near the flagpole where a red-and-white Ulster banner fluttered, spent cartridges scattered all over the flagstones among blood drops and pools of dragon drool. His stomach twisted.

He suppressed his anguish and cold-bloodedly considered his next move. No reason to stick around now. But the headland had sheer cliffs on three sides, impossible to descend without a very long rope once he got over the wall. And if he tried jumping into the lake, he'd be dashed to pieces on jagged rocks. The gate all the way down at the far eastern end was the only way out.

Pietersen sneaked in that direction. The fire continued spreading, erupting in a roaring orange inferno enveloping half the house. The ground was wide open beyond the hedge, but with the floodlights out, the area was pitch black beyond the lurid, flickering radius of the fire, the stars and moon obscured by the mist.

But the dragon somehow saw him and immediately slithered forward to block his escape. Blue flame stabbed at him, and he barely stayed out of range, heat washing over him. He smelled singed fabric, and was forced to dash back around to the rear of the burning house again.

But the dragon seemed to lose sight of him and after a short distance it gave up and resumed its demolition. It finished razing the south wing and began ravaging the main building as Pietersen hid behind the tool shed to catch his breath.

He was trapped. Once the dragon finished laying waste to the property – clearly its first priority – it would hunt him down, cleansing its sacred grounds of violators. *Where are the soldiers? Wolff ought to have come back by now. Maybe they didn't believe his story.*

But the more he thought about it, the more his blood boiled. This was actually how he wanted it. Pietersen had six dead comrades to avenge. He wanted to finish this himself.

But how? The monster seemed unstoppable. How the hell could he kill the damn thing?

His mind churned furiously. Summarized what he knew or guessed about the dragon.

How did it breathe fire? The blue color suggested methane, a byproduct of digestion. But instead of farting it as other animals did, it apparently stored the gas up, probably in a huge bladder. Source of ignition? Natural crystals, such as quartz, gave off sparks when struck. Maybe it swallowed them like gizzard stones. The slime it drooled could be a protective mucus coating the throat and mouth.

Other characteristics? Semi-aquatic, slow on land. Good night vision, possibly capable of detecting heat signatures – Pietersen had noticed two deep pockets located between the eyes and the flaring nostrils at the end of the snout, resembling those of a pit viper. Thick, bony hide impervious to small arms, similar to the armor on a tank.

Tank.

An idea flashed in his mind.

The north wing still stood but wouldn't for much longer. He streaked across to the far side of the building. The dragon, absorbed in its vengeful destruction, either didn't see him or maybe the intense heat from the raging fire poured out so much infrared radiation it couldn't detect him.

Pietersen fished for keys, unlocked the side door, and slipped inside, groping down the dark hall to the study. As he felt the wall to guide his way, his fingers brushed picture frames, proud portraits of the old man's supposedly illustrious ancestors. The din of destruction rocked his senses – the roar of flames, the crack of splintering beams and crash of brickwork, the clash of shattering glass.

Part of the ceiling crumbled, and a falling oak beam hurled Pietersen onto the carpeted floor, pinning his leg. He strained, managed with great effort to heave the heavy timber off, and struggled to his feet. Pain lanced through the outside of his lower right leg. He guessed the small bone was fractured, but he gritted his teeth and forced himself on, finally making it to the study and slipping inside. He shut the door and fumbled for a flashlight on his belt. Flicked it on.

He knelt beside the Soviet anti-tank rifle and checked to see if it'd been de-militarized. So far as he could tell, it hadn't. The long barrel ending in a squat muzzle brake was still clear and the firing mechanism appeared intact. But he didn't have time for more than a cursory inspection.

Armor-piercing .30-06 slugs from Dietrich's Garand failed to punch through the dragon's hide, but maybe this cannon could.

The display included a wooden ammo crate with Cyrillic stenciling containing five bullets. They were huge: 14.5-millimeter, around .58 caliber. The old man had told him once that from a hundred yards these armor-piercing incendiary rounds could penetrate over an inch-and-a-half of steel armor and set fire to anything flammable they hit.

But would they still work? The ammunition, like the rifle, was World War II vintage, which meant it was at least thirty years old. And there were just five rounds.

Only one way to find out. He scooped them up and thumbed them into the chunky clip one by one. The rifle was a semi-automatic PTRS-41. He swung down the magazine cover, snapped the clip in, and shoved the heavy bolt forward to feed the first round into the breech.

Pietersen dumped the submachine guns and magazine pouches and doused his flashlight. Leaning against the armchair, he clambered back up, almost fainting from the pain. He flipped up the rifle's carrying handle and tried picking it up. Damn thing weighed over forty pounds. With a broken leg it was impossible. He was forced to drag it along, gasping in agony, and struggled to maneuver it through the doorway.

Reeking smoke choked the hall. The building creaked and groaned, about to come down on top of him. Coughing, he limped out the side door into the fresh, clean air just before the roof collapsed behind him in a cloud of ash and cinders.

He limped a short way, then lost his grip and dropped the rifle. He couldn't go a step further. Pietersen dropped to his knees and laid prone, manhandling the heavy gun around and propping the bipod on a flat rock. He flicked the safety lever off. Only iron sights, and he couldn't read the increments on the flip-up rear sight in the dark.

As huge as the dragon was, even if these big bullets penetrated, Pietersen knew they wouldn't necessarily bring it down right away unless they struck something vital. Shooting it in the head would presumably kill it but hitting it there would be almost impossible. The beast moved relatively slow, but could swivel its head quickly, and an anti-tank rifle was hardly a precision weapon. It couldn't be used the same way as Dietrich's sniper rifle.

Pietersen's target was the methane bladder inside the trunk. If he was lucky, the incendiary ammunition might detonate it. Emphasis on 'might'. It could be similar to shooting a car's fuel tank, which, contrary to Hollywood movies, didn't explode very easily. And even if his guesses about the dragon's anatomy were correct, he didn't know the bladder's exact location.

It finished leveling the main house and began battering down the already damaged north wing.

He tucked the wooden stock firmly into his shoulder, aimed at the beast's flank at about mid-section, and squeezed the stiff trigger. The rifle boomed and savagely kicked, spitting out a huge orange muzzle flash. The ejected steel shell clattered on the stones.

The dragon flinched – a clear indication the bullet penetrated – and its head whipped around, seeking the source. Pietersen was evidently too far from the fire for the heat to blind its senses because it zeroed in on him immediately, those inhuman eyes shining an eerie, demonic red in the firelight. The dragon slithered from the rubble towards him.

Ears ringing, shoulder bruised from the recoil, Pietersen fired again. And again. And again. Slamming slugs into it, but the bullets weren't even slowing it down.

The old man called it a leviathan, and the pagans worshipped it. Was this even an animal, or something supernatural? Could you kill a god?

The dragon loomed over him. He gagged on its foul reek. The wicked black claws spread to seize and rend him; the head reared back, inhaling, poised to cremate him.

The white cones of headlights sliced the gloom. The Land Rover hurtled into view and jerked to a halt. Wolff sprang out and sprinted towards him, banging away with his pistol.

"No, no!" Pietersen frantically tried waving him away. "Get back, get back!"

Wolff screamed and fell writhing, wreathed in flames. The dragon swung back to Pietersen. Only one round left. "Go back to hell, you fucking freak!" He jerked the trigger.

The explosion rocked the earth. The blast wave scorched him, flying splinters from the monster's shattered bones shredding him like shrapnel. Chunks of flesh and gobs of blood sprayed everywhere.

The blunt steel snout of a Saracen armored personnel carrier lumbered through the smoke. The turret hatch clanged open and a stunned British soldier in a beret gaped at the towering mushroom cloud boiling up before his eyes.

As agonizing consciousness faded into blessed black oblivion, a grim, defiant smile on his face, Pietersen's last thought was a French song popular with Legionnaires: *Non, Je Ne Regrette Rien* – 'No, I Do Not Regret Anything'.

A SHARPENED DAGGER

Phil Scott Mayes

Vivid nightmares plagued Job Abrams for as long as he could remember. The doctor called them night terrors. As a kid, he could only run, hide, and survive the night. He got good at it, much better than his twin brother, Daniel. Oddly, it was the revelation that the monsters were real that finally gave Job courage. If they were real, then Job wasn't powerless. He could hurt real things. Real things bled. And if they bled, they could be killed. Unlike Daniel, Job took control. He went hunting in his sleep. That's when the Daggers found him.

Now, in the perpetual darkness of the Void with dozens of missions under his belt, an oily projectile zipped past in a near miss that split the air with a deafening crack. The black stubble on his head stood straight and his heart thumped against his sternum. He controlled his breathing and held his M4's green laser where the thin, fluttering skin of the demon's throat would soon be exposed. The beast reared up and coiled its six tentacles to send another volley of digested and packed human bone.

"Come on. Do it, you ugly bastard," he growled.

Demons were prideful beasts, and that was the only reason Daggers ever stood a chance. A demon never called for backup until gravely wounded, and sometimes not even then, but if it used its hive mind to call reinforcements, they would appear by the hundreds. The task force had lost more than a few good Daggers that way.

Job watched the demon's movements, waiting for the moment its body would begin to lurch. The creature's head was that of a warthog with the flesh peeled off – bone streaked with dried blood and fatty tissue. Its tusks were adorned with a

139

garland of human entrails that swung wildly with every flick of its snout.

It occurred to Job that Satan was a mad scientist. Jealous of the Holy Father's creative power, he vindictively disfigured His creation. That would make the Void, at best, a playground for his ghouls, and at worst, a training ground for his army.

The demon's body began forward, jerking like a whip's handle and setting its tentacles in motion. That's when its head rose, exposing Job's fist-sized target. He squeezed the trigger smoothly and sent a burst of 5.56 into the creature's throat. Ripples fanned out where each bullet punched through the hide and tore into the telneurum – its communication organ.

Its tentacles flailed wildly, sending the next round of projectiles astray, and Job recognized another opening. He fired rounds at the demon's joints and marched forward with weapon raised until its hind legs buckled. The moment it met the forest floor, Job slung the rifle, drew a wooden rod from its sheath, and sprinted to finish the monster.

As he raised the rod high, it lengthened, and in a swirl of black particles, the head of a broad axe appeared. He swung the weapon down, severing the tentacles like twigs from a tree. The demon twisted and let out a hissing type of growl that coated Job's face with blood and bits of masticated meat. It swung its head, bent on skewering Job. Face coated in blood, Job could taste the iron, could hear the beast's snorting, could feel the air stirring, but couldn't see the tusk careening toward his left flank.

It plunged into Job's side, snapping a rib before popping his lung. Its skull slammed into him and sent him tumbling across the clearing. Pressure built with each shallow breath. His ribs ached mercilessly, but it paled in comparison to the pain of the demon's tentacles coiling tightly around his legs, squeezing until he thought his calves would burst.

The surge of pain as his bones cracked forced thought entirely from Job's mind, immersing him in fleeting oblivion.

By the time he regained his wits, the demon stood over him. Job rolled his head and spied the cabin he'd come to raid. That was the mission: kill the demon sentry, retrieve the artifact, and beat feet. Job also spied his axe and reached for it, grasping desperately among the tendrils and twigs for the staff, the only weapon he possessed that had the power to truly kill a demon. The rifle was efficient, its range and firepower unmatched, but a demon would inevitably heal from any wound it inflicted.

The creature's jaws opened for a crushing bite, and Job's fingers closed over his staff. It shortened and swirled with black particles once more, the axe head becoming a sword blade that he thrust as deeply as he could into the demon's neck, sawing with every ounce of strength he could muster. Blood spurted and frothy pink bubbles appeared at the gashed windpipe. It gurgled, choking on its own blood, then collapsed sideways.

The demon sentry was defeated, but the mission was far from complete. Hot lightning shot through his legs and left side, reminding him of his powdered bones and punctured lung, but it was the tentacles pulling his feet beneath the loosened earth that would keep him from the cabin.

He dragged the sword's edge across the tentacles' rubbery skin and they tightened further, grinding the jagged shards of bone against his muscle. Job cried out and flopped to his back knowing there was only one way forward.

He sat up, grunting loudly through the stabbing pain in his ribs, and raised the wooden staff. Again, the particles swirled as the handle lengthened slightly, and when the conversion was complete, he gripped a hatchet in his right hand. He retrieved a stout twig from the ground and placed it between his teeth. Then, with the sheer madness of determination, he swung the hatchet straight through his left leg midway between knee and ankle. The fragment of tentacle that remained around his calf tightened reflexively, staunching the wound. The hatchet fell from his fingers as he fought unconsciousness, but he found the blade, raised it again in quaking hands.

His right leg blurred beneath his tears as he brought it down, but the swing lacked conviction. The lackluster chop bounced off the bone.

Before he could lose will, he chopped like a maniac, each hack weaker than the last. He lost count of his swings, and when he thought he couldn't swing again, the hatchet split the bone. One more swing and it was done. When Job's mania subsided, he felt an ironic gratitude for his tentacle tourniquets.

Returning the staff to its sheath, he rolled to his belly and rose onto his forearms. He repositioned the M4 to his back and fought through fatigue and agony as he high-crawled to the cabin with its dry-rot walls and crooked door. Behind him, trails of blood glistened like oil on the moonlit undergrowth. It was always midnight there, always bleak and hopeless.

Job dragged himself up to the stoop. The door was unlocked, scraping as it opened to reveal his objective lying unceremoniously on the old wood planks. At first, the artifact looked as ancient as it was – coated in thick dust that obscured its exact shape and details. It wasn't until he crawled closer that, he saw modern lines and a simple structure. It looked like a military-issued web belt, but from the pounding in his chest, he knew it was indeed The Belt of Truth. He prayed silently the other Daggers had retrieved their pieces of the Armor of God; ultimate victory would require the complete set. Job grabbed the belt, shook off the dust, and stuffed it in his pack.

A shrieking chorus pinballed off the viny trees of the hellish wood.

Job dug frantically under the neck of his uniform and followed the gold chain to the five-inch cross that dangled at its end. The beams were round, a half-inch in diameter, and ornately carved with ancient script and decorative flairs. He pressed the button at the top of the cross, releasing a spring-loaded dagger that extended from the bottom.

Job glanced out the door. An arm with bright red spots on glossy black scales reached around the trunk of a nearby tree. A pair of yellow eyes peeked from behind the trunk, an infected glowing in the moonlight. Job's heart dropped when he noticed the others. Hundreds of them – climbing, creeping, leering. The forest was alive.

He looked regretfully at the dagger in his hand. "I hate this part." He took a breath. "All things in Christ!"

He sunk the dagger smoothly into his chest, between the ribs, and through his heart.

Job gasped, bolted upright, grabbing his chest then his legs, which were still attached. No matter how many times he went in, he couldn't get used to the dual reality. The two monks assigned to pray over him during the mission rushed by candlelight to his bedside, offering him water and a pan for purging. The spirit's experience waging holy war in the Void was completely immersive. They felt everything as if it happened in the waking world.

There were only two ways back from the Void alive: waking up in the real world or dying by cross-pendant in the Void. Sometimes Daggers just woke up, pulling their spirit back to their body, but it almost always meant mission failure. Such wake-ups were rare, so most missions concluded with suicide by sacred pendant. It gave the Daggers control over their exit. You had to endure the pain of getting stabbed in the heart each and every time, but it beat not waking up at all.

Any spiritual death in the Void meant death to the body – flatlined in sleep. Those were the stakes.

"Anybody else back yet?" Job whispered, trying to catch his breath despite having two healthy lungs again. He sipped water and eyed the monks who nodded in unison.

"Okay… is anybody still out?"

The monks shook their heads.

"Oh, c'mon. I was the last one?" he asked in disbelief.

No response.

Job touched his bare feet to the cool concrete floor and the feeling surprised him, almost painfully so, like pins and needles. Though they'd never actually been gone, it was as if he stood on new feet just grown from his roughly-hewn stumps.

Seven years he'd lived in the bunker – a decommissioned

Cold War shelter. Now, at twenty-four, he found its cool cement walls warm and homey.

Job hobbled stiffly toward the bunker's entrance. The reinforced main door wasn't the only way in or out, there was also a web of escape tunnels the task force had carved into the mountain over the years. Though it had been almost a century since the Daggers' last real-world engagement, they knew Satan's influence had consumed the hearts and minds of people around the globe. The threat was ever present.

He pushed the heavy door aside and breathed the crisp mountain air. Light swelled from the horizon as daybreak approached, but the veil of night had yet to lift entirely. Job set out across the lot to the compound's main gate. Fresh air and exercise often flushed the Void's rotten aftertaste, and if that didn't work, a cup of coffee at the guard shack would do the trick.

The existence of the task force was one of the world's best kept secrets, but the existence of the bunker was no special mystery. According to public record, it had been converted into a monastery. Mechanical maintenance and food delivery were handled by outside companies, each vetted and monitored, and that part of the operation usually ran like clockwork. The head monk saw to that and was the public face of the operation.

Cover aside, security was still necessary, so the Dagger trainees worked rotations at the main gate. That morning, Job found Mike Winters pulling guard duty with Joey Chin. Mike stood to approach the food service truck, squinting at its high beams. Pursuant to their training, Joey stayed in the guard booth where Job slid behind him to pour a cup from the steaming pot.

"Morning, fella," Mike greeted. "Could you please shut off your headlights like the sign says." After a beat, the headlights flicked off. "Running ahead of schedule this month?"

It wasn't the usual driver, but judging by the curious tilt of Mike's head, he'd already noticed.

"Yeah, soup kitchen cancelled this month," the driver said, projecting over the engine noise. "Said donations were good and they didn't have room. Insisted we deliver it here free of charge. I was in the area, so I came early."

Mike nodded the way he did most things: slowly. "Very thoughtful. If I could see your driver's license, I'll make this quick and painless so we can get that food inside."

The driver's hands disappeared, rummaging out of sight below the window. "I'm new to this route. What is this place?"

"A monastery."

"With armed security and razor wire?"

"They value their privacy. Can't be too careful nowadays."

There was only so much chit-chat Job could take, so he patted Joey on the shoulder and whispered, "One o'clock. Rec room. Texas hold 'em ass-whooping. Invite Mike." Then he started back toward the bunker.

Job had walked no more than twenty feet when there was a brief rustling from behind followed by wet choking and what sounded like Joey's coffee running off the counter and onto the floor. Job spun to see Joey grabbing at his neck, eyes bulging as crimson ribbons of blood spurted through his fingers.

Fear punched Job in the chest as his gaze flicked to where Mike was staring down the business end of a suppressor. His forehead ate the bullet, the top of his skull flapping back like a toupee in a gust of wind. He teetered for a second, then slumped as his legs collapsed.

Job sprinted to a large safe just inside the bunker door, swiped his thumb, and grabbed a short-barreled M4 and a Glock 19. He heard the driver rap twice on the cab's door. The man yelled, "Let's go, you."

Job punched the red button beside the safe, sounding the bunker's internal alarm. He chambered a round in the rifle and raced outside just in time to see a shirtless, skeletally-thin man trot from behind the guard shack carrying a combat knife, wet with what had to be Joey's blood. A crudely painted pentagram glistened red on the man's bare chest as he moved for the back of the truck.

Job raised his M4 but glanced over his shoulder as feet

padded out of the bunker in double-time. When he returned forward, the gaunt man had disappeared.

"Hold your fire," Commander Solomon said, striding to Job's side as his fellow Daggers took position behind concrete barricades. "Job, I need a sitrep."

"Two-plus enemy combatants in a box truck. Mike and Joey are dead. Driver has a handgun, shirtless man, a knife."

Job watched as the driver exited the truck and slowly raised his hands, grinning like a fool.

"Permission to engage?" Job asked.

"Stand down, son. If this is who I think it is, Command will want him alive."

"Well, good morning, y'all," the man said. "Do you welcome all your delivery drivers this way or is it just my lucky day?"

"You're no delivery driver," Job said, "but I can tell you're not Fallen. Which groupie gang are you with?"

"You guys *are* good. Daggers, eh?" the driver said with another shit-eating grin. "Satan's Angels. I'm honored to finally find y'all."

The driver took several steps toward the bunker, and Commander Solomon ordered him to halt. The driver continued anyway, even after a warning shot cracked past him into the truck's grill.

Solomon motioned for a Dagger named Hannah to follow as he moved cautiously toward the driver who seemed unfazed by their approach.

"Cover us," he ordered the group. "Halt and turn away from the sound of my voice! Do it. NOW!"

"Commander Ramesses sends his regards," the driver said, bringing his arms behind him.

Job shouted, "Gun!" as the man produced a silenced handgun from his waistband.

A cacophony of gunfire erupted from the barricades. Little explosions of meat, bone, and blood painted the truck a chunky red as the bullets cratered the driver's body. He collapsed, the gunfire ceased, and the team moved in.

146

Solomon kicked the handgun clear of the driver who had been dead since Job's bullet popped through his left eye and tumbled around inside his skull. He turned to check on Hannah who was pressing a hand against an expanding dark spot on her thigh.

"I'm hit, sir," she called. When Solomon began to turn back, she barked, "I'm good! Check the truck."

"Hannah's hit. Left leg," Solomon bellowed to the others as he moved ahead.

Job and three other Daggers converged on the truck with weapons trained on the door. They opened it to find boxes of food, a bag of onions, and two dead bodies – the actual delivery drivers. The gaunt man was nowhere to be found.

Job began to circle the truck. "Anything?" he asked Commander Solomon, who was checking the cab.

"Clear!" Solomon responded.

Job continued around, weapon at the ready. He stooped for a view of the undercarriage, expecting to see the gaunt man clinging to the chassis like some humanoid bat, but once again there was no sign of him. Job finished his lap around the truck and bent down once more. That's when he spied the gaunt man behind the three trainees at the bunker's entrance.

With strength that defied his apparent frailty, he buried his knife in the base of a kid's skull and grabbed the trainee's M4. He unloaded bursts into the two remaining trainees then targeted the exposed team who scrambled for cover behind the truck.

For some it was too late.

The gaunt man fired round after round, ducking below the concrete, and changing his position at intervals. Several of them shot randomly at the barricades as they moved, but none came close to hitting the shooter. On her back, Hannah scooted across the ground, pushing with her good leg. As she drew it up for another push, supersonic lead hit her knee so hard, Job thought it was blown off entirely. She bawled in pain then laid without movement. For a moment, she appeared to be dead, but it was not so.

Job watched as Hannah slid her handgun free from its holster, laying as still as possible, playing dead. Once it was firmly in her grasp, she sat upright, took aim, and pulled the trigger.

Her shot split the gaunt man's ear and smacked the concrete behind him, but his return fire entered through her cheek and obliterated the far side of her skull on its way out.

"Shit! Hannah!" Job yelled. He hung his head. "Dammit, you almost got that fucker..."

Behind the concrete, the gaunt man killed with impunity, landing lethal rounds on five Daggers. He even had time to reload with the extra magazine the trainee had carried.

The truck was terrible cover and Job knew it. Not only were their legs dancing in plain sight beneath the chassis, the truck's box and cab weren't very likely to stop a bullet from passing through.

Job watched on as Solomon chanced a glimpse through the cab's windows and recoiled as the glass burst with a loud snap. The commander turned to them. "We have numbers, but he has position. We have to split up. Storm from both sides of the truck. One team should get a clear shot while he's focused on the other. Job, take Zeke. Naomi, on me."

"Wait. Sir, do you have a full mag?" Job asked, and Solomon nodded. Job laid prone, using the truck's back tires as cover. "Shoot through the truck's cab to draw his attention."

Solomon reached the weapon into the window's opening, aimed in the direction of the bunker, and held the trigger down. Job rolled out from behind the wheels, took aim, and fired one shot through the gaunt man's head.

✟ ⚱ ✟

Ramesses leaned against the fender of the Mercedes SUV watching his lieutenant, Crezik, and the rest of his four-man strike team load the Gulfstream with rifle cases and ammo cans. Ramesses took another drag from his cigarette; they had eliminated prayer groups, potential Dagger trainees, and even Void scouts, but they'd never had an opportunity like this. Victory at Mount Esther wouldn't end the war, but it would be monumental. After the bunker, they could begin hunting the young ones.

✢ ⚱ ✢

"The Fallen will send a team before we can relocate or reinforce our ranks," Commander Solomon said, then paused before gravely predicting, "They're probably already on their way."

Solomon stared at the tortured souls that, like Job, had become their only family. "We've never been this close to the full Armor of God. We have to go in tonight – one final push for the sword."

Naomi raised a hand. "Shouldn't we defend the bunker?"

"We will, but the bunker is lost. Tomorrow, we'll move on and by the time we're settled into the new location, the Sword of the Spirit will be gone. It could take the scouts centuries to find it again. Zeke, you'll come with Job, Naomi, and me. The others will play defense."

"I've never seen combat before," Zeke noted nervously.

"This operation was going to be tough with a full team of seven. Without you," —Solomon scanned the stale briefing room, and Job knew the commander saw the same thing he did: peaceful monks and pubescent youths. "We'll only have three. We need you, son, and I think you're ready."

Zeke stared downward and nodded with growing conviction. "Okay, let's do this."

They spent the day preparing their bodies for sleep with hard labor and intense training. At least a full hour before sunset, the task force convened one last time to reiterate the plan before heading to their individual alcoves. Job entered the candlelit space and slugged the sleep tea that the monks prepared. He laid staring at the ceiling before closing his eyes with a prayer and achieving a state of repetitive thought that lulled him to sleep.

He soon found himself back in the hellish wilderness. Though the sun still warmed the west peak of Mount Esther, it was vacuously dark within the Void. The only light was a dull glow that seemed to emanate from the air itself. He stood on a riverbed checking his gear as he awaited the others.

The Void was a half-step between the human plane and hell and wasn't meant to host the human spirit. It was a demonic space even the Daggers didn't fully understand. After centuries of operation, they knew little more than it contained hideous beasts that fed on humanity, and that those beasts could be killed.

Their ultimate target was an apocalyptic harbinger called the Abomination of Desolation, a creature of horrifying repute – the bastard mutant of hell's grief and torment. It was the head of the serpent, ripe for removal, but that would be impossible without the full Armor of God.

The stones beside him jostled, and when he looked, Solomon stood there.

"Just us so far?" the commander asked.

"So far," replied Job. "Hopefully Zeke finds us without trouble. I don't like his chances alone."

Naomi materialized in knee deep water and looked down with disappointment. "Insertions: never an exact science," she quipped as she stepped onto dry land. "Still waiting on Zeke?"

"Yeah, I already checked my gear," said Job. "Wouldn't mind a buddy check though."

Before Naomi could do so, the wall of tropical greenery rustled behind them, and they immediately spun and aimed their M4s. Their fingers rested on their triggers as the movement drew closer. The leaves shook violently, and Zeke plowed through, coming to an abrupt halt with his hands raised.

"Damn, Zeke. You almost got lit up," Naomi shouted.

"Missed the insertion point. Sorry."

"You'll get better with practice," Solomon said. "Let's get situated. That rise behind Naomi needs to stay on our left. Zeke, the jagged ridge behind you —"

Solomon trailed off, as dumbstruck as Job. The bald hill that was behind Naomi just moments before had been replaced by the jagged ridge he expected to see behind Zeke. Even the river flowed the opposite direction, though none of them had changed positions.

"You saw the hill behind Naomi, right?"

"A-firm," replied Job. They looked that way again and beheld the jagged ridge, then looked behind Zeke and saw the smooth rise that had been behind Naomi.

"It's reconfiguring to disorient us," Solomon said.

"It's working," Naomi muttered. "How are we supposed to navigate when the landscape keeps shifting?"

"The temple is along this river," Job said. "We could split up and go opposite directions. That, or we all pick a direction and hope for the best."

Naomi shook her head. "Splitting up helps our chances of finding the temple, but if we cross an alpha-class demon or the Abomination itself when there's only two of us…"

"Job's right," Solomon said firmly. "We have split up. Teams of two. We need the sword. Fight hard and remember your training. Punching out is a last resort."

Job grabbed Naomi and Zeke's shoulders, making eye contact with each before looking at Solomon. "All things in Christ."

"He gives us strength," they said in unison.

"Before we split," Solomon started as he dug through his pack and tossed item after item to Job, "you need to put the armor on."

"Me?"

"The monks had a vision. You need to wear it."

As much as Job wanted to argue, there was no time. He donned the Boots of Readiness, Breastplate of Righteousness, Shield of Faith, Helmet of Salvation, and Belt of Truth. Armored up, he looked like a special forces operator complete with body armor, combat boots, and ballistic helmet. Wearing it centuries ago would've made him look like a medieval knight, but the eternal armor changed to suit contemporary warfare.

Solomon headed off with Zeke, Job with Naomi, setting out in opposite directions. Hiking the riverbank offered ease of passage, but there was no cover, and every puff of moldy air stirred the walls of lush greenery on each side of them, revealing eyes that tracked their every move.

The jungle watched.

Maintaining their footing was difficult. The ground seemed to rise and fall with each step, as though they treaded the chest of a sleeping giant. This was not the Void Job knew. This was the umbilic epicenter through which the malignancy of hell transfused.

Black serpents slithered up a nearby tree, twisting around and through each other to become a noose that hung low from an overhead branch. It wiggled stiffly before them as an accusation wheezed within Job's mind. His twin brother also had the gift, but the terrors broke him at a young age. Substance abuse, depression, and schizophrenia followed. A little over a year ago, Job visited him during leave and saw his brother's hopelessness. The final night of his visit, Job had woken in a cold sweat and went for a drink of water. He had found his brother hanging from a rafter in the kitchen, face purple, eyes wide and bulging.

As far as Job was concerned, his brother had been dead since he found him with that extension cord cinched tightly around his neck. His parents, however, refused to let him go and had kept him on life support ever since.

The noose of serpents was a sadistic ploy to summon that pain, and Naomi could see it on Job's face. She stepped forward and drew her staff with a twirl, producing a katana blade from the cloud of black dust.

"Don't," Job warned. "I don't want to pick a fight we don't have to."

"It bothers me that it knows we're here but *it's* not picking a fight with us."

"Me too. It's like it's waiting for something."

✠ ⚱ ✠

Crezik and his team quickly loaded their gear into the Land Rover. Vigrim, the team's youngest member and best driver, took the wheel and peeled out of the lot toward the foothills of Mount Esther as Crezik briefed the mission one final time.

The concept was clear even if the details were lacking. Their gaunt assassin would have found one of the bunker escape tunnels and disabled whatever security existed, then attacked while the task force was distracted. The exact number of Daggers remaining was unknown, but Crezik and Ramesses knew the assassin would exceed expectations. They would infiltrate the bunker via the escape tunnel and quietly lay waste to everyone inside. It was a simple plan, but their enemy's complacency made it effective.

Crezik eyed the distant peak of Mount Esther and offered a prayer to the dark lord of hell. If Satan would delay attacking the Daggers in the Void, the Fallen could kill their sleeping bodies.

✟ ☗ ✟

Solomon and Zeke trekked along the stony riverbed, sensing the malevolent life beneath their boots. The air smelled and felt like steam rising from a corpse. Only seventeen, this was Zeke's first experience in the jungle, but no earthly jungle could've prepared him for this. Bile floated in his esophagus, threatening to erupt without warning.

"I don't feel good, sir."

"That's normal. It gets easier with time. In a few operations you'll barely notice."

"*If* there's another operation," Zeke muttered. "I've got a bad feeling."

"Sense of doom is also normal. You'll get used to it." Solomon clapped Zeke on the shoulder, but the commander looked as green as Zeke felt. Seemed more on edge, too.

Zeke's next step brought the thin crunch of a trampled eggshell. Where he'd stepped, a black rock had shattered leaving a gooey pink puddle. He knew exactly what it was and heaved violently.

"No, no, no," Zeke whimpered between bouts of retching.

"What's wrong?"

Zeke looked at Solomon with tearful, self-loathing. "It's a fetus."

"A *human* fetus?" Solomon asked in horror. He looked back at the pink puddle.

Zeke nodded, out of breath and riding the frothy lip of another heave. "It's my sister."

"That's not your sister, Zeke. The void is messing wi—"

A branch cracked loudly. Then another. Leaves in the surrounding trees swished violently.

A woman in tattered rags stood before them on the riverbed, silhouetted by the meager light's reflection off the turbulent waters. Her features were blanked out by shadow, and she breathed with a heavy rattle. She stood frozen, eyes locked on the fetus in existential devastation. Over the tranquil babbling of the water, she began to sob and step mechanically toward the crushed remains.

She lowered herself onto all fours, nearly burying her face in the viscous mass. In a guttural, shrieking timbre, she cried, "You killed her, Zeke!"

Zeke wept as he stumbled toward the woman.

"Zeke, stop!" barked Solomon, but Zeke was lost in a memory.

His parents loomed over him, aged eight, yelling. It had been a tragic accident but he felt deserving of their vitriol. He had killed his unborn sister. Despite numerous lectures, he had again left his toy trucks at the top of the staircase. This time, his six-months-pregnant mother had tripped over them while carrying the laundry basket. The fall down the stairs destroyed her baby and any hope of having another.

"Zeke!" Solomon's voice sounded very far away.

His mother abruptly stopped crying. She turned to face Zeke. Her tears were black tar, her eyes blacker still. "It's your fault she's dead! It's your fault I'm in this hell!"

She pounced on Zeke, knocking him to the ground. Two sharp reports sounded and the creature's head, that of Zeke's mother, popped like a water balloon. Her skin peeled back and dumped her foul, liquified insides all over him.

Zeke spat the gore from him as the demon fell away. "It got in my mouth!" He spat again. "What the hell is happening?"

"Hell is exactly what's happening," Solomon said. "The void is toying with us." The commander helped Zeke up, sighed in sympathy when he looked him over. "I'm sorry, son, but we need to keep moving. Are you okay?"

Zeke nodded and washed up in the river. The water was downright hot, turning his hands redder with each subsequent dip. He stood on rubbery legs, glanced at the broken rock and squashed unborn child, and felt something crawl inside of him.

✝ 🏆 ✝

Crezik's team bumped through the towering aspens to a small clearing far enough back to avoid detection. They geared up and hiked through the alpine forest until only a small mound and cluster of trees stood between them and the bunker. At night, it looked like it was a part of the mountain, blending into its rocky face.

They picked up their assassin's trail in the fallen pine straw and tracked it over the hill from the bunker's entrance, finding an exposed metal hatch where the dirt was swept away. Carefully, they pried up on the hatch. No traps or alarms. One at a time, they crawled through the narrow tunnel.

They were inside.

✝ 🏆 ✝

Shadows swayed ahead. Someone, some*thing*, was moving toward them. Job and Naomi froze. The shadows froze too. For a long, terrifying second, Job and Naomi stood rigidly still, staring into the darkness. Job had the unnerving thought that were looking at their own evil reflections. They dropped to a knee in unison and raised their weapons, painting the figures with their lasers.

The shadows did the same. Job's heart beat loud in his ears. He tightened his grip and aimed between the target's collarbones. The laser deflected off something shiny. A chain like the one he wore, the one given only to Daggers.

"Identify yourself," Job ordered.

Solomon's familiar voice called out for them to hold their fire, bringing Job a wave of relief that was followed immediately by foreboding. "What are you doing here? You should be miles away."

"We went opposite directions and never turned back," answered Solomon, his frown deepening. "This is impossible."

Job finally got close enough to see that Zeke was a mess. "What happened to him?"

Zeke's eyes were bleeding, he was sweating profusely – sweat tainted with blood – and he was shivering with fever. The kid doubled over with a coughing fit that soaked his hand red. Solomon shook his head at Job and Naomi; Zeke wouldn't survive.

They laid him on his back and warned him of the pain he would experience, assuring him that he'd awaken safe and sound in the bunker. Even with their reassurances, Zeke's face registered absolute terror as Solomon withdrew Zeke's pendant and released the blade. Despite his whimpered pleading, Job and Naomi held his arms down.

"It's going to be okay, Zeke," Naomi said.

Solomon raised the dagger, and Zeke's eyes grew wide with fear and panic as the commander drove the blade into the kid's heart.

✟ ♟ ✟

Zeke awoke projectile vomiting, and the monks rolled him onto his side. He pushed them away and struggled out of the bed. "I need some air, but I have to go back," he panted. "A demon was right behind Naomi."

He hit the door-release button and stepped into the eerily silent corridor.

There was blood on the cement floor.

At first it was just a few drops, but as he edged toward the common area, the drops became a trail. His heart pounded in his eardrums. Glancing from the end of the hallway, he saw the trail grow thicker in the direction of the chow hall. Zeke snuck to the armory, grabbed a vest and rifle, and emerged, peering through the holographic optic.

He posted up against the cafeteria wall and listened. The faint odor of urine, feces, and iron that permeated the air had grown potent, almost flavorful, and as it wafted into his nostrils he couldn't help hacking. He heard jostling and a muffled wail and turned the corner ready to fire, but before he could even register his targets, a shattering pain exploded in his right shoulder as a bullet cleaved the joint in two. The M4 hung from its sling and Zeke watched helplessly as a clean-cut man finished gutting his friend Jacob. They tossed the trainee, entrails dragging beneath him, onto the pile of bodies in the corner.

The Fallen were here. Just as Commander Solomon predicted.

Another shot rang out, and pain ripped through Zeke's other shoulder, then both knees. Zeke dropped, yelled in agony as he tried to move. The shooter stood over him and tilted his head inquisitively.

"I really hope you aren't just another trainee," the man said, pointing a bloodied knife.

Zeke responded in the way he thought might earn mercy, or at least make him valuable. "I'm… a Dagger," he said, fighting through the monstrous pain in his arms and legs. "Just got promoted."

The shooter's lips spread into a sinister grin. "Congratulations."

He cut off Zeke's index finger then slashed his throat. Zeke lay there squirming, each pulse sending a warm gush onto his chest.

"We're in," the shooter said, smiling cheerfully and holding up the finger.

Zeke's vision started to narrow.

Another Fallen stepped over Zeke and snatched the finger. Two more blurred figures followed.

A dull ringing sharpened in Zeke's ears, but he still heard one of them say, "The alcoves are this way."

Zeke's head rolled to the side, each painful heartbeat more sluggish than the last. He watched through fading vision as the dark shapes moved toward the alcove hallway. Delirium scrambled his mind, but two thoughts came clearly. His finger was programmed into the scanners. It was the key they needed to slaughter his family.

A single tear fell from Zeke's nose onto the concrete as numbness set in.

His world went black.

✝ ☖ ✝

The beast's jaws clamped down on Naomi's head, ripping it messily from her shoulders. Job and Solomon fired a volley of rounds from their M4s that had the wolf-like creature take a defensive stance. It stood nearly ten feet at its withers and had large flaps of scaly hide that laid forward from its neck, shielding its head. It looked canine, but its snout split vertically so that it splayed open four ways. Long barbs extended from its spine, the flesh over its ribs stripped away, revealing pitted and decaying bones.

When the men ceased fire, the scales that covered the demon's head bloomed outward like reptilian neck frills that shuddered as it roared. Job glanced to where Naomi's headless body still pumped blood onto the river's edge.

"Keep it occupied," Job snarled.

Solomon nodded, switched out magazines, then fired short bursts at the demon's head. It covered up again and shrunk back, exposing the telneurum at the base of its skull. Solomon targeted it while Job flanked to the beast's left. He slung his rifle and brandished his staff which lengthened in his hands to form a pike. Sprinting at the demon's side, he aimed the spear behind the shoulder blade, but the beast sensed his approach and razor-sharp ribs sprung outward, nearly impaling Job.

He slid under the demon's belly and, in one swift motion,

thrust the pike through its heart and out the other side of its body. Job rolled clear as the creature slammed to the ground.

Commander Solomon approached Job, helped him to his feet, then yanked the pike from the demon's carcass and handed it to him. Without a word, Solomon went to Naomi's body, and Job followed. He knelt as Solomon said a prayer over Naomi then collected her pendant. Rather than follow the river they decided to climb the bald hill, hoping to determine the temple's actual location. Turning their staffs to machetes, they chopped their way through the jungle to the clearing where the hill rose before them. Then they climbed.

As naked as he felt during the climb, and as vulnerable as they were at the summit, Job took the fact that they hadn't been attacked as a bad omen. Passage through the Void was never freely given. From the top they could see the temple in the valley below. It resembled a Mayan pyramid and glowed with a foul green ambiance. They didn't speak as they descended the hillside, said nothing as they braved the jungle again, but as they neared the temple, Job's sickness intensified and the atmosphere grew thick, making sight and breath a labor.

With every step, the jungle watched. Waited.

It was the waiting that concerned Job the most.

There were four doors on each side of the alcove hall. Some bore nameplates. After Zeke's, the Fallen entered the door labeled 'Naomi' to find a pair of monks praying over her lifeless body.

The monks died easily.

On the way out, Vigram stabbed Naomi's corpse for good measure.

The next two rooms were empty.

Only two rooms remained.

Job and Solomon reached the edge of the jungle and gazed upon the base of the pyramid. Burning torches formed a perimeter and lined each side of the staircase that ascended its face, but their flames flickered with an infected green. Job wondered if with every breath, he sucked disease into his lungs.

Weapons shouldered, they moved into the clearing, rifles sweeping left and right in search of threats as they crept toward the temple's steps They reached the pyramid's base, crouched low between the flickering torches. There was something in the sound of the flames, and at the edge of his hearing, Job could make out one word, chanted: des-o-la-tion.

Solomon's gaze snapped to Job, his eyes wild with fear. "We need that sword—now!"

Job bolted, but the moment Job's boot landed on the temple stairs, the entire jungle exploded in a blistering scream. Branches and leaves whipped violently, and both men startled at the unexpected sound—a scream that was not just one voice but billions coming together in a shrieking wail they could feel in their bones. The Abomination of hell had arrived.

They sprinted toward the pyramid's peak without hazarding a look back. At the top, they spun with rifles raised and hearts drubbing. It stood there in the torches' unnatural light, a grotesque behemoth beyond their darkest imaginings.

Almost twenty feet tall, it was bipedal and vaguely human in form, but only in the most macabre sense. Six human arms jutted from around its head like the points of a royal crown, their fingers stripped to the bone and splayed outward like antlers. Atop its bulbous head was a dense mop of blood vessels and veins that flowed like hair down to its shoulders. Black, stippled flesh was stretched tightly over its head, torn in several places revealing a patchwork skull with jagged, bloody seams.

It had hollow impressions where eyes would normally be and two small cavities in place of a nose. Only its mouth was clearly defined, but it was a lipless chasm, disproportionately large with several rows of razor-sharp teeth.

"Go find the sword. I'll hold it off," Solomon ordered. His

somber expression made it clear that this was his last stand; there would be no punching out.

With a nod, Job rushed into the temple's interior as the Abomination levitated up the steps. Like it had in the presence of the belt, Job's pulse quickened as he drew nearer to the sword. When gunfire sounded behind him, he sprinted down corridors, checking rooms along the way until he found it.

The Sword of the Spirit.

It wasn't what he expected. It was identical in shape and size to the staff he wore on his hip, but as he picked up the sword, the balance and efficiency of the weapon were perfection. The grip was a dark gray metal with decorative etching and gold inlay. Its beauty made him smile.

He rushed back to the temple's entrance, confident in their imminent victory over the Abomination and eager to see it finished. He reached the door just in time to see the meat fall from Solomon's bones like clumps of snow falling from a tree. The commander's bones dried to dust, crumbling and blowing away to become a part of the Void's everlasting terrain.

Crezik wiped the blood from his knife and lifted his boot clear of the expanding red pool. The door read: *'Commander Solomon'*. They were nearly finished with their good work.

"Wonder what that looked like inside the Void," mused Vigrim.

"What *what* looked like?" Brigner asked.

"When Crezik killed him, I wonder what happened to his spirit in the Void."

Crezik lunged and put his knife blade against Vigrim's jugular. "Stay focused, boy. We're not done yet."

Job had never seen anything like Solomon's death. Grief compelled Job to Solomon's remains. He knelt, holding the

Sword of the Spirit's bladeless handle while he scanned his surroundings, but didn't see the Abomination anywhere.

Turning back, he was struck in the chest by a whipping appendage. Airborne and falling backward off the temple's two-hundred-foot peak, he spied the Abomination standing atop the entrance roof, tucking a bony tail back out of sight. Freefalling, Job braced, fully expecting the impact to kill him, but when he hit the ground, it felt cushioned.

The Armor of God.

When he saw the Abomination's stinger broken off in the armor plate, he knew it had protected him. The pointed shard of bone was lodged deep, but he wiggled it free and tossed it behind him. Where it landed, the ground turned black and bubbled, and the stinger dissolved into the tar.

Job drew the Sword of the Spirit, twirling it as he would his own staff, and a broadsword materialized in a cloud of white-hot sparks. It was lightweight, perfectly balanced and engulfed with a rippling flame. He gazed up the pyramid as the Abomination floated down the stairs with its four arms stretching stiffly outward.

Then he felt the knife.

✟ ♗ ✟

Crezik loomed over the last of the sleeping Daggers, the cool stone walls still warm with the blood of slain monks.

Glancing back at the door he read aloud, "Job."

He watched Job's eyes flick around beneath their veiny lids and wondered what cosmic battle was being waged inside the Void. Crezik wished he had the Daggers' gift, wished that in killing Job, he could inherit it.

Sending his men from the room, Crezik knelt by the bed, closed his eyes, and whispered a prayer to Satan. Boldly, he asked that he might be blessed enough to enter the Void, to gaze upon the dark lord's magnificence as a reward for his obedience. Then he stood, cycled a cleansing breath, and stabbed Job in the head with enough force to send the blade's tip crunching into the cot below.

✝ 🏆 ✝

Job felt it the moment the blade entered his body's forehead, slicing open the hemispheres of his brain and releasing a fatal flood. In the Void it was a shooting pain that faded as quickly as it came, but afterward he felt hollowed out. He was a decal, peeled from his backing and stuck to the fabric of the Void. His body was dead, but his spirit remained; whether sustained by the protection of the armor or some other quality knitted into his being, he didn't know.

As the Abomination reached the ground, the skeletal fingers atop its crown of arms curled in waves, producing a black spark that grew to an empty flame above its head. The behemoth drew back and spewed scalding tar from its gaping mouth. Job dropped to a knee and extended his forearm before him. The Shield of Faith materialized from the cuff like a shimmering hologram, blocking the hellfire. He shook its venom from the shield, then stood to attack but the Abomination was only inches away.

Its four massive arms gripped Job with serpentine fingers and lifted him high. As Job's face approached the empty flame at the center of the demon's crown, he felt no heat and realized it wasn't a flame but a gateway. He had no intention of discovering what lay the other side. The crown of arms grabbed Job's helmet and neck, attempted to drag him into the gateway, but the Helmet of Salvation sparked like a grinding wheel, preventing his passage. It didn't prevent the flashes of hell on the other side. The crown kept pulling and the sparking swelled with blinding intensity until a small explosion blew the crown of arms to pieces, extinguishing the gateway and sending Job tumbling.

The jungle whipped and screamed. The creature shrieked as it stepped back. Power surged not just through the armor and the sword, but through Job's body. Calling on the Boots of Readiness, he pushed against the spongy soil, sprinting straight at the Abomination with impossible speed. He jumped and planted both boots in its chest, launching it back against the temple stairs that cracked upon impact.

Job marched at the Abomination, the sword crackling with flame. He raised it to strike, but the Abomination whipped its tail—a chain of meat and bones like an elephant's spine—to block the attack. The sword sliced smoothly through the tail and severed two of the demon's large arms. Tar-like blood splashed into Job's eyes. It burned like acid, and he tried to wipe it away, but it had merged with his flesh, welding his eyes shut.

Job was blind.

He heard the Abomination moving to strike and strained against the tar to peel his eyes open. Raw power surged through them, and they burst into flames, melting away the tar. The beast lurched upright, jaws open and razor teeth exposed.

Job sidestepped the first attack and then another. He dove, rolled right, gained position behind the Abomination. It wore a collar of human heads, their bare spines hanging like a shredded cape. They melded with its shoulders and were animated as if still alive. The faces wept, muddy tears running down their cheeks.

Job sunk the Sword of the Spirit into the demon's back. Then again. And again. He wound up to slice the monster in two but it collapsed, face to the earth. The ground beneath it turned black and began to bubble. It sunk slowly until it was swallowed completely. The bubbling settled and the black stain shrank as if draining into a cavern below.

A convulsive clamor arose from the jungle. Branches cracked, tree trunks bent, and leaves flapped furiously amid a chorus of growling, hissing, and screeching. Job remembered the horde of demons that approached when he took the Belt of Truth and, despite his confidence in the armor, wouldn't chance a battle against such numbers.

Job meditated. As he did, a thread snaked through his grey matter. His mind was reconfiguring, new connections forming. It wove a web of revelation. He knew the Armor of God as if he had crafted it himself. Knew the capabilities of each piece. Knew what he needed to do next. He turned toward the jungle, held the sword aloft, then plunged it into the dirt blade-first.

The ground cracked outward in branching bolts that glowed with a holy fire. It spread from his location in a shockwave that set the jungle ablaze. The inferno towered on all sides of the temple clearing, and though its heat should've cooked him alive, he found its radiance refreshing.

"That's for my family!" Job yelled. "For the Daggers and… my brother!"

As the fire raged on, he plopped onto the temple's steps, inspected the sword, and enjoyed the chorus of screaming demons.

"How the hell am I gonna get out of this one?"

Like his namesake, Job had lost everything, and the Holy Father had allowed it. His body was dead, the people who had become his family were undoubtedly dead, the bunker that had become his home was surely destroyed, and it'd be a miracle if he ever found a way back to the waking world. Still, the Holy Father had preserved his spirit and entrusted him with great power, and that was all the evidence of the Lord's goodness that Job required.

He didn't believe the Abomination to be vanquished, and had no interest in staying at that temple for all eternity. Death would be better. Job held his cross pendant and prayed for a miracle, mustering absolute conviction in its delivery. It rested heavily in his hand as he released the blade.

"One last poke to get me woke. Or not."

There was a quiet beep. Then another.

Something was wrapped around his arms, and he couldn't pull air into his lungs. Job's eyes sprung open. He was alive and in a hospital. Panicked, he pulled and gagged at the tube in his throat. He tried to sit up, but a nurse charged into the room and gently pushed him back, telling him to slow down. Two more nurses rushed in to assist the first as they took vitals and tended to him.

Something was in his hand.

The Sword of the Spirit's handle rested at his side, wrapped in his fingers.

"You've been out a while. It's quite a miracle you're even here, to be honest," a nurse said.

His body felt strong though, and he had spent enough time in bed. Job stood, almost shoving the nurse aside in the process.

"Sir, you need to stay calm. Please, lay back down and let us run some tests first." Job headed for the door instead. "Daniel!" barked the nurse.

Job stopped, his heart thumping. "What did you call me?"

"Your name. Daniel."

Job raced to the bathroom, locked the door behind him, and untied the knot at the back of his neck. The hospital gown fell to the floor and as he stepped in front of the mirror, a reflection slid into view that would've been his if not for the short beard and chest tattoo.

They were his twin brother's.

Remembering that he still held the staff, he gave it a twirl and the blade appeared in a shower of sparks. His face glowed hot with its radiance. Looking past the sword to his new reflection, he saw his spirit clad in the Armor of God with black-ringed eyes of fire that nearly startled him.

The Fallen had won the battle, but Job would win the war.

WHEN THE OAKS FELL

Kirsten Cross

The Welsh rain lashed the face of the Legatus. He scowled, ignoring the stinging, relentless tattoo beating against his skin. "Miserable fucking country." He spat and stared at the massed army of Druids facing him.

Lunatics, one and all. Fucking raving lunatics. If this had been Rome, they'd all be lion food by now. Hell, even the damn lions would probably turn their noses up at these stinking walking carcases. Hair stiffened into white spikes with lime and mud. Blue spirals painted onto twisted, contorted faces. Eyes like black tar pits, wild and wide, with bloody tears rolling down their cheeks. Naked. Covered in shit and mud, just like the entire fucking country. By Mithras, there was no doubt they were Britons, the filthy, stinking bastards!

They howled. Damn it, they wouldn't stop that incessant howling! They howled like cats being thrown into a sack and drowned. Howled like dogs being kicked off the walls of the fortifications of Gaul, closely followed by their masters and mistresses. They howled like the very denizens of hell itself.

And always the fucking rain.

What did that lunatic Nero see in this pathetic, backward little country? Tin? Copper? A smidgeon of gold in the Western streams? Surely that wasn't enough to warrant a second assault on this pox-ridden hellhole? Even Caesar, nine decades before, had had the good sense to return to his damn boat and sail back, leaving this festering little pustule of an island to the Druids and their barbaric ways.

The Legatus spat again and turned his back.

It was the last mistake he'd ever make in a less than illustrious military career.

The spear tip punched through his leather armour as if through slow-cooked pork. It ricocheted off a rib, sending a judder through his body. The tip slid through the skin and protruded out of the middle of his chest. He stared down at it, confused. "The fuck is this?" He looked up at his Praefecti, and then back at the spear. He curled both hands around the shaft and gave it a tug. "The FUCK is this?" He looked back up at the Praefecti, who opened and closed his mouth a couple of times.

"Sir! You're--" The Praefecti watched the Legatus's eyes roll into the back of his head, topple forward, and faceplant into the mud. "--Shit. Dead. You're dead. That means I'm in charge. Shit. Shit! SHIT!" The Praefecti unsheathed his short sword and locked his gaze with an old man. "You bastards! You MURDERING BASTARDS!"

✟ ♆ ✟

"Then they came."

The old man poked at the embers with his staff. "Like wolves. They had nothing on their mind except blood and slaughter." Hooded brown eyes clouded and dimmed with age reflected the flames and the shadows of so many blood-soaked memories. "She knew they were coming for us. The Morrigan knew. It was as if her womb opened up to welcome her children back into the darkness one last time." He paused.

"Then the oaks fell."

The clan sat silently, hanging on every word of the old man's story. Only the pop and crackle of the fire interrupted the quiet of a forest night muffled into silence by thick fog and the cold, ever-present fear of the next Legion patrol. A fussy baby was shushed gently by its mother, and the twins snuggled closer to their aunt, frightened by the images their imaginations were crafting in their young minds. They had already seen their fair share of blood and slaughter when the last patrol attacked their village. They had been touched by the Eagle's shadow as it spread across the country, its progress as relentless and as merciless as a winter storm.

But the old man was different.

He had been there when the Eagle finally landed on Mona's sacred shores. He had watched the Praefecti give the order to attack, a trigger that unleashed a flood of death bringers, all scrambling ashore from their flat-bottomed boats with the scent of spilt blood already in their nostrils, stoking the fires in their bellies. An organised, ruthlessly efficient killing machine. A war band intent on wiping out the 'viper's nest' of Mona and its murdering Druids...

The old man stood with his brothers and sisters, defying Rome and its filthy gods. He was ready to battle the foreigners who spoke in a multitude of strange languages, carried vicious short swords and who showed no mercy to man, woman or child. The Legion marched to a single order, with no option but to follow the lore of their Emperor. Kill them all. Spare none. And they were determined to carry out that command to the letter.

When the Legion attacked, the old man screamed defiance and raised the wind with the Furies. The black-clothed women flitted through the ranks, sometimes rushing forward and hurling curses at the enemy, then retreating and screeching like the owls of winter. The Legion faced the full force of the Morrigan's sacred harbingers – and for the briefest of moments, they stopped. Some of the more timid, don't-wanna-even-be-here, rank and file paused, confused, and took a step back. It raised hope among the people. See? The Morrigan was protecting her land! The Eagle was fearful! They mocked. They howled. They displayed their arses to the Legion, defiant and confident the Morrigan had touched their enemy's dark hearts and planted the seeds of doubt into them.

One woman, a Fury with wild eyes and straggly, unkempt red hair, stepped defiantly forward and grasped the neckline of her dress. With a scream that echoed across the shoreline, she ripped the cloth in two and let the tattered rags drop away to reveal a mass of blue tattoos writhing and snaking across her naked body. She stood in the torchlight, arms flung outwards, legs astride and head back, letting out a yowl that called forth the army of the Dead to pluck the Eagle from the sky and hurl it to the ground. The more superstitious of the Eagle's soldiers began to mutter. Dissent started to grow. The Fury heard the muttering and screeched again, fanning the flames of doubt and superstition. She squatted and urinated on the ground, pissing on the face of the Eagle and daring it to challenge the might of the Morrigan and her kin.

The Eagle accepted the challenge.

The Praefecti, who had faced down Vercingetorix and his Gaul hordes, had fought the demons of the east, and feared nothing except the gods, rushed forward. He spat some guttural words at the woman and thrust his short sword into her belly, tearing her open from navel to neck. Her shriek rang out towards the grove, telling the oaks that the slaughter had begun. Bubbling and spewing red froth from her mouth, she fell face-first into the mud. The soldier stood on her twitching body, the hobnails in his sandals scraping and tearing into the flesh on her back. Those closest could hear her ribs cracking as he stamped down. He raised his sword and roared, showing the Legion that the blood of the Fury had been spilt.

And the Morrigan had not answered.

No ghost army of wraiths burst forth to wreak a terrible revenge. No worms slithered up from the belly of the earth to wrap around the talons of the Eagle and pull it from the sky. All that happened was that her winged children, the ravens of the battlefield, took to the skies, cawing and gronking, circling and spiralling, before flying away. The sight of Morrigan's Children leaving hushed the defiant shrieks of the Druids.

The old man looked frantically around, as confused as his brothers and sisters. Had they not served her? Had they not fought like devils against the Eagle as it polluted her land? Why had she forsaken them when they needed her most? When the Eagle perched on the very shoreline of Mona, waiting to tear down the groves and slaughter her children, where was she? Where was the Morrigan? *Where was she?*

It was all the Praefecti needed. He watched their muted mutterings, their corkscrewing, their pleas to the ravens to return. And he smiled.

That moment of abject confusion. An army at odds with itself. An enemy on the back foot, who put their faith in false gods and spirits rather than cold, hard steel. He thrust his sword into the air again, the steaming blood of the Fury running down the pommel and onto the leather webbing that encased his forearm. He bellowed in a language he knew the Druids didn't understand and then, slowly deliberately, levelled the point of his sword at the ranks of the Britons.

That roar needed no translation.

It was the order to attack. To kill.

As one, the Legion roared in response and rushed forward, determined to do as their compatriot had and grind the Druids into the dirt under the Eagle's claw...

The old man paused again, staring into the flames.

The clan, mortified by the tale of the Fury's defilement, could not speak. A single tear slid down the cheek of the chieftain. It caught the orange light of the fire, shining like a droplet of amber on his skin. The old man knew the chieftain had heard the rumours, they all had. But to hear the truth in all its bloody detail from one who had actually been there...

The chieftain's gaze was almost too much to bear. "Was... was there no hope? No hope at all?"

The old man shook his head. "She abandoned us to our fate, my brother. She punished us for our compliance. For those who bend their knees and bow their heads to the Eagle." He paused and stared into the flames, seeing the faces of his brothers and sisters as the Eagle tore out their eyes and slit their throats. He wrenched his gaze away from the flames and looked at the chieftain. "No, my brother. It was not she who betrayed us, but us who betrayed *her*. This was her punishment. Her anger. Delivered onto our shores and into our bellies at the end of Roman swords and pikes. A holy war where the gods left us to our fate."

He paused again, his breathing laboured as the horror of that night's carnage bloomed fresh like a blood-soaked flower. As difficult as it was, the story must be told. It *must*. He drew a shaking breath and continued, painting a vivid picture in the minds of the clan, using the magic his old bones still had to put them right there, on that accursed shoreline, with him.

He reached into a pouch and pulled out a handful of dust. Muttering, he tossed it onto the fire and the flames roared, flaring up as red as blood. Smoke swirled and twisted, forming into ethereal, screaming Roman soldiers and surrounding the clan as they huddled closer together. One of the twins started to weep in terror. The old man snorted and rounded on the girl. "Silence, child! Lest the Legion rip open *your* belly!" He jabbed a bony finger at the swirling clouds of smoke. The child whimpered and stuffed the ragged sleeve of her tunic into her mouth to try and still the cries that simply would not be silenced. Her aunt pulled her closer, curling her hand around the child's head and letting the little girl bury her face in the warmth and dark protection of her cloak. The old man glowered at the still-sobbing child and went back to his tale...

He stood for a moment as the Legion attacked, disbelieving not just the desecration of the Fury, but that the Holy Island had been defiled by the Eagle in such a filthy and brutal way. Then self-preservation kicked in. He was a man who had lived beyond his years, armed with nothing but a curved sickle, a staff, and the will of the gods. He was facing a well-armed enemy of trained soldiers, driven not just by the discipline of Rome, but of their unspoken fear of what horrors the Druids might evoke if they didn't cut them down right now. That fear manifested in a fire that burned hot in their bellies, a blood lust that turned them into raging animals.

The Druids were outnumbered. They were facing trained killers. All their magic, all their power, could not save them now.

The Morrigan, her fury at the betrayal of her people, had left them to wallow in their own defeat.

So he turned, trying to flee the slashing swords and the slathering pack of wolfhounds the soldiers brought with them. The ferocity of the Legion was nothing they had ever seen before.

He stumbled, slipped, lost his footing and fell to his knees. A surge of bodies propelled him forward into, a maelstrom of swirling, scrabbling limbs interspersed with merciless Roman steel. The ground was already so slick with blood and mud that he couldn't even scramble back to his knees – the momentum of bodies tumbling forward pushed him down again and again and again. He rolled onto his back, hacking at the soldiers' ankles with his sickle, hamstringing them so that his brothers could cut them down. One last-ditch attempt at defying the Eagle and its demon soldiers.

Bodies fell across him, pinning him to the ground. Both Roman and Briton lay side by side, united in death if not in life. Their blood mingled and gave the sweet, peat-scented air a metallic tang that brought the circling ravens back, wild with bloodlust. These were the Morrigan's ravens. The Children of the Battle. They didn't wait for the bodies to fall. They divebombed the living, talons digging deep into flesh, powerful beaks pecking at eyes and skin. Many didn't see their death coming, blinded by Morrigan's ravens.

As the battle raged and the bodies fell, the old man was overlooked by the Eagle's gaze. To the soldiers he was just another blood and woad-covered corpse in the mud. They had moved relentlessly onwards, closer to the groves and the sacred oaks. The Eagle knew that if it destroyed the symbol of the people then their spirit would be broken. Subjugation would be complete – the Eagle would be victorious.

Not every holy war needed the death of thousands.

Sometimes, it only took the destruction of a symbol, a muster-point, to get the job done. The oaks *had* to fall.

The Eagle liked things neat and tidy. It craved order. Discipline. The Druids represented everything the Eagle hated.

They were chaos. Disorder. Untamed, wild, and uncivilised. And at the heart of the Druids was the grove. Destroy the oaks, destroy the Druids. So the Eagle soared onwards, over a carpet of twisted and broken bodies, towards the grove on the hill. Towards the mistletoe-covered branches of the oldest oak on Mona.

Towards the heart of the Druids.

Amid the mayhem and murder, hidden under the dying and the dead, the old man survived. He could do nothing except lay there, covered in the blood of his enemy and his brothers alike, weeping silently as he watched the Eagle alight in the boughs of the oak and call out across the land. The soldiers set fires at the base, and the oaks started to crackle. As the amber light danced across the battlefield, there was a boom as the king of the grove exploded. Sap boiled. Flames engulfed the entire tree. Finally, as the dawn broke in the east, the home of the Eagle, the oak shrieked one last cry of agony and crashed to the ground.

The Eagle's fires turned the grove to ashes.

The old man's tears dripped onto the dark earth, mingling with the blood. His right hand formed a claw, and he plunged his bony fingers into the wet earth, curling them around the peat and clinging to the sacred land, desperate and alone.

Who knows how long he lay there?

Minutes? Hours? Days?

Time stopped when the oaks fell.

Eventually, the Legion boarded their boats and left. The Eagle didn't even claim the island as its own. It merely desecrated its holy soil with the blood of the Morrigan's children, burnt down its groves – and then simply left.

That was perhaps the greatest insult of all.

The Eagle didn't even think that Mona was worthy of conquering. Just something to be crushed and defiled and then left to rot in darkness. The ghosts of the slaughtered its only inhabitants.

The Morrigan's Children still patrolled the battlefield, pecking at the corpses, squabbling over ribbons of flesh, and cawing to the wind, taking the message of the Slaughter of the Sun to the four corners of Britannia. The flies buzzed and swarmed as the corpses blackened. Nobody came to send these empty souls to the Otherworld. The army of the dead simply rotted into the peat, the battlefield running with the juices of their bloated corpses.

In a pile of bodies, something stirred. A flaccid, rotting arm flapped as if reanimated by the devils of Hell. A nearby raven, busily feasting on a juicy eyeball the others had missed, squawked in alarm and flapped backwards. The corpse shifted and a clawed, dirty hand thrust upwards. The raven, its curiosity quickly getting the better of caution, hopped forward and croaked questioningly.

The flaccid arm waved again and was gripped by a dirty hand at the armpit. There was a grunt and the arm, held onto the shoulder by just a few ragged strands of rotting skin, detached and was hurled outwards, just missing the raven. The raven flapped furiously, squawked angrily and gave the putrid arm a hard peck, before turning its attention back to the pile of bodies.

A much more alive hand scrabbled for purchase and finally, the old man emerged, battered and wounded. He roared, white-hot fury burning eternally in his chest at the memory of the flashing swords, the blood that flowed like rivers, and the screaming howl of the Fury as the Praefecti's sword had pierced her belly.

As he crawled out from under the rotting bodies of his brothers and sisters, puking from the stench, he remembered every single detail of the unholy battle with the Eagle. The sound of skulls as they cracked. The pleading of the dying, cut short with a slash of a blade across the throat. The roar of the fires set ablaze at the base of the oaks that boiled the sap until the mighty trees exploded into splinters. The wild screams of the Morrigan's ravens.

The fall of Ynys Môn.

The desecration of the most sacred place in the Druidic world.

And the beginning of the end for the people of Britannia.

He saw it all. Knew the end was coming. But right up until the moment that first snarling, spitting Roman bastard placed his sandaled foot on the shoreline, he had been certain that the Morrigan would protect her children from the Eagle's onslaught.

She had not.

For whatever reason, the Morrigan had seen fit to allow the defilement of her groves and the massacre of her children. The blood of the priests had not been enough to rouse her from her slumber. All but a handful had been cut down like a field of ripe barley.

But the Morrigan had seen fit to spare him from the final journey that night.

He finally pulled himself free of the bodies and stood, surveying the hell spread out in front of him. The raven gronked and hopped closer. The old man looked down at Morrigan's Child, who stared back at him with gimlet eyes full of intelligence. The raven's blue eyelids flickered, and it let out a soft caw. The old man whispered. "I hear you, Morrigan. I hear you." The raven cawed again and took to the sky, circling three times over the remains of the grove before flying east.

Now he knew why he had been spared.

Morrigan's Child had told him herself. His task was to wander her land, telling her people of how the Eagle had soaked the soil of the Sacred Isle in the blood of murdered children. How soldiers had hacked down women as they fled. How the Morrigan's priests had been butchered. How the Furies had been crushed under the hobnailed sandals of the Eagle's soldiers. The holy war that their Mithras, their pantheon of filthy gods, and their emperor had called down upon Britannia.

And how her oak groves had been burnt to ashes.

The flickering image of those burning oaks was seared into his eyes, and all who looked into those brown orbs would see the flames too. What was reflected in his gaze wasn't a mere memory of an old man, a storyteller, a bard from the Brotherhood. It was the embers that signalled the end of their days. The fall of Ynys

Môn, the Sacred Isle, and the wholesale slaughter of the Druids cut the heart out of the tribes of Britain. And a people without a heart were nothing but ghosts, haunting the rain-soaked forests, mist-shrouded marshes and the secret valleys of the west.

It hadn't been a golden time before the Eagle had landed on Britain's shores, make no mistake. The tribes had been at constant war with one another, battling for land and power. A suspicion that the Druids were manipulating events made them icons of mistrust, loathed by many, feared by all. But then the Eagle turned its gaze across the narrow sea and towards Britain's lush, green shores, and the people knew the Druids had been right all along. Those who didn't capitulate to the Eagle were enslaved and sent to the lead mines of the Summer country or the tin mines of Cornwall. The women and the elderly were spared the mines, instead packed aboard flat-bottomed boats and taken beyond the narrow sea and into a brief, brutal life of servitude and slavery.

There were rumours among the tribes that Britannia's warriors were highly prized as gladiators in the circuses of Rome itself. They fought ferociously. But they still died, just like any other man, ripped apart by wild animals or hamstrung and scythed down by Roman champions for the entertainment of the emperor and his baying masses. If they begged for mercy, so much the better. If they didn't, their deaths were slower and more agonising. The Roman gladiators were experts in the art of death.

To the Eagle, Britannia was a resource to be plundered. Nothing more. Those Britons who bowed their heads to the Eagle's overlords were rewarded like pet dogs with a titbit of power, carefully controlled and administered by the regional governor. It was an empty vessel filled with vapid promises and thinly veiled threats.

Some grew fat and prospered, keen to induct themselves into the Empire and all the advantages that brought. Little did they realise that the Eagle held them in utter contempt.

Those who didn't bow down were enslaved or slaughtered. The tribes dissolved into the forests and marshes of the borderlands, driven to the very edges of Britain by the spreading shadow of the Eagle. Now, only the remote reaches of Wales and the far tip of Cornwall were safe havens for the Britons. And beyond the northern wall – well, who knew what lurked in those dark lands where even the Eagle refused to fly?

Fleeing the carnage, the old man followed the raven's path, and headed east, away from the remote tip of Mona and into the remote hills and valleys of the western lands, earning a crust of bread or a bowl of broth by entertaining huddled families with tales and stories of old Britannia. Of worms and warriors. Of mythical beasts and marvellous mysteries.

And, if they were of the People, he would tell them the truth of the Slaughter of the Sun. He would tell them the bloody, violent truth of the time the oaks fell at the sacred isle. But he did it in a hushed voice lest some Roman spy should be hiding in the shadows, waiting to bring the Eagle's claw slashing down across the back of his naked neck.

Of course, they'd heard it a thousand times before. And they would hear it a thousand times more. Stories such as this had to be told, again and again and again. They had to stay alive in the minds of the people.

Those who were still left.

It was getting harder to find those who had not capitulated to Roman rule and swapped the torque for the toga. But the old man never gave up. As long as he had breath in his lungs and a stick to help him scramble along the stony paths between hidden caves, transient camps and the occasional unconquered hill fort, he would tell the people.

Tell them that the oaks may have fallen but Britannia was still their land. That the Eagle may have spread its shadow across the country, but there were still places where its gaze could see nothing but stones and scrub.

And there were whispers too.

Of rebellion and defiance.

Of a warrior in the east, defiled by Rome and stripped of her rightful title as Queen. Whose daughters had been publicly violated, and whose own back ran red with blood from a brutal lashing. Her husband, the traitor Prasutagus, along with ten other kings, had bent their knees to Roman rule. But the Eagle was cunning and had taken the death of Prasutagus as an opportunity to subjugate the Iceni once and for all. Buddug, Prasutagus' queen and mother of his daughters, had defied Rome and made good on her rightful claim to her throne, enraging the Eagle.

She had proclaimed her own holy war. She marched across the land at the head of a mighty army, laying waste first to Camulodunum and then the busy port of Londinium. None were spared.

She would be the one to put the Eagle to flight!

She would be the one to lead them to victory!

She would drive the Eagle from their land and unite the clans once more. *She* would be the embodiment of the Morrigan made flesh. The Morrigan would return to reclaim her land. The Eagle would flee, hounded to the very shores of the eastern sea by her ravens. The Holy War of the Druids would be won by a woman, bare breasted and feral, defiant and unyielding.

And then The Golden Time would begin.

The groves would be replanted and the Morrigan, her benign and gentle aspect once again dominant, would bless all of those who had stayed true to her name.

So, for a time, the people had hope. And the old man wandered the land, encouraging those pockets of resistance to the Eagle's rule to stand fast, to prepare for a great battle. To be ready to ride to the call of Buddug…

"When do we ride? Tell us, old man. When?" The chieftain leaned forward, his blue tattoos seeming to writhe and twist with anticipation at the thought of a battle. Massive muscles bulged, and the old man could see the passion and battle-lust in his host's eyes. The chieftain's hand went to his sword, as if ready to battle the entire army of the Eagle right here, right now, as they sat around the campfire.

The old man shook his head. "Buddug will lose."

"Traitor! She is a queen, a leader for our people!" The chieftain snarled. "Yet you doubt her? You who brought us word? For what? As a simple ghost story to scare the children and make them huddle in their mothers' skirts? If your words are not a call to arms, then what are they, old man?"

"They are a warning, you fool! A *warning*!"

The old man stood, surprisingly quick on his feet for one of such advanced years. He pointed a long finger at the chieftain, who recoiled as if the old man's finger was a poisonous snake. "Those of us in the west may be united against the Eagle, but this treachery you speak of? It is not mine, my friend, but that of the eastern tribes. They are the ones who will betray Buddug and her followers! The Morrigan came to me. She told me. Her child flew to me on black wings and whispered in my ear!"

Flecks of spittle formed in the corners of the old man's mouth. His eyes widened, the flames of the Slaughter of the Sun burning fiercely in his death-black pupils. "She cannot hope to convince them to rally to her cause, they will melt away like mist in the dawn at the first flash of Roman steel!" The old man's voice was sharp and harsh. "Betrayal, not the Eagle, has destroyed the Britons! Betrayal and a desire for a soft and comfortable life. And Buddug will find that out to her cost! Would you rush to the side of a doomed woman? A woman who has felt the lash of the Eagle on her own back? Who knows her fate is to be led through the streets of Rome like a trophy and then slaughtered at the feet of the emperor?" He leaned towards the chieftain. "Or would you save your people, ready to fight another day?"

The old man suddenly slumped onto his knees. Vision stories were so taxing now. He had told the story so many times. The blood. The scent of death. The bellow of the oak as it blew itself apart. He had stared for too long into the sacred fire. He had swallowed the Mother's gift; fungi that would break down the barriers between then and now and show the initiate what was to come.

The tears came.

He had seen nothing but shadows. Ghosts. A people both betrayed and betraying.

A people fading into the forests, the marshes of the west and the remote, jagged islands.

A people vanquished from the outermost reaches of their lands by an Eagle with steel armour and blood-red eyes.

He stared into the fire and saw the chieftain and his people enslaved and ripped from their camp. He saw the twins transported to a distant land full of heat and dust, where they would be playthings for fat old men. He saw their delicate, pale throats slashed and the blood running freely once the men had no further use of them. He saw the squalling baby ripped from its mother's arms and dashed against a rock. And he saw the chieftain, on his knees and with one bloody eye hanging from its socket, as a Roman sword flashed and severed his head from his neck.

There would be no victory for these people. Only more death. More betrayal.

And the old man would go on, living beyond his years as the Morrigan dictated, no grave to give him peace and rest, no death to embrace him – only blood-soaked memories to haunt him and a never-ending responsibility to tell his stories to those who were left.

This was his punishment.

This was how the Morrigan saw fit to burden those who had let her lands fall to the Eagle. For the crime of surviving, he was doomed to wander the western lands, telling the story of the fall of Ynys Môn, and bringing that same fate to every tribe that gave him food and shelter in exchange for stories of the People.

He was the messenger of the Eagle, not the Morrigan. His punishment was that of his people – to be eternally consigned to the darkness as the Eagle's shadow spread further and further across the land. Death would not lay a finger on him until his task was completed. Until all knew of the betrayal and destruction not just of the People, but of the Morrigan herself.

Their time was coming to an end.

The Druids were scattered to the winds. Most were dead. Others too afraid to identify themselves for fear of immediate reprisals from both Roman and Briton alike. No Druid would carry the Fey for the dead or whisper the words they needed to hear to find their way through the Annwn to finally drink from the Cauldron of Rebirth.

This time, there would be *no* rebirth.

This was the final death of the People.

The old man fell silent, fearful that the chieftain's wrath would result in his mission being cut short right here, right now. The Morrigan spoke in his soul, telling him to bow his head and say no more. Speak only the traditional words of thanks for the meagre meal the tribe shared with him, find a quiet corner to rest, and then slip away quietly before dawn brought the Eagle to the tribe's camp.

The chieftain, however, wanted to know more. "Speak, old man. What now? What do we do now?" He reached forward and grabbed the old man's cloak, shaking him like a dog shakes a coney. "Tell me! What do we *do*?"

The old man raised his watery eyes to the chieftain and held his gaze. In those orbs, the chieftain could see the end. He could see everything the old man had seen.

The death of the Fury.

The Centurion standing on her mutilated body, black blood running down the blade.

The exploding oaks.

The corpses piled on the shores of Ynys Môn.

The betrayal of the Iceni queen and her defeated army.

The death of his tribe.

So much blood.

So much slaughter.

The old man reached up and laid his hand on the clenched fist of the chieftain. The oracle may have doomed this tribe to death and exploitation, but damn it, he could change that! He could defy the gods and even the Morrigan herself one last time. He could make sure that at least some of the People would survive.

Damn the Morrigan! Damn her!

Had she not abandoned the old man and his brethren on the

shores of Mona? Had she not burdened him with a life beyond his years, wandering in the wilderness, bringing nothing but fear and despair to the few pockets of Britons who had managed to avoid the Eagle's gaze? Well, *this* tribe, this tiny band of kin, they would at least have a chance. He whispered to the chieftain. "Flee. Flee to the south. To the very tip of our lands. Take your people tonight. Don't wait for the sun to rise, gather up only what you can carry, and flee. Stay to the forest paths. Avoid the roads, the Legion patrols are many. Keep walking south until you reach the land of granite.

The chieftain frowned. "And then what?"

The old man stared at him, scowling. "And then? You survive, you fool, you *survive!*"

The chieftain slowly released his grasp and the old man dropped back. "That, brother, *that* is all we can do. Survive. Eventually, the Eagle will fly from this land. Not in our lifetime, not even in your children's lifetime. But one day it will be driven from Britannia."

"And then?" The chieftain looked broken. A lifetime of hiding like a pig in the forest, followed by death with no honour was all he could look forward to. That was all he could offer his people. No glorious victory. No triumph. Just a lifetime in exile in his own country. "What then, Druid? What hope can I give my people?"

The old man smiled. "That one day, brother, one day, Britannia will rise again. That our stories will be remembered. That the legend of our people will shine brightly like a golden torque."

He stood, tucked his sickle into his belt and picked up his staff. Despite his years, he stood straight and proud. He raised his hand in blessing. "And that one day the oaks will grow again." He tossed his cloak over his shoulder, ready to brave the night-time path through the forest, knowing the Morrigan would light his way with her silver disc.

"Fare well. And remember our tale, brother. Tell it to others. Tell them of the time the oaks fell. Of the Slaughter of the Sun. Remember, tell the tale, and *survive!*"

The Tower of Babel

Duncan McGeary

The Needle's dance floor shook on its rickety foundations. The noise was deafening – the shouts, cheers, and laughter of my people drowning out the metallic thud of the industrial music. Marcy weaved her way through the crowd, heading my way. Marcy Jackson, aka Velvet.

Shit. When did I learn the stripper's names?

Worse, looking out on the dance floor, I realized I couldn't remember the names of half my troops. How did that happen? In the beginning, I knew them all.

The promise of a lap dance was in Marcy's eyes, a free one since I was the commander of these soldiers, and we were the reason the bar existed. I shook my head and her smile faltered; she veered off toward my second in command, Sergeant Adams.

"Fuck this, I'm heading out," I muttered.

"Too much for you, old man?" Private Johns shouted from across the table.

"That's Lieutenant Winslow to *you*, Private," I snapped.

"I'm sorry, sir. I didn't mean…"

I stood, shaking my head. Dizzy. The table was covered with empty bottles. Fuck, how long had I been here?

Johns came to attention, almost tipping over the table. The bottles clattered in tune with the thumping music. I waved her off.

"No, no… you're right, Private. At ease. We're off duty."

I knew the platoon called me 'old man', but it didn't usually bother me. Even though I was only a few years older than most of them, it felt like a goddamned lifetime.

Time to muster out? No matter how much I drank, I couldn't banish the question. But what would I do then?

185

Visit Deena on the McAuliffe Space Colony? Sure, if she was willing to see me. Go even farther? I had enough credits to get to the moon station and to come back if I didn't like it. Enough credits to go to the Mars settlement, but not to return. I'd always wanted to go up on the space elevator. It seemed only fair since I'd spent most of my adult life protecting it.

I felt a vibration in my pocket, but for a moment couldn't figure out if it was the music booming or my communicator. I fumbled to answer, and could make out Deena's voice, if not her words. My daughter hadn't called me since... I couldn't remember the last time she'd called me.

I stumbled into the alley, then lean back against the vibrating door as it closed behind me. "Deena?"

"Dad! They're coming... they're coming. My... God! They're so beautiful!"

"Slow down, Deena. What are you talking about?"

"They're so beauti—"

"Deena? Deena?" Shaking the device didn't help. I was more stunned by the fact that my daughter had called than by being abruptly cut off. Communications between the space colony and Earth were always spotty.

A scurrying in the shadows distracted. I recognized Private Evan's mohawk; the beehive hairdo of Missy, the newest stripper.

Good for them.

I marched past them as if I hadn't seen them, ignoring their furtive straightening of clothes. The lights of Republic Avenue beckoned. I laughed at the thought of anything being called 'republic'. We weren't the 'United'" States anymore, even if both sides pretended to be democratic. When we invaded Ecuador to build the International Space Elevator, that had been the last straw.

Must be drunker than I thought.

I rarely looked up at the sky anymore. The Tower of Babel, The Eighth Wonder of the World, the Stairway to Heaven, the Heavenly Spire, the Needle, the Beanstalk, Sky Hook, God's Finger, God's... My mind balked at the obscenity, a holdover from my Catholic upbringing. Whatever you wanted to call the International Space Elevator, it was just part of the background to me.

But for once, the massive structure caught my attention, and I ran my eyes up the length of the ISE, its red lights every thousand feet blinking in the night sky, narrow at the bottom, thickening higher where the landings had been built. Roughly twenty-five thousand miles up was the counterweight, mostly constructed of discarded equipment from the building of the ISE, piled on a stray asteroid. But what really mattered was the space station, two hundred miles above, where Deena lived with her husband, Mario, whom I'd never met.

At the base of the elevator was the biggest structure on Earth; the Terminal, with its warehouses, hotels, and restaurants. Republic City had grown up around the base in concentric circles. The military district was the closest to the Terminal, surrounding and protecting it. The bar I'd just left was on the farthest borders, where even the military MPs rarely wandered. Opposite me on the circle's arc, off-duty Newcons were probably staring at the same sight. The New Confederate Army had their own bars.

"It looks like a fucking hypodermic needle," Madame Agnes, the Needle's dance club's owner, had once told me.

And sure enough, it did. Right now, it seemed to be vibrating, as if it had just plunged medicine – or poison – into the heart of the planet.

I blinked. It wasn't just my drunkenness. The Space Elevator really was vibrating. Hobart's Station, the first landing, only a mile or so above, was swaying.

That's impossible.

The ISE was anchored to the ground, its diamond nanothread cables as strong as the Earth itself. Not the fiercest hurricane winds, not the impacts of eight airliners manned by suicidal terrorists, not even the Earthquake of '54, had so much as shaken it.

Hobart's Station shuddered, and then I was blinded by a white flash. When the wavering stars in my eyes began to clear, the station was sliding down the Needle like a donut down a stick, breaking apart as it fell. It seemed to me that I saw bodies falling, backlit by flames, though it was too far away for that to be possible. The explosion's shock wave nearly knocked me off my feet, followed instantly by a deafening blast.

The ground shook as the station crashed into the Terminal. A second, an even larger explosion threw me to the ground. The factories and repair shops, the workshops and laboratories, the huge Republic Shopping Mall – everything that serviced the Space Elevator – all gone in an instant.

My apartment was in the terminal, as were most of my soldiers, sleeping in their barracks. The family housing, the schools. Most of the population of Republic City. Vaporized.

One by one, the ISE's amber warning lights blinked out. The Space Elevator was still visible in the night sky, and as the flames licked higher, the Elevator's cables glowed red.

A familiar calm came over me – the numb competence I always felt before battle.

"What the fuck happened?"

Sergeant Adams was standing behind me, her mouth agape, her face red in the light of the flames. Within that huge, glowing cloud, dark shadows soared in the updrafts. I calculated how big those human-shaped, winged creatures needed to be for me to see them from this far away.

An illusion. It has to be.

Adams seemed to be seeing it too. "What are those things?"

I almost answered: *angels or demons, take your pick*, then realized how insane that sounded.

Above, black spots swirled around the glowing figures. Ash, I figured. But then, as if guided by a single impulse, all the spots surged toward us. My pistol was in my hand before I was aware of drawing it. The crowd around me didn't seem to notice the approaching danger, and I grabbed Adams' arm, dragged her into the shadows.

The flock swarmed. The creatures were the size of vultures but though they had wings, their bodies were those of snakes, their skulls were sharp beaks, which came down on the heads of the humans, splitting and cutting and spraying blood in every direction.

It had been a long time since I'd been to church, but my Catholic upbringing came to the fore once again.

For, behold, I will send serpents, cockatrices, among you, which will not be charmed, and they shall bite you, saith the Lord.

Our backs were to the Needle's walls. Hidden beneath the eaves, we had some cover but the people in the open were being torn apart. A cockatrice dove at me, growing large, larger than I'd thought at first. My shot blew its skull apart, which attracted the rest of the flock's attention. I fired, again and again and again, hitting my mark each time. Adams was frozen beside me, so I drew her pistol, and emptied it too.

Just as the trigger clicked on an empty chamber, the flock wheeled around as one and speared straight into the air, swirling around the Needle before winging back toward the Space Elevator.

Adams stood slack jawed.

I shook her. "Round up everyone you can find, Sergeant! Now!"

Adams didn't budge. She couldn't tear her eyes away from the flames and smoke, and the winged creatures within.

"Move it, Adams! Everyone you can find, whether they are part of our company or not. Rally point at the armory."

"The armory?" She waved vaguely in the direction of the base. "Shouldn't we…?"

She had a wife in the Republic City. I faced her, put my hands on her shoulders, and looked her in the eye. "Don't you get it, Adams? Everything in the Terminal is gone. We have to secure the ISE before the Newcons do!"

She straightened up, grasping at my orders as if they could anchor her to the earth. "Yes, sir."

The armory and the munitions dump weren't far away. They'd been deliberately situated well outside the city limits. I'd once argued with General Conners about that decision. In

1842, the British in Afghanistan had located their armory across the city of Kabul from their barracks. The Afghans had figured it out: the soldiers were stationed where the weapons weren't. They'd exploited this weakness, and that had led to the British surrendering on the condition that they be allowed to leave.

Only one British soldier survived the long retreat. No one was ever sure if that was an oversight or a message.

"The British didn't have munitions that could blow up an entire city," the general had pointed out, "and the International Space Elevator. Besides, I doubt the Newcons are that smart."

General Conners was probably gone. The entire Northern Army was gone, except for a few off-duty soldiers. I took a last glance at the Space Elevator. The ISE still rose into the heavens, which meant my duty to protect it was still in effect. The Newcons, if any of them had survived on the other side of the city, would be thinking the same thing, and likely trying to figure out how to exploit this situation. I couldn't let them take control of the ISE.

✠ 🏆 ✠

The armory had been our last guard duty assignment; that's how we'd stumbled across the Needle dance club in the first place. That meant the munitions were now unguarded. I tried to remember which units had taken our place and decided it didn't matter. Half an hour later, only a squad's worth of my platoon – ten soldiers, including me – had mustered. Where was everyone? There'd been at least thirty soldiers on the dance floor.

"More will show up," Sergeant Adams said.

"We don't have time to wait," I answered.

I catalogued who I had to work with. Sergeant Pederson was a solid soldier with a huge handlebar mustache. Privates Sherman and Morgan, a pair of skinny new recruits who were always together. Private Johns, also skinny and nervous. A female corporal whose solid eyebrows reminded me of sticks; Cooper was her name. The rest I didn't know, except Hernandez, our communications specialist. I was glad to see him. Had a feeling we were going to need his skills.

We had to shoot out the armory's locks, and equip ourselves while the alarms blared. We took everything we could carry, loaded up two Humvees, and headed out. Dawn was breaking, though the sun, glowing red behind the curtains of smoke and dust, was no brighter than a full moon.

Hernandez sat next to me while I drove the lead vehicle. "Our equipment is fried," he said. "Some kind of electromagnetic pulse? I suspect there isn't an operational communicator within a hundred miles."

I nodded. My communicator felt like dead weight in my pocket. I thought about Deena and the strange call she'd made to me before all hell broke loose.

"What were those winged things?" Hernandez asked. "I mean, they *glowed*. They looked... they looked like..."

I didn't answer, concentrating on the road. There was no one else on the streets. Whatever survivors there were, stayed out of sight. It wasn't long before we reached the middle districts of the disaster.

There were no survivors. Everything was shattered, crumpled, twisted, burning, barely recognizable. No one could have survived the explosions, although there were no bodies to be seen. Not a surprise considering the metal lamp posts lay in melted puddles on the street corners.

The Terminal was a smoldering shell; only a few sections of the walls remained. Defiant. Deep grooves crisscrossed the roads, and what buildings still stood had been sheared off at their tops as if by a razor-sharp blade.

At the main entrance, the giant doors were intact, but the walls around them were missing. When I turned off the engine, silence fell over us like a shroud. The ticking of the cooling motor only made the silence deeper.

The Humvee's windshield shattered. Hernandez and I ducked reflexively. I turned the key, and blindly slammed my foot on the accelerator. The other Humvee followed. I poked my head over the shattered windshield just in time to avoid slamming into the remains of a building, and steered around the ruined walls and stopped.

The gunfire was a couple hundred yards away. It sounded like three assault rifles at the most.

Only three fucking enemies. But that was more than enough to defend the Terminal's entrance against a mere squad. Nor could I be sure that was all of them.

Sergeant Adams exited the other Humvee, and trotted to the driver's window.

"We can go around them," she said. "There can't be very many of them. The perimeter extends for miles."

"Except if they can see what we're doing it'll only take a couple of good shots to take us out," I pointed out.

"How the fuck are they going to see us? The net is down. We're getting nothing."

Hernandez said, "If I may make a suggestion, sir. If we split into pairs, we can approach from five different directions. Unless I'm mistaken, there aren't enough of them to keep us all out."

By this time, the other soldiers had scrambled out of their Humvees, crouching beside us. To my surprise, Private Johns, usually the quietest of them, spoke up. "Why? What's the point?" Her voice was hollow, bleak

I looked up. The Space Elevator was visible even through the veils of smoke and dust. *My daughter is up there.* "The ISE is still operational, and everyone in the space station, hell, even the moon and Mars bases, are still dependent on us for resources."

"So?" Johns said. "Let the Newcons take care of it."

"We didn't fight a war over this just to let the New Confederate Army win now. Split into pairs. Station yourselves one mile apart. At 0:700 we advance."

I was relieved when they obeyed my orders. For all I knew, we were all that was left of the Northern Army, and had half expected them to just leave. When the squad split into pairs, I wasn't surprised that Hernandez remained at my side.

"We'll take the center," I said. He nodded. It was the one position we were certain was defended. The most dangerous.

Forty minutes we had to get into position. I crouched down to wait, leaned against the wall, and closed my eyes briefly only to snap them open. "Take off your T-shirt, Hernandez," I ordered.

He obeyed without hesitation, and I tied the white garment to a stick and stuck the makeshift flag around the corner of the ruined wall, half expecting it to be blown out of my hands.

Nothing happened.

I glanced at Hernandez, who saluted, then eased around the corner into the open and walked toward the main entrance. The sky was starting to clear a little, and sunlight glinted off the metal doors.

From the jagged shadows stepped a soldier, dressed in fatigues and wearing a red armband.

I continued forward, my hand straying to my holstered Colt.

Ten feet away from him, I stopped.

The officer was middle-aged, which likely meant he was of higher rank, but there was no insignia on his uniform. His revolver was holstered, too. His eyes glinted as if in triumph. "You're a little late, lieutenant." He had a Southern drawl. "The New Confederate Army has taken possession of the Terminal."

I nodded, resisting the urge to salute. "Lieutenant Winslow. According to the treaty, neither side is in sole possession of the ISE."

He looked up at the cables overhead and smiled. "Too late, asshole."

I guessed the polite phase was over. Whether he was well-garrisoned or at ghost levels, once the fighting started here, so did the war. I reminded myself why I was there. My daughter was above me, and the only way to reach her was by using the Elevator.

I gestured at the Terminal. From this distance, I could see that the cables were still intact. "Just what do you think happened here?"

He shrugged. "Sabotage, obviously. And since I know it wasn't our side, that leaves you bastards."

It was clear he hadn't seen the flying creatures. "Why would we do that?"

"I gave up a long time ago trying to figure out why you fuckers do anything," he said. "I'm giving you one minute to retreat before we open fire."

I stared at him for another ten seconds. It was the longest ten seconds of my life, but it was a point of pride. Then I turned and marched back toward Hernandez, trying to look unhurried. In my mind, I was counting the seconds.

Thirty-four, thirty-five, thirty-six...

The twenty square inches at the center of my back held all my focus. I knew Hernandez had his rifle trained on the Newcon officer, but one signal from him and I was a goner.

Fifty-two, fifty-three, fifty-four...

I reached the Humvee, and ducked out of sight behind the wall. They hadn't fired. Was that a sign of strength or weakness?

Hernandez was staring at me. "That was a very brave and stupid thing to do, sir."

"I don't want to be the one who starts the Third Civil War." I checked the time. Ten more minutes. *Why the hell are we doing this? Even if we succeed in breaching their defenses, I wouldn't survive. Without me, would the others complete the mission?*

"You ready?" I asked.

Hernandez nodded, his face pale. He knew as well as I did that as soon as we left cover, we were probably dead meat. I stared at my watch, counting down. At 0659, I waved my hand forward.

Gunfire erupted before we could take a step. Despite being behind six feet of concrete and rubble, we both hit the ground. It took only moments to realize the bullets weren't coming at us. The gunfire sounded muffled, distant.

We both moved into a crouch then exchanged a look – which of us was going to poke our head around the corner? Hernandez, being closer, got there first. Since he didn't immediately yank his head back, I moved up next to him and stuck my head out, expecting it to be the last thing I ever did.

I'd been wrong in my estimate of how many enemy soldiers we were facing. A full squad was charging toward us — ten well-armed troops. But they weren't firing at us. They were turning and shooting at something behind them.

From the corner of my eye, movement. One of the shattered walls bulged outward. Then something huge and red burst into the Terminal's entrance plaza. It kept emerging, long and sinewy, a red, glistening carapace with hundreds of churning legs. It lunged toward two of the enemy combatants, sweeping them up in leviathan pincers that closed quickly with a snap.

The Newcon soldiers were cut in half, their bisected pieces flung to either side. The creature seemed not to feel the bullets slamming into it. Three of the troops turned and ran, the movement catching the creature's attention. It darted sideways, trampling them under its thrashing legs. To their dying credit the other Newcons stood their ground, continuing to fire until their last moments. The thing's pincers sliced through them so cleanly that their blood flowed downward and upward equally.

Only the Newcon commander remained standing. He'd been watching, in shock or stoic resignation. Now he reached for his holster, drawing his weapon with a smooth, practiced motion as the monster swayed sinuously toward him, in no hurry. The officer's bullets hit true but bounced harmlessly off the armored exoskeleton – except the last one. As the creature snipped off the man's head, that last shot sheared off one of its legs at the joint.

Hernandez and I had scrambled for cover. It had been mere seconds. Now Hernandez raised his rifle. Too late, I shouted, "Don't move!"

The creature swirled around and charged.

"Aim for the legs!" Hernandez yelled.

For every leg we managed to shear away, there were a dozen more. But as I replaced my magazine, the abomination was moving slower, though relentlessly forward. I grabbed Hernandez's arm and dragged him with me.

The Humvee was sheltered behind the wall. I don't remember how we managed to get into it so fast, nor do I recall turning the key, but we were moving before Hernandez had managed to close the door on his side.

We raced away from the Terminal, but a glance in the rearview mirror showed we were barely keeping ahead of the creature. We reached a wide spot in the road, and I tapped the brakes, decelerating, then yanked the handbrake and turned into the spin.

"What the hell are you doing?" Hernandez shouted.

I slammed my foot down, and the Humvee lurched forward, picking up speed. The creature was moving clumsily now, as if it belatedly noticed the absence of half of its forelimbs.

I'd aimed for the beast's head, but it was too quick, and we slammed broadside in its hind segments, the Humvee's defensive attributes closing around us. The vehicle had crumpled into half its normal size, but we stayed battered but safe within the extra protection of the seats. There were a few seconds of complete silence and then the engine whined and shuddered to a stop. The death throes of the creature shook the Humvee. Slamming our shoulders against the battered doors, we tumbled out, hitting the ground hard. The creature squirmed and thrashed and then rolled into a ball.

It stopped moving.

Hernandez appeared and lifted me to my feet. On shaky legs, I turned to the shattered entrance of the Terminal. "My daughter is on the station, Hernandez. But you've done enough. You don't need to come."

"My family is gone," he said, voice flat as he stared over the desolation. "If we can save your daughter, I'm in."

I nodded, not hiding my gratitude. It didn't take long to become quickly lost in the rubble. I'd only visited the base of the elevator once, to see my daughter off. Nothing was familiar.

Hernandez brushed past me. "I was stationed here on my first tour of duty."

He took the lead, and we quickly reached the station itself. To my relief, a Climber was already attached, miraculously undamaged. We moved to either side of the door, took stock of our ammunition and gear. Newcons and monsters could be behind any door. I nodded and Hernandez opened the door to the chamber. I dove in expecting the worse. It was empty except for two rows of seats.

Holstering his weapon, Hernandez moved quickly to a command panel beneath a large picture window. "We lucked out. A VIP Climber, prepped to go." He swiped his hand across the panel; the doors closed, and there was a soft jerk as the Climber began to ascend.

When I fell into one of the seats in relief, all my strength drained from me. I closed my eyes; the first station was a mile above us – no, not Hobart Station. Its fall had caused this carnage. The next stop was the space station, hours away. Unbelievably, I felt myself drifting off. I opened my eyes to find Hernandez still at the panel, staring out the window. I closed my eyes again and let myself go.

The Climber jerked, waking me up. We were swaying violently, and I fought back a surge of nausea. Hernandez was still at the window, and he turned to me, his face drained of color. Moments later, wall panels clattered to the floor, pressure suits popping out from behind them.

Hernandez ran across the Climber, and as I got to my feet, my ears popped and a loud hissing sounded. I stumbled toward Hernandez, who was already suited up. He helped me get my feet into my suit, but before I could get my arms encased, I was gasping. My vision narrowed. Turned black.

I woke on my back on the floor. The hissing replaced by the sound of screeching metal. Reaching into the busted window of the Climber was a long glistening tentacle. I clambered to my feet, and slipped toward the side of the Climber. Most of the wall was gone. Huge black tentacles were tearing the metal apart. I slid to a stop, my feet hitting the inch of metal that still rimmed the Climber along the bottom. It wasn't enough to stop my momentum, and I felt myself slipping.

A hard grip on my arm pulled me back from the brink. Hernandez dragged me to the center of the chamber.

"Help me up there!" he shouted, his voice deafening within the speakers of my suit. Hernandez pointed toward the Climber's ceiling. I managed to get to my feet and cupped my hands. Hernandez was a small man – fortunately, because I could barely hoist him up. He opened a round escape hatch near the center of the ceiling and pulled himself up and out of sight, then he lunged back into the opening, arms outstretched. He managed to lift me far enough that I could reach the opening and pull myself up the rest of the way. The Climber's roof of was slick with ice as Hernandez pulled me toward him.

Below was a swirling mass of tentacles. Very little remained of the Climber aside the metal nearest to the massive cable.

"There are tethers attached to your suit; at your waist," Hernandez said, his voice surprisingly calm. "Pull them out."

I found an opening and pulled out a long cord. Nanothreads. The same ultra-strong material that made up the ISE. Hernandez grabbed the end out of my hands, reached over his head, and clipped it to the same hook that held the Climber. Then he reached for his own waist.

The last of the metal gave way, and Hernandez slipped. Instinctively, I grabbed his sleeve, the two of us swinging wildly around the cable, Hernandez dangling from my grip. What was left of the Climber disappeared into the clouds below.

The cable shuddered and my grip on the cable started to slip. Damned if I was going to let Hernandez go. But I couldn't stop him when he reached up and put his other hand on my fingers.

"Save your daughter," Hernandez said, his voice calm through the speakers of my suit. He pulled loose my fingers and dropped away, his eyes still visible behind the faceplate. He didn't appear frightened, but at peace.

I dangled from the hook. For a few moments, I felt so defeated that I almost let go, but then Hernandez's sacrifice would have been for nothing. I felt my resolve snap into place, like loading a magazine into a rifle.

The hook was still drawing me upward, but now it was as if I was floating. I glanced up to see what appeared to be the ground coming up to meet me. It was an illusion; what seemed to be down was actually up – if either term meant anything in this weightlessness.

The opening was large and round, big enough for the Climber. The chamber beyond was huge, stretching off in all directions, but it was empty, no one to witness the hook pulling a single bedraggled human toward the ceiling, where I stopped and floated helplessly. The only light came from below. The space station was dead.

I reached up to detach myself, but though weightless, the opening below was intimidating. The clouds had parted, and the fires still raged far below, still devouring what was left of the Terminal.

A shadow obscured my view, and a creature flew through the opening, which scissored shut behind it. The figure was glowing, illuminating the chamber with a soft white light. The naked figure was tall, and quite definitely male, with a broad chest and muscular arms and legs. From his back sprouted white wings, which glowed even brighter than the rest of him.

But these were all incidental details compared to his face.

He was beautiful. There was no other word for it. In the way movie stars strove to be – flawless and yet distinctive. His eyes were wider than normal, perhaps, shining bright in the celestial light.

An angel. Of this, I had no doubt.

He glanced up at me and then looked away, uninterested. He walked away, as if gravity did not apply to beings such as him.

I detached myself and pushed off in his direction. He turned to regard me. I floated before him, certain now that everyone in the space station was dead.

"Why? Why have you done this?" My voice came over my speakers, but in frustration, I realized my words couldn't reach the angel.

Nevertheless, he seemed to hear me. His lips didn't move, but I heard his voice clearly in my mind. "I once stood at the Gates of Eden. Now I guard my master's domain."

"We never meant to trespass in heaven," I blurted.

"Heaven?" the angel repeated. "There are no boundaries to heaven, nor to hell. There is no up, no down. But from the realm of purgatory, the path of man is narrow. Thou hast not earned the right. Until mankind has learned to speak in one voice, thou shalt not pass into the heavenly realm."

And then the angel smiled. His teeth were sharp and pointed. His glow darkened and flames flickered around his head. An infernal halo.

His eyes turned black, and he reached out a taloned hand and pushed me away. I tumbled backward and slammed into the far wall. As I rebounded, I grabbed the netting that hung from the ceiling. The angel turned away and as he did so, the station shook. I looked down. The cable spooled away like the string of a broken kite, falling, falling and I knew that anyone alive near the Terminal was doomed.

The door closed. The chamber plunged into darkness.

The angel –a or was it a demon? – was gone.

I floated, knowing the darkness would never end.

✟ ☗ ✟

I woke in a hospital bed, my daughter at my side. Deena says the pressure suit almost killed me; the loading dock had air, but it hadn't been reaching me. Most of the space station's inhabitants have survived, but we're quickly running out of resources. It doesn't matter. We're slowly losing altitude and will likely burn up in the atmosphere. I believe most of us would prefer a quick end rather than slowly starving to death.

We have communications with Earth, but the last message from Mars – a pitiable cry for help – came a few months ago. Earth has tried to help us, but no rocket, manned or unmanned, has made it into space without being blown up.

I sent the angel's message to Earth, but instead of responding in 'one voice', the people there erupted into fighting over whose voice should answer and how. I suppose I shouldn't be surprised.

Deena is certain they aren't angels but aliens. "They don't want us leaving the planet," she said. "And who can blame them? They *can't* be angels; angels are good. Good is good and evil is evil."

The soldier in me doesn't agree. I think perhaps good and evil exist side by side, that, as the angel said, there is no up or down in heaven or hell. But the old Catholic in me wonders. The creature who'd spoken to me had had a certain air about him. I've run into his sort before.

He had the whiff of a mercenary. Perhaps God had hired outside help.

Forward Operating Cathedral

Case C. Capehart

The moment Toshiro and the other Lightsworn rolled into the forward operating cathedral, he knew something hunted them.

Conflict in the Haqar region had mysteriously died down months ago. Neither the Regime nor local insurgents claimed victory. Satellite images showed a calm landscape. Information coming out of the area was scarce. Despite the reports, the Lightsworn braced for enemy fire as they rolled through the last town before reaching the FOC. The locals glared wordlessly from the streets and through windows. No one fired on them, and the convoy of customized civilian Hummers passed through without stopping.

"The Haqar people are exhausted from war," Bishop Rinquist yelled from the rear of the second humvee to anyone who would listen. "The US tried to liberate them decades ago, but they refused. Can't say I blame them. You can't reach people like this through military might. You have to come for their souls. Once we re-establish the cathedral, missionary work can continue in earnest this time."

"That's gonna have to wait, Bishop." Sergeant First Class O'Malley turned around in his seat and lifted his visor to meet eyes with the holy man. "We're here to find out what happened three years ago, not to convert angry Haqari natives. For all we know, those townsfolk back there are the ones responsible."

"Of course, Sergeant," the bishop replied. "I am merely excited about the future, is all. These people... they deserve so much more. They deserve God's mercy."

The driver pointed ahead to a clearing in the gray trees. "We're coming up on the site now, Bishop."

Forward Operational Cathedral Haqar sat like polished ivory among weeds. The white walls of the building and its once carefully manicured courtyard contrasted the natural gloom of the surrounding mountains and forest, even years after its former residents went MIA. If not for the overgrowth and the busted front gate, one might think someone still lived within the manor.

A journalist from the Patriot News Corp and her film crew exited the humvee behind the bishop and approached him, getting footage and photos of the robed man as he reached out and touched the askew gate. Sergeant Toshiro Saiga exited his humvee and gave the spectacle a passing glance before looking out into the mountains. A sense of unease filled him, and he thought about the faces of the locals in the nearby village they'd passed through.

"Feels like Afghanistan all over again, huh, Toshi?" O'Malley clapped Toshi on the shoulder, jarring him out of his momentary lapse of awareness.

"Too much like Afghanistan." Toshi smirked at O'Malley. "The bishop doesn't allow booze on his deployments, either."

"Well, what the bishop doesn't know..." O'Malley popped open one of his ammo pouches and pulled out a 375mL bottle of Tullamore Dew.

"You son of a bitch. You don't need ammo?" Toshi shoved the big red-head.

"You know, when I first met you, I was not expecting you to be a fan of Irish whiskey," O'Malley laughed. "Figured you more for a saké guy."

"Yeah, 'cause you're a racist dipshit."

"I'm not racist, I'm just from Tennessee." O'Malley slipped the bottle back in his pouch and fastened it, checking to see if anyone noticed him. "I don't dispute the dipshit part, though."

Toshiro smiled for a moment before something in the trees drew his attention. "You hear that?"

O'Malley whirled and shouldered his M4. "No, but I felt something."

"Sergeant O'Malley? Is everything okay?" Bishop Rinquist had noticed the two react and turned to them.

"Everyone quit dicking around and get inside," O'Malley bellowed. "We are not secure yet."

Drivers pulled their humvees into a semi-circle formation in front of the busted gate and then exited toward the FOC. Toshiro and his unit took up positions behind the humvees while the Sapper began assessing the damage to the gate. Sergeant First Class Hecker's unit escorted the bishop and the other civilians inside the facility.

"You think the locals had time to arm up and make it here already?" Toshiro scanned the road leading up to the FOC. The only tracks were those made by their vehicles. Otherwise, it looked like no one had been there since the facility was sacked. "They didn't look like much when we rolled through."

"The locals never look like much until they're shooting at you," O'Malley replied. "But something about this isn't right."

"What do you mean?" Toshiro glanced over at his platoon sergeant.

O'Malley scooped a gob of tobacco out of a circular can and shoved it into his mouth, pushing out his cheek like a chipmunk. He clamped the can shut and shoved it back into his pocket, then spit brown murk onto the ground in front of him. "We don't know why the civil war just stopped. Conflicts like this don't just end. Yet here we are with a fuckin' news crew before we even know what's going on. Seems like a stupid move, if you ask me."

"You aren't in Delta anymore, Sergeant. We're under civilian command now. Well..." Toshiro looked around to see who was in hearing distance. "I meant to say divine command, channeled through a civilian committee."

"You almost slipped up there, Lightsworn," O'Malley chuckled.

"Contact front!" One of the privates called out and the others repeated him as everyone fixated forward.

"Eyes on your sectors, dammit!" O'Malley moved to the side of his humvee and drew down on the lone figure approaching on the road. He clicked the comm-link on his neck to 'on' and held the receiver up against his throat. "Hecker, this is O'Malley. We've got a target approaching the front gate."

A second later, Hecker's voice came over the comms. "Roger. I'm sending Garland up to the steeple to watch our ass."

O'Malley turned to Toshiro. "We'll cover you. Get up there and try to talk to them. Tell them to scram."

Toshiro nodded and moved to the front of the humvee. The figure continued to approach. Toshiro held up his left hand, and called out "halt" in the dialect he had learned while in Special Forces.

The figure approached him without halting. As it neared, Toshiro could see that it was a small woman, maybe a girl. She wore a cloak that dragged the ground and a hood concealing her hair. Black splotching framed what little of her face he could make out under the hood. Toshiro called out "halt" again, keeping his distance. This time the woman responded.

"I am unarmed."

Toshiro could make out what she said, but the dialect was different in the Haqar region than what he had learned.

"I need you to turn around and go back." Toshiro kept his M4 at the ready, but not levelled at her.

She kept approaching.

"Get your fucking weapon up, Toshi," O'Malley commanded over the comm.

Memories from his time in Afghanistan shot to the surface in his mind and he shook his head, trying to physically push them back down. "Please go back. No one here needs to get hurt."

"Liar." The look that the petite woman gave cut him through to the bone. For a moment, he felt like an insect caught in a web, staring down the spider as it approached.

Toshiro flipped the visor up on his helmet and looked the woman in the eyes.

"Please," he begged, remembering the fearful expression of the Afghan girl as she bled out at his feet all those years ago at Checkpoint Charlie. "Please stop."

The woman drew to a halt and Toshiro exhaled, lowering the barrel of his rifle an inch in response.

"They're not coming for you, Lightsworn," the woman said. "But they are coming."

With that, the woman turned and headed back down the road.

"Who's coming?" Toshiro yelled after her. "The Regime? Do you know what happened here?"

She did not reply and after a few minutes he returned to the gate.

O'Malley called into the comms, advising them the target was retreating. He then turned to Toshiro. "What happened out there? What did she say?"

Toshiro scanned the trees. "She said someone was coming. She said they weren't coming for the Lightsworn, though."

"She specifically said 'Lightsworn'?" O'Malley scowled at him.

"Affirmative." Toshiro took up a position behind his humvee. "Sergeant, I think we're about to find out what happened to the residents of this FOC."

Sergeant Hecker came over the radio. "O'Malley, we need Saiga in here."

O'Malley pushed his receiver to his throat. "We might have incoming threats, Hecker. I'm going to need every man I've got out here. You need to wrap it up in there."

"I'll send U'Butu out to replace him," Hecker replied. "We need a translator in here. Now."

O'Malley looked at Toshiro and shrugged. "You heard 'em. Get back out here as soon as you can, though, Toshi. I don't like the tidings that local brought us."

Toshiro entered the front doors of the FOC and made his way past the security team. A corporal pointed him farther into the cathedral. Hundreds of spiderwebs coated the inside of the FOC and grew larger and more dense as he reached the inner sanctuary. Inside, Toshiro drew to a halt as he took in the scene.

Thick, silky webs spanned from wall to wall, disappearing into the dark, vaulted ceiling above. Bones, some with withered skin, littered the pews and the black-stained floor. Most of the corpses could be seen from inside dilapidated cocoons. Ichor coated the walls. Toshiro looked up at a massive portrait of the current High Cardinal. Filth had long ago been smeared across his pleasant-looking visage. The other portraits were ravaged, as if some beast had clawed at them. Faint light spilling in through the stained glass cast the whole room in an eerie red glow.

"Over here, Sergeant." Hecker emerged from a hallway between bookshelves. To the side, remnants of another shelf lay scattered and broken. Scuff marks in front of the hallway hinted at a door being present at some point.

Toshiro followed Hecker down a stairway that went on for much longer than he expected. As the stairs ended and the hall opened up into a room, Toshiro dropped to a knee and extended his right index and middle finger, putting them against his chest in the symbol of the Holy Candle.

"Merciful God... what is this?" Toshiro looked around the room. Pop-up halogen lamps cast a sterile, ambivalent glow on the grisly scene before him.

Several surgical tables sat in the middle of the room. Along the walls, various machines were crusted with years-old gore. The machinery seemed a blend of contemporary tech and arcane devices yanked from the days of the Inquisitions. Blackened filth coated the floors, creating a faint spiral pattern toward a large, central drain. As Toshiro hovered over the stainless-steel drain, he swore the darkness below stared back at him. He let his imagination explore what horrors might await him if he were to dive through that ominous drain.

"I cannot fathom the evil that must have overtaken them... that they could do something like this."

Toshiro pulled his gaze away from the drain and looked to where the bishop stood in front of the cameraman. The man wiped at his red eyes with a trembling hand as he spoke to the journalist.

"It's clear you had no idea what was going on here, Your Grace." The blonde journalist consoled the bishop, glancing at the cameraman for a brief instant to make sure he was focused on them. Toshiro scowled as he noticed the American flag patch the journalist had sewn onto the sleeve of her blazer. She continued as Hecker's unit investigated the room. "Can you at least speculate? Are we talking torture? Was this the work of the Regime—"

The bishop held up his hand, cutting her off. "I want to be perfectly clear. This was not the work of a heretical regime. Look around, Ms Pullen. Do you honestly think an enemy faction built an underground facility within our cathedral just to torture clerics?"

"I…" The journalist looked at her crew with confusion before turning back to the bishop. "Your Grace, the majority of our viewers are patriotic Americans who belong to your Church. I'm one of them. I'm sure you don't mean to imply that... that *we* did this."

"I'm not saying the atrocities committed here were done by faithful servants of God like your viewers," the bishop said. "Nevertheless, it very much appears that the victims of this room were locals; that this was some terrible way to try and—"

The bishop raised his hand and turned away from the camera as he attempted to regain his composure. After a moment, with a shaky voice, he spoke. "These people may have been non-believers but they did not deserve this. This is not how we bring people to God, and I will not allow this to be covered up."

The bishop pushed past the journalist and spoke directly to the camera. "I, Bishop Archibald Rinquist, denounce the acts that we have found here. I denounce the men and women who lived at this cathedral. It is clear they strayed from God's merciful ways a long time ago. They are dead, but true justice cannot occur until we, the truly faithful, have drowned these horrors with our good will."

The bishop's voice quivered with anger as he lifted his fist in front of him. "We will make this right. We *must* make this right."

"Let's take a break, Jamal." The journalist lowered her mic and the cameraman shut down his equipment. She turned to the bishop. "Your Grace, I have to say, I thought you were going off the rails there for a second. But wow, did you turn it around. I have goosebumps."

Toshiro pushed forward and interrupted the exchange. "Your Grace, you needed me for something?"

"Ah, Sergeant Saiga. Yes, I am in need of your linguistic skills." The bishop waved off the reporter and led Toshiro over to a wall. He pulled a schematic free that had foreign words scrawled all over it. "Can you decipher this?"

"What is it?" Toshiro asked, looking over the faded paper.

The bishop lowered his voice and looked over toward the journalist as he whispered. "I can't be fully certain, but they appear to be plans for genetic experimentation. I believe the cleric in charge here was interested in something other than conversions. But never mind that. I am interested in what has been written on it."

"Genetic experiments?" Toshiro frowned as he studied the notes and symbols. None of it made any sense to him. "How the hell could clerics be doing something like this without anyone knowing? And how did you figure this out?"

Bishop Rinquist stared at Toshiro with a confused expression before blinking, the smile returning to his face. "Oh, my boy, pardon me. I assumed you had read my dossier. I am the Church's leading geneticist. Well, it's more of a hobby, really. The hard sciences don't make up a very large section of the 'Evangelical pie', you might say. Nevertheless, it is what I obtained my PhD in. But, back to the writing, Sergeant."

"They don't seem to be words. At least none I'm familiar with." Toshiro traced a gloved finger over one of the words. "Like this one: 'Neera'. That sounds like a name."

Toshiro looked up at the wall. Jars of body parts adorned the shelves like something out of an old horror movie he saw as a kid. He felt like he stood within the lair of some mad scientist. Directly in front of him sat what appeared to be a female hand and forearm, perfectly preserved. Part of a floral tattoo adorned the upper portion of the arm.

Just then Toshiro's comm crackled. "Incoming! We've got incoming!"

"What's happening?" The bishop glanced around as the Lightsworn ran to the hall, checking their weapons en route.

"Alpha team, cover the bishop. Everyone else, get topside." Sergeant Hecker barked orders, kicking a private in the ass as he passed by.

O'Malley came over the comms. "Waker is down. Toshi, get your ass up here."

Toshiro took the stairs three at a time and burst through the inner sanctuary as more reports came across the comms. Everything he heard on his way through the cathedral confused him. Someone opened fire with a M240-B machine gun just before Toshiro made it outside.

"What the fuck is that?" Toshiro heard O'Malley out loud and over the comms as he exited into the front courtyard of the cathedral.

A figure broke through the trees to the left and slammed one of the Lightsworn up against the humvee with such force that two of the tires lifted off the ground. Toshiro drew down on the figure but couldn't get a clear shot without hitting his teammate. He watched through his day scope as something resembling a cross between a person and an alligator shredded the screaming Lightsworn. The figure had green, armored skin and spiked ridges down its back. Toshiro stared in shock as it lifted Private Simmons with one arm and slung him over the back of the humvee like he was a dusty rug.

Simmons' guts burst from his open torso, showering the closest Lightsworn. Toshiro and the others opened fire on the creature a second later. It dodged behind the humvee and emerged on the other side, faster than anything Toshiro had seen. It slammed into the two Lightsworn positioned in front of the vehicle. Shrugging off the rounds that managed to hit it, the lizardman grabbed one Lightsworn by the arm, ripping it off at the shoulder with ease. It dropped on the screaming soldier, biting his face off with its jagged maw. The adjacent Lightsworn adjusted his aim, but a clawed foot shot out, disemboweling him with a single kick.

"Take it down now!" O'Malley screamed, dropping to his side around the corner of the humvee and unloading his carbine into the creature.

Toshiro dropped the empty magazine from his M4 and loaded another as he moved closer to the reptilian berserker. From the side, Private Joon-Park dashed in with one of the M240-Bs. Before he could open fire, some kind of metal hook burst through his shoulder, knocking the machine gun from his hands. The hook yanked tight against his chest, and he flew backward through the air, into the trees beside the cathedral. Toshiro saw only a blur of movement intercept Joon-Park before the screaming soldier disappeared.

"Contact left," Toshiro shouted as he scooped up Joon-Park's machine gun.

The berserker rose between the humvees, blood flowing down its face and pale chest. Toshiro levelled his weapon at it and unloaded. Roaring in the face of the monster, Toshiro held the trigger and pumped round after round into the beast. To his shock, a few rounds ricocheted off the behemoth, hitting the vehicles on either side of it. One bouncing round clipped Toshiro's helmet, but he continued his assault. The other Lightsworn joined alongside him, emptying magazines into the monster before them. Another machine-gunner opened fire and within seconds, the berserker dropped to its knees, riddled with puncture wounds.

Sergeant Patel, pushed through the men with a 12-gauge pump and hammered three slugs into the creature's head. With its skull busted open and brain matter leaking out, the creature hissed in defiance at the Lightsworn until the fourth slug put it down for good.

"Watch the woods," Toshiro yelled, scanning the trees to his left. "Something got Joon-Park and it's still out there."

"What the hell is that thing?" O'Malley came up next to Toshiro, his .45 trained on its destroyed head. "You're telling me there's more of them out there?"

"I don't know." Something about the creature drew Toshiro's attention. In its last moments, its eyes seemed very familiar to him. He had seen that same, hateful defiance before in Afghanistan. It was a look only another human could give.

"Merciful Light, it took down four of us in seconds with only one arm?" O'Malley kicked the corpse over and Toshiro's breath caught in his lungs.

The beast was missing its right arm from the elbow down. Running up the tricep, from the nub to the shoulder Toshiro made out a floral tattoo against the leathery armor of its skin.

"She was here." Toshiro barely breathed the words, fearful of what they meant.

"This thing's a 'she'? How can you tell?" O'Malley leaned over, looking at its crotch with all the grace of a little kid inspecting a dead cat. "And what do you mean 'she was here'? You think this thing killed the missionaries?"

Toshiro pulled on O'Malley's shoulder, getting his attention. "Protect the humvees. I'm getting the bishop. We've got to pop smoke."

"Agreed," O'Malley replied as he pulled M4 magazines from the blood-splattered pouches on Simmons' vest. "We're not at all equipped for this threat. No dicking around in there, Toshi. Let's get the fuck out of here."

Toshiro took a fresh magazine from O'Malley, popping it into his M4 and passing the M240-B off to O'Malley before sprinting back to the cathedral.

Sergeant Hecker emerged from inside. "We're holding our position inside, but I need a report, Sergeant Saiga. What are we—"

Something dropped from above and punctured Hecker through his collar with a bullet-like impact. The sergeant jerked forward, the M4 dropping out of his grip as he tried to raise it. His eyes widened and his right hand fumbled for his sidearm. Toshiro noticed the silky cord trailing out of his wound and lunged forward, pulling his combat knife free. Before he could reach it, the cord lost its slack and jerked Hecker back a few steps. Toshiro froze as Sergeant Hecker clawed at his chest and stomach.

"...what?" was all he managed to say before the cord tightened and yanked him into the air.

Hecker's body shot upward, past the stained-glass windows and into the arms of a petite, naked female standing atop the cathedral. Toshiro lifted his rifle, peering through his scope. The woman's body appeared segmented, like that of an ant or spider. Dark splotches seemed to spread over her, starting from the sides of her stomach and breasts. The coloration of her skin resembled a bodysuit torn away at the front.

Toshiro looked for an opening, but Hecker's body blocked his shot. He watched through his scope as the slender woman lifted the sergeant – who must have weighed two-hundred fifty pounds in full gear – up by his collar. As Hecker struggled in her grip, three pairs of 'spider legs' pulled away from her sides, just below her armpits and flexed against the overcast, midday sky. Toshiro yelled and fired wide of his target as the spear-tipped legs plunged into Sergeant Hecker. With a shudder and a flex, the woman ripped Sergeant Hecker in half, right up the middle. Toshiro looked on as she pulled him apart like a grilled cheese sandwich. Hecker's blood splattered over her as she puffed out her chest. She lifted her head and exhaled, showering in the gore of Sergeant Hecker's bisection.

Before Toshiro could adjust his aim, she dropped onto all eight legs and skittered back across the cathedral roof, disappearing over the ledge.

"They're on the roof," Toshiro yelled. "Watch the roof."

"They're in the trees!"

Toshiro pushed the receiver of his communicator to his throat. "No, the roof!"

As he turned back to the front gate, another monstrous form dropped from the treetops overhead onto one of the Lightsworn taking cover near the gate. It landed on the man in one instant and in the next it had jumped away, back up into the trees. Behind it, the Lightsworn screamed, a bleeding stump where his leg should have been.

Toshiro abandoned his quest to reach the bishop and ran to the injured Lightsworn. Pulling a zip-tie from his belt that he normally used for detaining prisoners, he used it as a tourniquet for the maimed soldier. Slamming an injection pen of morphine into the Lightsworn, Toshiro looked around and saw two more men missing limbs.

"What the hell happened?"

Lieutenant Zamaki, their Sapper, dropped down beside him. "A fucking shark happened."

Toshiro stared at him, trying to gauge if the young officer had gone into shock.

The Sapper shook his head. "Yeah, it sounds stupid, but I know a Carcharadon when I see one. Whatever that thing is, it's got a shark head. And it jumps like a damn flea."

Toshiro looked over at the corpse of the reptilian berserker. He could still make out the floral tattoos on its arm. "They were making... animal people here?"

"What are you talking about, Sergeant?" Zamaki asked. "You think this is some kind of Dr Moreau shit?"

"Get everyone inside." Toshiro stood and shouldered his rifle. "We'll be slaughtered out here in the open like this."

"I don't think that's the plan," Zamaki said, pointing behind him. "What the hell are they doing?"

Toshiro turned to see Hecker's Bravo Team escorting Bishop Rinquist and the news crew out the door of the cathedral. Then he heard O'Malley over the radio.

"Hecker, what are you guys doing? Get those civilians back into the cathedral. This zone is fucking hot as hell right now."

"Hecker is KIA. We're working on orders from command, now," Sergeant Russo came back over the comms. "We're taking Humvee Five, O'Malley. Cover us and then fall in behind."

Toshiro yelled over the chaos, "Converge on five! Eyes up!"

He and Zamaki helped the wounded private to the designated humvee, scanning the tops of the trees for the spider woman and the shark jumper. He almost collided with O'Malley as the platoon sergeant rose from behind the humvee.

"This is a terrible call, Sergeant," Toshiro said, taking up a position on the right flank of the vehicle.

"This whole thing is a shitshow, Toshi. But having an argument out in the open like this will get us all killed." O'Malley waved Bravo team forward. "If we can get moving, we can lose them on the road. Unless one of them is a were-cheetah."

The journalist and Bishop Rinquist loaded into the humvee. Even as he piled in, the bishop wouldn't stop talking. "Demons! Light guide us, the heretics have summoned demons to stop us!"

"Shut up and get inside, Your Grace," O'Malley yelled, slamming the door shut and banging the roof. "Move out. We're right behind you."

O'Malley turned to issue orders to the ones covering their retreat when a Lightsworn came over the comms. "There's one in the road. What the hell is that?"

Toshiro could hear the bishop over the comms, screaming about demons in the background as they looked up the road. The humvee picked up speed and then slammed into something strong enough to stop it in its tracks. It looked as if they had hit a light pole; the whole vehicle buckled, and the hood flew off and over the top of the humvee.

Someone yelled, "save the bishop," but Toshiro was already moving. He and O'Malley sprinted, weapons drawn, toward the crash.

No one got out of the humvee, but Toshiro could hear the screams from inside. As they came up on the vehicle, O'Malley opened fire on what Toshiro could only describe as a demon. Black fur covered the woman's legs, which ended in massive hooves. Thick, red horns curled over the top of her head from underneath long, dark hair. Her lower face protruded forward into a bovine snout. From the bottom of flaring nostrils, smoking orange fluid dripped like lava to sizzle against the destroyed engine below her.

Flinching away from the rounds O'Malley sent her way, the demon reached into the humvee and ripped the radiator out, flinging it directly at him. The spinning radiator clipped O'Malley on the arm, nearly taking it off. He dropped the machine gun and hit the ground, crying out in pain. Ignoring him, the demon turned back to the humvee it had single-handedly stopped at full momentum. She sucked air into her lungs and opened her mouth, vomiting what looked like lava all over the front of the vehicle. The liquid began eating through the interior.

Toshiro opened fire on the demon, emptying his magazine. Other Lightsworn were either engaging the demon or wrenching the doors of the humvee open. Toshiro's M4 halted with a click as smoke curled from the empty, open chamber. Letting the weapon drop against its sling, he reached down and pulled O'Malley to his feet. The sergeant roared in Toshiro's ear and shoved him aside. An instant later, the demon slammed into O'Malley, goring him through the middle with her horns.

Even lifted off the ground, O'Malley fought back, slamming his right knee into her face. He pulled the combat knife from his hip and drove it into the demon's shoulder. She cried out, shoving the big man off of her horns, and onto the ground. Toshiro charged, firing his Beretta as he ran. The demon dodged to the side and ran into the woods, grabbing at the knife still in her shoulder.

Toshiro and Zamaki dragged O'Malley back toward the cathedral. The other Lightsworn escorted those from Humvee Five. The bishop and Sergeant Russo sprinted ahead of the others, passing even Toshiro to reach the safety of the FOC.

Behind the fleeing bishop, the blonde journalist had gotten her hands on a M4 and was firing wildly at the trees as she ran. Something in the sky caught her eye and she pointed her rifle at it.

Suddenly a screech blasted Toshiro's ears unlike anything he had ever heard. He dropped his weapon and O'Malley, gripping the sides of his head. It felt as if every bone in his body were cracking under the intensity of the sound. Something whooshed by and he hit the ground, certain someone had opened fire on them.

The screech stopped and he opened his eyes in time to see a winged creature slam into the journalist as she recovered from the audio blast. All he could see were leathery, flappy arms and white hair. The journalist screamed in terror and pain as she tangled with the creature. In front of them, Toshiro noticed two of the news crew and a Lightsworn on the ground. Their heads resembled burst watermelons.

Others opened fire at the creature, unbothered by the journalist caught in the crossfire. The soldiers were past the point of waiting for a clear shot. These monsters had to be put down no matter who might be in the way.

The creature turned its grotesque, pig-snouted face toward them and bellowed another bone-wracking screech, dropping them to the ground with another audio blast. Then the beast scrambled into the woods, taking to the trees and disappearing.

Toshiro instinctively ran to the journalist. The bat-thing had shredded her with its claws. Her bright blue blazer with the obnoxious American flag patch on the arm was soaked through with blood and her innards poked through the tears in her once-white blouse.

The journalist choked on blood, clawing at Toshiro as he knelt over her. She was beyond saving and her wide eyes seemed to acknowledge as much. She clawed at his chest, grabbing his hand and shoving a cell phone into it. Feebly pushing the cell phone at him, she looked skyward and then was gone.

Toshiro looked down at the phone. She had it open to a half-written text message. The recipient section read 'MOM' in large letters across the top. Below a text showing her flight time and a response reading, 'Be careful' was a text she must have been in the middle of writing when they hit the demon.

Something went wrong. If I don't make it out, tell the boys I l

Toshiro looked back at the woman; he guessed her to be in her thirties. 'The boys' were most likely her children.

Shoving the phone into his breast pocket, Toshiro bolted back for the safety of the cathedral.

Inside, several of the Lightsworn knelt before Bishop Rinquist as he said prayers over them. Toshiro looked around until he found Zamaki knelt over O'Malley along the wall. A wide trail of blood led up to him.

The bishop was going on about demons, but Toshiro suspected something more to the monsters outside.

"How's he doing, sir?"

Zamaki looked up at Toshiro and sighed. "Our two medics are out there lying in the grass somewhere, missing limbs. Even if they were here..." Zamaki shook his head.

O'Malley laughed, spitting blood onto his web gear.

Toshiro knelt beside his friend. "What can I do?"

"You can get that bottle out of my pouch, if you want," O'Malley replied.

Toshiro chuckled and unsnapped the ammo pouch, pulling the whiskey out. "At least her horns didn't get this."

"Halle-fuckin-luyah," O'Malley sighed.

"Merciful Light, the bishop is right over there," Lieutenant Zamaki huffed.

"What's he gonna do, kill me?" O'Malley lifted the bottle toward Toshiro. "You better take the first sip and make it a good one. I'm liable to get blood in it on my turn."

Toshiro took the bottle and tipped it up and then passed it back.

"I'd offer you some, sir, but I don't want you in trouble for fraternizin'." O'Malley halfheartedly raised the bottle.

Zamaki glanced at the bishop and then reached for the bottle. "Screw that, Sergeant."

Zamaki took a long pull and then handed it back, coughing into his sleeve. "That... is not very good, you guys."

Toshiro and O'Malley laughed. Just then the screeching came back, locking them all up for a few more seconds before it passed. The pain wasn't as bad this time, inside the cathedral. However, when Toshiro looked up, he noticed fresh cracks in the walls.

"The demons are breaking the walls down around us." The bishop grabbed Sergeant Russo by the shoulder. "We need to move deeper into the sanctuary. That is holy ground. We should be safe there."

"I don't believe this shit." Toshiro pushed to his feet, facing the bishop. "Those aren't demons out there and he knows it. Why is he still lying to us?"

The other Lightsworn scowled at him, but none of them replied. O'Malley coughed up more blood. "What are you going on about, Toshi?"

"Earlier, the bishop called me down to this secret basement they found. All kinds of wicked shit was going on down there; place looks like a freaky science lab. There was equipment like I've never seen and jars of body parts all on the walls. One of those jars had an arm in it with floral tattoos. The lizard woman out there that got Simmons?"

"The one with the missing arm." O'Malley grunted and spat to the side. "I saw the tattoo, as well. Fuck! This whole thing's been FUBAR from the get go."

Toshiro looked around to see if anyone else from Russo's group had hung back. "The bishop had me try and translate words written in blood on these genetic schematics he found. I think they were written by the victims here. I think the experiments broke out."

"How the hell does a bishop know anything about genetic schematics?" Zamaki asked.

"He said he was the leading genetics expert in the church," Toshiro replied.

"You're telling me that clerics in here were doing genetic experiments without anyone in the church knowing," O'Malley grunted, coughing up more blood. "...and the bishop they send to reclaim this place just coincidentally happens to be a genetics expert?"

"I didn't even know we had any geneticists in the church." Zamaki glanced nervously between the two sergeants.

"They fucking knew about this." O'Malley grabbed Toshiro and pulled him close. "Toshi, you gotta get out of here. What did that girl say to you earlier? That they weren't here for the Lightsworn? You make a run for it... if you're not a threat... they might let you through."

O'Malley's hand faltered and his head lulled. "Take the

sappy lieutenant... forget about the bishop and Russo... you guys get the hell away from here."

Gunfire erupted within the inner sanctuary and Toshiro pulled away from O'Malley. He looked to the lieutenant. "Watch him. Keep him awake. I'll be right back."

✝ ♆ ✝

"Take it alive!"

The bishop's voice rose above the chaos before Toshiro even entered the room. As he rounded the corner, every Lightsworn in the room was dog-piling a raging figure in the middle of the pews.

"Watch its mouth! Holy shit, watch its mouth!" Russo bellowed orders as he pulled every zip tie he had off his belt.

"What is going on here?" Toshiro yelled, stepping closer with his rifle drawn.

Bishop Rinquist approached him worriedly. "We found one of the demons attempting to ambush us. They're subduing it and taking it to the basement."

"You're what?" Toshiro asked, pushing past him and approaching Russo. "How is that supposed to help us get out of here?"

"We have a live demon right here," Russo said, overseeing the men as they struggled. "No one's ever been this close to one. We have to learn all we can from it. Even if we have to send the information to high command for others to use."

Toshiro looked down at the monster. It was the shark-headed creature. He couldn't tell if this one was also female, but its body was lithe and covered in faded cloth wraps. It thrashed in the dozens of zip ties but seemed contained. Just as Zamaki had said, its head resembled that of a great white shark. Goopy mucus pooled around its opal eyes, and it wheezed like an asthmatic with every labored breath. Toshiro wondered if it was even supposed to be on dry land at all, least of all high in the mountains.

Russo turned to Toshiro, a maddened look in his eyes. "This could be our best chance at learning true evil's weakness."

Three Lightsworn carried the monster down into the basement.

Toshiro returned to the bishop. "You've got to stop this."

"I agree. We must kill this thing." Bishop Rinquist clutched at Toshiro's chest. "You have to kill it. Before they can react. Please Sergeant, we cannot allow it to live."

"What?" Toshiro shoved the man's hands down. "No, I mean you have to tell them the truth. They think they're capturing a demon. They're not and you know it."

"I don't know what you're talking about at all." The bishop backed away, shaking his head.

"I'm talking about human beings," Toshiro pressed in on the man, backing him against a pew. "That's what these things are."

"That's what they used to be, Sergeant," the bishop hissed. The worried look dropped from the man's face and with it fell the innocent guise he had been wearing this whole time. "They refused salvation. They chose darkness over the Light... and then God changed them to reflect the monsters they were on the inside."

"God didn't turn them into monsters," Toshiro growled. "We did that to them. They aren't being punished by God. They *are* God's punishment."

The bishop looked Toshiro over with wide eyes, appalled at his accusation. With a trembling voice, he called out. "Demon. Sergeant Toshiro has joined with the demons!"

Sergeant Russo and the other looked up from their positions near the entrances, with a few turning their weapons toward Toshiro.

Toshiro held up his free hand and gawked at the bishop. "What are you doing?"

"Sergeant, drop the weapon," Russo said, training his rifle on him.

"He is already turning, can you not see it?" The bishop was nearly wailing at this point. "They have corrupted his soul and his body is turning, just like those heretics outside."

"Drop it, Toshi," Russo yelled.

Toshiro looked around. Russo's entire team had their weapons trained on him. He lowered his M4 and placed it on the ground. "Russo, don't shoot. Don't shoot, man."

"Kill him. Kill the demon before he infects the rest of you." The bishop tugged at the arms of the privates closest to him.

"Hold your fire, men," Russo barked. "Toshi, don't move."

"Sergeant, you are putting us all at risk. I order you to execute this demon." Bishop Rinquist turned and strode toward Sergeant Russo as an object from above slammed into him, nearly knocking him over.

The bishop stumbled and looked up. "Merciful Light..."

The pale, silky cord straightened, yanking the shocked bishop off his feet and into the shadow of the vaulted ceiling. The Lightsworn opened fire above them as chunks of the bishop rained down.

Toshiro reached for his rifle, but one of the Lightsworn opened fire at him. Running for cover, Toshiro bolted through the open doorway and down the stairs toward the basement.

The three Lightsworn that had carried down the shark-head monster halted on their way up as they saw him, but he waved them past. Not willing to question it, the three privates ran up the stairs. Toshiro reached the bottom and entered the brightly-lit room.

On one of the surgical tables lay the monster. From the look of things, the three privates had already started their own 'investigation'. A lot of the wraps had been pulled off, revealing heavily scarred flesh. The mucus around its eyes had gotten runnier and trailed down its bruised, pummeled cheeks. Toshiro could not understand how any person could survive such a transformation.

As he approached, the monster thrashed and snapped its jaws at him. He backed up and raised his empty hands. In the language the woman outside the cathedral had used, he tried to reassure the monster. "I'm not here to hurt you." Toshiro turned toward the sounds of gunfire continuing upstairs.

He looked back at the monster on the table. "We'll leave. If you tell the others to stop, we'll leave."

The monster thrashed at him again. He had no idea if it could even hear him, much less understand. Toshiro glanced around. There were no other exits to the room. His Lightsworn brothers had opened fire on him earlier without hesitation. No matter what happened, he was likely going to have to climb those stairs into the waiting arms of an enemy.

Kneeling, he lifted his fingers to his chest and prayed. He asked the Light for wisdom; beseeching God to tell him what to do.

No divine inspiration hit him. No booming voice reached out to him. All he heard was gunfire and the monster thrashing on the table. All he felt was the cold floor against his knees. He opened his eyes to the sight of the stainless-steel drain in the middle of the floor.

How much bodily fluid had run through that drain? How much blood had carried the anguish of its owner through that gleaming, indifferent portal? How many tortured souls had spiraled that metallic maw?

Toshiro looked up at the monster. He rose to his feet and pulled the knife from his belt. The monster grew still and stared at him as he approached. Without eyelids, it could only watch as he closed in on it, blade drawn.

"I am so sorry," he said in the local dialect.

Toshiro's knife easily cut through the plastic ties in a few quick tugs. He cut through maybe five of them before the monster's powerful legs broke through the rest. Before he could react, the monster jolted forward, its toothy jaws open wide.

The monster slammed into him, its weight crashing him to the floor, and he waited for the end to come.

Seconds felt like hours, and Toshiro fought the fatigue threatening to drag him into the darkness. At some point, he'd lost that fight, and realized he was still on the floor. Still alive.

His vision came back slowly. One of his eyes appeared to be swollen shut, and looking around as best he could, there was no sign of the shark monster. He thought he heard more gunfire up the stairs, but he couldn't be sure.

"Fuck," he breathed, nearly puking. "I need... I need to get out of here."

Toshiro got to his feet and immediately fell. He had been in some pretty bad fights before; he knew this feeling well enough. With a more focused effort, he got to his feet and stayed there. Steadying himself on the wall, he made his way into the hall and up the stairs.

"This is like being drunk," he muttered, and he pushed himself up, one stair at a time. "I'm just knock-down drunk. I've done this before. I made it all the way to the third-floor barracks at Fort Carson like this. First Sergeant never even saw me. I can do this."

His head rang like a grenade had gone off beside him, but he could tell the gunfire had stopped. Pausing in the doorway of the sanctuary, he looked around.

"Looks clear."

He stepped forward and turned to see the demon woman standing in front of him. Her nostrils flared and leaked more of the lava-like acid.

"Shit."

✟ ♟ ✟

Toshiro awoke to sharp tugging at his neck. Before he could open his one good eye, he felt the bindings all over his body – wrapped tightly, preventing any movement. Toshiro's mind went to the images of desiccated bodies in cocoons then to the spider woman on the roof.

He forced his one good eye open to see thick, fibrous hair in front of his face. Looking to the side, he could just make out the face of the girl from before. She was the spider woman all along. And she was sucking the blood from his neck.

With a gasp, she released and lifted her head, breathing heavily, as if she had just surfaced from underwater. His blood coated the front of her face. Without the cloak, he could see the extent of her transformation. She tucked her extra 'legs' into her side, against her ribs; the discolored skin on her sides resembled a spider's chitin.

She sneered at him and took a deep breath, ready to resume draining him. Toshiro sighed and turned his head to the side. He was ready for this day to end.

A strange noise stopped the spider woman and they both turned to see the shark-head monster standing in the room. It made a noise that was a cross between a squeak and a bark; nothing one would expect from a great white shark. The spider woman pulled away from Toshiro and approached the shark-head. Behind them, more monsters came into view. Toshiro saw the demon, who wore a ragged tank top; her red arms were heavily muscled. She stared at him, the orange mucus practically glowing in the dark of the room.

Toshiro also spied the banshee. Its wispy white hair reminded him of a picture of Albert Einstein. It hunkered in a corner, the leathery flaps of its arms draped around it like a blanket.

There were more shifting in the shadows. Toshiro couldn't see them clearly, but he could hear them. The spider woman seemed to be arguing with the shark-head monster, though its squealing seemed completely unintelligible. Who knew how long these monsters had been together. Even deprived of human language, they would have figured out how to communicate with each other.

Toshiro looked forward as the spider woman approached him again. She looked him over and then huffed through her nose.

"Neesa claims you rescued her. Why?" The woman's voice seemed so young, yet incredibly hard.

"We didn't know," Toshiro murmured. "We didn't know what they were doing here."

"So you feel guilt, is that it?" The woman hissed in his face.

"No," Toshiro replied, locking eyes with her. "I knew I was going to die. She didn't have to."

"Mercy." The woman glared at him. "Your people claim to have a god of mercy. I think you are the only one who actually hears this god."

The woman motioned behind her, and the demon stepped forward. Rubbing her nose on the webbing, her acid ate away at the bindings until they came loose, and Toshiro spilled onto the floor.

The spider woman lifted his chin to look into his eyes. "Take the road through town, but do not stop there. They sheltered us when we escaped. They will not shelter you. They will wonder why we did not kill you like all the others who brought war here."

"The civil war..." Toshiro muttered. "It was you who stopped it."

She tilted her head and her eyes narrowed. "This is our home now. We have purchased it with blood. Never return here."

The monsters backed away from him, allowing him to get to his feet and stagger out of the cathedral. On his way out, he noticed the bodies of O'Malley and Zamaki, but he did not stop for them. He feared any hesitation might void the pardon granted him.

Outside, more monsters crept in from the woods, but these were not like the others. They appeared more humanoid, but still disfigured. Some walked on stilted legs while others pushed makeshift wheelchairs. None of them seemed capable of fighting; not like the ones he and the Lightsworn had faced. Many appeared to be children. They all regarded him with fear as he passed through the busted gate. He got into Humvee Three and started it up.

Without looking back, Toshiro drove away from Forward Operational Cathedral Haqar. He passed back through the local town, past the glaring locals, and he did not stop.

GOD GIVETH NO QUARTER

J.G. Grimmer

The midsummer sun began its slow, red burning death behind us. Its light still potent enough to blind those waiting for us, flintlocks primed and ready to fire out the windows of the black meetinghouse that loomed larger as we approached—perfect for our coven's attack. We twelve formed an arrowhead as we sped forward; the wind whipped our hair behind us, our skirts fluttering like black wings. Our bare feet skimmed mere inches above the earth that was scorched brown, dead and brittle by Inferno's breath. It had been a hot, dry summer.

Entering the village proper, we locked the families within each house we passed, hexing fast every window, shutter, and door.

Just before the village commons, the darkness of the Puritan faith descended upon us, engulfing our number whole and entire, blotting out the meetinghouse.

As one we opened our Third Eye. I searched ahead, the wondrous witch's sight piercing the blackness of ignorant theology and hatred of all not like them. Small figures clad in white robes emerged from the meetinghouse and lined up in front of the black-washed two-story building.

"Begin attack?" Raveneye said.

"Stand fast, sister," I replied. "Those are children." I slowed my approach.

"No, Ravenheart!" Raveneye hissed, her head whipping around as she turned on me, Third Eye blazing. "They are Puritan spawn and stand between us and our sister imprisoned within! Tear them apart, I say, children though they be!" Her words were a spray of spittle that sizzled like fat in fire when

229

striking the ground, her black hair a halo of snakes that whipped about her head.

Low growling rose from our sisters, akin to that of a hungry tiger, and I placed myself between them and the village. "*I said. Stand. Fast.*" My voice the sibilant warning of a copperhead coiled to strike.

"What about Ravenborn?" said Ravenwing.

"Aye," said Ravenbeak.

"Aye," said them all, Third Eyes like lanterns shining between brows – human eyes white and blind stared behind nearly invisible lids.

"Shut up, you quims!" Ravenclaw hissed. "What shite out of the world's arse is this now?"

Two of the children stepped forward, trembling, holding hands. Each I reckoned to be ten summers old. A boy and a girl. They became wreathed in undulating coal-black tendrils of smoke that detached from the darkness. Those finger-like-wisps savagely poked their way into their nose, ears, eyes, and mouth; silent screams were clearly writ upon their young faces. They started shaking uncontrollably. Bones cracked in their hands as they gripped tighter and tighter. They didn't cry out, though the pain must have been fearsome indeed. Their mouths stretched so wide the corners split and bled.

Sweat ran freely. As did tears.

Their eyes filled with blood then blackness as their heads suddenly collided with a sickening crack. Their heads merged; the twisting flesh of their faces blackened as a heavy bone-ridge formed across their foreheads.

Horns, sharp and black, pushed out the sides of that monstrous head then curved forward. A thatch of white fleece-like ringlets draped down above four black eyes set in a line above a wide black nose. The thing snorted, nostrils flaring above a lamb-like mouth.

I stared, struck dumb by the unholy yet most impressive sight before us.

All the other children were in the midst of the same metamorphosis.

Their tattered robes split to reveal a heaving, muscular chest as the children's bodies drew together. I blinked at the mino-taur-like abomination. Something large and knuckled could be seen moving beneath the skin of the chest. A sharp cloven hoof struck the ground, and it bellowed. Part roar, part bleat that built to a crescendo of the children's screams.

A chill coursed down to the very center of my heart.

"What the f…?" Ravenclaw said, the rest of her word carried away by the guttural bleating and screaming of the grotesque creatures arrayed before us. "Are those…?"

"Sodom's whores!" Raveneye exclaimed. "*Bulls?! Lambs?!* No, *both!*"

Eight bull-lambs stood before us on five legs, each measuring from six to eight feet at the massive, hunched shoulders; each with four black eyes which held a bright star-like light in the centers. Sharp curved horns, and great snapping teeth charged toward us.

One rammed Raventree into the ground, her head exploding in a mist of blood, brain, and bone. Another tore away half of Ravenfeather's face. Her Third Eye glowed fiercely, and with a look she broke the beast's legs, shattering them at the knees, then punched a hole in its head before collapsing onto the carcass's twitching side.

"Fall back!" Raveneye shrieked, as her right hand disappeared into a blood-stained maw.

"No!" My banshee-scream pierced through the sounds of battle. I grabbed one of the beasts by the throat, and with a word my hand doubled in size, morphing into a raven's talon. "Kill Them All!" I yelled, tearing the head off the beast.

"Be a kindness indeed if someone would disperse this Puritan-fouled darkness!" Raveneye complained, turning just in time to impale a charging monstrosity through its two center eyes. Her skeletal hand broke off and lodged in the beast's skull. "Fuck!" She held the stump up to her vex-writ face as the creature fell dead at her feet. "That was just growing back!"

Ravenwing, dark of complexion and often mistaken for a

child, darted about the commons, laughing and taunting the snorting bull-lambs into a hackle-raised fury. When two charged at her, she leapt into the air, pebble-textured flesh ending in claws sprouted from her legs and arms.

Spinning like a pinwheel, she removed the head of one bull-lamb as it passed beneath her. Its head spun off its body in a red spray, while its huge black and white fleeced body lumbered a few steps before collapsing, thick dark blood pumping from its ragged neck. The other bull-lamb charged from the darkness behind her.

"Ravenwing, look out!" I cried and moved to protect her.

She replied with her customary insolent smirk and took to the air once more. The bull-lamb's horns missed her by the slimmest of margins. "Oh Ravenheart, that's so sweet of you," she replied, and scythed down like a falcon, her claws slicing the beast neatly in two. Its blood and entrails spilled hot and steaming onto the ground, front and back halves falling to lean forlornly against each other. "No need to fuss so." She smiled gleefully, hovering in the air.

I rolled my eyes at her and shook my head; *this is what happens when you indulge a child* – but I wouldn't change it for the world.

Ravenstar, Ravennight, and Ravenstone – sisters of the Coven of the Unkindness, but also by birth – stood together as always. They let loose hobbling spell after killing spell at the stampeding bull-lambs circling them. The beasts emerged for mere moments before vanishing again into the darkness. The sisters three cursed and blasphemed the creatures while criticizing each other's conjuring prowess and aim. Their voices shrill and sharp as a flock of common bats.

Ravenstar and Ravennight both cruelly berated Ravenstone when one of the largest bull-lambs, its four black eyes glittering fiercely, lurched from the darkness. Its horns impaled Ravenstar and Ravennight together, threw them off and trampled them into the ground. It struck down Ravenstone with its massive head, who joined her sisters in the thunderous roar under the beast. Gouts of blood stained that pure white fleece crimson and spattered the ground.

As one we screamed in fury as the beast returned to the safety of the darkness.

Ravenmoon, the fairest of us after Ravenborn, rose into the gloom, singing a spell devised by Morgan le Fay; rumor had it that the Lady of the Lake was as easily distracted by the female voice as well as face and form. Ravenmoon's voice was as beautiful as her fair countenance, and halted the beasts attack just long enough until...

Wait, wait...

Ravenmoon blinded them with spears of the quicksilver light of a full Harvest Moon, casting the meetinghouse and all around it in stark relief.

Twenty Minutes Earlier...

"Make ready, brothers," Lieutenant Josiah Goodoath said, standing at the pulpit dressed in an ordinary soldier's open-necked shirt, wool stockings and trousers all shades of brown as he consulted the watch he'd pulled from his black waistcoat. "The sun is setting. The Witch Daughters of Eve will come at us with it behind them, make no mistake." His storm-gray eyes rendered all the more wild-looking, magnified by the thick, yellow-tinted discs of his handmade spectacles secured to his head by a length of tanned witch flesh.

"Sharpshooters, make ready," Sergeant-Major Trask barked up at the four men atop ladders spaced two feet apart, each at a window with a clear view of the village commons.

Forged in the three-year bloodbath of King Philip's War, formerly in the Essex regiment, the militia men loaded their flintlock carbines; with powder and ball rammed down the smoothbore barrel, they primed their flash pans as though one man.

"Ready," they reported in unison.

Goodoath strode to stand behind the witch they'd captured cavorting naked with her familiar by a brook. He pressed the muzzle of his pistol hard against the back of her red-haired head.

Even though the iron of her shackles was thought to impair her powers, he was loath to take any chances – the only good witch was a dead witch.

"Still nothing to say, hmmm, devil's strumpet?" he whispered, his breath hot and foul.

The witch swallowed down a choke, his body smelled worse. She stood mute, still naked. Mercifully, her hair was so long it covered much of her body, including her arse.

Goodoath stared at the meetinghouse doors, averting his eyes from the naked woman with an effort of will he convinced himself was worthy of a Puritan Saint, one of God's Elect. As he backed away from her, he pressed the pistol's barrel against her head for emphasis and directed her attention to the meetinghouse doors where eight pairs of white-robed children he and Trask voluntarily (or by force) took from their homes when they marched into the village at twelve of the clock this day.

"Look at them, Witch," Goodoath said. "God's children, innocent lambs; knowing only God's goodness their pure faith and hearts will be you and your sisters-in-sin's undoing, as your unholy Godless knot will soon discover."

While he ranted, she opened her Third Eye, which rushed through the 'lambs' and out the doors seeking her sisters, the Coven of the Unkindness, she knew were coming for her. Even though the cost was that the iron manacles that bound her wrists and arms seared her flesh like the stings of a dozen hornets, the pain drove her on. After all, agony untold was the currency of magick.

At last, she heard it – the raven's plaintive call for one thought lost to the Unkindness.

A single tear fell down her dirt-smudged cheek.

"That will avail you nothing, Witch," Goodoath sneered. "Soon you will join your infernal whores in the flames of the pyre – nothing compared to the eternal flames awaiting you in Hell."

"I'm looking forward to reveling in your screams," said Sergeant-Major Trask. "Wicked wench."

A sound like the rustle of silk filled the meetinghouse.

"They're here." Goodoath smiled broadly. "All right, children, take each other's hand, go forth and stand outside where I told you. Have no fear, our God will cloak us in the darkness of His wrath – *you* will become the instruments of His Holy and Righteous Judgment!"

Trask opened the doors, scratching his arse through dark brown trousers as the children filed out.

Goodoath raised his arms high. "Protect and defend Your servants, Oh God, in our battle to smite the Enemy!"

A black cloud formed overhead and descended from Heaven upon the children and commons, and in the instant before Trask shut the doors, Goodoath's eyes beheld the wild-haired witch women floating above the ground, their black skirts snapping like banners in the wind. "God's Love goes with you into battle, my lambs," he whispered fervently.

The village commons echoed with sharp reports of cracking bones louder than a concentrated volley fired by battle-hardened troopers.

"Sir," Trooper Thomas Wheeler said, his voice nearly lost in the fearful din.

A rumbling, horrific bleating rattled the windowpanes and coursed the innards of the men.

"SIR!" Wheeler shrieked, close to hysterics.

"What is it, private?" Goodoath replied, lipless mouth pursed in annoyance.

"The children, they... they're... God in Heaven, have mercy on us!" The young man's eyes bulged as he stared out his window, unable to look away from the snorting horrors that moments before had been *human – children*.

"Steady man!" Trask shouted, as he stomped bow-legged across the floor and kicked Wheeler's ladder, causing the private to hang on for dear life. "You question Lieutenant Goodoath's orders or God's purpose here again and I'll pitch you off that ladder myself!"

"This is God's Mercy, Wheeler," Goodoath said, quietly. "He is protecting us, just as He's protecting those children."

The floor shook beneath their feet. The troopers shuddered as the meetinghouse filled with the diabolical shouts of the witches without; their shrieks set their skin crawling.

All except Goodoath and Trask, who went about calmly checking their pistols were loaded and ready; Goodoath's sword and Trask's hatchet and knife honed to flesh flaying sharpness, the two preened and strutted about, jabbing their blades at their witch prisoner laughing like inmates in an asylum.

Buffoons, the witch thought, her Third Eye watching as they capered about, smirking that they thought themselves expert swordsmen. Her confidence came abruptly to an end when she realized that this band of buffoons, Goodoath's Witch Finder Irregulars, had tortured and burned scores of medicine men, as well as dozens of witches.

The Puritan leaders of the Massachusetts Bay Colony had commissioned other like forces in their campaign to destroy the Devil and all his agents – meaning all unbelievers.

Turning her Third Eye outside, she shuddered when her witch sight came upon her sister Raventree, her eyes staring out of a face made as flat as parchment, a halo-like spray of blood and brain matter around it.

Sister Ravenfeather's body lay sprawled across the carcass of a gigantic malformed lamb, the right side of her face gone. Blotches of bone showed through blood – her Third Eye glowed ever so feebly until going dark altogether.

The surviving monstrosities snorted and stomped about the commons; their black hooves scarring the ground in their relentless desire to trample her sisters into dust.

So this is what the Puritan God does to His children. Always knew he was a perverse old maniac.

Searing pain snapped her Witch Eye shut, and her human eyes opened, streaming with tears. Her head was yanked back so hard she thought her neck would snap.

"Didn't think you could ignore that," Trask said, looking into her eyes as he gripped a fist full of her hair, the blade of his large knife cool against her throat. "Would you like to hear what

I'm going to do to you with my knife before you burn, witch harlot?" he whispered, breathless, his coal-black eyes alight but as soulless as any demon.

"Sergeant-Major!" Goodoath shouted.

Trask snapped to attention, releasing her. "Sir!"

"Attend to the battle at hand first. Afterwards…" Goodoath said, standing close, "you may indulge your love of butchering, as always. But do leave enough of her alive, mind you. Mustn't cheat the flames," he said, winking.

"Thank you, sir!" Trask replied with a malignant smile, suggestively waving his knife around the witch's mouth. "Sharpshooters, make ready to aim and fire at Lilith's Daughters," he said, hands on hips. "*Witches only!*" he added.

"Sir!" The four men answered crisply, opened their windows and sighted targets down the barrels of their flintlocks, elbows resting on the sills.

✞ 🍷 ✞

Troopers Woodcock, Fairchild, and Hopkins had been with Goodoath and Trask since the summer of 1675, the outbreak of King Philip's War; while Wheeler was only recently drawn from the Essex Regiment to replenish their ranks and had been with them for a fortnight. Though even the veterans had never engaged in an all-out battle with an entire knot.

Despite the wonders and horrors their eyes beheld, they had an unshakeable faith in Lieutenant Goodoath. Surely only one of the Elect could perform such miracles in His Service.

Woodcock had taken aim at a pretty, fair-haired witch, while Corporal Fairchild's barrel was pointing at a one-handed sorceress whose hair looked like slithering black snakes. Hopkins kissed the stock of his flintlock while peering down the iron sights at the ebony-haired witch in the center, one of her hands a monstrous black talon dripping red. A bull-lamb lay in a widening pool of blood at her feet.

And Private Wheeler held a shaky aim on a witch so

slight and small he at first feared was a child; then the devil's handmaid leapt into the air and put down one then two bull-lambs, removing the head of the first and cutting the second in two with black claws while cackling in a most dreadful manner.

Woodcock's target, the pretty witch, rose suddenly into the air, disappearing into the darkness. "Mr Trask," he whispered urgently.

Suddenly rays of light brighter than the full moon at harvest time lanced down, blinding the bull-lambs and troopers alike.

"Fire!" Trask shouted, hands shielding his eyes against the unnatural illumination. "Fire at will!"

✟ ⚱ ✟

The Present...

The village commons trembled as we, Sisters of the Coven of the Unkindness who lived still fell upon the remaining bull-lambs as they stood bewitched by our radiant Ravenmoon.

As we tore through the beasts – now defenseless as lambs – we bathed naked in the blood that spattered our bodies, delighting in our red orgy.

A shot rang out.

"Ravenmoon!" I cried when her light winked out, and she spun through the dusky sky. Snarling, I whipped my head back to the windows where I saw a shower of sparks and heard another blast of musket fire.

Raveneye's mouth fell slack, her blood-stained fingers clawing the powder-scorched edges of the hole that opened in her throat. Her eyes bulged, mouth working mutely as she fell face first into the dirt.

Another shot.

Ravenwing cackled uproariously, then darted effortlessly out of the ball's path.

"Sisters! With me! The windows!" I shouted; sharp ebony talons extended from my fingertips.

Ravenbeak, Ravenclaw, Ravenwing, and Ravenstorm

joined me, unleashing the grating war cry of the Coven of the Unkindness, and we shot forward, a ball narrowly missing my head.

Reaching the meetinghouse, we scaled its surface, black talons digging easily into the planks.

At the window above the doors, I snapped the musket barrel pointed at my head, in two. The soldier's eyes widened as I squared my shoulders and brazenly thrust out my breasts. I smiled fetchingly at him, then showed him my true face. My skin turned gray-green, my cheeks hollowed, exposing the bones of my skull. Then I opened my Third Eye.

The man's face turned white, his eyes glazed over, drool dribbled down his chin.

I caressed his flaccid face with my talons, leaving behind long open cuts which did not bleed. *"You're mine now."* I whispered. Then lifted him off his feet and threw him out the window.

Woodcock, Fairchild, and Wheeler watched with horror as Sergeant Hopkins' body flew from the window, twisted in the air, and hit the ground with a sharp crunch.

"Report!" Trask shouted, pistol in one hand, hatchet in the other.

The three troopers pointed their muskets at the raven-haired witch bobbing in the air outside Hopkins' window, and fired together.

"Ravenheart!" Ravenwing screamed.

"Don't carry on so, little one," I called down, safe from my perch at the roof's edge.

Ravenwing laughed so hard she held her belly.

"Shall we, sisters," I said, "while they're reloading?"

✟ ♆ ✟

Trask watched as, one by one, black talons grabbed the troopers by their heads then yanked them out of the windows. "We've been breached, sir!"

Lieutenant Goodoath tsked loudly. "I find your conduct in the face of the enemy unbecoming, Sergeant-Major Trask," he said, every word a blade.

The stout, bulldog-featured aide de camp turned to see Goodoath stroking the witch's red hair like he was petting a favored hound. "SIR!" he shouted in consternation as four witches pulled themselves in through the windows – a nightmare vision.

"That will be quite enough, Master Trask," Goodoath said, raised his pistol, and put the ball between the sergeant-major's surprised eyes, the impact snapping his head back. As his body fell, the witches dropped to the floor.

✠ ⚱ ✠

I gazed down at the corpse with the hole in his forehead, and tucked hair behind my ear. "Well that may not have been my choice, considering," I said to the man who stood behind and to the right of Ravenborn.

Ravenwing, Ravenclaw, and Ravenbeak surrounded the Puritan witch finder, Third Eyes alight, their faces hideous.

He shrugged and dropped his smoking pistol to the floor. "I don't need him, or the others."

Ravenwing laughed in his face and spit. "Just *you*, against the five of *us*?" She turned around, bent over and farted.

I laughed along with my sisters.

"Six," the witch finder said and removed Ravenborn's shackles. They fell to the floor with a clang.

"You're insane," Ravenborn said as she stepped to my side.

"No, red Jezebel," the Puritan replied calmly. "I am a Saint." His gray eyes were wide and large as an owl's behind his spectacles.

"Not for long," I replied. "My sisters."

Ravenborn's hair formed into a halo around her head, then burst into flame. Her Third Eye red as a smoldering coal, crimson talons extended from her fingertips as she levitated above the floor.

The rest of us followed. "Let's make this nice and slow," I said.

The Puritan backed up a step, then two, his giant eyes darting frantically. "My God, give me the strength of your killer angels!"

Ravenwing closed on him a dark blur, opening a gash on his cheek that bled profusely. She smiled, examining her handiwork. "You want to be a martyr?" she asked, leaning in. "*Good. Martyrs die slow.*"

I backed the witch finder against the pulpit and lifted him off his feet, pinning him there while Ravenwing, Ravenstorm, Ravenclaw and Ravenbeak flayed his legs and scourged his torso, black curved talons removing strips of flesh that curled up before fluttering to the floor.

"God... God... God." The witch finder wept, then started laughing like a maniac.

I dropped him to the floor.

"At least he's enjoying himself," Ravenwing quipped, then doubled over, eyes bulging, black blood spraying from her mouth.

The witch finder's laughter turned into a growl. His bottom jaw cracked and jutted out, two large fangs slicing through blackening gums.

We backed away, hissing and slashing. Ravenwing coughed her last as the Puritan pulled out his silver fur-covered claw from her stomach. His lantern-yellow eyes examined the blood dripping from the long claws with curiosity. As his other hand transformed, he ripped off his spectacles and howled.

His nose flattened; a silver widow's peak of coarse fur raced over his head. His eyebrows thickened, arched extending to the temples as his ears blurred then became black and pointed. His shoulders broadened, ribs cracked as they expanded and he howled in pain and rage, rising to a height of eight feet of fury.

Ravenbeak leaped at him, the shadow of black wings shredding the air, her talons extended like sabers.

The transformed witch finder batted the talons aside with ease and grabbed her by the throat, squeezing until snapping Ravenbeak's neck. Snarling, he threw her body against the pulpit, rendering the wood to splinters. Growling low, he marked my sisters and I with amber eyes.

We answered that challenge with shrieks.

Ravenborn distracted the man-wolf with the allure of dancing flames about her head, while Ravenclaw and Ravenstorm dropped and scuttled across the floor.

The wolf's right ear twitched, then his left. He blinked.

"Stop!" I cried as the beast pounced.

His clawed foot crushed Ravenclaw's head in an explosion of gray and red.

Ravenstorm, hissing and spitting, coiled herself around him, her fangs flipping forward like blades – beads of venom glistening the tips.

The man-wolf seized Ravenstorm's serpent-like neck and twisted it savagely, then roared his triumph holding her body aloft like a trophy.

Ravenborn's Third Eye flared like the sun as she speared toward him. The wolf-man swung Ravenstorm's body like a lash; her fangs still dripping with venom narrowly missing Ravenborn's taut stomach.

At my command, the meetinghouse doors swung open. One by one, four shadowy figures filed in.

The man-wolf stared, sniffed, and growled when the four former troopers stepped into Ravenborn's light, their movements stiff and lurching.

Poppets, we called them.

The wolf-man howled, but their corpse-gray faces didn't flinch.

I inclined my head, my Third Eye setting the hex marks on their foreheads alight. "Now poppets. *NOW!*"

Pinning his ears back, the lycanthrope snarled and slashed

at the closest poppet. I raised it into the air like a marionette and swung its hand down hard, breaking the beast's four fingers. The wolf-man howled in pain. Ravenborn's light blinded him, and I inched my poppets closer. Closer.

A bestial scream of red agony slashed the stillness.

The yellow eyes of the beast darted frantically over the poppets encompassing it– the blades of silver that had once been their hands slowly twisted in its innards.

Slowly, whimpering miserably, the human Puritan slowly emerged. The pain of transformation no doubt terrible, but he didn't feel it – the agony of the silver blades eclipsing all else.

Ravenborn and I floated down, settling gracefully on the floor.

"We wanted you to know that *you* didn't lure *us* into this battle. *We* lured *you,* and *I* was the *bait,*" Ravenborn said, leaning in close.

The witch finder's eyes widened, and he choked on the blood flowing from his mouth.

With a blink of my Third Eye, my poppets set to butchering.

"Burn this unholy meetinghouse to the ground, my sister."

✠ ♟ ✠

Firelight turned night into day as my poppets gathered our dead. On our way out of the village, we unlocked each house, freeing the villagers; after all, we are not monsters.

We felt the heat of the fire on our backs, the smell of burning wood filled our noses as we sought the comforting coolness of the night, and the feathery embrace of Raven's wings.

SPEEDLIGHT

Mike Barretta

We can't leave an enemy behind us. We take it out," said Captain Jonathan Graves. He glassed the Speedlight project with his binoculars and saw only the tip of the iceberg. Nondescript, windowless, concrete buildings, empty parking lots, overgrown vegetation, weedy and yellow, whether from the drought or blast effects of the nuclear strike, he didn't know. Ninety percent of Speedlight lay safely hidden underground in a limestone cavern, undiscovered by the Aculeata. They had no idea the instrument of their death was beneath their feet.

"Pretty risky waking up a hive," said Staff Sergeant Mike Polanski. "We could work our way around to the entrance."

"This many humans, this close to a hive? They'll smell us out no matter how much neutralizer we use. We need to give Dr Stone time to work uninterrupted."

"Your call," said Polanski.

"Only one sentinel," said Graves. "Lightly armored. Unarmed. Two or three inside. The rest of the hive should be responding to the diversion or foraging. Quigley's the best shot. He can take the sentinel out and assume overwatch. The rest of us breach, destroy the hive, and save the world."

"What's left of it," Polanski muttered.

Three billion people died in the initial attack. Another billion or so from starvation, disease, petty human conflict, and worst of all, Aculeata predation.

They retreated to the cover of the 100-car pileup on Interstate 10 east of Pensacola, Florida. Door were ajar, belongings strewn. Silvery craters and heat scars blasted into sheet metal. Dried crusts of brown blood and diamonds of shattered glass. No bodies, though. The escaping civilians were overrun and over-whelmed. Even if killed, the Aculeata did not waste protein. Those captured alive were carried off to an even worse fate.

Dr Amanda Stone spoke up. "Encountering any Aculeata jeopardizes the mission. Combat command opened up an entire front to pull Aculeata forces away from us. We shouldn't risk it."

She would know, thought Graves. She was the mission. But she wasn't in command. Not yet anyway.

"I ain't opposed or nothing," said Sergeant Nathan Flynn, "I got a hard on for killin' bugs, but I got concerns. They got antenna like a radio. They can read each other's minds."

"They are sensitive to electro-magnetic energy, but that has nothing to do with their antenna. And they can't read each other's minds, " said Dr Stone. "And they can't read ours either."

The Aculeata were not a hive mind, but they did chemically transmit information with perfect fidelity from one to the other with their antenna. Their culture, their collective memory, their god was molecular. Each Aculeata was highly conforming but just as individual as any human.

"But we don't really know that, do we?" Flynn offered conspiratorially.

"We do, Sergeant. I know. I've had plenty of time to study the Aculeata and you've killed enough of them to know they aren't magical."

If anyone knew the Aculeata it was Dr Amanda Stone, polymath of the highest order.

"EMP warheads have fried this theater of ops," Graves said. "No Aculeata dropships have come down so the only way any message is getting out is if it is walked out. We can't leave a hive right on top of us. We destroy it."

Two days ago, Graves had watched hedge-hopping cruise missiles carrying EMP warheads streak in, pitch up into the lower atmosphere and detonate, frying any unhardened electronic equipment with massive jolts of induced voltage. Aculeata tech was far more sophisticated than humanity's but much less robust. The EMP attack and precision munitions reduced local

Aculeata forces to parity with humans. Now, they had a chance. None of Aculeata's fancy beam-weapons would work and they had yet to field reliable, chemically-driven, projectile weapons in decisive quantities. The only functioning soft electronics within 300 kilometers were theirs. Speedlight's systems were safe from the attack. The ultra-hardened equipment was buried deep in a limestone cavern. It would take a direct hit from an Aculeata bolide, like the ones that took out Earth' major cities, to destroy it.

"Captain?" Polanski interrupted. The man was clearly irritated at the delay "Your orders."

"Quigley, take out the sentry and assume overwatch. The rest of us stay undercover until the deed is done. Then we assault the hive."

The team took their positions under cover of the wrecked vehicles while Quigley and Graves belly crawled back up to the ridge.

"Goddamn it," said Quigley. He wiped sweat from his brow then sighted through his scope. Graves knew Quigley's field of view was filled with the triangular black and yellow head of the alien. Unlike humans, the Aculeata didn't have a proper brain, but there was a sufficiently large cluster of neurons in the space between their eyes that a headshot would drop one instantly. In that regard, they were pretty much like humans.

Graves spotted with his own sight. The creature's wasp face turned and looked directly at him. Relaxed antennae tasted the air. Serrated jaws worked back and forth gnawing on nothing but the creature's own fear. Aculeata were not inclined to conversation. In their cosmology, humans were somewhere between vermin and sacred cow, but enhanced interrogation techniques suggested an interior life just as complex as any human's.

"Take her when you are ready," Graves said.

"You got it," said Quigley.

Graves watched the Aculeata through his scope. Aculeata were quite beautiful in a murder hornet kind of way. Deep, shiny black skin, graceful limbs with translucent serrations that caught the light like jewels. Bands of red or gold or brilliant emerald green. Faceted crystal eyes. Even their wasp-like faces were pleasant until their mandibles scissored open and clamped down hard enough to cut through bone.

He heard Quigley exhale, emptying his lungs, and, in the span between heartbeats', the silenced Remington chuffed and the .308's bullet smashed into the Aculeata's head at twenty-seven hundred feet per second. Vaporized brain matter and blood misted the air in a pink cloud. Shattered chitinous fragments spun away. The Aculeata dropped into a messy tangle of limbs as if touched by the hand of God.

"It ain't my Blaser, but it will get the job done right, " said Quigley.

"Good shot."

"And just so you know, if a bug cavalry comes over the horizon, I am going to be pissed," said Quigley.

"Noted. Get comfortable. We'll be back in a minute." Graves waved the team up to join them.

"I'm going in," said Amanda.

"You do not want to go into a bughole," said Flynn. "They'll get in your head with them antennae."

"Captain?" asked Amanda.

He had just assumed she would stay with Quigley. No one volunteered to go near a hive. Take her in or leave her out seemed like pretty even propositions. Endless mental debate was not his style. No one survived vacillating in occupied territory. She had basic tactical training. She might be useful.

"Stay close, keep up, and don't make me regret it." Getting her to the project was the entire point of the mission. With a single push of a button, this woman could wipe out the Aculeata high ground and turn the war.

She nodded acknowledgement.

He shouldn't worry too much about her, he rationalized. Farm girl. Trim. Athletic. Not your typical egghead. Pretty deft hand with rifle and sidearms on the range and a survivor of the evacuation when the Aculeata overran the area. That had to count for something. Besides, she would be surrounded by guns.

Graves reached the entrance first. Flynn flanked the entranceway opposite. The team split up: Polanski and Dr Stone lined behind Graves. Corporal Murphy and Petty Officer Grace took position behind Flynn. Sculpted representational figures of divine Aculeata and agonized humans decorated the hive entrance. Pheromonal scent signals, indecipherable to human senses, accompanied the sculpture. Before entering a hive, Aculeata touched the lintel with their sensitive antennae to reaffirm their faith and identify the occupants. Aculeata hives were home, temple, and military production facility.

"What does it say?" asked Polanski.

"Enter unto our temple, where the flesh of this world is made holy," said Amanda.

"Nice," said Polanski. "Let's start desecrating."

"Will, grab that fucking body and drag it out of here," said Polanski.

Petty Officer Grace grabbed the dead Aculeata by one of its six limbs and dragged it behind a cluster of palmettos. The alien's limbs were wrapped in a silky fabric that shimmered like oil on water. Light armor plated its segmented body. Its holster was empty. Any gun it had would have been neutralized by the EMP attack. Will kicked the pieces of shattered skull out of sight and scuffed his feet to dust the ichor before spraying a chemical neutralizer to cover any pheromone death signals the creature's body exuded.

Graves surveyed his team, looking each in the eye, checking for readiness. He nodded and descended the dark, smooth-walled tunnel in a slight crouch. Glowing glyphs and sigils offered messages of greeting and faith. The pheromonal stench was so thick that even a human could smell it. If it had a message for humans it would be: Get the fuck out.

Graves held a hand up to stop his team. A thick fibrous curtain separated the hive proper from the entrance. He pressed his back to the wall. He didn't have much time. The Aculeata did not need to see to be alerted. They would smell him. The neutralizer spray could only delay recognition of an intruder. He parted the curtain with the tips of his fingers and peered in. Silvery light, more than enough to shoot by, suffused the room.

Naked human bodies, pale with reflected light and shimmering with sweat, lay about in random formation upon the birthing room floor. Two Aculeata stalked the living bodies. Caregivers. Their delicate antennae caressed the humans, tasting their sweat. One bent low and hovered over a man. It cradled the man's face with delicate forelimb pincers and turned the man's face to meet its own. It opened the man's mouth and extended its rostrum, the tubelike structure used for fighting and feeding.

The Aculeata vomited up a bilious, gray palp. The man gagged, choked and swallowed reflexively like a sleeping, suckling baby. The Aculeata, tenderly combed the dribbling palp from the sides of the man's face. It moved on, surveying the rest of its charges.

Aculeata were all born warriors. Their bodies hard and chitinous, festooned with sharp ridges and serrations. Powerful oversized jaws designed for ripping and tearing. If Aculeata lived long enough, they became like these caregivers. Softer. Fatter. Slower, but still immensely dangerous. Graves held up two fingers and designated the general direction Sergeant Flynn could expect his target.

Flynn nodded.

Graves held three fingers up and indexed them into a fist. One. Two. Three.

They stepped through, sighted, and shot near simultaneously. Graves' target twitched its head towards him and caught the bullet just below its left compound eye. Hydrostatic pressure exploded the crystal eye. The creature squealed in unexpected pain and shook its head casting gooey strands of clear ocular fluid. It was probably dead, but it refused to fall – its limbs locked in a supporting geometry. Graves fired again and the head came apart. The creature collapsed.

Sergeant Flynn downed his target with a single round to the skull. Right in the center, hitting so hard that remains of the head hyperextended the neck and snapped it backwards. The headless Aculeata pitched back, spewing blood from its slender neck in an arc before sprawling across captured humans.

Sergeant Polanski, Corporal Murphy, and Petty Officer Grace, followed a step behind, flanking left and right along the circumference of the circular chamber, opening each other and providing cover.

Graves and Flynn advanced deeper, stepped over paralyzed humans, rounding the central supporting pillar.

"I think we got 'em all," said Flynn.

An Aculeata warrior dropped from a concealed perch on the ceiling. It landed on top of Flynn knocking him to the floor. It hoisted its abdomen for a killing strike with its ovipositor. Two shots rang out and the alien's body bucked from the impact. Then Polanski fired a three-round burst and cut the alien in half. The creature's upper body twisted and sheared away, the lower half's legs kicked a furious, impotent tempo, carving bloody chunks of flesh from silent humans.

The upper half of the alien, a warrior and not caregiver, spun about to face him.

"Hooman," it said.

It clambered over bodies, stabbing its forelimbs into captured humans to pull itself forward, dragging a tail of bloody viscera. The alien opened its serrated jaws wide enough to cleave a human thigh. Its rostrum extended.

Flynn shot it through the mouth.

"Clear?" asked Graves.

They both looked to the ceiling, expecting to see more alien horrors.

"Yea, clear now," said Flynn.

Dr Stone held her H&K .45 two handed. Instinctively aimed. She was the one that had fired the two shots that saved Flynn. Graves looked to Flynn and then her. She nodded back.

"Good idea taking the lady in with us, huh?" said Flynn. "Thanks. You can holster that now."

"No, I'm going to hold onto it little longer. It makes me feel better." She pointed the gun wherever she looked. Her trigger finger lay along the slide. Her wrists were strong and she had confidence in her ability to handle the weapon. No timidness at all.

Light emanated from the stained-glass wall. The birthing room had the sacred hush of church. In the center, a five-meter, thick luminous gray pillar served as structural support and point of focus for Aculeata faith. Aculeata scripture wrapped the pillar. The room would have been beautiful were it not for the paralyzed humans swollen with Aculeata larvae. Most were dead-eyed, catatonic and given over to the horror of being eaten alive from the inside out. The Aculeata had a symbiotic reproductive relationship with another species that did not survive the journey to Earth. They were forced to parasitize themselves to survive. When they got here, their promised land, they discovered humans were acceptable hosts. It confirmed their belief that Earth was a divine gift.

"I knew," said Amanda, "but it's different seeing it. It's horrible."

"No loving God could design such a monstrous reproductive cycle," said Murphy.

"No human God anyway," said Graves.

"That's not exactly true," said Amanda.

✠ ♆ ✠

"Over here. I found someone," said Amanda.

Graves joined her and they knelt by the side of an older man, mid-sixties, though it was hard to tell given his condition.

Petty Officer Grace joined them.

"Dr Linus Beckett, Senior Project Scientist at Speedlight," said Amanda. "Can you wake him?" she asked Petty Officer Grace.

"Atropine should do it, but do you really you want me to?"

"We need to talk to him," said Graves, trusting Amanda's request.

Petty Officer Grace took an atropine injector from a side pocket on his uniform trousers, bit the cap off and spat it out. He stabbed the man in the meaty part of his thigh and held it until the injection hiss stopped.

The man's eyes drifted open as the atropine released his muscles from the Aculeata toxin.

Amanda took the man's hand. Tears glistened in her eyes. "Linus," she said. "It's Amanda. Can you hear me? Linus?" Her voice quavered such that it was hard to understand.

"Amanda?" asked Linus. "I dream. Amanda, I dream of the stars and they are horrible. It takes eons to cross space. They made it here because they believed."

"I know, Linus," she said.

Interrogations suggested the Aculeata were once an advanced, rational society, having forsaken the supernatural. They calculated the time required to voyage to another star but did not account for the effect such vast amounts of time would have on them. Somewhere between stars, on a failing starship, they succumbed to the terror of the endless night and rediscovered God. Who else could deliver them?

The old man's stomach bulged and twisted, and his eyes widened with abject horror as realization hit.

"No, no, no," screamed Linus. "No, dear God, get it out, get it out, Oh, Jesus, I'm sorry. Get it out. Get it out. Getitoutgetitoutgetitoutgetitout."

Whatever information she wanted to get from the man was irretrievable. "Give him a pill," said Graves.

Petty Officer Grace pressed a .22 caliber handgun to the man's skull and pulled the trigger. Linus Beckett's head bucked but the low velocity round did not exit the skull. It bounced around chewing up the brain. Humans did not recover from an encounter with an Aculeata.

"No," said Amanda. "No. Oh, God. How *could* you?"

The old man's belly distended hideously as the larvae panicked.

Amanda scrambled backwards as the larvae self-aborted. A translucent sack bulged from Dr. Linus Beckett's abdomen split like a pale mushroom erupting from the earth. It flopped out of the man's belly and rolled to the ground. Fibrous umbilicus feeds that connected the sack to the doctor's intestines tore away leaking blood and nutrients. The sack ruptured gushing yellow liquid and squirming, mewling Aculeata larvae.

Amanda gasped.

Graves stabbed a pale larva and held it up. Strings of mucosal amniotic fluid dripped from the wriggling, half-formed Aculeata. He twisted his wrist to ensure she saw the creature from all angles. Pale multi-jointed legs kicked the air. Soft mandibles worked back and forth. Even this young they were capable of severing a finger. The rostrum, a tube-like stabbing structure hidden behind the mandibles emerged and dribbled pre-digestive fluid. The Aculeata dissolved their prey and slurped them up. He had trod through many a greasy puddle that used to be people or anything else Aculeata thought worth stabbing. There wasn't much Aculeata didn't find appetizing on Earth. No wonder they thought it a promised land.

"This is a holy war," said Graves. "There are no compromises. We can't reach an accommodation with a species that has a divine mandate to do this to us."

The dying grub let out a kitten mewl, and he flicked it off his knife against the wall. It stuck for a moment and then slid down leaving a shiny trail of fluids from its burst body.

One of the larvae had taken to gnawing upon a sibling. "A plague of demons," said Graves.

A plague of unarmed demons thanks to portable EMP devices. Without their energy weapons, Aculeata relied upon speed, ferocity, and the razor-sharp serrations that edged their limbs. Every human they took could host five or six Aculeata. Their army built rapidly. Aculeata were born formidable and chemically indoctrinated with all they needed to know about Aculeata faith and culture. The hard chemical coding made them extremely resilient in the face of adversity and terribly resistant to innovation. Even after five years, they were poorly equipped for war with humans, but that god-forsaken starship gave them an insurmountable high ground advantage.

SPEEDLIGHT

Sergeant Polanski stepped on each larva, adding pressure until their exoskeletons burst open with a satisfying gooey pop.

Amanda took a deep breath and calmed herself. "Linus refused to abandon the project when we evacuated. If Speedlight works, we can thank him."

"We just did," said Graves.

✝ ♟ ✝

Quigley wiped sweat from his eyes and thought this whole operation was a bad move. He understood Captain Grave's concerns. He just didn't agree with them. His home, Sydney, Australia was in a completely different hemisphere and he didn't know what had become of it. Quigley had come to America as an exchange instructor for the US Army Rangers, but when the Aculeata struck, all air travel had been cut and he found himself trapped on the wrong side of the equator. As a sergeant with the 2nd Commando Regiment, his skills put him in high demand. His American comrades gave him the call sign 'Quigley', and he knew better than to fight it otherwise a worse one was coming his way. Maybe 'Dundee'. The best way home was to kill the nasty buggers as fast as possible.

He caught movement. Three Aculeata warriors emerged from a tree line of oak and sycamore. The last in the procession dragged a stung human, a woman as far as he could see.

Keying his radio would alert the team and the Aculeata. They had a highly developed electromagnetic sense that contributed to the myth of a hive mind. Two more, unencumbered with human prey, appeared.

He keyed his radio. All five of the Aculeata froze, antenna erect, forelimbs curled back tight to body – an alert posture, trying to divine the bearing of the broadcast.

"Foragers. Five. Incoming."

He took advantage of the freezing behavior and shot the one closest to the tunnel entrance. He fired again and another fell. Three remaining. The survivors ducked into the hive entrance, abandoning their human prey. He shot her in the head.

The spot between his shoulder blades itched, a shadow dimmed the light. He rolled fast swinging the muzzle to bear on the source. The Aculeata seized the end of the muzzle and pushed it up and away as he pulled the trigger. The Aculeata stabbed its head down, rostrum extended from between splayed jaws. Quigley dodged his head away and the needle mouthparts buried in the dirt. He released his weapon and grabbed the extruded organ with both hands and pushed it viciously to the side against a gaping mandible, wrenching the creature's head sideways. He heard the cracking of cartilage. The creature shrieked, backpedaled with its four legs, pulling him up to his knees. He shot a foot out to dig into the dirt and yanked hard on the rostrum, hyperextending the organ. The Aculeata screamed a few octaves higher in response. Something gave in the back of the Aculeata's throat and the organ pulled from its attachment point like the sudden release of a bush breaking from the soil. The creature coughed pale, pink blood and pelted him with weak panicked blows that slashed his body armor and helmet.

"HOOMAN DIE!" said the Aculeata from its tympanic organs at the base of its throat.

The creature vomited an acidic pre-digestive from its rostrum that coated his ceramic fiber gloved hand. A bit of the vomit leaked through at the wrist and if felt as if his hand was immersed in fire. Quigley released the alien and peeled the burning glove from his hand. He punched the thing in its faceted eye and shattered it, sinking his fist into thick goo. The wounded alien backpedaled again. Its rostrum swung loosely as it retreated. At least it couldn't bite him without severing its own organ.

"Got a fuckin' dick in your mouth, mate," said Quigley panting.

Vestigial wings no bigger than a human hand buzzed, pumping air through the cooling chambers that used to be spiracles

"Sucks, doesn't it?" said Quigley. He was breathing hard himself. "I ain't here for a fair fight, mate." Quigley reached for his sidearm to finish the creature off. Gone. He crouched lower for his boot knife.

Something hit him hard from behind pushing him toward his enemy. He sprawled forward and another Aculeata, a flurry of entangling limbs was upon him. The Aculeata rolled him to his back and straddled him, seizing his arms and legs by ankles and wrists, pinning him down spread-eagled so hard it threatened to dislocate his joints. He was stronger, but Aculeata could mechanically lock their limbs into position to facilitate a stab with the smooth, sharp ovipositor extending from the abdomen. The alien curled its segmented abdomen and hoisted it high.

With panicked strength he pulled his acid burned right hand, tearing skin, lubricating his hand with blood. It slipped free of the Aculeata's grip. He punched the creature in one of the left forearm's elbows, buckling the joint. He threw his weight carrying the momentum of the collapsing alien and rolled even as the creature stabbed into his body armor with the force of a boxer delivering crushing body blows. He rolled on top, face-to-face with the giant insectoid. Jaws snapped inches from his face. The other Aculeata having differed, charged in to help. Quigley saw his Glock 21; reached for it. Since his arm was conveniently pointed in the right direction, he fired three rounds into the abdomen of the charging Aculeata. The Aculeata beneath him bit down on his gun hand severing tendon, muscle and bone as the serrated mandibles meshed. He screamed and head butted the alien. The alien curled its lower body tighter and stabbed its dagger ovipositor. He felt the ovipositor slide along armor plate and through a gap. He felt a burning pain in his hip as the Aculeata pumped him full of venom. The Aculeata wrapped him up, pulling close. Quigley's leg muscles stiffened, pulling his limbs into contortions. His stomach muscles and sphincter seized cramping his whole body into a tight rictus of pain.

His transdermal trigger sensed the Aculeata toxin spreading through his body.

"Fuck you, mate," said Quigley before his jaw locked up.

No one recovered from an Aculeata sting. No one would want to.

The wearable Anti-Aculeata mine detonated spraying high velocity tungsten ball bearings vaporizing the middle third of the Aculeata's body. The small backblast of the shaped charge was enough to blow apart his descending aorta.

"Incoming," said Graves.

Two Aculeata tore through the curtain, taking huge leaps faster than the eye could follow. Corporal Murphy let loose with the M280 squad automatic weapon chewing up the wall just behind the blindingly fast Aculeata with the 7.62 rounds. The glass-like panels shattered into razor sharp shards.

The third entered. Hesitated. Graves shattered its jaws with a single shot. Another caught it in the throat and it went down shrieking, spraying blood. It rolled to its back and death spasmed.

One closed on Petty Officer Grace. Bullets spanged off appliquéd armor. The alien slashed with its razor-edged arm and opened a gaping red wound across Grace's throat. Arterial blood sprayed. Grace dropped his weapon wrapped both hands around his throat to stem the flood and collapsed, making wet, gurgling sounds.

Back at the central pillar, Amanda took a weaver stance and emptied her magazine at a jinking Aculeata. Her firing pin fell on an empty chamber. A long, sustained burst from Murphy's SAW and the Aculeata blew to pieces before it reached her.

The last Aculeata hit Graves like a runaway truck, bowling him over backwards. Hard appendages grappled for his wrist and ankles even as they tumbled over impregnated humans. The creature slammed its ovipositor into him trying to find a gap in the armor. It was not the careful hypodermic insertion to deposit eggs but a vicious stab intending to disembowel.

Graves punched the alien between its eyes, stunning it. He punched again and again shattering the creature's face and knocking the jaws crooked. The alien lost its fight and lay still, panting. Its vestigial wings buzzed. Graves got up out of reach of the dangerous ovipositor and rostrum.

"Are you all right, Captain?" asked Polanski.

"Yea, fine."

Sergeant Polanski reached over his back and grabbed his daddy's sawed-off Mossberg 900. He pressed the barrel to the head of the alien and pulled the trigger.

Chunks of Aculeata sprayed. Gun smoke and the pheromonal stink of dead Aculeata fogged the room. Every breath tasted bitter.

Graves recovered his weapon and gave a long last look at Petty Officer Grace. "Motherfuckers," he cursed. "Get to Quigley," he said, though he knew what they'd find. Suddenly it didn't seem like such a good idea to destroy the hive.

✝ ♆ ✝

Their mood was sullen. Grim. Two team members down for no effective gain. Graves took point and led them to the Speedlight Complex in silence. Amanda overtook him when it came into view. This was her backyard and the sooner they got inside, the sooner she would be in charge.

"This way," she said, leading them to a rather innocuous, unmarked metal door that hung half open. Dried, brown leaves and dirt lay in drifts. Aculeata hoofprints marred the dusty floor around the emergency generators, switchboards, and mechanical pumps. Aculeata had investigated the building and found nothing. She walked to a large circuit breaker panel and flipped select breakers to off and was rewarded with the sound of bolts withdrawing.

A panel swung open.

A secret door yawned into darkness.

Amanda headed toward the door. "No one thought the Aculeata would attack the Gulf Coast of the United States and overrun the project except for Yuri, a Russian mechanical engineer on the project. He built this little bit of maskirovka."

"What is maskirovka?" asked Polanski.

"Russian doctrine of military deception and camouflage," said Flynn.

"Good thing he did," said Graves. "What happened to him?"

"I don't know."

They entered, shut the door behind them, and descended a spiral metal staircase bolted to the circumference of a deep shaft. Fluorescent lights provided weak pools of light that did nothing to alleviate the impression they were descending into hell.

"Speedlight is built from repurposed cold war infrastructure," Amanda said, leading the way. "Eglin Air Force Base was for testing and evaluation. The locals called it Area 52. Gulf Breeze, Florida, just down the road a bit, was once the UFO capitol of the world, probably because of the work they did here."

At the bottom of the shaft, she typed a code into an armored door's high security lock. She reached into darkness and flipped switches. Banks of stanchion-mounted lights illuminated the gloomy outlines of an immense limestone cavern. Towering stalagmites reached for descending stalactites. Pillows of rock and frightening organic shapes painted in mineral pastels glistened wetly. A gigantic sphere, like a chrome football wrapped in scaffolding centered the immense space. A path led to a windowless blockhouse atop a shock-mounted platform directly beneath the sphere.

"We're here," she said.

Cool, damp air chilled Graves' skin. Water droplets falling into puddles broke the silence. At the blockhouse entryway, she opened another code locked door. Slumbering consoles crawling with low bandwidth data streams illuminated the interior.

"Sergeant," Graves said. "Form a perimeter in case we have guests."

"Give me your mine," said Polanski.

Graves unclipped his anti-Aculeata mine from his chest and handed it over.

Polanski turned to Flynn and Murphy. "Let's go. Nothing in here but science shit."

Amanda sat at a console and brought up the illumination. Graves watched over her shoulder. The computer woke at her touch and she typed: SPEEDLIGHT ONLINE to Space Force Command at Wallops Island, Virginia. '"Response will be slow," she said. "Communications are by extremely low frequency antenna buried in the ground. It's not good enough for timely targeting data but it's undetectable."

She typed commands in the console and brought up a large, wall-mounted monitor of Earth.

"Orbital parameters," said Amanda. "There's a network of optical telescopes tracking the Aculeata starship." She touched a line of data. "This is telling me, no change. They haven't moved a goddamned millimeter since we evacuated."

"They don't think we can touch them," Graves said.

"We can't. Not with anything physical. The Aculeata have been shooting down dust motes at relativistic velocities for millennia. Our fastest rockets climbing out of a gravity well are really no problem for them."

"We have eighty-seven minutes to install the initiator and fire if we're going to hit them in this orbit, otherwise we wait another cycle."

A chatroom window opened. 'ACKNOWLDEGED. PROCEED', responded Wallops Island. All of humanity's eggs were in one basket and Dr Amanda Stone was the hand that carried it.

"Now what?" Graves asked.

"When the system goes active, a network of S-band radars and LIDAR will paint the Aculeata starship, and a patched together network of cellular antennae, hardlines, and HF burst transmissions coordinated by Wallops Island will provide real-time targeting data to Speedlight. Those facilities will get one or two transmissions out before the Aculeata detect and destroy them."

"Is that enough?" asked Graves.

"I have faith."

"Come on, let's install the initiator," said Amanda.

They exited the blockhouse and climbed a ladder mounted on the exterior of the building and another to the bottom of the sphere. Graves spotted Polanski, Flynn, and Murphy deployed in an arc facing the silo entryway. Power cables as thick as a telephone poles and blocky waveguides converged upon the sphere, rose up, and wrapped it in a chaotic embrace.

"The cables lead to buried banks of ultra-capacitors," she said, drawing Graves' attention. "Aculeata Tech. They'll jump-start the magnetic compression cycle."

At the bottom of the sphere, she opened a hatch and they climbed in to stand upon a metal grate platform. She shrugged off her back pack, set it down, and took out a polished sphere the size of a softball.

"The initiator," she said, "is a Bose-Einstein condensate of positronium stabilized in a room temperature super-conducting matrix wrapped in a shell of iron." She set it in a fixture attached to a skeletal arm.

"Looks like a small cannonball."

"And about as heavy."

The arm redeployed, elevated until it reached the center of the sphere.

"You can't see them," Amanda continued, "but at the top of the sphere there's a bundle of hexagonal rods made of the same superconductor that shrouds the condensate. That bundle is the collimater array. It focuses the released energy into a single, coherent beam."

"It's big. I'll give you that, but it doesn't look impressive enough to destroy a starship made of solid rock."

She looked a bit disappointed in him. "The sphere captures a 100-megaton detonation pinched by an ultramagnetic field. The collimater array focuses the blast in the form of hard ionizing radiation that will burn every organic molecule on that starship to ash."

"I stand corrected."

✛ ☗ ✛

Dr Stone sat down at the firing console. "We only get one shot at this. The Aculeata will respond fast." She typed. INITIATOR

INSTALLED. SYSTEM NOMINAL. SWITCH ACTIVE MODE?

With a nod, she said, "Fifty-eight minutes until the Aculeata ship enters the projected beam path."

"Will they find us?"

"Yes. Definitely."

ACTIVE TARGETING ENGAGED. PROCEED.

The ninety-inch tactical display symbology switched from blue passive optical tracking to red active radar – laser tracking. The orbital track of the Aculeata starship was calculated to the hundredth decimal point. Secondary displays showed live images of the ship, a craggy spindle of ancient rock wrapped in mining equipment, manufactories and weapon stations. Aculeata, highly tolerant of vacuum exposure swarmed the hull. The Aculeata starship swung in its constant orbit as S-band radars and Lidar beams swept across it. A pulse of light flashed on the surface of the ship.

"Aculeata bolide and energy fire," Amanda explained.

Columnar text data vanished as stations and data nodes were destroyed from orbit.

She armed the weapon. The clock decremented. Active targeting stations dropped off line. Her display flickered back and forth between red and blue. Active and passive. "I argued against active tracking. A passive track is good enough even for a beam as narrow as Speedlight, but the increased cloud cover from atmospheric debris hasn't settled out and imperfections in telescopic sights convinced my superiors to use active tracking."

"What does that mean?"

"Red data is best. Blue is good enough. Yellow is project-ed. Projected means that we can't see the starship and calcula-tions are made as to where we think it is based upon last known parameters," said Amanda. "They're maneuvering."

Engines flared on the Aculeata ship.

✠ ☗ ✠

An explosion rocked the blockhouse and it went dark. Screens blinked and came back up. Standby warnings flashed.

Gunfire erupted from outside.

"Breach," said Polanski over the radio.

Graves gathered his rifle.

"John," Amanda said, grabbing his arm. "When I fire this weapon nothing outside the blockhouse survives."

He nodded and exited, ensuring the door was secure behind him. He heard the sustained ripping of the M280 SAW at a rate that would burn though the ceramic barrels. The atmosphere was hazy with shattered limestone and gunpowder. Crimson beams of Aculeata energy weapons slashed the cavern.

Rapid responders. Fanatical Aculeata troops that probably came down from the starship. Graves probably triggered the response himself when he destroyed the hive. He leapt from the blockhouse platform into a puddle. Murphy poured M280 fire into the doorway and Aculeata bodies piled up. No sooner did one go down, two others took its place. They pushed through the kill-zone by holding up the bullet-soaked corpses of their siblings as augments to their armor.

Graves filled the gap between Flynn and Polanski. Aculeata were through and moving with blinding speed, leaping from stalactite to stalagmite and diving behind cushions of accumulated minerals. He didn't need to win this fight, he just needed to delay losing it. A beam of crimson light raked across the rock in front of him. Molten spall splattered his face and the odor of cooked meat filled his nostrils. An Aculeata leapt from cover, suspended in space and he fired a wasteful burst into its center of mass. The creature hit the ground, legs kicking in agony. Another appeared and he shot it with greater discipline.

Despite the gaps in the line, they held. A single Aculeata carrying something flanked far left out of contact heading for the sphere. He shot. Missed. Flynn caught the leaping Aculeata with a burst of fire. The alien tumbled out of sight and exploded. It was carrying demolition charges.

"Fire in the hole," said Polanski over the radio.

Graves instinctively ducked as Polanski set off the Anti-Aculeata mines. Explosions shook the cavern. Aculeata body parts hurled through the air. The pheromone stink of their ruptured bodies permeated the cavern.

Flynn dashed from cover and landed breathlessly at Graves' position. "I think we lost Murphy. I'm almost out. Got Ammo?"

Blood-red emergency light filled the blockhouse. The primary display flickered blue. Passive tracking. Good enough as they still had eyes on the starship. It was changing its orbit with agonizing slowness. It took a lot of energy to move a rock that big. They knew the Aculeata were fast, but they'd thought the active sites would last longer. Nothing from Wallops Island. Its lifespan was measured in minutes once it went active. More disturbing to Amanda was the lack of ELF signals – broadcasts pumped directly into the ground, impervious to detection unless the right earth-bound equipment was in place.

Speedlight still reported nominal status. All of the components were operable and ready to fire. Even through the thick reinforced concrete walls of the blockhouse she could hear the sustained gunfire and explosions and wondered how long before something critical was destroyed.

At zero time, she would fire. Inside the block house, a calculated detonation null point, she gave herself a 50% chance of survival. It was all theoretical. Outside, there was no chance.

An Aculeata leapt to stalactite and clung. A commanding position. It fired down, beaming through Sergeant Flynn. In a nanosecond, his body's water molecules superheated and exploded, blowing his armor off like bark from a lightning-struck tree.

Graves moved as beams of light trailed him. He took cover and found Murphy's M280 SAW. Blood and greasy stringers of gore slicked the weapon. He swung the barrels to the overhanging Aculeata and released a sustained burst of 7.62 rounds that disintegrated the Aculeata. Body parts rained down. Burned blood steamed from the rotating barrels of the empty gun.

"John, get your men inside the blockhouse. Three minutes until I fire," said Dr Stone over the radio.

Graves didn't answer her. Polanski, the only surviving team member would either retreat to the blockhouse or hold position until the end. Cordite and the stink of burned meat hung in the air.

Graves reached the blockhouse platform and used the elevation to shoot Aculeata. Red beams scoured the blockhouse, but it took more than a Aculeata-portable weapon to penetrate six feet of steel-reinforced concrete. Polanski limped into view, dragging a blood-soaked leg. Graves covered him.

The door opened behind him. Polanski climbed the steps, and they backed in, firing. An Aculeata leapt from the roof of the blockhouse, spinning like some horrible falling angel. It landed on the platform and its arms lashed out like a sparing boxer with its fingers squeezed together to form a natural blade that punched into Polanski's throat and face. It hooked Polanski and pulled him out.

"No," Graves screamed, and pointed his weapon. A crimson beam lanced out, melting the SAW and spraying his face with molten metal. The pain was excruciating. Amanda seized him by his collar and yanked him backwards until he sprawled on the floor. She body slammed the door shut and leapt back to her console.

Graves took in a secondary screen, his face afire. The aft end of the needle shaped rock of the Aculeata ship was bathed in actinic bright light. They were maneuvering out of the beam's cast. Amanda adjusted the collimater array to keep the ship targeted.

The secondary screens blinked out. The primary display icons turned yellow. Projected data. No one had eyes on the ship. "Please, God," he said aloud, speaking to a God he had stopped believing in when his family disappeared into the Aculeata onslaught. "Please, God," he said with the fervent hope of the reborn. "Let them die."

Amanda looked at him, eyes wide with disbelief.

SPEEDLIGHT

The timer indexed to three, two, one.

Zero.

She pressed the button.

Ultra-capacitors discharged with a roar that shook the shock-mounted blockhouse. His head burst with pain from the sideswipe of the ultramagnetic field. Meteors streamed across the underside of his eyelids. The matter and anti-matter matrix collapsed to a point singularity.

Annihilation.

In a fraction of an attosecond, before the sphere was destroyed, the collimater captured and focused the immense energy from the detonation. A beam hotter than the creation of the universe burned through the roof of the cavern. Unnatural light erupted. Vaporized rock fountained into a fifty-kilometer-high cloud. The shock wave of super compressed air rolled out, flattening everything from Tallahassee to Mobile and setting the panhandle of Florida ablaze. A beam of pure white light jacketed the invisible gamma and x-rays that split the sky.

In the null point of the detonation, Captain Jonathan Graves and Dr Amanda Stone lay on the floor screaming, hands clasped to ears to block the very sound of obliteration. The vibrating roar, the voice of a vengeful, angry God filled their skulls to bursting.

Graves couldn't tell how long had passed when he finally opened his eyes. A single point of light was all that he could see. His head pounded and he could taste blood in his mouth. He lay quietly as his eyes adjusted to the dark. The void took form. He saw Amanda, reached for her. He took her hand and they pulled close to each other. His throat was raw and angry. Her breath was warm on his neck. "Did we win?" she whispered.

He didn't know the answer. How could he?

"Yes," he said. "I have faith."

SERPENT'S ROT

Justin Bell

Greece, 432 BC

Lightning slashed, bright and wicked, like the gleaming blade of Zeus slicing open the dark demon's belly of night. Screams shattered the still air, a rolling bellow of angry thunder threatening to drown out the pilgrims' misery.

"To the temple!" the old man shouted, his withered arm extended towards the stone structure barely visible in the fading electric heat of the storm.

"They are upon us!" another voice screeched, this one shrill and female, etched in hard fear. Figures hurtled through the night, men moving like whispers, sliding between shadows.

"Mercenaries!" shouted Lajos, turning and drawing his short sword, metal sliding from leather.

"Lajos, no!" his young wife pleaded, pressing her hands onto his shoulders. "Run with me! With us! With our children!"

"There are too many of them," Lajos said, "we will be overrun. Better to die looking my killer in the face than to take a spear in the back!"

"Lajos, please!"

"Take the children, Rada. Take the children and run. If I can hold them off, even for a moment, it could be just enough—"

His words broke. A spear shot through the darkness, its broad, metal tip colliding with Rada's left shoulder, a jet of dark blood erupting from the wound. Her scream, like the wail of biting wind, cut off as a second spear buried itself in her sternum, pinning her to the ground.

"No!" Lajos screamed, throat raw with fury. He dropped to the ground next to his wife, her body twisted above the hard ground. Clasping her hands in his, he squeezed and held tight, struggling to find the words to bid her farewell.

Not that it mattered. No light shone in her eyes, her lifeblood twisting down the shaft of the spear thrust through her.

Lajos drew in deep, sharp breaths, expelling air from his nostrils and whipped up and around, clutching his sword in two firm hands. "Show yourselves, mercenaries! Show yourselves!" His vision blurred with tears, his rage bulging his muscles, tendons pulsing beneath rain-slicked flesh.

More pleading screams echoed left and right, desperate cries choking off into wet gasps, the distinct sound of metal on bone and ripping flesh halting every voice one by one. Lajos charged forward, pulling his sword close, his eyes narrowing on the silhouette of a tall man huddled over the fallen form of an old woman, her cloak colored in deep crimson.

"Begone!" he shouted and leaped into the air, deftly avoiding a spear, and swinging his sword with all the might he could bring to bear. The mercenary whirled upon him, but his weapon remained buried in the body of the woman, and he faced Lajos unarmed.

Lajos' sword raked out and down, hewing flesh and muscle, ripping open the man's chest, engulfing himself with a jet of arterial blood as he crashed into the man, already dead before he hit the ground.

Lajos let his knees strike his enemy's mangled chest and threw himself forward into a tight roll, coming up in a crouch, sword held close, eyes searching.

Already, carnage littered the flattened rocky terrain surrounding the temple. They were pilgrims, nothing more, desperate to visit this holy place, to bend their knee before the oracle, to swear fealty to Apollo and pledge themselves to—

"Fiend!" another man burst from the darkness, his sword slashing. Lajos lurched backwards, his blade clashing against the other, sparks dancing in the night. His hands hummed with each rattling impact, the blades banging hard, he and his foe performing an awkward, deadly dance.

Lajos slipped under a swift, flat strike and drove his blade deep, running the man through, stomach to back shoulder. Warm gore ran over his hands and arms, splattered the rocks at his feet, his toes wet within the threadbare sandals. Something squished between them, but he ignored it as he sprinted forward, yet more darkened shapes converging.

"Hadrian! Padma! My children!" He screamed into the night, already knowing he'd hear nothing in return. There was too much chaos, too many screams of the dead and dying, voices audible over the banging of swords striking stone and spears ramming bone.

Somehow Lajos slipped beneath another spear thrust, narrowly avoided two deadly sword strikes, hurtled through the crowd of approaching mercenaries, thirsty for blood and desperate for death.

"The temple!" a voice cried from the darkness, a voice high off the ground, and Lajos heard the shrill neighing of horses, the thrashing gallop of hard hooves on ground. Chaos surrounded him, corpses splayed about the earth, enemies descending upon men and women who were his friends and family— fellow pilgrims in search of something to believe in.

Horses charged from the night, large beasts, hooves pummeling those too slow to get out of the way, a large group of them galloping across the rock-littered ground, barreling west towards the temple.

The Temple of Apollo. Residence of the Oracle of Delphi. The place Lajos and his fellow pilgrims had sworn to travel despite all the dangers.

But they weren't the only ones traveling. Mercenaries from the surrounding villages, rode on horseback and carried swords, shields and spears. Up against them, Lajos and his pilgrims were little less than chattel.

Lajos turned left and right, searching for his children, searching for rescue, but saw only blood and death.

Thrusting his sword to the ground, he dropped to his knees, tears stinging his eyes, his bones weary, his body weak.

Another horse screamed from the night and Lajos lifted his head, watching its rider. A large, bald man who would have been taller and broader than Lajos even off of his steed. His head ducked low, a leather cape snapped in his wake. There was a long sword in a sheath strapped over the man's arched back as he guided his horse toward the temple at top speed.

Lajos watched him go, remaining on his knees, quietly begging Apollo, but fearing the only answer he'd receive would be silence.

✦ ☖ ✦

The mighty steed galloped towards the steps of the temple, the broad, white columns surrounding the structure, pale in the low light of dusk and storm.

At the steps of the temple, he saw two of his men clasping an old, robe-draped pilgrim between them. Despite the pilgrim's advanced age and his crooked spine, the man jerked in their grasp, his leathery face a mask of rage.

"Release me, dogs!" he bellowed as Valter swung down from his horse. He gripped the hilt of his sword sheathed at his back, which had a dramatic effect on the withered old man, who seemed to shrink, drawing into himself.

"Please, kind sir," he whispered, his voice fragile, suddenly subjecting to Valter's imposing form. "We are but lowly pilgrims, coming to offer fealty to the Gods... Apollo watch over us and —"

"You are but lowly sheep braying at the altar," Valter spat. "And what are sheep but to be slaughtered?" His hand tightened on the hilt of his sword, a flash of metal slewing through the scattered rain.

The old man fell with a wet thud, his head separated from his shoulders to tumble down the dirt slope from the temple. Valter climbed the steps, his two men falling in behind him. All around, other mercenaries dismounted, taking up arms and following him toward the temple.

"Pythias? Is she here?" Valter asked, his voice a low whisper.

"Aye," his man replied with a curt nod. "She'll not be pleased to see us, especially with blades covered in pilgrims' blood."

"I have no care to please her," Valter replied, threading his way between two massive columns to breach the inner sanctum of the temple. "She simply stands in the way."

As they entered the inner chamber of the Temple of Apollo, Valter could almost taste the low thrum of electricity permeating the entire structure. Hair stood up on his arms, and a low tingle rippled through his teeth, his cracked lips spreading to a crooked grin beneath his dark beard.

They stepped into the threshold – a large, open chamber surrounded by columns and in the distance, the vague, robed shape of Pythias, the Oracle of Delphi. Energy crackled from her as she stood; strange, rippling waves of heat emanated from her and the chalice mounted upon a platform to her right.

Valter's heart hammered and he felt a low pang of deep need, a hunger that went far beyond mere food. A hunger for power.

"Who goes there?" Pythias asked, her voice a low, slithery inquiry.

Valter strode forward without fear, sword in hand, his eyes narrowed and focused on the chalice at Pythia's right hand.

"You dare?" she asked, turning towards him, her green eyes narrow, gleaming slits from the darkness within her hood.

"I do," Valter replied without hesitation. "Ares compels it."

"Ares? This temple is a testament to his brother — the power I draw from Python's rot, a mighty serpent slain by Apollo himself. What would Ares have with it?"

"Ares cares not for slain pythons or for withered old hags draped in robes. He sees the pilgrims flock to this place, Apollo basking in the adoration of these religious zealots, and it sickens him."

The oracle stepped forward, a strange, sliding grace to her gait, a withered staff clutched in her left hand.

"Ares treads dangerous ground, mercenary," she hissed. "He knows not the power that lies—"

Valter lunged. His sword struck, a swift bolt of slashing metal. A muffled, hissing grunt came from the robed woman, and she stumbled backwards uncertainly, then collapsed, her robe flattening around her slender corpse, dead on the temple floor. Strangely colored, viscous blood eased out from beneath the piled cloth, following the strange, lined contours of stone.

The mercenary smiled, eyes scouring the chalice, and he stepped forward, clutching the metal cup within his palms. Wisps of pale steam stroked the air, like hot springs on a winter morning. Valter leaned forward and inhaled, drawing in the potent fragrance.

"Lord Valter?" one of his men asked, taking an uncertain step backwards. "Are you certain that is a good idea? Ares demanded that—"

Valter shuddered, his bones locking, muscles tensing and twitching. Pain raced through him, tiny daggers stabbing from within, every limb and every fiber suddenly aflame with hot, sharp agony.

✢ ☗ ✢

Lajos stopped, stared into the temple. "No," he whispered as he saw the corpse of the Oracle of Delphi splayed upon the floor. The large man on horseback, the mercenary leader was drawing in from the chalice, the secret energy that provided Pythias with her visions.

But… something was happening. Something the man hadn't expected. He went rigid, his face twisting up to the sky, a deafening shriek of horror and pain splitting the relative silence. Lajos could hear the man's bones snap, a brittle cracking like dried sticks, his limbs twisting apart, splintering and reforming.

Skin burst open along his arms, ripping from tendon and muscle, blood spilling to the stone floor of the temple as the man's scream curdled like spoiled milk. It broke into a wet, hissing snarl and as Lajos looked on, the torn flesh began knitting into thick serpent's scales.

Vapors began filling the chamber – a thin cloud of pale, purple smoke slid from a fissure in the stone, rolling over the floor like thick morning fog. Each mercenary within its grasp shouted and screamed, clutching at their face, doubling over, skin boiling, popping, then knitting back, bones ripping askew like the sallow drumbeat of stone on skull.

Figures emerged from the vapor, scale-covered and slithering, and Lajos' eyes widened, his own fearful shriek forming on his thin lips.

✦ ⚱ ✦

Fear chilled his veins to ice, but Lajos forced himself forward, sprinting through the narrow trees of the forest, the wails of dying pilgrims fading low in his ears.

The wails were horrific, the stuff of endless nightmares, but it wasn't the wails that gripped him in the iron grasp of terror now. It was the hissing. The relentless, piercing hisses of their pursuers; rasping, throaty snarls of the men— no, not the men— the *things* chasing them. Perhaps they had been men once, but Lajos had watched their transformation with his very eyes.

"Faster, Lajos! Run faster!"

"My children," he gasped, ducking a branch, looking at the man shouting to him, "did you see them? Are they alive?"

"Nothing is alive!" the man shouted, and as if to punctuate that fact, one of the beasts lunged from an upper branch, slamming into the man, driving him down, jaws closing around bone in a sickening wet crunch that temporarily clouded the screams.

"No, oh no no no," Lajos pleaded, his eyes stinging in pain. For a moment he considered returning to the temple, searching for his children among the dead and dying. But he knew he would not find them alive. There was no one alive back there. As evil as the men who attacked them had been, these creatures were worse.

A shrill screech pierced the forest and his head snapped right, watching just in time to see another escaping pilgrim enveloped by a leaping monster, dragged kicking to the ground, claws slashing.

Lajos tried to push the terror from his mind, tried to focus only on escape, only on his legs pumping.

He didn't even hear the low hiss of the serpent to his left, the sudden blur of movement catching him by surprise. Then it was above him and on him, gaping mouth filled with ivory knives. Fangs punched into his neck, pierced his skin and the swirling crimson darkness of agony swallowed him.

✛ ☗ ✛

Rain and wind whipped at the surrounding tents, cloth snapping beneath the churning roll of thunder.

A lone soldier stood at the north edge of the small encampment, a lean, bearded man in battered armor, his fingers closed around the slender shaft of a tall spear, shield clasped to his left forearm. He wore leathers over bare arms and thick, metal shin guards above his sandaled feet.

"Markos, do you see something?"

Markos turned and watched the approaching figure, a slender, but tall woman, cloaked in deep green, a hood pulled over long, brown hair. Her eyes gleamed softly in the starlight.

"I hear it," Markos replied. "Screams. I fear our travel to the temple has taken too long. We were meant to defend the pilgrims, but—" he turned his head slightly, straining to listen.

The woman came up next to him. "I hear them as well. We would have reached them by daylight. Were they not ordered to wait for our signal?"

"They were. But when it comes to visiting the Oracle of Delphi, men are sometimes compelled by forces beyond their own choosing."

He turned back to the village, which was little more than a scattering of thatch-roofed huts, several smaller tents erected throughout the dirt covered roadways and narrow passages. Several figures moved between buildings, most of them women, tending to and assisting Markos' men.

"It was kind of you to offer refuge," he said.

"The village is not ours," the woman replied, "we are passing through, same as you. On our own voyage."

Markos nodded, his eyes roaming over the various women tending to campfires, offering food or drink, providing nourishment to his small group of Spartan soldiers.

"Whatever the circumstances, we are in your debt, Demetria."

"There is no debt, Spartan," she replied, "it is our honor to provide."

Markos nodded, deep in thought.

"What bothers you?" she asked.

Markos continued looking out toward the trees, his eyes staring off at some unseen item in the distance.

"I have family in my village," Markos said quietly. "My wife is ill. The village elders— they are not certain she will still be of this world when I return. She watches over my two sons, and I fear for them."

"Then why come? You owe the Delphi people nothing."

Markos scrutinized her. "Delphi asks for our help, so we come. My duty demands it. Honor demands it. I could not very well say no."

Demetria nodded in seeming understanding.

"What of you? This camp of your women. Are you pilgrims, like the others? Traveling to bend you knee to the oracle?"

An expression passed over her face that Markos couldn't decipher, a shadow coloring her features.

"That burden is not mine to share," she said quietly, looking in the same direction as Markos, back out into the trees. She tilted her head slightly, squinting into the dark forest.

"What do *you* hear?" Markos asked, facing the thick forest separating them from the Temple of Apollo and surrounding buildings. "The screaming has stopped, has it not?"

"Someone approaches," Demetria whispered, and Markos stepped between her and the trees, brandishing his spear, dropping into a fighter's stance.

"Approach with caution!" he bellowed. "Or I shall run you through!"

A shadowed figure moved through the forest, stumbling forward, barely holding himself upright. Leaves rustled in the low rain and he burst free, a pale-skinned man, covered in dirt and smeared with what looked like fresh blood.

"Gods," Markos hissed, taking a step back as the man stumbled to his knees, palms pressing into moist mud. A murmur spread throughout the nearby camp and figures came forth, approaching with caution, the Spartan warriors with swords in hand.

"Are you injured?" Markos asked, dropping to one knee. The man looked up at him, his face so white it could be transparent, blood raked down his face, his neck reddened and swollen with injury.

The man gasped, his cracked and bleeding lips trying to form words. "I— I am Lajos," the man gasped. "We were on a pilgrimage to the temple."

Markos lowered his head. "So I feared. It was our job to protect you."

Bubbles of spit and blood formed on Lajos' lips as he tried to speak, but instead broke down into a wet, ragged coughing fit. It took him a moment to compose himself. "We were attacked," he gasped, "they— they left me for dead."

Markos glared through the dim light, the wound at Lajos' neck was no ordinary cut or bruise. There were two gaping gashes in his flesh, festering slashes the size of knife wounds, pulsing with pale, green puss and viscous blood.

"What attacked you?" Markos asked.

"An— evil is afoot," Lajos said, struggling with the words. "Pythias— the Oracle of Delphi is dead. Murdered by mercenaries."

"No!" Markos said. "Why?"

Lajos' head shook. "I know not. But in doing so— they've unleashed horror— I—" Lajos coughed again, his lungs tearing with deep stabbing coughs. He spasmed, and vomited blood into the dirt at his hands, convulsing.

"Lajos! Speak!" Markos drew closer. "What did this? What evil?"

There was one more violent, choking shudder, then Lajos collapsed to the blood-covered dirt and lay still, the life finally seeping from his weary, wounded body.

✟ ☗ ✟

"Is this course of action wise, Markos?" Demetria studied the Spartan as he walked the line, scrutinizing the large gathering of men in his group. She tagged behind him, head lowered, trying to appear subservient as she probed him for answers.

"What would you have us do, Demetria? There are women and children in Delphi. We traveled all this way to protect the rights of these pilgrims, to allow them their religious worship. Does it matter whether they are attacked by mercenaries, Athenians or... something else?"

"Perhaps it doesn't matter," Demetria advised, "but it would do well to proceed carefully."

Markos' men were not a full army, but the vast numbers nearly filled the camp clearing. He turned to Demetria again, guiding her away from where his soldiers gathered. "Your advice is appreciated, Demetria. But battle is a man's world. Once we are victorious, we will return, and I look forward to your food and your healing. That is how best you may serve our cause."

Demetria's jaw flexed. "As you wish," she said quietly, a glint in her green eyes.

Markos nodded his agreement, then turned and strode towards his men. Some held spears, others swords. A large, broad-shouldered warrior at the end carried twin axes, one clamped tightly in each fist.

"Adelrick!" Markos said, nodding to the man. "You are our strongest. You will lead the charge toward the temple. Leave no mercenary standing, am I understood? Drive them apart, send them scattering, and we will follow your lead."

"By your command," Adelrick replied, his voice thick and deep, a curt nod emphasizing his agreement.

Moving down the line, Markos took in a smaller soldier,

narrow shoulders, trying to draw himself upright, to look taller and larger than Markos knew he was.

"Rajosh," he said quietly, and the young man flinched imperceptibly. "You are our fastest. Hang by the rear of the formation."

"But—"

Markos held up a single finger. "You heard me, boy."

Rajosh nodded firmly, his jaw clenching beneath the iron helm.

Markos lifted his sword and pointed it towards the trees. Lajos no longer lay on the ground by the edge of the forest, he had been carried away by the women, prepared for burial, and Markos hoped he would see his family again in the afterlife.

"We wait no longer," Markos said. "To the temple!"

His men shouted in unity, thrusting blades to the darkened sky, then fell in behind Adelrick as the large warrior charged toward the trees.

✝ ♱ ✝

Adelrick drew close to the edge of the forest, peering out at the pale ivory glow of the temple's columns. Figures milled about, roaming the grounds surrounding the structure. There was something odd in the way they moved – strange, jerking gaits, lurching and sliding. The men in his sights were not walking, they were— slithering?

"Markos," he whispered, turning back to face the leader of his group. "What I see— they are not men. They are—"

Leaves gently rustled around them, the trees shifting with motion. Not just before them, but behind and beside, the whole forest moving at once.

Markos' eyes narrowed, fingers closing on the contoured hilt of his sword. "Spearmen," he said, "at the ready."

The forest settled into a deep, dark silence, the leaves' rustling halted. The night drew down around them like a thick blanket, a void of light or sound, as if swallowed by oblivion.

Markos felt a narrow, cool bead of sweat track down his forehead, cling to the hard contours of his jaw and dangle there for a moment, hovering above the hard ground.

Suddenly there was a wet, rasping hiss, a breathy, gasping snarl from his right, in the thick cypress. Markos whirled that way, two of his spearmen converging on his location. Leaves exploded outward. A figure leaped. A man-shaped silhouette streaked from the copse, sword in hand.

Markos lashed out, sword swinging, then whirled and lifted his shield. Sword struck metal with an echoing crack, but the leaping man continued forward, landing too gracefully before streaking low and swift, slipping back into the trees on the opposite side.

"What in Zeus' name?" Markos gasped, twisting to look at where the figure had vanished.

"Did you see that?" another voice gasped. "The way it moved. It was not human!"

"He was a man, you fool!" Adelrick barked. "He had arms and a sword, I saw him!"

"He had no legs!" a shrill voice echoed. "He had only—"

The leaves burst again, coming from the direction the attacker had vanished, and again a figure leaped free. This time, in the soft glow of the pale, full moon, his face was clearly visible, much to Markos' horror.

It was a vaguely human face, oval-shaped, taut, thin flesh, leathery in texture, stretched over a narrow-tapered skull. His skin was a mottled green, the shade of rotting limes, eyes pulled wide with vertical pupils. The flesh on his face was not flesh as Markos knew it, but a myriad of layered scales, and that mouth pried open impossibly wide, revealing throngs of jagged, curled fangs.

Through the sharpened fence of teeth, a narrow, forked tongue flicked as the thing lunged, slicking along its pointed chin. As the abomination descended upon Markos, he saw that the shrill voiced warrior was right – it had no legs. Only a thick, meaty snake's tail, which struck the ground with a hard thud as it landed, before surging forward, sword in hand.

"By the Gods!" Markos shouted and lunged back and right, narrowly dodging the creature's wild swing. He got a better look at the beast; rigid scales covered most of the creature's body, its torso shrouded by scraps of torn cloth, what looked to be a shirt before it had been ripped asunder.

Narrow, bony arms ended in thick fists holding the handle of the sword, every inch of visible flesh was that same strange rotting green as its face. Against the drab muck of that skin, the pale eyes almost glistened like broad diamonds.

"Gorgons," Markos whispered, his voice tinged with fear. "The legends are real." Markos clutched his sword, dropping into a battle-ready stance.

The creature drew back, sneering, a facial expression somehow blending between human and serpent. Its massive tail supported it as it rose, lifting far taller than even Adelrick, pausing just for a moment before surging forward, swinging its blade yet again, hissing wildly.

Markos ducked low, the blade whispered over his hair, then he planted a foot and twisted around, swinging his own sword wildly. Somehow, the blade found its mark, steel biting scales, ripping free a small clutch of them and tossing them in the air like coins as the sword ripped into the yellowing torso beneath.

Dark green blood spewed forth in a wide arc. The creature howled and hissed, its single voice like a battle between python and man.

Holding his strike, Markos shifted, then stabbed, sinking his short sword hilt-deep in the creature's gut, right where its tail met its torso. The skin popped like ripe fruit, another broad jet of dark blood sprayed Markos.

"What manor of creature—?" the shrill voice shouted again, but then the leaves were moving again. All around them the forest shook, and then the serpents burst free. All around them, men with scales and claws and teeth and swords.

"They're in the trees!" a voice screamed from somewhere in the horde of Spartans, a voice Markos didn't recognize, but then again, he had so rarely heard stark fear in the tenor of his men's words.

"Adelrick!" Markos yelled, barely deflecting a spear strike with his angular shield.

The large man bellowed, leaping into the fray. Serpents had surrounded them, thick men with thick tales, scale-covered membranes slipping over fallen trees and dirt. Several were armed, but many weren't, lashing out at the Spartan warriors with claws and teeth.

Markos knocked his attacker's spear away and Adelrick lunged past him, swinging his axe, burying the blade deep in the crook of the creature's neck, embedding sharpened curved steel into bone and scale.

Ripping it free, the large warrior spun, swinging his second axe, this following strike ripping through the thick leather of the creature's neck, tearing through its spinal column and sending its narrow skull twisting into the air.

Markos turned back towards the others just in time to see one of his men raked with gorgon claws. The hooked talons tore ragged gashes through flesh and muscle. Another Spartan leapt over his fallen comrade, barely wincing as claws slashed at his armor, sending sparks dancing into the air.

Rolling with the impact, he landed in a low crouch and spun with his spear, crashing it into the rear of the creature's tail to little effect.

Drawing the blade back, he balanced, twirled the long weapon, then lunged, piercing the snake man's throat with its broad, metal tip, tearing scales and skin.

War ripped through the trees. Spears lanced the air, hurtled with swift ferocity, barbs embedding themselves in the chest of the gorgon enemies. Some of the snake men fell, others slithered atop their twitching corpses, hissing and slashing with claws, swords and fangs.

"Rajosh!" Markos shouted, seeing the young man through

the trees. He deftly dodged a sword strike, then drew his own blade, advancing on the gorgon.

"By your lead!" Rajosh shouted, clanging his sword against the others.

"Go back to the camp! Warn the others! They must fall back to Delphi, take shelter in the village!"

Rajosh bashed his sword against the snake man, then lunged forward again, his second strike sweeping clear.

"Now, Spartan!"

Rajosh looked as though he were going to argue, but finally just nodded, ducking away from a sword blow, then falling back. Another Spartan charged between him and his enemy, fighting off the attacking beast, then Rajosh spun and vanished into the trees.

Markos dodged a spiked flail hurtling just above his head, connected by a chain to a thick shaft clutched in the palm of a scale-covered fist. The spiked mace rammed into the narrow trunk of a nearby tree, embedding into the wood, splinters bursting splinters free.

His attacker hissed an angry, ragged sound, struggling to free the spiked ball, tail curling around the roots of the tree for leverage. Markos swung his sword, cleaving both hands at the forearm. The creature squealed and lurched backwards, splintered bone and torn flesh spurting pale, green blood.

"Fight, Spartans! Fight!" Markos roared, dodging the wild slash of another snake man, swinging his sword, but missing. The narrow skull of the enemy creature pitched forward, fangs bared, but Markos dodged the strike.

A man behind him wasn't so lucky. The Gorgon buried its fangs in the soft tissue of the warrior's leg, puncturing skin and breaking the leg. With a growling hiss, the beast yanked back, pulling the man from his feet and tossing him spine-first into a thick tree.

Markos charged the beast, sword flashing in a swift, two-hand arc. The creature spun back toward him – fast – slipping under the strike and lashing out with his tail. It struck Markos in the ribs like a hammer, lifting him from his feet and sending him tumbling sideways, his sword cartwheeling into the air.

"Halt, creature!" another Spartan shouted, leaping above Markos, spear in hand, thrusting it toward the Gorgon. The spear sunk deep into the creature's stomach, the snake man's mouth opening wide in a silent scream. Wrapping narrow, bony, green fingers around the shaft of the spear, the beast looked at the man who stabbed him, its mouth narrowing to a thin, upward slit. Grasping the spear, the creature pulled himself forward on it, impaling himself deeper, but drawing himself closer to the warrior.

The Spartan's eyes split wide, and he let go of the spear far too late. Surging forward on the shaft of wood, the gorgon dug his claws into the man's forearms then drove his gaping, tooth-filled maw onto his neck, ripping and tearing.

Blood spilled down onto Marko's face and he sputtered, rolling swiftly and crawling to his feet. He scanned the surrounding trees. Violence was all that he saw. Humans versus gorgon. Swords raked flesh, spears ramming through muscle and bone, teeth and talons shredding. The screams of the injured and dying flooded his ears, and he blinked away the red hue of death.

Two more creatures slithered over the uneven ground on their thick, unnatural tails, one held a broadsword, the other a pair of narrow, needle-sharp daggers.

Markos spotted a throwing axe resting in the dirt not far from him and he ducked low, bolting towards it as the creatures attacked. Sharp pain lanced along his left shoulder as one of the daggers hewed a jagged gash through his flesh. Dropping low, he slid over the dirt feet-first, one knee tucked beneath him, narrowly dodging a blow from the hacking sword of the second gorgon. Markos grabbed the wrapped handle of the throwing axe and planted his foot, stopping the slide, then turned, swinging the axe and burying it into the leathery hide of the serpent man with a wet crunch.

The beast howled, a mournful wail as Markos thrust a foot against the creature's chest and wrenched the axe free, spraying gore in thick strands. Continuing his backwards spin, he brought the axe back up and around, ripping the curved, metal blade through the thin tendons of flesh beneath the serpent's elongated jaw. Its head snapped back, separated from its spine, and tumbled to the dirt as the rest of the body slumped forward, convulsing.

Markos swept away from the falling corpse, releasing the axe. It tumbled end over end, wedging into the skull of the second gorgon.

Markos yanked a broadsword out from beneath the lifeless, headless body as chaos swirled around him like a tornado. Clasping the sword in both hands, he took stock. His men dwindled, forces shrinking by the moment, and though they took their pound of flesh, it was clear the gorgons were winning.

A brutal battle cry echoed from Markos' left, and he turned in time to see Adelrick barrel into one of the creatures, dodging a second beast's attack before using both axes to sever its head.

"There are many!" he gasped, down on one knee. Like Markos himself, his face was streaked with blood, red, black and green, his armor dented and scarred from numerous blows narrowly deflected. Markos nodded at him, his mind racing, not knowing what to do or how to react. Just beyond Adelrick, a young Spartan valiantly rammed a spear through the throat of a gorgon before three others descended upon him, driving him down then feasting on his writhing corpse.

"The temple," Markos gasped, "Lajos said— the evil had come from the temple."

Adelrick nodded.

"To the temple!" Markos bellowed, his voice raw with anguish. "Fall back to the temple!" He had no idea how many Spartans remained, it was difficult to tell in the hellscape of battle, but he saw the movement of men peeling away from their battles, giving themselves some space so they could run for the trees, make their way east.

The temple was near, Markos knew that, though he had no doubt the serpents could likely slither far faster than his men could run. Still, they could use the trees to their advantage. Dart back and forth, slide between trunks, move in ways the snakes, with their large, cumbersome tails, could not.

"Now!" he screamed, even louder than before, and his men sprang, charging for the trees. Markos ripped free a spear embedded into the corpse of a Spartan, holding tight to the broadsword in his other hand. Gorgons screamed and hissed, slithering forward in pursuit. "You, too, Adelrick!" he said, nodding toward the large man.

Markos threw the spear, impaling the first charging gorgon, its sprawling corpse slowing the progress of two others behind. Taking advantage of that momentary lapse in the action, he followed his brothers into the trees.

✣ 🏆 ✣

"Where did they come from?" Adelrick asked as he leaped next to Markos, ramming his axe blade into the skull of another serpent. Blood sprayed over his face, peppering his teeth and clinging to his long, dark hair.

The temple loomed just beyond the trees, its large shape shadowed in pale moonlight. Their charge through the trees had been quick, but came at a high cost, several more of his warriors falling beneath the slithering onslaught of gorgons.

"I know not," Markos replied, blocking a claw strike, then ripping his blade through the forearm of an attacking creature and severing its scale-covered hand. "The man at the camp— Lajos! He claimed evil was afoot!" He glowered in the direction of the temple, a place he had always thought of with a sort of awe and inspiration, but in its current shadowed state it looked only dark and ominous.

"Evil, you say?" a voice shouted from nearby, a voice deeper than the other shrill screeches of hissing beasts. There was a cadence to the voice, a low rolling slur, but the voice was distinctly human. The snake warriors before them parted, sliding away, creating a path between them and a large man stepped through. He was clearly serpentine, but different than his apparent minions. He had no tail, still sporting his two legs, though his skin was rough with thick brown scales.

The man-creature glowered at them through darkened flesh, a tangle of black facial hair growing from the hard contours of his jaw. A face of bone and slick skin, he smiled wickedly as he looked upon them, his own sword in his hand.

"One man's evil is another's force for good," he snarled. "You may call me Valter, and I serve at the altar of Ares, God of War."

"You are a mercenary!" screamed Markos. "Nothing more."

Valter's narrow eyes scanned the clearing beyond the trees, already littered with the bodies of Spartans and gorgons alike. The battle had carried from beyond the forest and Markos hadn't realized the carnage wrought in such a short time.

Men he knew – brothers – lay dead and dying, some with their stomachs ripped open, entrails spilled out onto the leaf-covered ground. He recognized the face of a man who might have even been his cousin, the face staring at him from a head separated from its shoulders. The stink of blood and feces filled the air, crawling its way up his nostrils, churning into his guts.

The thrill of battle was already fading, the curtain pulled back, revealing the stark, visceral reality left behind.

"What is your cause, snake-man?" Markos asked through gasping breaths. "Why do you come? Why do you kill?"

"Why indeed?" Valter asked, fingers flexing on the hilt of his blade. "Power, of course. Why else? The Oracle of Delphi drinks from it – the rot and ruin from the python Apollo slew eons ago. She steals it. Takes it for herself, uses it for her own vile wishes."

"She is the oracle!" Markos shouted. "She offers nothing but service!"

"Service? These filthy pilgrims pay fealty to her foolish visions. She demands they bend their knee to Apollo while they turn their back on others. You call it service. It is no service, it is *zealotry*."

"What concern is it of yours? Or Ares? Delphi owns this land, they can do with it as they—"

"Silence!" Valter hissed, fangs parting, the narrow tongue snapping like a cracked whip. "I do not welcome debate. I welcome only obedience. If you cannot provide that to me, then this conversation is over."

Markos flexed his own fingers on the handle of his stolen broadsword, his blood-covered brow furrowing. He said nothing. His expression and movements were all the words Valter needed to hear.

The serpent sneered, his lipless mouth parting into a crooked, fang-filled grin and he lunged, sword slashing.

✟ ☒ ✟

Adelrick saw Valter brace and surged forward, axe at the ready. There was an echoing clash as Valter's blade struck the hard steel of Adelrick's axe, a dance of sparks bursting from the point of impact. The force of Valter's strike drove the large Spartan's weapon down, pulling him off balance and Valter whirled towards him, lashing out with one clawed hand.

His scaley fingers clasped the exposed throat of the warrior, squeezing, tendons bulging on the back of his pale, green hand. Talons dug into the tender skin of Adelrick's throat, narrow trickles of blood coursing over the serpent's bent fingers.

"No!" Markos swore as he charged. Valter turned towards him, his mouth splitting wide, an explosive, sinister hiss ripping free. His fingers clenched, piercing Adelrick's throat, tearing flesh and blood from the large warrior's exposed neck, cutting his strings and dropping him to the ground.

Valter's speed was inhuman, his sword around even before Markos reached him, blade clashing against blade, sparks flying. All around them, the war reignited, serpents leaping, claws raking, the deafening screams of dead Spartans a recurring nightmare in Marko's ears.

His sword struck near the hilt and knocked Valter's blade from his narrow, bony fingers, his talons clawing as the weapon tumbled away. Behind the leader of this motley crew, Markos spotted two snake-men descending upon an over-matched Spartan, one of their jaws dislocating, opening wide then engulfing the poor man's face in a single, tooth-filled bite. Blood sprayed and flesh peeled from cracked bone as he ripped the man's face from his skull and spat out his eyes.

"There are men— women and children at Delphi," Markos gasped. "I will not let you—"

"Don't act as if you have a choice, meat bag," Valter snarled and lunged, slicing at him with long, hook-shaped claws. Markos spun away, the serpent's claws hacking at the metal armor covering his back, throwing sparks into the darkness.

Markos peered into the surrounding blackness; the moon shone pale light upon the battlefield, blood soaking into the ground, turning it to mud in places. Many more of his men littered the landscape, bent and twisted forms dead and dying, the low moan a chorus of suffering beneath the starlit sky.

Breath stabbed in his lungs as he leaned upon his broadsword, rammed deep into the soft ground, his head low. Valter loomed above him, claws curled, preparing for his next strike, a strike likely more carefully aimed and more deadly than the last.

They had beaten down many of the gorgon horde, slaughtering scores of the snake-men with swords, axes and spears, but several of the humanoid reptiles remained, and his men had been whittled down to but a few. As he lifted his head, Markos realized just how hopeless the battle was.

"Have you given up?" Valter snarled, looking down at him, kneeling in the dirt.

Markos shook his head. "I will not let your vile beasts descend upon Delphi. If it is with my dying breath, I will stab your heart out with my blade."

A low, rattling chuckle clicked in the mercenary's serpentine throat, his clawed fingers flexing. "Your death rattle will be like a lullaby to my ears, you useless sack of skin." Valter bent low, finding his sword in the dirt. Bones cracked as he closed his hand around the hilt, the twisting membranes of serpentine muscle clenching in his arms.

Markos drew and held a deep breath, body tensing, and he leaped up and around, swinging the broadsword in a two-handed grip.

Valter moved like lightning, a swift slash of green, his curved kopis banging hard against the mighty swing of the broadsword. The impact forced the broadsword up and back, exposing Markos' torso to a secondary strike. Valter slashed the sword back down, spittle flying from bared fangs, the blade cracking against Markos' chest armor. Markos stumbled back into an ungainly twist that had him sprawling forward.

Ahead, a gorgon wrapped its long tail around a fallen Spartan, slowly squeezing the life from the man. In the low din of battle, Markos could hear the bones snap, ribs caving in under the constriction. There was a final barking shout of pain, then the Spartan slumped lifeless within the reptile's embrace.

"The battle is lost," Valter sneered.

Markos tasted metal in his mouth with each stabbing breath.

Striding forward, the snake-man glared down at him through the vertical slits in his pale eyes. "You were a valiant opponent. I will make your death fast and as painless as possible."

Markos twisted his head around, clenching his jaw and refusing to show a hint of fear as he stared his killer in the eyes and prepared for the swift fall of the curved blade.

✛ ⚱ ✛

Somewhere in the darkness, a shrill, shrieking cry. It was loud and long, a piercing wail, but not one of pain. One of war.

Markos' would-be killer turned slightly at the sound coming from the trees, the initial shriek followed by a chorus of others.

Suddenly a figure leaped from the high branches, lithe and swift, arcing gracefully in the air, drawing a hand back—the figure had a bow and arrow and as Markos watched, the arrow was loosed.

It streaked straight and true, the shaft striking a gorgon in the face with a bone-splitting crack, the broadhead arrow bursting through the back of its skull in a shower of blood and splintered bone.

The figure flipped smoothly, then landed in a low, elegant crouch, scantly visible in the dim light. Markos saw her face—yes, it was a woman, and one he recognized.

"Demetria?" he whispered in disbelief, knowing she was too far to hear. The woman smiled at him, crooked and confident and a host of other figures burst from the trees behind her.

"Amazons!" she shouted, standing to front her gathering horde, all of them women in iron armor and battered helmets, many holding swords, many others bow and arrows, a few gripped long, sharp spears. "Attack!"

There were at least three dozen, maybe more, and with the shouted order, they charged towards the gorgons, weapons drawn.

"Hold your ground!" Valter bellowed. "Drive them back!"

A fleet of arrows launched into the sky, a cloud of narrow shafts arching upward and plunging down, then the hissing screams of snake men filled the air, bodies twisting away and down, arrows drilling into soft flesh and hard bone, piercing, ripping and breaking.

Demetria hollered another violent war cry, discarding her bow and retrieving a short sword from her sheath then charged into the fray.

Three snake-men converged on her, lunging and slashing. Almost effortlessly, she spun away from the first attack, severed a scaley arm with an expert sword strike, then ducked a second attack, placed her hand on the shoulder of the creature and vaulted over it, landing behind to ram her blade through its tail, pinning it to the ground.

The third swung a fist full of jagged claws, and Demetria ducked away from the attack, ripping the sword free from the other snake's tail, springing backwards only to punch forward and thrust her bloodied sword hilt-deep into the creature's gut.

Piercing cries echoed throughout the attacking Amazons as they pressed their assault, pushing forward against the scattered remains of the serpentine mercenaries. Another barrage of arrows, and Markos watched as another group of gorgons fell, sprawling to the dirt, clawing and gagging.

He pushed himself to his feet, lifting the broadsword, scanning the battle, searching out a target. Demetria's back was turned as she clashed swords with an orange-hued snake-man, metal on metal, paying no attention to Valter who stalked swiftly from behind, sword in hand.

Markos ran, pushing past the pain, his crimson-tinged vision clouded by blood and rage.

Valter lifted his curved kopis aiming for the exposed back of the Amazon. Markos threw himself forward, swinging his heavy sword in a nearly uncontrolled sweep.

CLANG!

Kopis clashed against straight-edged steel. Markos landed in a crouch, blocking the would-be death blow. Demetria glanced back, blocked a strike, smirked her thanks at Markos, then plunged headlong into conflict, her sword dancing a gleaming dance of death and blood.

"Some life in you yet," Valter sneered. His mouth split wide, jaw dislocating as his venom-smeared fangs extended.

Markos brought a hand up, his metal gauntlet catching the clamping jaws, teeth banging against iron almost hard enough to pierce the armor. His arm exploded in pain; though the armor held, he struggled to counter with only one hand on the heavy sword. Valter pulled back and this time lunged with his sword. Markos barely ducked beneath the strike, getting both hands around the hilt of his own weapon and driving it upwards.

The swords collided, a stark vibration humming in his hands. The kopis sprang free, tumbling into the air and landing with a thud in the dirt. The impact shattered his own broadsword, leaving the jagged remains of steel blade jutting from the useless wrapped hilt.

Regardless he swung, but Valter's thick palm blocked his arm, fingers curling around his limb and squeezing like a bound rope. Markos grunted as the snake-man forced his arm down, pulling him off balance, his open jaw inching forward, searching for a tender place to bite.

Markos stretched to the ground, his arm in agony as the creature tightened his fierce grip. Valter drew closer, fangs discolored with pale, green venom. Thick droplets spattered on the dirt next to the Spartan as he twisted around, reaching for the dropped kopis.

It was too far away. Valter was dragging him back, teeth clicking in anticipation, the narrow tongue slurping hungrily.

"Your fight is over, Spartan," Valter hissed. "As is your life." His head shot forward, fangs bared.

Markos' fingers closed around a hard rock wedged in the dirt. He ripped it free, and swung with as much might as his weary arm could muster. The hard, ragged stone blistered into Valter's exposed teeth with a jarring explosion of shattered ivory and flying blood.

Hissing, the creature writhed backwards, releasing Marko's arm. Valter clawed at his face, his mouth now filled with broken teeth as Markos continued to grasp in the dirt.

Valter screamed in rage and leaped forward, mouth full of blood, gleaming eyes narrowed in pure hate. The Spartan's fingers dusted the hilt of the kopis, and he ripped it from the dirt, swinging it up in wild arc. The curved blade bit into the hard flesh of Valter's neck, burying deep within the meat, jetting dark blood into the air.

Valter stumbled back, dropped to one knee, his scream choking into a ragged, wet rasp. Markos pushed to his feet, keeping the kopis lodged into Valter's flesh. He loomed above the snake-man, kicked him onto his back, ripping the curved blade free.

Valter glared up at him, menace in his eyes, blood littering his lipless mouth. He sneered and began to speak, but Markos had no interest in hearing his words. He rammed the sword into Valter's face, splitting skin and bone, punching all the way through to the earth beneath.

The snake-man jerked, vomited green and red gore, then

stilled. The hilt of the blade pointed towards the low thunder in the heavens above.

The weight of battle dropped Markos to one knee, around him lurked the stink of death and the fading screams of his men. But that was all he heard.

Fading echoes.

There were no current screams, no battle cries, no sounds of weapons clashing, shields battering, or blades ripping flesh. Lifting his head, his eyes confirmed what his ears were saying.

The gorgons lay dead or dying, sprawled along the ground, scores of them. Several Amazons had joined them, lying amongst serpents and Spartans, some dead, others wounded, but still a number of them standing. Two slowly roamed the corpses, thrusting swords into exposed chests, ensuring the creatures were dead.

Still others helped the wounded to their feet.

"Let me help you," a low voice said, and Markos looked up at Demetria, who held out her hand. He accepted her help, pulled to his feet, leaning on her shoulder, the world swirling and threatening to pitch back into darkness.

✝ 🏺 ✝

"I had no idea," Markos said to Demetria, who stood at the base of the temple. She wore armor on her torso, her arms and her legs, a leather skirt scattered with drying blood.

"That was the point," she replied coldly. "We were to be the last line of defense for Delphi should your men fall."

"I never expected," Markos said, staring in awe over the battlefield. "I apologize. The way I spoke—"

"You did not know. You could not know. Fortunately, neither did they." She nudged Valter's motionless corpse with her leather boot.

"What are they, do you think?"

Demetria drew a breath, lifting her eyes to look at the temple. "Men. Evil men tempting forces they had no right to. The oracle knows how to consume the power contained with the temple. These mercenaries were corrupted by it. Apollo slew the great serpent, the python, and the oracle draws on that power for her visions. Clearly, it had a different effect on these men."

"Where these men come," Markos said, "others will follow."

Demetria shook her head. "I will not allow it." She stepped up the stairs to the temple and Markos followed.

They approached the row of columns on the exterior, the inner chamber within. Demetria continued on, heading into the temple.

"What power do you hold over what men do or do not do?"

Demetria halted, framed by the columns, shadows falling over her narrow form, sword still in hand. She glanced over one shoulder. "A new oracle will be needed. One pure of heart and clear of mind."

"Someone…like you?" Markos asked.

Demetria placed her palm on the stone column to her right, her head lowered slightly as if deep in thought. She looked back over her shoulder. "Return to your family, Markos. To your children. Don't sully their lives by what happened here. Just know that the temple is safe. Delphi is safe."

Markos opened his mouth as if to protest, but eased his lips closed, nodding curtly. Turning away from Demetria, he strode down the steps leading from the temple and rejoined the last few survivors of his men.

THE ENEMY OF MY ENEMY

Kevin Wetmore

The City of Baghdad, in the year of 552 at-taqwīm al-hijrī, in the Name of Allah, the Beneficent, the Merciful...

The scimitar flashed in the torchlight and another head fell, the body tumbling after. To the soldiers watching from behind the gate, the four men seemed to work as one – a single warrior with eight arms striking in all directions in perfect synchronicity. Swords slashed faster than the eye could follow, and the mob of bodies surrounding them split apart in a rain of blood and flesh.

For half a year the siege of Baghdad had brought skirmishes, but the threat at the south gate was of the new kind. The guards watched while the four warriors pushed back against the small, advancing horde. Safe behind the gate, they ignored their three comrades crying out from their wounds, begging for help. Their enemies had no weapons but were all the more deadly for it. Jambiya whirled, scimitars struck home, but not every wound stopped the enemy.

At long last, the final two enemies stood before them. Malik went to face them alone. Hassan cried out for him to wait, but Allah had willed a different path. A quick strike with his jambiya missed the head, plunging into the woman's shoulder as she staggered at the last moment. She turned and bit the hand holding the dagger, even as the man missing an ear, an eye and an arm grabbed him from the side and sank his teeth into Malik's shoulder, tearing his thawb and drawing blood.

With a cry of rage and pain, Malik spun and in a single move both jambiyas entered the eyes of his opponents. They dropped and moved no more.

The biggest of the men approached Malik, who stood, unmoving.

"At least I ended the ones that ended me," Malik told him.

"Your place in paradise is assured," the other said simply.

"Inshallah," Malik whispered. Then, "I do not wish to be like them."

"And you shall not," the other replied, and faster than any at the gate could follow, he whipped his scimitar through the air in front of him, and Malik's head fell from his shoulders.

"He died on his feet, like a man," said Hassan.

"No man should die like that," said the general. "End the suffering of those at the gates while I collect heads. The Wazir will be awake in a few hours and must know of this."

Hassan turned and walked towards the three soldiers on the ground.

✟ ♆ ✟

The sun blazed down on the seven heads nestled on the rug, each upon a clay plate so as not to mar the Caliph's magnificent carpet. The Wazir surveyed the heads – four men, two women, and a child – and the man who stood behind them, arms folded over his black thawb. The only man allowed to keep his blade in the presence of the Caliph stood unmoving, his scimitar hanging from his belt on his left side, three jambiyas lining the belt around the front. His keffiyeh, also black, wrapped around his head and hung down his back. Although it was early morning, the Wazir could see the keffiyeh and thawb were soaked with sweat or perhaps worse. He absentmindedly wondered if the man wore black so the blood did not show as readily. Did these things even have blood?

"More last night," the Wazir said. It was a statement, not a question.

"Yes," replied Abu Ibrahim Ibn Sulayman. "The Caliph must be told. The *alhay almayit* are in Baghdad, and each night their numbers grow."

Alhay almayit – the dead who walk.

The Wazir studied the faces. They had already begun to decay in the heat, and each one had dried blood around the mouth, as if they had been chewing on raw flesh when Sulayman removed their heads.

"Where did these come from?" the Wazir asked.

"The desert in the direction of Hillah. They were part of a group that attempted to enter the city through the southern gate."

"There were more?"

"Yes, Wazir. These," he pointed at the heads, "are for your inspection. There were a few dozen. We ended them all, but three of the Caliph's soldiers and my companion, Malik, lost their lives."

The Wazir paled. Hassan and Jawad, the other companions of Abu Ibrahim Ibn Sulayman dropped their eyes and said silent prayers, their anger and desire for revenge no less visible for it.

"I thought the *alhay almayit* were slow. I had been told they were easily defeated."

"Yes, Wazir, one-on-one. But this one has never encountered just one *alhay almayit*. They travel in packs and wherever they are their numbers grow. As I said, we defeated a few dozen that came from the desert last night, but not without cost. Malik had been bitten by two of them. When all the *alhay almayit* were defeated, I took his head myself."

"We will bury him with great honor."

Abu Ibrahim Ibn Sulayman nodded his gratitude but then pointed to the heads on the carpet. "And will you tell the Caliph of the growing threat from the desert?"

"The Caliph has much on his mind. This never-ending siege has tasked him. The armies of Sultan Muhammad of Hamadan and Qutb ad-Din of Mosul, three times ten thousand men sit across the Tigris, watching, waiting. The Caliph cannot be bothered with an insignificant number of frail beggars from the desert when our food and supplies dwindle."

"There is no such thing as an insignificant number of *alhay almayit*. Where there is one there is soon ten. Where there are ten there are soon ten hundred. They breed by biting. All who die by their hands become as they. If they enter the city, the armies of Sultan Muhammad and Qutb ad-Din need not lift a finger for Baghdad to fall. And if the *alhay almayit* encounter the armies of Sultan Muhammad and Qutb ad-Din—"

"Then our problem may be solved," interrupted the Wazir.

"Or we may wake to find an army of thirty-thousand dead surrounding Baghdad."

"I shall think upon what you have said. In the meantime, continue to keep your city and your Caliph safe from all enemies, living and dead."

Abu Ibrahim Ibn Sulayman bowed his head. "It shall be done as you say." He turned and strode from the courtyard.

✟ ⚱ ✟

The heads were now the Wazir's problem.

After washing up, putting on fresh clothes, kneeling in prayer, and having a quick morning meal, Abu Ibrahim Ibn Sulayman and his companions rode towards the south gate again.

"What makes them walk?" asked Hassan.

"I do not know," responded Abu Ibrahim Ibn Sulayman. "Perhaps it is a disease. Perhaps it is a djinn in the southern desert using dark magic to make the dead walk. Perhaps Iblis has found a new way to torment the children of Allah. In the end, it does not matter. They must be stopped, else the entire city becomes as they."

"They come from the south," observed Jawad. "Perhaps it is something to be found there."

"*Alhay almayit* from the south; the armies of Sultan Muhammad and Qutb ad-Din from the north and west. Baghdad is surrounded on all sides by those who would destroy it."

"Perhaps the Wazir is right and we can turn our enemies against each other."

"No," countered Abu Ibrahim Ibn Sulayman. "The dead who walk are the enemy of all, who become the only enemy. It is for them we must prepare." He had spoken, and Hassan and Jawad fell silent, the discussion over.

As the horses came up upon the crowds at the southern gate of the city, the men slowed and approached the man in armor watching all passing through the gate. Guards were everywhere, but it was clear from his demeanor and considerable moustache that this man was in charge.

"As-Salam-u-Alaikum wa-rahmatullahi wa-barakatuh, Bader," Abu Ibrahim Ibn Sulayman called in greeting.

"As-salamu alaikum wa rahmatullah, Abu Ibrahim Ibn Sulayman," responded Bader Ibn, commander of the south gate. "What brings the Caliph's great general back to our humble post," he added with a hint of a smile playing about his mouth.

"I wish to see if the way is clear to the south. Have the Seljuk infidels attempted to attack this gate?"

The smile, if indeed it had ever been there, vanished. "Not for at least a week, Allah be praised. I have heard from my brothers that they have begun to rebuild the bridges across the Tigris, and if we do not stop them, they will be able to enter the city from the west before the month is out."

"Worry not about that," admonished Abu Ibrahim Ibn Sulayman. "We are surrounded by infidels. What I want to know is, how did the *alhay almayit* get past their camps and reach this gate?"

"I am certain I do not know, my general, but this gate will not fall, either to the dead that walk or the infidels."

"I wonder," responded the general absent-mindedly, staring across the desert at the Seljuk camps a mile from the city walls. "Either the infidels sent them this way themselves, or there are holes in their lines."

"Holes we might pass through as well?" asked Hassan. "To what end?"

"Strike from behind?" asked Jawad.

"No," said Abu Ibrahim Ibn Sulayman softly. "No. We may seek to pass through in order to bring a different solution to both of the enemies that confront us."

The sound of loud destruction echoing across the city suddenly reached their ears. All four men turned to the west to see smoke rising over the city and sounds of devastation and damage. From a great distance came the screams of many.

"What do you think that could be?" asked Jawad.

"The Sultan must be attempting to enter the city from the west again," surmised Abu Ibrahim Ibn Sulayman. "Come!"

Without waiting, he turned his horse and took off for the western walls of the city. Hassan and Jawad followed.

The screams intensified as their horses raced to the site. Children, women, and grown men crying in pain and horror. Within minutes they came upon the chaos of the western wall. A squad of the Caliph's soldiers stood atop the wall, another group stood below, attempting to keep those who had been armed by the Caliph to defend the city, from fleeing. As they approached, a large rock sailed over the wall and crashed into a building, knocking the wall open and raining debris upon the soldiers and civilians below.

A loud scream echoed from above and a body crashed down from the wall – a soldier with a six-foot-long bolt driven through his chest. The crowd grew more panicked by the second.

"Ballista and catapults," said Hassan.

"They must be on the bridge leading to the wall!" said Jawad.

"Join the soldiers down here. Get control over the crowd, get them to clear the square as much as possible and then join me on the wall."

With that Abu Ibrahim Ibn Sulayman draw his bow from its case, grabbed a handful of arrows and leapt from his horse to a low wall. Without losing momentum he leapt up to a balcony, pivoting to jump to one of the ladders lining the wall and climbed the last few yards to the top.

The bridges over the Tigris had been destroyed by the Caliph's troops when western Baghdad fell to the Sultan's army. The wall itself was makeshift – wood, stone and brick intermixed in an attempt to provide some safety and protection for the people of East Baghdad. At the moment, it was doing anything but.

Another bolt flew over the wall and struck a minaret, shattering it. Another rock hit the wall itself, creating a hole and showering bricks and pieces of wood down upon the few soldiers still at the base of the wall. A scream from the square suggested the rock kept going and found another target. Abu Ibrahim Ibn Sulayman looked back and noted it was a piece of bridge used as ammunition. It had struck a soldier, crushing his pelvis and legs. Turning back, he saw arrayed before him the armies of the Sultan lining the western bank of the Tigris, lining the bridges as far as they still crossed the Tigris.

He shouted to the captain of the wall, "Do you have anything to strike back?"

"The walls are not solid enough to hold catapult or ballista such as theirs."

"Do you have arrows? Slings?"

"Yes. But…"

"Then do not try to destroy buildings or bridges – make them pay for being on the bridges."

"We have always fired back, but—"

"Stop making excuses. Drive the infidels from the siege weapons and set the weapons on fire! Make them think twice before attacking this place again!"

Without waiting to see if he would be obeyed, Abu Ibrahim Ibn Sulayman wedged his arrows into the top of the wall. Knocking one, he drew his bow. He focused on an infidel drawing back the cord on a large ballista. Letting fire, he did not even wait to see if it struck home before pulling another arrow. He heard the captain calling for slings, arrows, and buckets of pitch as his third arrow dropped another body into the Tigris.

Soldiers on the bridge noticed him and begin to adjust the catapult. Several more paid with their lives as his arrows rained down with deadly accuracy. Suddenly, a great number of arrows began flying from the wall as the guards finally organized a counter-attack. Several soldiers on the bridge fled, giving Abu Ibrahim Ibn Sulayman time to cross the wall, gather several arrows, coat the heads with pitch, thrust them into a torch a civilian pressed into service held for that very purpose, and fired them into the ballista, which began to burn in the heat of the day.

He turned to the other archers on the wall. "Do the same to all the siege weapons on the bridge! Make them regret challenging Allah and his Caliph!"

It was then he noticed a group of the Sultan's soldiers moving back across the bridge in a group. Those in front carried large shields. Several also held shields above their head as they crossed the narrow span towards the catapult. Between the gaps in their defense, they carried some kind of ammunition in a large blanket. Although the Caliph's guards poured arrows down upon them, most either missed or skated harmlessly off the shields.

Abu Ibrahim Ibn Sulayman watched as they stayed behind the shield wall but clearly pulled the burning arrows out of the catapult and began to set it to fire again.

"Brace yourselves," he called to the warriors as the catapult launched its bucketload high in the air over the wall.

A human form sailed through the air before hitting the building opposite the wall and dropped to the ground, inert.

Then he saw it try to stand.

He immediately began to swing down the ladder to the square calling out for Jawad and Hassan. "They are catapulting *alhay almayit* into the city!" he cried. "Jawad – stop it before it attacks!"

Jawad turned to the unsteady creature, attempting to stand on broken legs. He drove his jambiya into the back of its skull just as another two came sailing over the wall.

Abu Ibrahim Ibn Sulayman reached the ground, drew his scimitar, and split the skull of the first. The second had landed directly on one of the citizens of Baghdad who had been armed to fight. They both went down in a tangle of limbs. Jawad pulled the *alhay almayit* off the man and Hassan crushed its head with a piece of fallen masonry. The man was screaming and bloody, but one could not say if he had been bitten.

"Did it bite you?" asked Hassan as the man kept screaming.

THE ENEMY OF MY ENEMY

Abu Ibrahim Ibn Sulayman crossed the square. "Look at me," he said to the screaming man, who turned just as the scimitar separated his head from his neck.

"We cannot risk this curse entering the city." He cleaned his blade on the man's tunic.

"Catapulting *alhay almayit* over the wall is foolishness," observed Jawad. "The bodies will be too damaged too attack. Broken legs will not allow them to chase."

"No," said Abu Ibrahim Ibn Sulayman. "They do not need to chase, they just need to be able to bite. If they bite one person inside the walls, that one will become many."

"They are not afraid to use *alhay almayit* to attack us. We should do the same," said Hassan.

"No," replied Abu Ibrahim again. "They are foolish to think the dead who walk can be used in such a way. *Alhay almayit* are a knife that cuts the user as much as the target. This is an act of desperation."

Another horse approached quickly, its rider a solider in the Caliph's army. "As-salamu alaikum, my general," the man called. "Bader Ibn said you'd be here. His eminence Ibn Hubayra instructed me to bring you back to the palace. The Caliph desires your thoughts."

Abu Ibrahim turned to the soldiers. "Should they send more over, cut the head off or split the skull. Do not let any of them survive for more than a few seconds. And if they should bite someone, take that person's head immediately, even if it is your own brother. Indeed, take the heads of these and throw them back over the wall onto the bridges. But be careful, do not let yourself be bit!"

He then called out to the captain of the wall, "Continue to shoot arrows at them until your arrows are no more, then throw your bows at them if you must. Throw pieces of the wall if you have to. Stop them from attacking here. If you cannot then I will have the Wazir send someone who can and we shall send you against them," he said, and pointed at the bodies of the *alhay almayit*.

Jumping on his horse he yelled, "Come, friends." Without another word, he and his companions galloped with the soldier back to the palace as another body flew over the wall.

✠ ⚲ ✠

"The son of a whore is using catapults and ballistas! Hundreds have been killed already. It is bad enough the city is starving, that son of a jackal now rains death from above."

Caliph al-Muqtafi raged in his palace. The Wazir and his generals knelt on the carpet before him. To the side knelt Abu Ibrahim Ibn Sulayman and his companions. Al-Muqtafi sat upon his ebony throne covered with brocade. His unmoving personal guards stood behind him. His son, Al-Mustanjid, destined to be the next Caliph, sat lower and to his left.

The Caliph turned to the Wazir. "Did I not arm the people of Baghdad, giving them weapons and armor?"

"It is as you say."

"Is not every man, woman, and child within the city walls a soldier now?"

"It is as you say."

"Then let them fight. Remind them, the Sultan's army is nothing but a pack of infidels!"

"Infidels?" asked General Mauhūb. "Are they not Muslim?"

The Caliph turned upon him in rage. "They dare attack their Caliph, the successor of the prophet and the leader of the ummah! By attacking me, they attack Allah!" Turning to the Wazir he barked, "Ibn Hubayra, tell the people, this war is a holy one we wage against the infidel. If one dies fighting them, they are promised to awaken in paradise, beloved of Allah."

"It shall be done."

"Give five golden dinars to every wounded soldier. For every person who falls in the fight against the infidel, tell their family the Caliph will care for them the rest of their days."

"It shall be done."

"And get this ignorant dog from my sight," he commanded, pointing but not looking at General Mauhūb.

"It shall be done."

Without another word spoken, Mauhūb stood and left the room, no doubt to be sent to one of the gates, demoted. He would not be killed – the Caliph needed as many soldiers as possible and Mauhūb's sword would be missed, even if he were as foolish as his careless remark suggested.

Turning to the three men kneeling off to the side, the Caliph asked, "Abu Ibrahim Ibn Sulayman, my Wazir tells me you think there are enemies worse than the Sultan's infidels."

"Yes, your eminence. The *alhay almayit* are far worse than the Sultan's army, for the Sultan's men are but men and can only destroy the body. The *alhay almayit* destroy both body and soul. When a soldier of the Sultan dies, he is a corpse. When a man is killed by the *alhay almayit*, he rises and joins the fight on their side."

"And you say these *alhay almayit* are in the city?"

"No, my Caliph, but like the Sultan, they try to enter it. And as with the Sultan, if they ever do, it will mean worse than death. My men and I have just come from the walls of the Tigris where the Sultan's men used catapults to send them over the wall."

"So they are in the city?"

"No, my Caliph. We sent their heads back over. But it is only a matter of time."

The Caliph considered him, then leaned forward. "What do you propose?"

Abu Ibrahim Ibn Sulayman took a deep breath and began. "There are things older than the faith," he said. "Three days ride into the desert to the southwest of Nasiriyah lie the ruins of Ur. To the south of that a lost city without a name extends into the waste. It grew out of the cemeteries of Ur, it is the city of the ghuls. It is they who might be our only chance at stopping the *alhay almayit*. I will sneak through the army at the Southern gate and ride there this very day with Hassan and Jawad."

The Wazir looked incredulous. "You would bring us one monster to fight another? Or do you seek to bring a third army here to complete the siege of Baghdad?"

"No," responded Abu Ibrahim Ibn Sulayman simply. "I wish to defeat the armies of the Sultan. I wish to defeat the *alhay almayit*. I do not wish for the *alhay almayit* to infiltrate either the army of the Sultan or the walls of Baghdad. Both would be fatal to our city. But..." He looked the Caliph in the eye, an infraction that could lead to punishment, should the Caliph take offense, "But... the enemy of my enemy can be my friend. I believe the ghuls would despise the *alhay almayit*. If we can convince them to fight the dead that walk, we can then destroy the armies of the Sultan without fearing they will rise again and continue to fight."

The Caliph considered. "Why do you think ghuls will fight *alhay almayit*?"

"It is simplicity itself, your eminence," said Abu Ibrahim Ibn Sulayman. "Ghuls consume the bodies of the dead, but if the dead rise and walk, there will be nothing for them to eat. The *alhay almayit* threaten the existence of the ghuls. Perhaps I can convince them to undertake a holy war of their own."

The Caliph reflected. "It is sensible. I will allow it." Gesturing in the direction of the barracks, the Caliph said, "Take a dozen of my soldiers with you."

Dropping his head, Abu Ibrahim Ibn Sulayman quietly said, "No." After all, one does not contradict Al Muqtafi with impunity if one wishes to keep one's head. "If it does not go well three of us are enough to lose. You will need those soldiers here to protect the city and yourself, my Caliph."

"Very well. I expect you back within seven sunsets."

The camps of the Sultan were easy to avoid. Fires marked each outpost. By silently traversing the dunes to the west of the road, they were able to head for a large gap in the line.

As the crested a dune, a snarl broke the silence. Stumbling through the sand towards them was an *alhay almayit*. He was dressed in a Seljuq uniform, and it was obvious he had died recently.

"Looks like the Sultan is missing a soldier," whispered Hassan as Jawad silently unwrapped his scimitar and took the head of the man quickly and quietly.

"I think he went this way," came a voice from across the sand.

Abu Ibrahim Ibn Sulayman gestured to the others to move quickly away from the body and hide in the shadow of the next dune.

"Here he is!" came another voice.

Three soldiers approached the beheaded corpse. "His head is off."

Abu Ibrahim Ibn Sulayman slowly unsheathed a jambiya and gestured for the others to do the same. Then marked each of the Sultan's soldiers for his men.

"Someone must be here!" said the one obviously in charge. "Kabir, stay with me to hunt for him. Ghasaan, run back to the camp and tell the commander there may be men out here."

Abu Ibrahim Ibn Sulayman's dagger struck the leader in the throat. His expression of surprise as he reached for the hilt faded as he dropped first to his knees and then the ground to bleed out onto the sand. Jawad's jambiya struck the second in the chest, and he, too, fell. The one called Ghasaan turned to run.

Hassan launched his jambiya, striking the man in the shoulder as he stumbled in the sand. Ghasaan screamed in pain but kept his feet and continued to run, calling a warning to the Sultan's warriors nearby.

Hassan did not have to be told; he flew after the man, catching him after a dozen yards and running him through with his scimitar then slit the man's throat with his jambiya to stop his screams. Hassan cleaned his blades on the dead man and quickly and carefully rewrapped them within his thawb as he returned.

"This one is sorry, my general," Hassan whispered.

"It cannot be helped now," Abu Ibrahim Ibn Sulayman responded. "They will have heard. We must hurry if we are to get through the line. Four dead soldiers will give us away, and it is clear they were not killed by *alhay almayit*."

Sticking to the shadows and running low through the sand sea between the camps, they heard men and saw torches moving in the direction of the bodies. They sped down the erg, sticking to the slacks when Hassan signaled the general.

Abu Ibrahim Ibn Sulayman nodded and as one, like a flock of birds, they changed direction, heading in a circular path to a small encampment. Once again daggers were drawn, and three more Seljuqs bled out on the sand.

"Thank you for the gift of your horses," said Hassan. "Give my regards to the Sultan." A glance from the general silenced any further joking and they rode south, stopping after only half a mile as they approached a zariba.

This animal enclosure did not have goats or sheep or horses or camels. Instead, three dozen *alhay almayit* wandered aimlessly while two guards slept at the pen's gateway. They did not stir at the sound of approaching horses. If they heard, they did not seem to care.

"Now we know who has been sending them towards the south gate nightly," Hassan said through gritted teeth. "And that the Sultan's forces are lax in their discipline after this long siege."

"Burn it, and them," said Jawad simply.

"No," said the general. "The fire will draw more troops quickly and they will know we went this way. As I said, *alhay almayit* are a knife that cuts the wielder." He pointed to several of those in the zariba in Seljuq uniforms. "Those who handle them get bitten and end up here themselves. If this place still stands when we come back this way, Allah willing, we will burn it."

"Why not simply set them free to attack the Seljuq from behind?" asked Hassan.

"A knife that cuts the wielder, friend. Have you not listened?"

They quietly dismounted and approached the two sleepers.

"About time you dogs arrived. I thought the captain had forgotten we've been sitting watch here all day," one muttered, not opening his eyes until it was too late. The last thing he saw was Hassan's knife flashing by firelight as it came to slit his throat, Hassan's hand on the enemy's mouth so as not to alert anyone nearby.

The Seljuq guards dispatched, they turned and rode south-west, through the sand sea, spreading out empty and endless before them in the moonlight.

✜ 𝔜 ✜

They rode for three days, encountering and avoiding a few caravans, circling around cities but finally reached the outskirts of the ruins of Ur.

"Now what?" asked Hassan.

"Find a cemetery. Wait," came the reply.

Near the edge of the city they discovered a cemetery with a number of aboveground crypts.

"Good as any. Now we wait."

They watered the horses, set up camp, built a fire and sat as dusk set in.

The half-moon rose high in the desert sky, a cadaverous smirk casting a sick glow on the broken stones and abandoned crypts below. The ruins in the distance formed contorted silhouettes, an ugly echo of what had once been a shining empire. Allah had turned his back upon this place, and even in the pallid moonlight, the sand pulled and brightness and life from the light.

"It is said ghosts haunt this place," mumbled Hassan.

"Think on Allah, and worry about the living who can hurt you far more than any spirit," responded Abu Ibrahim Ibn Sulayman. "We are here to perhaps find an ally against the infidel."

"Things that live beneath a ruined city might fight thirty-thousand?"

"Might stop this siege from being against an army of the living and one of the dead."

"Silence," whispered Jawad, picking up a flaming branch from the fire and staring off in the darkness.

Growling. Just out of the firelight's range. Eyes reflected, teeth visible in the moonlight.

"Jackals," said Hassan, whispering a quick prayer to Allah.

"A pack." Jawad turned slowly to the encircling growls.

Hassan and Abu Ibrahim Ibn Sulayman rose deliberately, pulling a weapon into each hand. The men moved back-to-back as the jackals drew nearer. One snapped at Jawad, who brandished his makeshift torch at it. Another charged in, attempting to bite Jawad from the other side, only to find its skull staved in by the general's sword. Another closed in and bit at Abu Ibrahim Ibn Sulayman's sword arm, he swung his dagger at that one, and it switched its attack at the last minute, closing its jaws around his left forearm. He grunted in pain and slid the scimitar into its throat, shaking his arm to displace the dying animal.

The jackals backed off but stayed just outside weapons' range and continued barking and snapping.

"My general?" asked Hassan.

"We will worry about wounds later. This night will be very long if we must fight off a pack of jackals."

Suddenly, the jackals stopped growling as one and all heads turned in the same direction, looking east toward something the men could not see. They turned and darted off noiselessly into the darkness.

The men reset themselves, weapons at the ready, prepared to face the new threat, but for several long minutes nothing happened.

"Show yourself," Abu Ibrahim Ibn Sulayman called out.

A scuffing was heard in the direction of the largest tomb, followed by footsteps.

A strange creature lurked at the edge of the darkness just beyond the flickering glow. It stood on two legs like a man, but its face resembled a jackal. Its claws glistened in the firelight, clicking against a tombstone it grasped, wary, and emitting a low growl.

"You do not belong here," it finally said, its Arabic flavored with guttural tones – part dog bark, part Damascus streel scraped against ancient stone. The men shivered at the sound of words spoken by something that should not know the tongues of men. "This is a place of the dead, of the ghuls. Not a place for you."

"I am Abu Ibrahim Ibn Sulayman, general to Caliph al-Muqtafi of Baghdad the Great. I come in the name of Allah, the beneficent, the merciful."

The creature spat. "Speak not to me of Allah. He has cursed my kind and in return we turn our backs on him."

"Be that as it may, I come bearing greetings from Caliph al-Muqtafi of Baghdad the Great to the Ghuls of Ur, and an offer of allyship."

"These words mean nothing to me."

"Baghdad the Great is under siege from its enemies. What's more, the *alhay almayit* threaten the city."

The creature gave off a noise that Abu Ibrahim Ibn Sulayman realized was a laugh. "What care I for the affairs of men? You may all kill each other, and my people will feast for decades."

Abu Ibrahim Ibn Sulayman nodded. "If Allah wills it. Were I you, I might be worried about the *alhay almayit*."

"These words mean nothing to me," the creature growled again.

Abu Ibrahim Ibn Sulayman nodded once more and lowered his sword, instructing the others to do the same. "They are the dead that walk."

Again that barking laugh. "Ah, yes. Those I know. They trouble us not, nor do we trouble them. Again, I ask you, what care I for the affairs of men, even dead men?"

"Can you eat them?" the general asked.

"The dead who walk? We have not tried. There is no need. The desert provides. Perhaps before the sun rises, I will clean your bones with my tongue and teeth."

"If Allah wills it. Let me ask you, what happens if the dead that walk bite you?"

The ghul tilted its head. "None have. But if they tried, what man tooth could penetrate a ghul's hide? Again, I care not for them or you."

"But think. If the dead do not die, but walk forever, what will you eat? If there is no carrion ever again, no cemeteries, no bodies buried, do you not starve?"

The ghul stared at him a long time. He seemed to pull away from the men, no longer visible. They heard footsteps, then he was no more.

"Is that it?" Hassan asked.

"Wait," said Abu Ibrahim Ibn Sulayman.

The silence of the desert was weighted. As if the moon, wind, and even the sand held its breath. Only the crackle of the fire filled the hush. The men stood as statues, waiting, swords undrawn but hands near them, ready.

After what seemed an eternity, the ghul was suddenly at the firelight's edge again. "Could this happen?" it asked simply.

"The end of all food for you? Yes, I think if Allah wills it, it could. But..." He sat next to the fire and with a subtle gesture encouraged the other two to do the same. "But... perhaps Allah wills that we work together. We are engaged in a holy war and —"

"No war is holy," barked the ghoul.

"Perhaps," conceded the general, staring into the fire. "But perhaps this one is existential."

"These words mean nothing to me."

"I simply mean perhaps this one will determine whether or not there will be men or ghuls in this desert when you and I are old, and those who would descend from us have nothing to eat."

The ghul considered the general's words. "What does your Caliph offer?"

"Come to Baghdad, defeat the *alhay almayit*. Consume them if you can. If not, end them all. They cannot harm you, but they can make the ghuls starve if their numbers grow too large."

"And this vast army of men?"

"We will fight the men." The general threw another piece of wood on the fire. "But during and after the battle, there will be many fallen men. If you were to stock your larders with the bones of Seljuq dead, I would not curse you before Allah."

"Why the ghuls?"

The general looked up, staring into the ghul's black eyes. "We cannot safely fight the dead who walk. Their presence makes the siege of my city even more dangerous and unendurable. We learned on the way here the enemy is using the *alhay almayit* as a weapon. Both must be stopped. Come fight for us and you return here with food for yourselves and your pups for a generation. Stay here and the last ghul will perish with an empty belly and leave Ur empty and your kind but a legend spoken of by none, for no one remains."

The ghul edged closer and squatted on its haunches.

"If you speak true, I will talk with the ghuls. If we believe you, we shall come to your city. We will end the dead who walk. We will take our food. In exchange, you must promise no ghul will be harmed by you and yours."

"Done," said Abu Ibrahim Ibn Sulayman. "The ghuls are not to be touched and in exchange you may have all the Seljuq you wish."

"No," said the ghul.

"No?" asked the general.

"Ghuls are not to be touched and we take the dead. We do not know who is Seljuq and who is of Baghdad. We take the dead. All dead. For this, we stop the dead who walk, and you can have your city."

Hassan whispered, "Our fallen brothers cannot be eaten by such monsters."

Ignoring him, Abu Ibrahim Ibn Sulayman never stopped staring the ghul in the eyes. "The dead are yours. No ghul is to be harmed. You will end the *alhay almayit*. If but one remains, we shall return here with an army and make the city under Ur look like the ruins above it."

The ghul nodded once and stood. "This I will tell the ghuls."

The general nodded. "How will we know if they agree?"

"The fourth moonrise from tonight, look to your cemeteries. If you see the ghuls emerge, then you will know we have agreed."

"And if not?"

"We will feast after the battle anyway."

The general studied the beast. "What are you called?"

The ghul barked a short series of coughs.

Abu Ibrahim Ibn Sulayman nodded. "I will call you Abdul Baith. It means 'Servant of the one who raises death'. It is no insult."

The ghul returned that studied stare, what seemed to be a smile playing about its snout-like mouth, and responded, "Very well, I shall call you…" and released a short series of barks, unpronounceable to the human tongue. "It means, 'he whose bones we shall eat with honor' – it is a mark of respect of my kind."

"As you say," replied Abu Ibrahim Ibn Sulayman, touching his forehead as a sign of respect in return. "I hope to see you at moonrise in four days, Abdul Baith."

"As do I, human. You are interesting among your kind. I hope someday to eat your bones with honor." It looked around, regarding the cemetery. "Stay not here tonight. The jackals will be back, and in greater numbers. They prefer their meat fresher than I."

With that, it was gone.

Dousing the fire, the men gathered their possessions. The general bound his arm after rubbing ointment on the jackal bite and said a quick prayer to Allah that the beast did not have water-fearing disease. They led the horses out of the cemetery. Once safely beyond the gates, they remounted and rode north-east toward the city.

"My general, I fear this bargain you made," said Hassan. "What will the Caliph say?"

"The Caliph need not know the details. He wants the city saved. The ghuls, Allah willing, will fight alongside us and the siege will end. Victory forgives a number of choices one makes during war."

"As you say." Hassan was silent a moment, then asked, "How will they get through the Seljuq lines?"

"They need not," said the general. "The desert is filled with their tunnels and catacombs. It would not surprise me in the least if they emerged from our tombs and cemeteries rather than march across the desert. This is preferred. Gives us the element of surprise."

Jawad simply pulled his robes tighter about him and kept an eye out for jackals.

They returned to the city at dawn on the morning of the third day, having only stopped to slay the guards at the zariba but leaving the dead that walk alone in the pen. The Wazir had not been happy with the general's non-answer regarding the ghuls' arrival, and Abu Ibrahim Ibn Sulayman told the Caliph the ghuls may come that night, may not. He spoke nothing of the bargain and the Caliph did not ask.

The Wazir leaned close, speaking confidentially to the general, "There are rumors the Sultan's brother seeks to displace him back in Hamadan. He must end this siege or lose his throne. He must attack soon or leave in defeat."

"Inshallah the latter. But we must prepare for the former."

As the sun began to set in the June heat, Abu Ibrahim Ibn Sulayman mounted the newly reinforced walls on the bank of the Tigris, looking out at the siege machinery arrayed against him. In the dying light he saw thousands of men, armored, not passing the time of a siege but preparing for battle. Lining the streets were the citizens of Baghdad, armed and ready to defend their city. The soldiers had also moved catapults and ballista to the squares below the walls – pieces of ruined buildings transformed into ammunition for the catapults. Thousands of arrows had been amassed and distributed along the walls. Soon the air would be filled with them.

With Jawad and Hassan, the general rode from the wall to the south gate, the east gate and the north gate before moving to the center of the city.

"Do you not want to be at the wall when the battle begins?" asked Hassan.

"We will be at the wall soon enough. The battle will truly begin here, Inshallah."

They stopped and Hassan realized where the general had led them. Qureish Cemetery, in the heart of Baghdad.

From the western wall arose a cry. Men shouting. Then the sound of rocks crashing into walls. Screams. The clash of swords.

"They must have put ladders up the walls," said Hassan. "We are needed there."

Abu Ibrahim Ibn Sulayman did not speak. Instead he pointed at the moon, rising above the city walls.

A rider approached. "General! Greetings from Ibn Bader. The *alhay almayit* attack the south gate in great numbers. He begs your help in stemming the tide, but it is like trying to catch the wind I fear."

"Ride back to Ibn Bader. Tell him Allah will send help soon! Hold the gate and remove the head of any man, woman or child bitten by them." The man reeled his horse around and rode off.

"They are not coming, I fear." Hassan's horse sensed his unease.

"Which do you fear more? Them not coming, or them coming?" asked Jawad.

"Just one was hideous. Can you imagine an army of those things?"

"No need to imagine," smiled Abu Ibrahim Ibn Sulayman. "Our allies have arrived."

A rumbling was heard, and the earth beneath the cemetery seemed to shift. Tomb doors opened, the soil rolled like waves in a storm and from them emerged a wave of dozens of ghuls.

One ran to the general and stopped about ten feet away. He sounded a series of short coughs.

"Abdul Baith, it is good to see you as well. Thank you for coming, friend. Tell your people that the *alhay almayit* are at the gate that way." He pointed to the street that led to the south gate. "The battle with the Seljuq lies that way." Again, he pointed west. "They may take any food they think fit."

The ghul may or may not have smiled – it was hard to tell. "Some of the ghuls are already feasting below." He chuckled.

Hassan drew his sword. "The Caliph's family is buried there, filth!"

The ghul snarled, but the general held up his hands to both, pushing Hassan's sword down and placating the ghul. "We will honor our agreement, but he is right. The Caliph's family is in the royal tomb. Touch them not. What you do with other graves, I need not know."

The ghul smiled again and barked at the others, who began running, some on all fours, to the south. The men followed on horseback as quickly as possible. They arrived to screams.

Drawing their weapons, they stopped. The screaming was from the defenders of Baghdad but not from pain or agony but abject horror. The ghuls scaled the wall, leaping on the dead that walk surrounding the gates. The sound of tearing, rending, and laughter came from beyond. The ghuls skittered back up over the gate carrying pieces of *alhay almayit*, some already chewing on their prizes. Others dropped the food and clawed their way up the city walls. They began to lope around the walls, occasionally jumping down to the places outside.

Ibn Bader approached Abu Ibrahim Ibn Sulayman. "What creatures cursed by Allah are these? We must kill them all!" he screamed.

"NO!" commanded the general. "These are our allies and guests of the Caliph. They are here to rid us of *alhay almayit*. Tell your men to stand back and let them work. Better yet – send as many of your men as you can spare to the western wall and aid the people fighting the Sultan's army there."

Too shocked to do otherwise, Ibn Bader ordered his men to the wall and stood watching the carnage.

The ghuls scurried in and out of the city, gathering the dead who walk in pieces, cutting them down with their claws and bringing it all to Qureish Cemetery, where it was fed into open tombs to those ghuls waiting below. Abu Ibrahim Ibn Sulayman prayed they would take the meat to the city of the ghuls and not make permanent residence under Baghdad.

He then rode to the western wall where the battle raged fiercely. Rocks and debris came over the wall, destroying buildings and crushing people in the squares, some of whom fled. There was heavy fighting on the walls on the Tigris – spears piercing human flesh, scimitars flashing, denting armor or cutting off limbs and heads. The bodies of the dead covered the top of the wall and lay at the base of it.

Al-Mustanjid rode up to the general.

"The Sultan has ordered his men to climb the walls and take the city," he shouted. "Has your army shown up? The people of Baghdad bleed this night."

Just then, through the alleys leading to the center of the city, dozens of ghuls burst forth. Their appearance terrified the soldiers and citizens, some of whom dropped their weapons and fled. The ghuls did not touch the living, however. They ran straight to the bodies at the base of the wall and dragged them back to the alleys, disappearing within. Others scarpered up the ladders and grabbed hacked off limbs and heads. They even began to pull the screaming mortally wounded behind them.

For a moment the battle ceased at this horrific sight. The Seljuqs on the ladders fell off in shock, terrified at the beasts atop the walls. Other ghuls jumped down and into their ranks, grabbing any *alhay almayit* they may have intended to use as weapons. The Seljuqs also panicked and fled back across the bridges, but the ghuls did not pursue. They did not touch the living at all. They simply carried their prizes back up the ladders in the torchlight, in the moonlight, and cackled as they hauled them to the cemetery.

"NOW, MEN OF BAGHDAD," bellowed Abu Ibrahim Ibn Sulayman. Defend your city! May these enemies of Allah pay for attacking his Caliph and his city! You see, even the cursed of Allah, the ghuls, fight our enemies, as they know the Sultan and his armies are infidels!"

A man at the top of the wall looked back over at the bridges and knocked an arrow. "Infidels!" he screamed as he fired it off. Like a dam breaking, the soldiers ran back to the walls and the siege machines. Catapults were loaded with debris and fired. Rocks that had come over the wall were carried to the buckets and sent back over again. The ballista sang, sending bolt after bolt over the wall. Hundreds of arrows flew. Three struck Abu Ibrahim Ibn Sulayman; one in the right shoulder, one in the thigh and one in the abdomen. He stayed on his horse, however, breaking off the arrows, tossing them aside and refusing medical attention while the battle continued.

The heavy fire did not stop when the ghuls emerged a second time to mount the walls, drop down, claw apart more corpses and carry them back into Baghdad. The people of Baghdad knew that this was a fight against the infidels, and Allah willed they win. While some arrows returned over the wall, the Seljuq warriors continued to flee across the bridges. Within an hour the side of the city had emptied out and the army, now considerably less than thirty thousand settled down miles from Baghdad.

Abu Ibrahim Ibn Sulayman was helped down from his horse. "Take me to Qureish first."

"Surely you should go to the Caliph," insisted Al-Mustanjid. "My father's surgeons can save you."

"Qureish first," the general told Hassan, who placed him in a litter and he and Jawad carried him to the cemetery.

The ghuls had disappeared back into the ground, save one.

"Abdul Baith, you are a true friend and a great warrior. I will make sure the ghuls of Ur are spoken of with honor and gratitude among men.

"You are not long for this side of the soil, friend," replied the ghul. "We may see each other soon. But still, you have kept your word. No ghul has fallen and we shall feast for years on what we have taken today." He coughed out the general's ghul name, "will be honored among our people as well. We return to Ur tonight. May Allah keep you, human."

"Salaam, Abu Baith."

The surgeons saw Abu Ibrahim Ibn Sulayman at the Caliph's request, but it was too late. Hassan and Jawad were with him to the end and received his final instructions.

Three rather strange things followed, however.

First, the Sultan lost a third of his army that June night, and then learned that in his absence during the long siege his brother had taken his throne. He and his army departed to retake his kingdom, and Baghdad was freed, the siege over. The *alhay almayit* were not seen again in the city.

Second, a half dozen years later, when Caliph Muqtafi passed and his son Al-Mustanjid became the new Caliph, the royal tomb at Qureish was opened and discovered to be empty. The dead Caliph was quickly entombed and the doors sealed. The men who had seen the empty tomb were all put to death to ensure their silence. An order quietly went out to find and seal all tunnels beneath Baghdad. The ghuls were not seen again in the city.

Third, after the siege of Baghdad had ended, Hassan and Jawad were seen loading a wrapped body on the back of a horse and riding southwest out the south gate of the city. Rumor has it that the placed it outside a broken tomb in a cemetery near the outskirts of Ur, although traders who have passed by Ur have said no such body was ever seen in the cemetery. Perhaps the jackals took it, they wondered. Hassan and Jawad were not seen again in the city.

THE EYE OF GOD

B. Michael Radburn

Order of Teutonic Knights, 1st Ecclesiastic Airborne Regiment (The Blood Red Cross).

Founded in 2224 during the First Off World War (OWW1) and noted for its Battle Honours of the Siege of St Paul where the 17th Vatican Settlement of Amatus (*see Addendum 1*), a colonised planet in the Antares territories, was raided by a first contact race known Terrestrially as the Skat due to their home planet's proximity to the star *Skat* in the constellation of Aquarius.

Addendum 1: Militarisation of the Catholic Church. The Papal Isolation Policy of 2172 was introduced to utilise the Church's vast resources and wealth to fund a program of off-world migration and the establishment of a chain of self-defended planetary colonies dedicated to Catholicism.

Teutonic Knights Compendium, 5th Edition

D-Day minus 1 hour…

Peter, a lowly Novice, stood with his platoon on the trembling flight deck of the Deployment Vessel CSS *Mary MacKillop* as she made a slow arc towards the armada's target planet, Tycolus I. It was the first beachhead assault in the Blood Red Cross's planet-hopping campaign towards the Skat's home planet of Aquarii Major. The mission? To neutralise the Skat's forward base, sever enemy supply lines, establish a Knight's tactical support base, and deny those Skat devil's access to the Church's Aquarius Colonies. It was going to be brutal, but no less fierce than the legacy left in blood by those alien aggressors across the colonies. As was custom before each battle, Peter rested his right palm over the Teutonic Knight's Blood Red Cross insignia on his uniform's left shoulder. He was honoured to be one of the many hands to wield the Lord's sword.

Their Platoon Sergeant, Father O'Donnell, barked his orders and Peter stepped in line towards the open ramp of their assigned Armoured Personnel Lander (APL). Battle helmet in hand, he tapped it nervously with his fingers. The ship's gravity had been gradually adjusted over the past 170 hours to acclimatise to the planet's surface conditions, while Peter's deployment pressure-suit regulated its exoskeleton to better take the weight. His pack and blaster were nearly twice as heavy as they should be, and despite the supportive suit, they still bared down on his 19-year-old shoulders with the pressing weight of the mission.

The flight deck was bordering on chaotic as the convoy of APLs were loaded with columns of troops. The Fire Support Landers, or 'Beasts' as they were better known to the ground troops, idled ready to deploy. Ahead of them, the Fighter Escorts were lit up, the growl of their thrusters shuddering through Peter's body.

His boot hit the ramp as the sound of the ship's blast screens began rolling down to shield the observation windows. Peter glanced up just as their target came into view. Tycolus I, in full sunlight, had a strange red hue about it. Behind it, like a gateway to the heavens, lay the great Helix planetary nebular, better known to mankind as The Eye of God due to its shape of an unblinking heavenly eye. Peter crossed himself and patted the Blood Red Cross one more time for luck.

Platoon Lieutenant, Deacon Gabriel ushered them ahead from the top of the ramp. "Stay in your three sections!" he barked. "Alpha, Bravo, Charlie from port to starboard!"

"*SIR, YES, SIR!*" came the collective cry.

No sooner had Peter taken his seat with Bravo Section, than the rear ramp groaned shut and the red battle stations light replaced the white. This was going to be a hot insertion in broad daylight. It was every soldier's nightmare, and not exactly by the book, but the book was thrown away when the Skat began their night raids on the colonies.

THE EYE OF GOD

The enemy's habitable planets were closer to their sun than earth was to its star, thus driving their species underground during the day, venturing to the surface only during the cool of their 40-hour nights to work and plot their schemes. Peter checked his blaster one last time before take-off, counted his pulse grenades and ammo clips again to ensure he had enough firepower for the mission. *They attacked us while we slept*, he recalled with bitterness, having experienced their raids first-hand, the only survivor in his family. *An eye for an eye, and a tooth for a tooth, states Leviticus.*

Deacon Gabriel strapped in last. "Launch in five seconds, gentlemen," he cried. "See you on the beachhead."

Peter leant back into the netted seat and crossed his arms over his chest with the rest of the Knights, braced for the launch.

"Three... Two... One..." Gabriel sounded.

Peter clenched his eyes shut as the force pressed him back into the netting, breath expelled momentarily before he could breathe again. When he opened his eyes, he was staring out through the row of viewing slits that ran along the APL's gunnels. It was his first view of the armada, and it was magnificent.

Above them, slowly contracting into the distance, the destroyer escorts began their barrage of suppressive fire, cannon trace slicing through the blackness like flaming arrows. Soaring vanguard on the APL's flanks, the fighter support squadron flew in defensive formation, comforting as the force drew closer to the landing site. Peter's adrenalin stirred as the landing zone on the surface began to light-up with the destroyer's cover fire. The platoon roared with martial delight in one voice, but perhaps a little premature.

As the force approached the atmospheric arc, explosions of plasma flack began to burst ahead, creeping closer until the fleet of landers were in the thick of it.

"Brace yourselves," barked Father O'Donnell.

And as Peter did so, a plasma blast rocked the lander with a monstrous tremor, the shockwave whipping his head back into the webbing, a sharp pain biting into his neck.

"They know we're coming, boys," cried Deacon Gabriel. "Lock and load!"

Another explosion took out the lander to their starboard, debris raining against the hull, the twisted bodies of soldiers hitting the viewing ports like bugs on a windscreen. Peter clumsily loaded his first clip amidst the turmoil and engaged his blaster's prime toggle, the indicator light switching from green to red. He prayed in a whisper as he crossed himself.

"Dear, God. Just get me to the beachhead and I'll take it from there."

Delta Aquarii Sapiens. Common English name: The Skat.

Delta Aquarii Sapiens are an alien species from the Skat solar system located in the Aquarius constellation. The system contains several exoplanets in the star's habitable zone, their indigenous world being Aquarii Major. A space-faring militarised race, the Skat have successfully colonised three habitable outer plants: Tycolus I, Tycolus II and Aquarii Minor. They are a nocturnal humanoid species possessing a leathery grey flesh and exposed horn-like bone structure protruding from their joints and cranium. First contact with the human race was in 2218. Second contact was six Earth years later when their militia forces raided the Catholic colony of Amatus in 2224, killing 128 settlers. To date, no official declaration of war has been tabled by either party.

Teutonic Knights Compendium, 5th Edition

Two years earlier…

Peter, just seventeen, woke to the call of a bleating cow. Light from the twin harvest Moons streamed across his bed through his open window. The cow whined again. Peter glanced at the time ball that hovered above his side table. It was way too early for milking.

"What in heck are you bellyaching about?" he moaned.

He drew the pillow across his face against the bleached light that flooded his room. The cows fell silent. He lifted the pillow and noted that the light had changed, its white hue transforming to a rippling orange.

Then came the screams.

Peter sprung from his bed to the window.

The outbuildings were ablaze, the barn well alight, spreading quickly to the transit quarters where the seasonal workers from St Paul slept.

Raid!

The next sound confirmed it, the unmistakable *womp* of Skat blasters, their unique red tracer rounds firing from the cornfields behind the barn, pockmarking the outbuildings to a chorus of collective screams.

Peter ran to the bedroom door and punched the red panic button. Every farmhouse outside the walls of St Paul had them installed, a direct mayday link to the city barracks. But nothing happened. The expected siren remained mute. He hit it again. Again and again and again. Then tried the lights.

The power had been cut.

Ma! Pa! He needed to get them to the basement saferoom, and fast.

But the cacophony outside pressed through the walls and into his flesh. It took all Peter's strength to break the paralysis that held him. He sprang to the gun rack above his bed and snatched the hunting blaster his pa gave him for his last birthday. Good for potting blind corn bats in the fields at night, but yet to be used against any larger prey. He checked the cartridges as he returned to the window. The light of the fires raged with his fears, casting shadows of the advancing raiders across the compound.

The fields of corn parted as the Skat crawlers tracked across the open ground, their turrets seeking out targets and blasting at will. Behind the crawlers came lines of the Skat in their shimmer-suits, a reactive camouflage that varied with the local environment. Not quite invisible but distracting enough to spoil a man's aim. At least their demonic faces were hidden behind those oil-black helmets, left only as anonymous silhouettes before the flames.

A surge of rage engulfed Peter, unsure if it could dominate his fears as he clutched the blaster's stock to his chest. There was nothing random about the attack. They had strategically set the cornfields alight behind them. *Scorched earth.* Their typical calling card while murdering the transit workers as they fled the burning quarters. It was a goddamned turkey shoot. The merciful among them used their blasters, the more sadistic tearing flesh and limb with their ceremonial L'aumé knives.

The cries of the dying had reached their crescendo quickly, and now descended into a morbid quiet. That was the only way Peter could have heard the creak of the veranda boards outside his window. It gave him enough time to step aside as the distinct shadow of one of the aliens shifted across his bedroom floor. He held his breath as it passed, switched his blaster to fire, then ran to the hall.

The front door was open, the frame forcefully buckled.

It took every ounce of strength to hold his ground until the Skat devil stood clearly in the doorway, shimmer-suit breaking its lines and distorting the air around it. Peter fired before it could see him, the distinct blue trace of the terrestrial ammo slicing the dark as the shimmer-suit dissolved and a fist-sized hole splintered through the creature's chest. It collapsed, lifeless. Peter counted the bloodied scalps tied to its utility belt just as a scream rang from his parents' bedroom down the hall.

Peter recharged the old blaster for another round. Only two left in the chamber. As he reached the bedroom door of his parents' room, one of the Skat fighters barrelled into him. They fell together, tangled for that moment, the alien scurrying for its misplaced weapon. Peter aimed in haste and fired, the blue trace ripping through the side of the creature's helmet. Its shimmer-suit blinked in and out. It bounded to its feet and peeled the smoking helmet from its barbed head as its camouflage halo vanished, one leathery cheek blistered and torn. The coward then abandoned its own weapon and scurried to the window at the end of the hall, bounding through it in a shower of glass.

One shot left. Peter took a deep steadying breath, could feel himself drawn into a pit of utter silence. For that breath, his world seemed transfixed, only the quiet light of the fires moving across the walls. "Ma? ... Pa?"

Peter could smell the coppery blood from the doorway; of opened bodies and excreted wastes. He couldn't move, not until a ribbon of blood snaked out from the open doorway and beckoned him forward. Grief now fuelled the rage as he stepped inside. He could see... something... lying on the bed in the darkness, unsure where Ma's rose-patterned quilt stopped and the blood began. But the scene was exposed in a sudden flash of red as a round grazed his leg, the scene of carnage vivid in that split second.

His parents' bodies, torn, gutted, and splayed across the bed in some macabre butcher's display. Peter's legs gave out, and he slumped to the floor just as a second shot flew over his head. This time the flash gave his foe's position away. *In the corner.* Peter fired his final round. The red streak smashed through the alien's neck, its head and body parting ways in a gout of crimson against the wall.

The only thing they had in common was the colour of their blood.

There was a moment of quiet, of unspoken grief that threatened to crush him. No time for goodbyes or tears as a booming crash of shattered timbers exploded through the doorway. Peter leapt to his feet, his leg burning from the wound as he was confronted with the splintered opening at the end of the hall where the southern wall once stood. Through the smoky haze came crawlers, columns of troops marching behind. No option left now but the saferoom.

He took up the abandoned alien blaster and high-tailed it towards the kitchen, the warped stairs groaning beneath him, ready to collapse, his leg searing with every step. He ran the hall, could see the entry hatch through the kitchen door when another crawler-blast shattered the timbers around him, the floor above partially collapsing. One more hit like that, and the farmhouse would be nothing but cinders.

Have to get below. FAST!

Peter dove forward, momentum sliding him along the floor. A heavy beam fell, catching on the overturned fridge to suspend just a metre above him, the only thing stopping the rest of the debris from burying him alive.

The hatch was on battery power and sprang open with the four-digit code, the interior light flickering on below. Peter slid down the ladder rails, landing shakily on both feet, the pain in his leg biting hard. He punched the lock button on the wall just as another explosion rocked the building and threw him to the floor, his head smacking the concrete, then he knew nothing more…

…Peter woke to aching bones and ringing in his ears, but even through the chimes he could hear a scraping at the hatch cover above. He had no idea what time it was or how long he'd been out. The Skat blaster was at his side, and he snatched it up, aiming towards the hatch. The scratching stopped, only to be replaced by a shower of sparks as the hinges were being laser sliced. There was no time to grieve, no time to be afraid, and only a few seconds left to take out at least one of those devils when they charged the saferoom.

The laser cut the steel with ease and the hatch slid away in a cascade of dust and shards. Peter fired at the opening, but the blaster remained cold and mute, no doubt damaged in the fall. Streaks of daylight streamed through the dust cloud as a figure stared down at him.

"You okay there, son?" An arm reached inside, hand opened in an invitation.

Peter stared in disbelief at the blood red cross of the Teutonic Knights displayed on the shoulder patch like a symbol of hope. He pushed unsteadily to his feet, took shaky steps forward, climbed the ladder and clutched the Deacon's hand, bound forever to the symbol of the cross.

THE EYE OF GOD

✠ ▼ ✠

Order of Teutonic Knights, recruitment process.

Unlike other branches of the Ecclesiastic Armed Services, the Order of Teutonic Knights is not open to voluntary enlistment by civilians. If potential knights are not recommended by their commanding officers through active units, then the Order exercises its own internal enlistment programs where recruitment scouts seek out candidates that meet their strict criteria. The process is discreetly carried out across selected bootcamps, officer training colleges, and victims of Skat raids. Many Teutonic Knights have lost family and friends to the invaders, creating an added incentive to defend the colonies.

Teutonic Knights Compendium, 5th Edition

✠ ▼ ✠

D-Day…

The APL pitched nose-up for the landing. Peter slipped on his helmet and fastened the chin strap. The lander then yawed violently to the left, dust and sand momentarily blurring images of the congested beachhead through the viewing slits. The craft hovered a moment longer amidst an onslaught of heavy fire, countless rounds skimming the APL's thin armour.

Peter focussed on the ramp-locks, his heart pounding beneath the confines of his pressure suit as he waited for them to activate.

"Line-ahead formation, Knights," cried Deacon Gabriel as he took his position beside them.

Peter stood with Bravo Section, struggling for balance upon the pitching deck as the APL descended the last metre towards solid ground. This drew more fire, a brief wave of rounds pounding the hull. He supressed his fear by recalling the image of Ma's bedquilt of roses and blood, then crossed his chest for the Lord's guidance. Better to feel rage right now rather than fear.

Platoon Sergeant Father O'Donnell began the assault prayer. "Who are we, Knights?"

"Sir, The Blood Red Cross, Sir!" came the collective cry. The APL's skids hit the beachhead with a jolt.

"And what is our destiny?"

"Sir. To hunt the Skat, Sir!" The ramp-locks disengaged with an echoed clunk.

"And what is Skat?"

"Sir. Animal shit, Sir!"

The ramp slowly opened, and the martial sounds of war flooded the deck in a discord of explosions, blaster fire, and shouting men.

The ramp hit the rust-coloured dirt as one of their Beasts crept forward, cannons blasting at the defences of pillboxes and dug-in crawlers ahead. Father O'Donnell had to shout the last verse as the men shuffled forward. "And what do we do with that shit?"

"Sir! Scrape it off our boots, Sir!"

A Skat crawler canister round hit the first wave in a shower of jagged pellets, blood-red rain spraying across Peter's visor. The shockwave threw him back onto the deck. The next thing he knew, Deacon Gabriel took his hand and lifted Peter to his feet.

"If you want to live, son, then get off this lander." It was the Deacon's last word, as a red tracer round dissolved his chest and threw him to the forward bulkhead.

With a roar, Peter lurched from the APL, firing his blaster through the gaps of charging Knights until his first clip was spent. Many of his brothers were cut down quickly, while others, by miracle alone, seemed immune to the onslaught of Skat fire. Peter went to ground in the depression of a shallow shell scrape, pressed himself as close to the dirt as he could. From the rim, he spied a Skat crawler ahead through his blaster scope, the turret traversing its arc of fire as it searched for targets. Peter used the moment to take stock and assess.

Beyond the boundary of thick smoke and rising flames of the enemy defensive line, the Eye of God filled the skyline, an unblinking witness to the Blood Red Cross's hand of vengeance. He rolled onto his back and replaced the ammo clip in his blaster, stared up at the ever-present nebula through a curtain of red tracer rounds. "Guide me," he whispered, then rolled back onto his belly and scanned the way ahead.

The Skat crawler held the right flank, no longer in line-of-sight of their own Beasts, and well positioned to leave a channel of dead and wounded Knights between the APLs and Skat defences, effectively pinning them down. As futile as his rifle blaster might be against the crawler's armour, Peter took the shot anyway, hoping he might draw it out into the gun sights of their own forces.

But instead, the machine exploded in a fiery ball of flames and molten metal.

What the...?

As Peter attempted to rationalise the limits of his personal fire power, two of the armada's fighters screamed across the beachhead, having released their plasma bombs. Their bombardment had opened several gaps in the defences, the knights quickly taking the advantage and regrouping into their units. Peter found Bravo Section, or what was left of it, and they gathered behind one of the Beasts as it edged closer to enemy lines with progressive bursts of cannon fire.

The ground was pitted with craters and shell-scrapes from the armada's opening barrage ahead of the assault, and as the Knights breached the gaps, it became evident that there were less of their dead, and more of the Skat's. Peter looked up at the Eye of God and patted the Blood Red Cross on his shoulder in a silent prayer. *I'll take it from here, Lord.*

The Beast's cannons suddenly fell silent as their turrets scanned the Skat's forward base – a series of engineered earthen mounds and walled compounds. According to army intel, it was the subterranean base to the raiding parties that destroyed his family farm and murdered his parents.

Sergeant Father O'Donnell crouched low behind the shelter of the nearest Beast and called the depleted platoon to join him.

"We had hoped to catch the bastards sleeping, men," he told them, "but you saw how well prepared for us they were during the landings. Most of their soldiers would have been on the defensive line, but rest assured there will be enough remaining within the barracks to make life difficult for us."

O'Donnell's brief was interrupted by several cannon rounds barking from the line of Beasts, explosions breaching the compound walls before they fell silent again. "The Beasts will remain here in support. They'll lay down a barrage of suppressive fire. Then we charge. This is not a mission for taking prisoners. Is that clear?"

In one voice. "Sir. Yes, sir!"

Peter felt a surge of unit pride, the *Esprit de corps* they preached about at his passing out parade. It surged with the blood in his veins, and the rush of adrenaline fuelled just one need: to avenge his parents.

O'Donnell stood, as did his men. "We have the beachhead, Knights, now let's take the barracks!"

And with O'Donnell's last order, the Beasts rained Hell down on the Skat barracks ahead of the first great Knight's charge of their planet-hopping campaign towards Aquarii Major.

The scent of ionised air pervaded Peter's helmet filters amidst the fog of war and broken wreckage that lay underfoot. The platoon had divided into its three sections, each penetrating an isolated breach into the barracks. Skat blaster fire was minimal, but enough to separate each of those sections into yet smaller groups. When the Knight next to Peter was shot, he took refuge behind the remnants of a collapsed dwelling. At his feet was a partially concealed body buried in the rubble, the thorny Skat face and lifeless eyes staring up at him. It wore no shimmer suit and bore no weapons, perhaps a soldier caught off guard during the attack. In its hand was a spade-like implement, no doubt the only weapon it could muster when the attack came.

Peter noted where the enemy trace was coming from, an opening in the collapsed mound across the way. Several random blasts were discharged as a number of Skat fled the ruins unarmed and in tattered clothes under the cover fire. Three in all, and Peter took them out one after the other; swift, clean kills, which was more than those devils offered his parents.

This is not a mission for taking prisoners.

Clean kills or not, his exposure drew a flurry of incoming blasts, singeing the air above him, way to close for comfort. He dropped behind the rubble and secured a pulse grenade onto his blaster's launch sleeve, then waited for a lull in the shooting. Peter counted to three, then sprang to his knees, took a hurried aim, and fired into the opening. The wood-be sniper's lair exploded, and the Skat's torn body was thrown into the road like a bloody ragdoll.

A group of Knights to his left sprang from their cover and took the advantage, charging over the ragdoll and into the now cleared cavity. Separated from his own section, Peter followed them down the rabbit hole. Difficult to keep up, the Knights took swift advantage and rolled through the labyrinth like a devastating storm.

The narrow burrows to the barracks descended steeply, lit from the walls by florescent crystals. Reaching a fork in the passageway, Peter became disorientated, could sense the tonnes of earth pressing down on him when he paused at the intersection. The pounding echoes of gun blasts and exploding grenades surged up through the passages ahead of the assault with the dying cries of the Skat. It was a mad house, a charnel house, the true direction of the sounds undiscernible. He raised his blaster sights and chose the right-hand passage, drawn towards the discord of sounds until the path opened onto a wide rock shelf that overlooked a vast domed clearing below.

The ceiling was crowned with an immense cluster of light-emitting stalactites that hung like the teeth of a monstrous animal. They illuminated the carpet of green below with a radiant warmth, row upon row of lush vegetation divided by shallow irrigation channels that were fed by a streaming aquafer from a fissure in the wall. Most notable was the Skat bodies that floated in the blood-streaked channels and lay among the foliage like rotten fruit fallen from the vines.

The rock shelf was a dead-end, one of many protruding from the walls that surrounded the clearing, one of many where groups of Knights had taken up fire positions above the fleeing Skat. Blaster trace cascading down on those below, and Peter found himself suddenly spent and weary as he watched the carnage. *This doesn't make sense.* He lowered his weapon. *Where were the barracks? The armouries? The soldiers?*

He noted some of the fallen clutched the same tool as that of the Skat body he first saw topside. They were spades or hoes of some kind. "This isn't a military base," he murmured. "It's a farm." Sure, Skat soldiers defended the perimeter, but was that any different to their own colonies? The sense of rage he suddenly felt slowly dissipated, replaced with frightful understanding.

"*We're* no different to *them!*" Peter shouted, his words barely competing with the cacophony of destruction that filled the dome.

But he did manage to hear the hurried sound of footsteps nearing through the passage behind him. Peter swung around, afraid now and confused. He raised his weapon just as one of the fleeing Skat ran panting from the opening, scarcely stopping in time. The creature wore no shimmer suit or helmet, just loose-fitting garments stained with blood, soil and sweat, a weeping cut above one eye. But it did hold a weapon, an antique blaster that Peter doubted even worked. For a moment they stood face to face, weapons raised point blank, and in that moment, Peter recognised the fear in the Skat's eyes, the same fear Peter had felt when his own farm was raided and his parents murdered.

In the end, Peter couldn't do it. The rage that brought him to this place, this moment, no longer fuelled him. He couldn't be responsible for one more drop of blood, either Skat or human. Peter lowered his weapon, unsure of what would happen next, leaving his destiny in the hands of God alone.

The Skat held its aim for a little longer, frowned, then cautiously did the same. Peter pointed to the passageway behind and simply nodded. "Go," he said, hoping it would somehow understand.

It did; turned and fled back the way it came.

Peter returned to the surface. On two occasions pockets of Knights passed him in the passage, their blood lust heightened by news of the massacre below. When finally he escaped the labyrinth, Peter paused in the opening and stared around at the carnage. He removed his helmet and let it fall to the ground. The Beasts were parked around the perimeter, many of their crews sitting atop each turret like tourists as they ate from their K-rations.

The Skat dead were being dragged into the middle of the compound, rows of them on display for the official body count as many of the Knights cut the L'aumé knives from each aliens' belt for souvenirs. A Novice, no older than Peter, was gouging out Skat facial horns with such a knife – another grim keepsake. Peter sighed, recalled the Skat trophies of scalps hanging from its belt the night his own farm was raided. Another Knight held a tattered Skat flag aloft as his buddy prepared to snap a holopic ensuring that the now familiar Eye of God was prevalent in the background sky.

Peter turned his back to the carnage, began the walk back to the beachhead when he came across yet another Skat body and paused, his shadow cast upon its face.

A cut above one eye.

Peter's breath caught in his throat, a cold tremble coursing through his body. "Too much," he murmured as he let his blaster slip from his fingers, determined never to fire it again.

Peter fell to his knees before the Eye of God, exposed, betrayed, his faith shattered under fire, his beliefs stained with the blood of both species, too deep to ever be clean again.

BESTING THE BEAST

Scott Forbes Crawford

As the sun chased off the last of the dawn fog, Kai studied the raggedy mob of foot-soldiers resolving into view. At most, a strength of two thousand. "A shame we outnumber them so," Lord Issei sighed next to him, gesturing to his formations of archers, spearmen and cavalry poised on the hilltop. Kai's master was still teaching him the virtues of the samurai – humility, self-mastery, honor – yet Kai struggled to abandon the virtues he'd once cultivated as a bandit, rather preferring to face the enemy four-to-one as they did today.

From the foot of the hill the Guardians of the Sleeper, clad in their blue-dyed armor, shambled forward. Their standard-bearer hoisted the banner: a woman's head with a curving, distended neck rising from water. Kai first saw that banner as a boy when, hiding in a pig corral, he watched the Guardians ride into his village to claim sacrifices for their goddess. Orphaned, Kai became a brigand preying on travelers until one day he attacked Lord Issei and his retinue, knocking down two soldiers only to stare at the lord's sword at his throat. Recognizing a warrior's mettle, Issei inducted him into his army, and now Kai stood at his side in this final battle, ready to grind that banner into the dirt once and for all. Yet something nagged at him.

"Why have they chosen *this* place for battle, master? We control the high ground. We outnumber them decisively. Yet they've constructed no defenses, dug no trenches. They are bunched up with forest on either side. Something is wrong."

The smile Issei gave was more proud father than canny commander. "You have come far, Kai. The Guardians, bah! Last spring I thought they might sweep the whole of Japan, but after defeat upon defeat, they're an army no more. Only fools and fanatics wailing about some false sleeping goddess. Ah, here we are, the Hierophant himself, come to beg quarter!"

From among the enemy's front ranks emerged a lone rider of stocky build – Jomon, Hierophant of the Guardians. He trotted his horse out ahead of his army. "Issei! You tried to stop the Mother but she has awakened! You will know her wrath!" Jomon lifted a horn to his lips and blew. At its bellow, the enemy soldiers reached into their belt-pouches and produced bright yellow sashes they fastened across their torsos.

"What's this madness?" Issei muttered.

"Master... Up there!" Kai jammed a finger at the sky, even as his mind revolted against what he saw.

Swiftly from the horizon they flew on slow-beating feathery wings. As they sped nearer, Kai spied their tremendously long noses, their legs stretched behind them while muscle-corded arms bore javelins. *Tengu.* Bird-men. Kai had heard of *kaijin*, the uncanny men who once haunted the land in ages vanished in the mists of ancient memory. Mere tales for children! Yet as each flying fiend released his javelins, the deluge piercing skulls or pinning targets through their legs to the ground, making hardened warriors into shrieking puppets, none could now dispute the kaijins' existence.

Issei froze.

Kai spotted a tengu squadron overhead and shoved his master from a javelin's flight. He scanned for a cover. Goggled at the maelstrom erupting out of the forest below. Dozens of *oni* – huge, misshapen mockeries of the human form. The shortest stood at eight feet. Their skin was of a sallow green hue. Horns, some half the length of a man's arm, jutted from their foreheads. Kai's mind sputtered as the oni rushed up the hill, their over-sized weapons raised, while Guardian troopers fell in behind their assault.

"Archers, loose volleys!" It was Issei, restored to cool command. "Infantry, get in Badger Formation! Spears braced to the ground! Don't think about what's coming," he called to his trembling men, tearing his sword free from its scabbard. "They are only more enemy to kill!"

Those words jolted confidence back into Kai. Action now, the meaning of what was unfolding for another time. He unslung the war-hammer strapped to his back. It had carried him through many battles. It must again today. It was not elegant, not noble or finely crafted, but, like Kai, it was steadfast and savage.

Arrows whooshed at the onrushing beasts but the iron broadheads mostly bounced off the creatures' coarse skin. The monsters plowed through the first ranks, spraying bodies like whipped seafoam. With their horns, and the mammoth clubs, axes, and mauls they swung, the oni made a gory mess of Issei's men. Then the tengu joined the oni on the ground. Javelins expended, the winged-men drew swords and engaged at close quarters.

A knot of Guardians moved on Issei. Kai crushed their skulls and shattered limbs with his devilish arcing hammer. The old man's sword blazed, slashing enemies as he wove among them. Sword sliced and hammer smashed, Issei's blade swift and controlled, Kai's weapon as blunt and brutal as himself.

A swish of wings above. Kai spun. A tengu hit the ground, bounded at him and slashed. Twisting, Kai caught the blow on the hammer's haft. As nimble grounded as airborne, the winged fiend twirled clear of Kai's counterstroke. With unspoken coordination, Issei and Kai closed from either side. Kai lunged. The creature leaped backward out of danger – then darted suddenly back and thrust his sword in Issei's chest.

Howling, Kai pounced. His skill was honed enough by Issei that even in a fury his tactical mind pulsed, and he sold his feint at the tengu's midsection before stepping wide and throwing all his force into a high backhand. The hammerhead passed through the tengu's face in a burst of bone and flesh and feathers.

Kai crouched beside his master. Blood flooded from Issei's mouth and nostrils, his battle-dress was soaking crimson. Throwing Issei over a shoulder, Kai hauled his master toward the forest. When an oni with a scythe blitzed at him, Kai braced for a fight he could not win.

Arrows sprouted at the oni's flanks. It stumbled and snarled at the five Issei soldiers dashing to Kai, including the archer who further enraged the oni by placing another arrow in its gut.

"Tell us what to do," barked a hulk with a battle-axe. Where his left ear had been now gaped a ragged hole.

A moan wisped out Issei's lips as Kai set him down. "Mind your range and wait for my command. You." Kai turned to the archer. "Go for the eyes. I'll draw it away, then the rest of you go in."

The oni barreled at Kai. He sidestepped, then smashed the side of its knee with his hammer. "Now! Move!" Kai ordered, evading a string of terrifying blows, allowing the others to carve up the oni from behind while the archer peppered it with arrows. Still the beast caught a spearman with the scythe, halving the man at the waist. Kai and the squad sliced, jabbed, smashed, and at last brought the monster to a knee. As Kai busied the creature in front, the axe-man hacked into its neck, stroke after stroke like a woodcutter chopping a stubborn tree, until he gave a guttural roar and with a final swing the gargantuan head slid from the shoulders.

"I'm Haru, sir." The hulk bowed, shaking his axe clean.

"Mito, sir," said the archer, short, wiry, with ever-scanning eyes. The two others gave their names.

"We're taking the commander away from here," Kai said. "Haru, you men, carry him. Mito, cover. Follow me." As he led the squad away, he noted how the oni and tengu held off from attacking Guardians. "Wait. Take sashes from the Guardians and put them on. And swap out your armor." Stripping the items from enemy dead, they made their way toward the forest. Just before reaching its boundary an oni thundered at them. Kai's guts turned to ice, but he kept moving, and upon spotting the sash, the beast ran past, and they entered the forest.

In a glade, Kai propped Issei against a tree then tore his tunic into bandages before stopping, knowing it pointless. Clenching blood-stained teeth, Issei craned his head to take in the battlefield. "My army... gone?"

Kai took his hand, surprised at the strength in it. "Gone, master."

"You've gone far with me, boy. Now go… alone." Lord Issei stared into him with such vigor and feeling, it was only when the hand went limp Kai knew his savior had made the final passage.

Issei had taken in Kai as a boy, when he was nothing but a wicked heart and beastly mind, and from those crude parts fashioned a human being. Kai wasted no time now on useless words of farewell. His duty and debt to the man could be fulfilled only by action. He addressed the four soldiers who were all that remained of Issei's once-mighty army. Though none showed obvious fear, Kai sensed they needed gingering up, just as he had during the battle. "Lord Issei swore to free the Japanese lands from the wicked shadow of the Guardians. Today we carry on his vow and finish our fight. Maybe you doubt we can strike a blow after our army has been destroyed. Do not let doubt take station in your hearts. We know our enemy now. We will take the head of Jomon. Blunt our blades slaying these kaijin. All that will come, my brothers, and soon. But for now, we must be wise, so we hold, we watch, we hunt for our moment."

Using a trick from his bandit days, from branches and leaves Kai wove a camouflage screen to cover the ditch in which they hid, watching the grisly aftermath of the battle. The field rose now in a series of rolling hummocks, each made of dead Issei men. Monsters and Guardians scoured for survivors, binding the uninjured and leading them off, brutalizing the wounded. Its work done, the human-kaijin force quit the field, flying and marching south. "After the last man goes by, we follow," Kai said. "We have the sashes to muddle the kaijin, but don't let any officers see you. I don't want to chance it."

They seamlessly fell in with the column, tromping through the forest and down into a gully. A stone wall as thick as any fortress defense spanned the width of the gully, protecting a massive rock formation ahead. The Guardians passed through an open gate in the wall and into a wide tunnel gaping into the rock. As they approached, Kai whispered to his men. "I don't know what's waiting in there for us. Stay close, watch me. If it gets hot and you don't see my signal, or I'm dead, strike at Jomon – or whoever truly commands these fiends."

Scattered torches jammed into the wall gave just enough thin light to discern their next step. Kai sniffed the dankness of centuries-trapped air as they descended a wide, spiraling stair. Murmured chant softly echoed. At the foot of the stairs began a long path of rock alongside a channel of deep black water. The chant loudened, the words growing clearer as they incessantly repeated.

"Arise, Great Mother, we beseech you with blood upon our hands
"Arise, Great Mother, be again one with your land."

The stone pathway brought Kai and his men to a giant cavern. Ranks of Guardians knelt in supplication before a giant elliptical pool of water. The chamber walls, the height of a score of men, were honeycombed with dozens of caves or tunnel mouths. Near the lip of the pool stood Hierophant Jomon, who raised an arm to end the chant and spoke toward the water. "Mother of the Sleepers, I have great tidings! We have done as you bid us! Issei was gulled into the ambush, his army is crushed! I beg that you reveal yourself. As tithe to you I dedicate these lives." Jomon nodded to a man, who oversaw Issei prisoners driven at spear-point to the pool's lip and forced to kneel. A Guardian stood behind each of them, dagger bared.

Kai's men turned to him, the yearning for daring action plain in their eyes. He shook his head. Those men were doomed, and any action now would win nothing but their own deaths; Kai needed a greater goal. Biting back his rage, he winced as Jomon give the order: "Exalt the Mother." As one the execution-ers dragged their blades across the prisoners' throats, their life-blood jetting into the pool.

"Show yourself!" Jomon pleaded to the still water. "We ask that you..." The chancellor trailed off, bewitched by a gentle rippling on the water's surface. "Yes, rise, Great Mother, rise! Witness my fearsome soldiers before you! Together with your children, no one dares stand against us! All the kingdoms shall be brought to heel!"

A blur of motion.

On an impossibly long, spindly arm, a hand shot from the water, snatched a Jomon trooper from the front rank and yanked him screaming into the pool. A red cloud mottled the surface. Another arm whizzed out. Another. Long fingers raked in Guardians. Now the water swirled and frothed. A head broke the surface and swooped up on a lengthy, sinuous neck.

The whole of the chamber released a collective, ecstatic sigh. Kai reeled at what hovered above the water – a woman's head, in some demented fashion, with strings of blue-black hair. Eyes like moons filmed in the hue of blood, a jumble of sharp teeth set in an outsized mouth. What form of body lurked beneath the surface? Kai shuddered.

The Mother spoke in a primordial dialect, her voice a demonic trumpet echoing in the cavern. "Once, the whole of your kind worshiped me and my children. We ruled these lands, receiving reverence. That faded and for centuries we slept. Issei could have caused mischief had he united the kingdoms against me. Now he is no more, I will take my place again." The Mother turned toward the honeycombed cavern walls. "Wake, my children, wake!" Oni and tengu appeared at the tunnel mouths. They might have numbered fifty.

It was clear they relied on the Mother to direct them. Perhaps their sole vulnerability. "She's our target," Kai whispered, "above all else." His men nodded grim understanding – striking her would be suicide.

Jomon stepped forward. "Yes, Great Mother! Wake all your children! Behold the strength of our combined forces… none can defy us!"

The Mother looked over his ranks. "Is this the whole of your army?"

"For now. Many will flock to our banner now that all know our power. Then we must—"

A hand snapped out of the water, seizing Jomon by the skull and lifting him off his feet. "Brazen sack of meat! You would dictate commands to me?!" the Mother seethed, and she yanked the flailing Hierophant into the depths of the pool. A moment later he surged from the water trailing a red spray from the shreds of his arms and legs. "Feast, my children," the Mother cried. "Feast!"

From the cave mouths the oni flung themselves savagely upon the Guardians. Tengu launched, swooping and slicing with their blades. If Guardians ran from one closing kaijin it was only into the fatal clutches of another. A triple-horned oni barreled at Kai. Into its path he shoved a Guardian, who readied his spear, only to have the behemoth rip the offending arm from its socket.

"Go!" Kai commanded his men, driving towards the Mother's pool. Seeing the massacre was well in hand, she slipped deep into the water. "Faster!" Kai yelled, weaving among the pockets of Guardians, using them as a screen against the kaijin. Yet the Guardians steadily dropped, leaving Kai and his squad exposed. A tengu dipped down ahead of them, swung its sword and flew on, leaving the head of one of Kai's soldiers bouncing in its wake. An oni veered for them. Though Mito pinned two arrows in its chest, still it barreled on.

"He's mine!" Hiro roared, and he rushed the oni, his great axe held high. Kai pulled his men along, Hiro's sacrifice buying enough time to reach the edge of the pool.

"Dive in!" Kai yelled to Mito. "Get ready to—"

Mito suddenly dangled upside down. His ankle was gripped by the oni with two arrows in its chest. The monster plunged its free hand into Mito's belly, ripping out his guts before tossing him aside like an emptied husk. With its gore-smeared hand, the oni snatched at Kai.

He leaped into the water. Weighed down by his plundered Guardian armor, he sank until he ripped off his breast plate and bits of his own armor, then pushed back to the surface. The oni had forgotten him, lofting a Guardian, and biting a chunk from the man's thigh. Gulping air, Kai went under again. His hammer secured on its strap across his back, he dived and probed the ink-dark water with the spear. No contact with the Mother, but Kai detected a break in the wall – a submerged tunnel. Surfacing for a deep breath, he dived once more and swam in, picking up speed as the tunnel wound on and on. His lungs burned, and panic edged his mind at the fear his air wouldn't last. His flailing hands met only more black water. Would the tunnel lead on and on until his air gave out? He stifled an urge to scream in panic, knowing it would only hasten his doom. He swam on, his boiling muscles clamoring for air.

Ahead, a lightening of shadows – a shimmer of hope.

At last, the tunnel ended. Kai surfaced in another enormous chamber, grabbed a handhold on a rocky slab. In the silence here his panting resounded dangerously, until he bit down on his fist to kill the noise. After his breathing steadied, he scanned the cavern, anemic strands of sunlight leaking through tiny faults in the roof offering scant detail. Stone shelves or ledges studded the high walls, each holding a humanoid form in repose – tengu, oni, and other types of kaijin. Sleepers, waiting to be stirred. What terror they would visit on the land.

Kai kicked quietly toward the narrow, rocky floor ringing the water—

Something clamped around his legs.

The Mother.

Kai was dragged under, managing a shallow breath. Fighting her in the water was like grappling a swarm of eels, her hands too many to fend. Sudden agony in his left shoulder – tendons strained to keep hold of his arm as she wrenched at his left wrist. He reached for his war-hammer, gripping it below the head, knowing that underwater he'd achieve little power. Another moment or two and the Mother would tear off his arm, and so without faith in his aim he thrust with the hammer's spike. He felt metal plunge into tissue and instantly the Mother's clutch slackened. Kai kicked desperately to the surface and clambered onto the ledge, greedily sucking air.

The water rippled.

Kai slid his hand through the hammer's wrist loop. He'd been lucky down there but struck no mortal blow. The Mother's head quested out of the water. "Your race has much to answer for, and it shall begin with you." Her voice was monstrous yet eerily calm as she stepped to the floor.

She was worse than Kai had imagined. All was sinewy, spidery, a narrow trunk with four limbs the length of lances, each curling and twisting. White, sun-starved flesh like mildewed marble, hands tipped with serrated talons, and those moon-and-blood eyes taking his measure, gleamed with an awful lust. Giving an earsplitting cry, she dropped to all fours and came scuttling. He jinked away from a lashing hand, heaved his hammer. Missed. Another swing, another miss. He glimpsed a fleeting opening, swung at her face, missing by inches but striking home in the chest. She staggered, quailing.

Strapping his hammer back on, Kai hauled himself onto a shelf above, across the tengu laid out on it – perhaps for centuries asleep – and then sprang for the next shelf. Below, the Mother shot a hand to a shelf and began an arachnid climb up the wall. From shelf to shelf holding tengu and oni and other nameless monstrosities Kai clambered higher. It was not cowardice driving him, he hoped, but the simple certainty that if he stood his ground against the Mother, his luck and reflexes would soon give out. He had to find another way to fight.

Vaulting to the next shelf, Kai paused, glancing at the long-nosed visage of the tengu it bore. An idea. He rolled the monster over the ledge. There came a scream, midway between rage and fear, and Kai peered over to see the Mother clinging tenuous-ly to the wall, gripping the tengu with a single arm, her child hovering over the rocky floor.

The next shelf Kai scrambled to held a hulking oni, and he felt the ledge wobble at his added weight. Scraping up the last dregs of his strength, he heaved the slumbering form off the shelf headfirst. It plummeted like a stone into the Mother and the tengu, the three crashing to the ground in a heap. The tengu's wings and spine snapped, the oni's skull pulped on contact, and the Mother ensnared among her own limbs and her dead, mangled children.

The shrill scream she summoned melted Kai to his knees and, off balance from shoving his ungainly improvised weapon, he lost his footing. With more luck than skill, he seized the lip of the shelf, dangling. Her voice sharpened, became even more jagged, and it breached into his veins like some vile phantom. Blood trickled out his ears, his nostrils. All he wanted was to clap his hands over his ears and dampen the penetrating horror of that voice – but that would drop him right into her clutches. He could only hang on, praying to withstand a few more moments of the agony.

When her scream ended, Kai hoisted himself onto the shelf and retched, but knew that must be the extent of his recovery. Setting aside the broken bodies of her children, the Mother began to climb again, this time the *clack-clack-clack* of her taloned hands coming more swiftly than before. She alighted at a slumbering oni and crouched over the creature, her hands pressed to its temples as she lowered her face and pressed her lips, blowing. The supine monster's hands jerked alive, then its legs shook. The Mother was waking her child to aid the hunt.

Kai needed to act, now. He needed something else to drop. There was a fracture where the shelf fastened to the wall. Furiously he hammered at it, chips and shards spattering as the Mother left the waking oni and scaled closer.

At the shelf's tremble, he leaped. The force of his jump snapped the shelf from the wall, dropping and slamming into the Mother's hideous face.

With jellied limbs, Kai climbed. Nearing the top of the chamber he spied a narrow tunnel that led into darkness. He paused at a cracking sound. The seam he'd exploited in the rock was splintering into a web of fast-spreading cracks.

Below, the Mother pushed to her terrible feet. Kai chiseled at another shelf of rotten rock, his hammer barely holding together now. When the stone sheared off, the Mother, halfway up, screeched as the falling projectile glanced against her torso, yet she maintained her grip.

Another crack rent the air as the first seam widened. What started as isolated breaches fused into a chorus of splitting rock – something long silent finding its voice. The whole cavern tremored, rumbled, a cascade of rock.

Though she dodged and weaved, the Mother couldn't avoid the raining rock. She battered flurries, bore the brunt of sharp-edged stone until at last her strength failed and she fell with a wail. Desperately, Kai scrambled up and up. His finger jammed into a fissure, embedding there, and when he yanked it free his bone broke and the nail was ripped away. Whimpering but fighting on, he clawed finally into the high tunnel. A point of sunlight twinkled at its end, taunting Kai as he raced for it. The ground swayed, fragmenting underfoot and he was thrown to his knees.

A thundering roar as the ceiling collapsed behind him.

Kai scurried forward. A chunk thudded against his head, spangling his vision. Another crushed his knee. He stumbled on, tripping out the tunnel mouth and crumpling to the dirt as the masses of rock behind him tumbled down and away, entombing the Mother and her monstrous children for their endless sleep.

DOWN MEXICO WAY

James A. Moore

listering heat pounded down like a hammer blow on the wagon train. The horses and mules continued on just the same, plodding hoof after hoof through the sun-dried air. They could smell the water coming closer. At least that was what Culver told himself. All he could smell was dust.

Corporal Dennis Culver rode with the wagon train, fully expecting the trail in front of his horse to melt, or just possibly to burst into flames.

"This is Hell, Jerome. I'm certain we died back in Colorado."

Alvin Jerome looked in his direction and shook his head sadly, his long mustache making him look even sadder. "You should not mock the punishments the Lord inflicts, Culver. He might take offense."

Jerome still believed in God. Culver did not. Surely a god would have stopped the atrocities they had both seen in their time. However, Jerome was a sergeant. His faith outranked Culver's atheism.

"All due respect, Jerome—" He was cut off by a scream coming from ahead of them. The only sound he'd been expecting was the shrill whistle from the lead wagon, a signal that they were done for the day and could come to a rest.

Up ahead, the night had taken over. The sun was setting, its rays devoured by a rare cloud that swept the horizon, a possible promise of much needed rain.

"What in the name of Heaven?" Jerome was alert, and he pulled his rifle from the side of his saddle where it had been resting and waiting. He may look like he was ready to cry, but the man was as prepared for battle as anyone Culver had ever known.

Culver reached for his own rifle, prepared to do what he had to despite a powerful need for peace in his world. He had promised to deliver the priest and the nuns and the whole congregation to a safe place, and he aimed to do so, whether or not there was a God. The doubt in his mind did not overwhelm the hope in his heart. Not yet at least.

The Lord apparently needed more priests in Mexico, so he'd do his part.

The sounds coming to him made no sense. First there was the scream. That was strange enough, but the other sound, the high-pitched whine that actually hurt his ears, made no sense at all.

A horse shrieked and the team bolted. The wagon capsized after a dozen paces, pulled too sharply off course for the wheels to compensate. The boy trying to control the horses let out a yelp that was cut short when his head hit the hard-packed trail.

Jerome stood in his stirrups and took aim with his rifle, though what exactly he aimed at was a complete mystery to Culver. Jerome fired; cursed under his breath.

"What are you aiming at?"

"I don't know. There's something up there. In the sky." Jerome scanned the darkness ahead of them and his lips worried at his drooping moustache.

There were dark clouds, nearly black, but beyond that? Nothing that Culver could see. He kept looking until… "There." He wasn't sure what it was, but he saw it. It was big, he knew that much, and it made noises.

No. Not it. *They.* They were big. There were several of them up in the clouds. He'd heard a scout talking about the Thunderbirds once, great birds that rode in with storms and carried off whatever they could eat. That'd be about the worst thing he could imagine.

Even as that thought came to him, one of the dark shapes dropped lower and caught a woman by her head and shoulder. He knew the woman well enough. Sister Catherine, a heavyset lady with a kind smile and the coldest eyes he'd ever seen. She screamed as she was pulled from the wagon where she'd been perching, and was lifted into the air.

"Good Lord." Jerome took careful aim, but then hesitated. While he considered his chances of hitting that dark shape and not hitting the nun, both vanished higher into the clouds.

"What are they, Jerome?" He couldn't see them clearly; he knew his sight was going. They made spectacles to fix such issues, of course, but he never quite had the time to take care of the situation before something else came along and now he was paying for that reasoning.

"I don't know!" Jerome was screaming now, trying to drown out that horrid, painful, ringing noise. He fired at something in the darkness and Culver flinched at the sound.

Darkness was spreading at an incredible speed. The sun had set now, and whatever was out there was growing bolder. More people screamed, and the air was filled with wet sounds of flesh tearing, cloth shredding, and bones being pulled one from the next.

Culver aimed at the darkness and fired. He had no idea if he hit what he was aiming for, but he could see men climbing from wagons now, grabbing firearms and preparing to fight against whatever the shapes were dropping from the sky.

A dark silhouette alighted on the capsized wagon and from inside it someone screamed. The boy who'd struck his head was lifted into the air by the darkness and carried higher, higher, following the same path as poor Sister Catherine. More shapes landed on the wagon even as another of the carriages was suddenly lifted into the air in fits and jerks and then dropped back to the ground, simply too heavy for whatever was trying to carry it away.

Culver aimed again and fired, hitting something that let out a shriek and flopped backward. He might be losing his long-distance sight but he wasn't blind yet.

Something caught his shoulder, and the beating of massive wings shredded the air around him, the winds so harsh from the flapping that he could not keep his eyes open.

Culver tried to stab at whatever was above him with the barrel of his rifle but it did little good. He felt the end of the rifle strike flesh, but it was as unyielding as stone.

Before he could try to defend himself a second time the ground and horse were ripped away from him. Thick talons cut into his flesh, piercing his uniform with ease. The pain was sudden and overwhelming, and Culver let out a yelp of pain as he was lifted into the air. His eyes grew wide as he rose higher and higher, the darkness above him flapping powerful wings and hauling him into the nighttime skies.

Something black lifted into the air and came toward him with the direct approach of an arrow.

A moment later, that something caught hold of him.

There was pain, and then there was darkness.

✝ 🏆 ✝

"I have considered the situation carefully, Mister Crowley, and I have decided that Hell is not likely to be quite as hot as this place." Lucas Slate spoke as softly as ever, which is to say his voice was just above a sepulchral whisper. Happily, for all involved, Jonathan Crowley had excellent hearing.

Slate removed his top hat and wiped a handkerchief over his pale brow. He was an albino, and that was the least of the things that made him stand out. He was overly tall and bore a powerful semblance to a cadaver.

"Your ability to state the obvious never ceases to be a source of entertainment, Mister Slate." Crowley's voice was as dry as the air around them but substantially cooler in temperature.

They were at the edge of a massive river. According to the crude map they'd procured, the river was the Rio Grande. The scale on most of the map was hideously out of proportion, and it was an effort on Crowley's part not to hunt down and kill the man they'd purchased it from. He might have done it too, but hunting the fool down would have required at least two weeks of back-tracking and a good deal more energy than he wished to expend.

Instead they followed what appeared to be a trail left by a caravan, that coincided with the trail on their map.

They had followed a path drawn out on the map that showed approximately two days' worth of travel time. It had been twelve days longer for them to reach the river than expected. That was the first reason for Crowley's poor mood. The other reason was simply that Slate was right. It was extremely hot and, aside from the river, the area was bone dry.

They called it a short day for travel and took their time bathing and letting the horses rest up from the arduous journey. There were fish in the waters, and they ate fresh meat for their supper.

The night was dry and hot, just as the day had been, and though sleep did not come easily to Crowley, or to his companion, both managed to rest for a while. When the sun rose, they readied themselves and rode south again, crossing the wide river and traveling toward what was supposed to be a caravan route that would take them to see several spectacular wonders.

Instead, four hours into their trek, they found bodies.

There had, indeed, been a caravan of travelers ahead of them. Several wagons were overturned and ruined, their contents spread out far as the eye could see. Clothes, vital supplies, parts of human bodies and several horses as well, decorated the landscape. Looked as if most of the horses had made good on escaping. The same could not be said for the people.

The slaughter was fairly fresh. Wet blood baked in the heat of the day, swarming black flies filled the air with the buzz of their activity. The vultures and carrion crows had made themselves known, though they'd surely only been there a short time.

Crowley looked the area over carefully, and Slate joined him. Neither man felt the need to speak as they studied the cadavers and considered the wounds. It was not the first time they'd had occasion to stare at bodies together. It likely wouldn't be the last.

"Should we bury them?" Slate spoke softly, as always.

Crowley shook his head. "It's too hot."

"It's the decent thing to do."

"Granted. But it's still too hot and I'm not being paid to be decent."

"Last I checked you weren't being paid."

"As a matter of fact, I am not. That makes me less inclined to do the decent thing." Crowley squinted against the glare from the sun and looked to the south. All evidence led to whatever had done the damage heading that way. It wasn't an easy assessment to make, as there were no prints of any kind to follow, merely a few stretches of bloody ground that seemed to trail that way.

"Hardly seems right."

"Seems to me the things that did the slaughtering should clean up their own damned messes." Crowley adjusted his gambler's hat and continued to look south. "I've got different ideas in mind." He looked at Lucas Slate and shrugged. "And last I checked you normally left the bodies above ground if you weren't getting paid."

"I was an undertaker, sir." His voice was stiff and bore a heavier southern drawl than usual.

"The longer I know you, the less you seem capable of taking a joke."

"And the longer I know you, Mister Crowley, the less you seem capable of telling one."

Crowley smiled and nodded. "I've a mind to find these things."

"To what end?"

"Why, I expect to deliver some mayhem, Mister Slate."

"And is it not true that you can't come to the aid of others without being invited to do so?"

"I cannot come to the aid of others without being asked, if I expect to use my more unusual abilities. That does not mean I can't come to their aid. And I'm not coming to the aid of anyone." Crowley gestured. "They're all dead."

Slate's eyes narrowed and he stared hard at Crowley. "I am not sure what you are up to, Mister Crowley, but I expect I won't like it."

Crowley smiled and climbed back on his horse. Despite his words, Slate followed his lead.

"What do you see, Mister Slate?" The question was one Crowley often asked. Lucas Slate knew the question well enough to understand he was expected to find the unusual in any circumstance and state *why* it was unusual. Crowley was his teacher in many things, not the least of which was how to use his expanded senses.

And so he looked around carefully, frowning in concentration. "There are no footprints. No sign that anyone came through this way." He scanned the terrain. "No footprints that are coming from anywhere else that is. Plenty on the trail." He continued to examine the area. "But there are still paths of blood."

"And what does that tell us?"

"I have no idea." Slate shook his head, the long, fine white hair sweeping back and forth in the arid air.

"Either our prey have an incredibly light tread, or they did not walk."

"That makes me ponder two things. You think there's more than one of whatever did this? And what other methods are there?"

Crowley pointed to the sky. "There are many creatures with wings, my good man. And while there might only be one creature, I have my doubts as there are different markings. Some are claws. Some are teeth. The bite marks tell me more than one creature did this. Teeth are different in different mouths."

"Well then, I suppose one of us should look to the skies." Slate pulled off his top hat and ran a hand through his long hair, shaking his head in the process. He did not look at all pleased by the notion.

"I could be completely wrong, Mister Slate. Stranger things have happened."

Pale blue eyes under heavy eyelids regarded him for a long moment. "That's true enough. However, you are seldom wrong in your logical deductions, Mister Crowley. I am simply not pleased by the idea of something dropping from the sky that is large enough to lift a horse off the ground."

"Nobody who is sound of mind would be, Mister Slate. I suggest we have our weapons at the ready. Just in case."

Crowley stopped talking long enough to gather several baskets and fill them with untainted food and supplies. He added two barrels of water, and then with Slate's help attached a wagon to Slate's horse. The horse, being dead and reanimated by Slate some time back, did not seem at all bothered by the additional weight. Crowley noted that the dead animal seldom so much as swatted at flies, though they often tended to draw near the beast if there was nothing else nearby that was dead enough to capture their attention.

Sometimes, he wondered exactly why he let the animal continue on rather than simply burning it and buying a new horse for his companion. Possibly, he mused, because he wanted to know exactly what Slate was capable of, and the horse had caused no harm to anyone as yet.

They rode on in silence for well over an hour before they found the ruins. They were, to be kind, completely unexpected.

Slate saw them first. Crowley studied the man's face as he spotted them. The man's eyes flew wide open and his mouth dropped into a O of surprise.

Rather than ask what was wrong, he looked in the same direction and saw what there was to see.

The ground in the area had broken and pushed forth a ruined structure. The very center resembled the pyramids he had seen so long ago in Egypt, but there were obvious differences. The stone here was cut differently and of a dark gray coloration. There were trails of steps leading to the top of the structure, or there had been, at least. What was left was a fractured hint of previous glories. On either side of the main shape, a long bend of stone ruins formed the arm of a horseshoe shape. The soil around the structure was freshly ruptured, as if the whole thing had pushed from the ground like a sapling grown from a seed. Thick dirt trails and mud covered large portions of the structure, and trailed the roots of various plants that had come out of the ground and fallen away in most cases.

At the very top of the pyramid was a large stone carving. The design was very stylized, but whatever it might be, and despite a very humanoid shape, it had wings instead of arms.

"I have to say, I'm not the least bit sure what the hell that form is supposed to represent." Crowley spoke in a purely conversational tone as he looked at the effigy. "I can't say if that's a crow, or something else entirely."

"Does rather look like it was sculpted by a toddler playing in the mud," Slate agreed.

"It's not a bad sculpture, just... very far from anatomically accurate." He squinted against the sunlight and studied the thing carefully. "It has bat wings, I think. Look at the arms and the shape of the wings."

"I don't know that I've ever seen a bat in my life, Mister Crowley."

"I study flora and fauna. I've seen at least a dozen varieties. Looks like a leaf-nosed bat to me. Or a vampire bat. Which, when you consider the blood and shredded meat we encountered, makes a bit of sense, really."

"While I acknowledge my ignorance of the actual form, aren't bats night-dwelling creatures?" Slate spoke calmly enough but there was an edge now.

"They are indeed."

"As the sun looks to be with us for a while, we might well discover the truth of whether or not this is a bat of some sort only if we are patient."

"That merely means we have time aplenty for examining our new ruins." Crowley looked toward the sun just barely approaching its zenith.

"We could also take this time to eat."

"I'd think all that bloodshed would have turned your delicate stomach from the notion, Mister Slate."

"I find very little makes me hungry these days, Mister Crowley, but sustenance is always a good notion if one wishes to be prepared for an extended battle."

"What makes you think we'll have an 'extended battle'?"

Slate looked his way with those half-lidded eyes. "Mister Crowley I also find that very few conflicts where you are involved end quickly. You tend to make a great number of enemies wherever you go."

"I'm not the one who offends the Indians merely by existing."

"I certainly can't control the opinions of savages."

"Savages?"

"A group comes at me with plans to skin me or burn me, they earn the title savages."

"So sensitive, Mister Slate." Crowley tsked. "One would expect more forgiveness from a Christian."

"I'm very forgiving of those that do not approach me with a desire to cause harm."

"Well said, sir."

Crowley took the time to eat an apple and several strips of dried beef. Slate joined him in his repast.

They then walked around the entire newly erupted structure.

The earth was still damp around the base, though the exterior of the soil had formed a hard, dried crust. Crowley estimated no more than a day or so in the baking heat of the sun. "Whatever happened, Mister Slate, it happened recently. Much longer and the soil would be as cooked through as the rest of this area." He pointed to where the ground was hard-baked and cracked from a lack of moisture.

There were no entrances to the temple that they could find on the ground level. There were, however, many elaborate carvings in the stone that told a story of sorts. There were two men, and one vast thing with a stylized mouth full of fangs and with the same sort of blade-like nose and overly large, rounded ears. Whatever it was, it wore a necklace of skulls, carried a dagger in one hand and what looked to be a heart in the other. Around it there were many smaller shapes that bowed and held out offerings to it.

If there was sense to be made of the images, if they told a story, neither Crowley nor Slate could understand the tale told.

"I would dearly love to spend a few weeks examining this place, Mister Slate." Crowley spoke with an odd longing in his voice that Slate found both curious and oddly endearing.

"I daresay we're not in a hurry to be elsewhere, Mister Crowley."

"True enough, but I expect the setting sun might change your mind, Mister Slate. As we have discussed, whatever attacked came out at night."

Slate looked to the sky and was surprised to see that the sun had lowered considerably.

"I didn't realize we had spent so much time here."

"We have been busy, Mister Slate. A busy mind often fails to keep track of the passage of time."

Slate squinted at the stairs leading to the top of the pyramid. "Time to arm ourselves?"

"I think that would be for the best."

They walked back to the horses. Flies once again swarmed around Slate's unusual steed, which continued to ignore them completely.

Crowley scowled at the lack of wood for a fire.

From the ground near the pyramid in the distance, the first noises came their way. Crowley looked at the figure on the pyramid's top again. It had large ears, or the strangest looking crown he had ever seen.

"I'd suggest making sure your weapons are loaded, Mister Slate." He pulled his own Peacemakers even as he spoke, and checked that both were fully loaded.

Slate looked to both his rifle and his shotgun and nodded his satisfaction. "Should we do something to protect the horses?"

"I'd say that would be wise, Mister Slate."

Whatever it was that Slate did, Crowley felt it but heard and saw nothing. As he did his best to see what Slate did at all times, for like it or not, Slate was potentially a very dangerous man, he did not like the notion in the least.

The sounds came faster now and louder, more plentiful, a series of high-pitched screeches and squeaks that seemed to carry from the pyramid and the whole of the horseshoe-shaped structure.

"I have to say, Mister Crowley, that I do not like these incessant noises."

"Nor do I, sir. I find them very disconcerting." Almost as unsettling as the notion that Lucas Slate might well perform magics to which he was not privy.

"Prepare yourself, Mister Slate."

"I have not been standing here admiring your beauty, sir."

"I would certainly hope not."

"Here they come."

Lucas Slate was right. Whatever they were, they came fast, spilling from the top of the pyramid like smoke from a campfire. They were little more than dark shapes against the deepening night but neither Crowley nor Slate had any trouble seeing them for what they were.

The creatures were emaciated, thin from far too long without food. If they had been buried in the ground as Crowley suspected, they had likely been starved for a long time. Possibly they had been hibernating and had simply used up whatever supplies of body fat they might have accumulated.

Whatever the case, they were very thin, and their features were drawn as tight as those of Lucas Slate, as if they bordered on the edge of death.

They had long, humanoid bodies, but where arms should have been the limbs were too long, and the fingers were stretched to impossible length and sported dark membranes between each, the sails of a ship, or the wings of bats.

They flapped their arms and the wind caught and up they rose, massive, bat-like nightmares made flesh. The high-pitched noises erupted from them, and they carried themselves higher into the air before drifting in a widening gyre.

"We could well have a problem on our hands, Mister Crowley." It may have been that Slate wanted to break the tension with his words, but what he accomplished instead was to capture the attention of the things soaring in the air above them.

Crowley cursed but did not answer. He was too focused on

the creatures circling in the sky, and how some of them changed course and began dropping toward the sound of Slate's voice.

"Scold me later, Mister Crowley." Slate knew he'd made a mistake and tried to compensate by aiming with his rifle.

The first of the creatures to descend toward them let out one last screech before its head exploded. It dropped from the sky like a stone, and several of the other creatures followed it. As it smashed into the ground its brethren dropped to feast, long tongues lapping at the hot blood spilled from the body. Crowley and Slate alike noticed but ignored them for the moment. There were far more of the creatures coming for them now, and they took precedent.

Closer up, the creatures looked diseased. Their fur was patchy and their skin mottled with areas both darker and paler than the majority of their flesh. Crowley took note of that fact as he aimed carefully and fired.

The shot caught one of the creatures in the neck and it dropped, screaming in an unsettlingly human way as it fell toward the ground, trailed by several other bat-things. It had not yet struck the ground before they were feasting on its remains. The frenzy for blood was apparently severe in the beasts.

They kept coming, more and more of the nightmarish things spilling from the top of the pyramid, a nearly continuous stream. Slate methodically tracked one and fired, missed and fired again with better results. Crowley shot and hit another of the beasts, this time in the chest, and as before the things followed their fallen kindred to the ground, quickly and efficiently making short work of attacking their own wounded.

Crowley shook his head. It simply didn't happen that any healthy creature attacked its own kind, with the exception of humans. Some animals might fight for territory, but beyond that? And to cannibalize their own? Whatever the things were, they were not healthy. They were too frantic to be anything but desperate.

Slate put down another of the things and then raised his shotgun and aimed as more of them came in closer.

There was no time for conversation. The things were coming in too fast now. The air was filled with the muted thunder of too many massive shapes beating wings to stay aloft and then with the sudden explosive noise of Slate's shotgun releasing a hail of death upon them. One of the creatures spun backward and dropped, another veered from the sky and fell, with one wing shattered by buckshot.

Slate had insisted on trying his luck with the slide action shotgun they'd found in Carson City and neither of them had reason to regret the decision. He pumped the slide action again and fired, undaunted by the weapon's kick. Another of the bat creatures fell back, eviscerated by the hail of buckshot.

Crowley emptied his first Peacemaker and then the second, delivering death as quickly as he could. His hands moved with practiced speed, sliding new bullets into their chambers, feeling the heat of the shells as he pulled spent bullets free and replaced them.

Before he was finished, one of the creatures caught him. Thick talons snagged the fabric of his shirt and tore through it easily, hooking into his flesh. Crowley hissed, and snapped the cylinder in place for his revolver. He aimed and fired; watched the wound that blossomed in the flailing nightmare's stomach. It released him before it could manage to become airborne, and then the thrice-damned thing fell back, slapping and screaming, a massive wound bleeding out from the bullet hole.

The wound in Crowley's arm started mending, and he was grateful to feel it happen before the scent of his blood caught more unwanted attention.

Wind and dust crawled higher and higher in the growing darkness as the great shapes neared. Several of the things had landed and were feasting, but they barely seemed to matter in comparison to those gathering around the two men. There were so very many of the nightmares still in the air and more boiling from the pyramid by the moment.

"We are going to lose, Mister Crowley!" Slate was yelling but could barely be heard over the sound of the numerous things flying around them.

Crowley called out words that had not been heard in the world for centuries, and stepped closer to Slate as he did so.

The albino stood perfectly still, frozen, his eyes wide in shock as whatever it was that inhabited his body reacted to the incantation.

"What have you done?"

Crowley didn't respond. Instead he braced himself as the winds picked up and howled. The dust, already thick enough to choke a man, grew stronger and he squinted and lowered himself into a squat as the bats fought to resist the air currents now pushing them to the west.

The creatures squealed and screeched and flapped their wings furiously as the winds caught them and hurled them westward. Many of the things fell to the ground and rolled, but just as many were cast along by the howling tempest. Not far away Lucas Slate braced himself against the winds and held tight to his top hat as if the loss of it would mean his life. His teeth were bared, eyes squinted shut and his hair whipped manically, but the man stayed where he was.

The bats were not as fortunate. Those that fell to the ground struggled to keep their place and the ones foolish enough to attempt flight were thrown about as if they were wheat thresh in a tornado.

After almost two minutes the winds abruptly ceased. Crowley stood as the dust settled. Lucas Slate didn't speak. He merely stared at Crowley.

"I created a means by which we would not lose, Mister Slate. What did you expect me to do?"

Slate carefully wiped the dust from the brim of his hat and from the top of it, then gingerly placed it back atop his head. "I might expect a bit of warning, Mister Crowley."

"If I expected you could have heard me over those damned things, I might have given it, too." There were a great number of the creatures on the ground, most of them bloodied and broken. One of them tried moving closer, and Lucas Slate walked over to it and promptly blew its head away with a blast from his shotgun. Others moved, and when they did, Slate repeated his action. Crowley joined him in short order. Broken did not mean dead, as both knew from experience.

"What are they, Mister Crowley?" Slate asked the question as he reloaded his shotgun. Crowley studied the closest of the things. It had the basic shape of a bat, but that form was distorted as if by a funhouse mirror. The bodies were too thin, the legs as long as a man's. The faces were longer than expected, too. It was neither human nor bat, but an odd collection of both.

"I assure you I've never seen their like before, Mister Slate." He gestured to the pyramid. "Though I expect the answer is one that has a long history. Given enough time and inclination I expect I could tell you at least a tainted version of that history. Looks like whatever they are, they were worshipped by the locals at one time. How they got buried, how they survived being buried, and why they have now risen to the surface again? Those are questions that might take a good deal more time to explain."

Slate looked away from the broken bodies surrounding them and stared at the pyramid again, his cadaverous face lost in thought.

"What's bothering you, Mister Slate?"

"They do not look like the sorts of things I would expect to be worshipped as gods."

"What do you mean?"

"Firstly, these creatures look diseased."

"Well, if they have been hibernating they might well have used up any and all sources of food some time back. They could have resorted to cannibalism and, as we have already witnessed, they are not above such actions. Malnutrition would likely explain the patchy fur and skin."

Slate nodded. "We have already determined that I am what some of the local tribes have referred to as a 'skinwalker'."

Crowley nodded.

"Given the rather spectacular level of abilities the more experienced of my kind have shown, I could almost see them being considered as god-like, but the locals we have encountered with knowledge of their type have treated them as demons, devils or worse, not as gods."

"Well, to be fair, the ones we've met were hardly god-like in their demeanor."

"And have you met gods before, Mister Crowley?"

"I have met several creatures that wanted to be worshipped as such."

"And did they, as a rule, look human?"

"No, but neither do these things."

"And did they come in such vast numbers?"

"Your point is taken, Mister Slate. They did not."

"And surely if this temple was not built as a house of worship for the bat creatures, there might be something that they worshipped?"

Crowley shook his head and said, "Damn me for a fool."

"You have been rather out of practice for some time, Mister Crowley."

"No, Mister Slate. I have grown comfortable with being among more civilized peoples and among monotheistic societies."

"I beg pardon?"

"I spent too damned much time among the Europeans, and before them among the Asians and Chinese. I have grown accustomed to a certain level of civilization and stopped considering the more isolated places in the world."

To the east the moon rose, a heavy orange orb that cast its light upon the landscape and brought more detail to the carnage around them. The dead were numerous, but the injured were more common.

"I fear we are not yet finished with this grisly work." Slate sighed the words.

Crowley nodded. "I expect the worst is yet to come, Mister Slate, especially if you are correct in these creatures being the worshippers and not the worshipped."

"I dream of a day when you say that the very worst is behind us."

"I assure you, I would only ever say those words in jest."

"Sadly, I do not doubt your sincerity." Slate sighed again as he looked around.

It wasn't long before more of the bat-things exploded from the pyramid. These, however, looked less diseased and better nourished. They rushed from the top of the structure and rose high into the air before circling, doubtless seeking fresh food. Unlike their predecessors, they did not need Slate to speak before they found the two men.

Once again, the sound of gunfire quickly filled the night as both men took aim and fired at the vile things. Just as with their predecessors, however, these nightmares took to the idea of cannibalism easily. Their wounded and their dead were easier prey, and so they became a feast for the creatures.

Crowley observed the damned beasts and shook his head in wonder. They were stronger, healthier, but still too diseased. They had discolorations and weaker spots, and they stank of infection. Like as not they were far healthier than the previous wave of creatures and he wondered if they came from deeper within the bowels of the pyramid. Did they just now awaken from their long sleep? Had they been moving all along deep within the ground? Some of them even wore rudimentary clothes. Loin cloths and skirts designed to work around their wings.

"What are these things, Mister Crowley?" Slate bellowed to be heard over the constant noise. Crowley heard him but could only shake his head in response. He still didn't know, only knew that he was rapidly running out of bullets as he fired again and again.

Slate fired one last shell from his shotgun and then let it drop to his side.

He swept up the rifle he'd strapped across his back and aimed carefully before firing.

"Mister Slate, I think this might be a good time for you to consider what your abilities might allow you to do."

"I thought you might summon another wind, actually."

"Let's see what you're capable of, Mister Slate. I am quite tired."

"I don't know that there's anything I can do here."

"You won't know, either, until you try, sir!"

Slate bared his teeth and considered the situation. He looked at a complete loss, which was perfectly understandable considering the circumstances. That didn't do a solitary thing to make Crowley happy about the situation.

Sometimes the man needed a push to connect with his other, darker half. Lucas Slate was a good man. His other part, the Skinwalker, was not. "Now, Mister Slate. Do something now!"

"Do not pressure me, Mister Crowley!" The voice that came from his companion did not sound right. It was deeper than usual, and certainly louder.

Slate swept a hand outward and roared, the sound of his voice impossibly distorted, unsettlingly loud.

The air around him burned, and the creatures flying in that air burned with it. Crowley defended himself automatically, deflecting the eldritch power sent toward him. Fires ignited on flesh, and membranous wings exploded into flame even as the things around them veered and tried to find a safe place to extinguish the sudden pain. Crowley smiled despite their predicament. Slate listened to him, and as dangerous as that might be, it was a momentary salvation.

"Mister Crowley!" Slate's eyes grew wide in his cadaverous face, and he reached for Crowley as if to take back the harm he'd caused. He relaxed noticeably when he saw Crowley was unscathed.

The creatures did not concern themselves with food. They worried instead about escaping the sudden, hideous pain they were experiencing. Their cries were worse than they had been as they flipped madly, flew in new directions or collapsed on themselves and crashed to the earth.

Through it all, Crowley smiled, a dark and sinister grin that had driven more than one person from him in abject terror. It was not something he was even aware of, merely an expression that came naturally to him in times of stress.

Slate saw it, and cringed inwardly, but at that moment he

was less Lucas Slate and more Skinwalker. His eyes rolled in his head, and he looked on as the things that had been attacking fell and burned. One of the bats slammed into him from behind, shrieking in pain. Wide, triangular teeth were bared in that beast's mouth even as it smashed into Slate's side and pushed against him, clawed its way up his ribcage in a blind effort to escape its pain.

Slate fell to his knees and cried out as claws cut through fabric and into pallid flesh. His reaction was instinct, not planned, and Crowley observed as one of Slate's long arms lashed out, slapped the beast aside and then caught its head in his long-fingered grip.

The creature let out another shriek and then stopped making any noise at all as Lucas Slate, one of the gentlest souls Jonathan Crowley knew, shattered its skull in his deadly grip.

Embers and ashes filled the air along with the stink of burning fur and roasting flesh. The bat-things retreated, their cries of pain filling the air in all directions. Many of the things flew away, but others dropped where they were and shivered as they died.

After that, the night was overwhelmed with silence, and the two men had a chance to rest.

✤ ♗ ✤

Crowley slept.

Slate slept.

Neither intended to do so, but sometimes exhaustion beats even the mightiest into quiet submission.

They awoke to the sound of horses and men. Crowley opened one eye and saw a complete stranger staring down at him. The man had pistols, but they were holstered. That was a good start to the day.

Slate, on the other hand, had three men staring at him, and while they did not have weapons drawn, they looked decidedly nervous. Lucas Slate, being a wise man, sat up slowly and left his hands in sight.

"You speak Spanish?" The question was aimed at Crowley. The man doing the speaking was in a uniform that was dusty but otherwise in excellent shape. He and the men with him were all in uniforms, leading Crowley to believe they just might be the local military.

"I do," he responded in Spanish.

"Why are you here?"

"We're heading down Mexico way. The city, I mean."

The man nodded. "Have you been inside the pyramid?"

"No we have not."

"That's very good. You need to leave here immediately."

"But—"

"No! Right now the government is broken. There's a lot of debate as to who is in charge. That means that here and now, I'm the law and you will not dig into that pyramid to find any treasures, understood?" The man was genuinely angry at the notion.

"I just wanted to warn you that—"

"You do not listen! You will leave here, or I will bury you!"

Crowley closed his mouth and nodded. Then he mumbled, "As you say, you are in charge."

Slate looked his way and almost spoke, but then nodded instead.

Five minutes later the two of them were riding to the south at a slow but steady pace.

Slate waited five more minutes and then spoke. "I know they didn't want to hear it, but we could have warned them."

"Far be it from me to tell a fool what he doesn't want to hear, Mister Slate."

"And do you intend to ride away, Mister Crowley?"

"Of course not. We're going to leave the horses a ways off and then we're going back to the pyramid and wait."

"And what are we waiting for?"

"Sooner or later the bats will come out. When they do, they'll be plenty hungry. While they are distracted by their newest feast, we'll go inside the pyramid."

"You'd let those men die?"

"No sir. I'd gladly offer assistance if they were to ask for it. As they have not, I am powerless to do anything to help them."

Slate nodded and his thin lips drew a hard line across his gaunt face.

Crowley said, "You're upset with me. Feel free to tell me what I've done wrong."

Slate shook his head and sighed. "You have followed your own code of conduct, sir, and while I can respect that, those men will very likely die for it."

"Those men are not following the law of their land, Mister Slate. They are planning to find whatever profits are there to be found and to desecrate that pyramid for their own gains."

"And how can you be certain of that?"

"Because I better understand the nature of man than you do, I expect." Crowley sighed this time and shook his head sadly. "If they were here for the proper reasons, they would not have warned us away to avoid plunder. They would have told us the area is dangerous, or they would have found another reason. Instead we are accused of the very crime they will be committing."

"And how do you know that? I would like to believe in the better nature of men."

"So would I, Mister Slate. If only men would give me a solid reason to believe it."

"I find your cynicism unbecoming, Mister Crowley."

"As do I, sir. Sadly, that does not change the nature of my beliefs in the least." He stopped his horse, climbed down from the saddle, and then tied the reins to a rare tree in the area. Slate simply dropped the reins and climbed down from his saddle. His horse would go nowhere without him, and they both knew it.

In strained silence they started back toward the ancient temple. Crowley said, "Perhaps they will prove me wrong, Mister Slate. We'll know for certain when we get there."

Slate nodded but did not speak. He kept himself busy checking the various weapons he was carrying. Entering the pyramid meant chaos, pure and simple and bloody at that.

It was nearly an hour before they reached their destination and they approached cautiously. Simply put, neither was in the mood to be shot by federales.

The federales, it seemed, were already busy. As Crowley had predicted the men had started into the pyramid, and while there was little to hear, he had no doubt that things were going to get interesting before anyone settled down.

Slate opened his mouth to make his opinion known and Crowley said nothing. After several seconds, the retired undertaker followed his example and then shook his head and sighed.

The first shots were followed almost immediately by the first screams.

✝ 🍷 ✝

Hernandez shook his head and bit back a scream of frustration The men were doing the best they could under the circumstances. The way into the old stone structure was narrow at the best spots and narrower still in the areas where they needed the passageways to open properly.

Marcos, moving ahead of him and doing his best to remain calm in the areas that felt like a tomb, cursed softly and took rapid breaths. Marcos did not like enclosed areas, but like everyone else, he liked the idea of gold enough to overlook that fact. Still, the small man was sweating heavily and his complexion was pasty under his tan.

"Are you well, Marcos?"

"I'll survive, jefe, as long as the fortune we hope for is here."

Somewhere below them the chaos started. Whatever it was that made that noise, it was enough to make Hernandez shake his head to escape the ringing vibration that tickled his ears. "What is that noise?"

Marcos looked back his way for a moment and started to speak, but before a word came from his mouth, a black-fingered hand reached up from the shadows and slashed at his chest and stomach.

Marcos screamed in surprise and pain, and fell back against the stone wall. The long fingers clawed at him a second time, opened his belly as if he were a fish being cleaned for dinner. Whatever it was that killed the man wasted no time beginning to eat. The face was shoved into Marcos' stomach and wet noises spilled from the man, even as he let out a death howl.

Hernandez was not a coward, but whatever killed his companion was savage and fast and looked as far from human as anything he could imagine. He saw little beyond the large ears and the reflected gleam in the eyes of the beast.

His pistol was out and firing a second later. It might not be human but the creature bled and screamed as a bullet sheared away part of its face.

Whatever the monster might be, it retreated. Too late to save Marcos, who trembled and bled, and spoke directly to God, begging for mercy that was not destined to show itself.

Hernandez looked past the dying man and waited. If what had been there seconds before came back, he would kill it.

That sound again, louder this time, more insistent. He knew the noise, of course. He had grown up not far from caves where the bats came out in the night and searched for insects to eat, but this was different. Louder for one and coming from below him instead of from a cave. He had seen the statue of a winged man and scoffed at the notion, but he wasn't laughing any longer.

They came from below, singing their bat-songs and crawling up the sides of the tunnel. Lopez and Luis both opened fire as the things neared, and Hernandez saw them in the light of each muzzle flash.

The faces were hideous, masses of wrinkles around noses that pointed upward, against dark eyes that gleamed in the meager light, but worse were the mouths filled with dagger-sharp teeth. Each time those terrible mouths opened, fangs were bared, and the ringing-screech of the demon-bats came to his ears and sent him reeling.

Luis screamed and tried to retreat, but there was nowhere for him to go. A dozen men were ahead of Hernandez and fifteen more behind him. They had expected a simple enough task, finding the treasures buried in the great structure and carrying them out. What could possibly be alive after so long in the ground? But no, this was so much worse than anyone could have expected.

The faces of the things opened to bare those nightmarish teeth and then three of them were on Luis, biting, tearing, feasting.

Arturo Luis, a good man, a brave man, died screaming. Hernandez doubted he ever hit anything with his bullets or, if he did, the creatures hardly seemed to care.

"Retreat! Back the way you came!" He motioned for the men above him to climb, but they continued pressing against him.

Somewhere above him one of the men tried repeating his orders, but if anyone was listening you could not have proven it to Hernandez. "Get the hell back up and out of here, do you hear me?"

He dared look back just as the shadowy shapes crawled over Lopez and pulled him from his feet. Lopez shrieked and tried to fire his revolver, but he'd run out of bullets. While he tried to reload the demons tore at him with claws and teeth. The poor wretch was pulled down by the hellish things and, a moment after, his screams ended. Below there was only darkness now, as the men who'd been ahead of Hernandez, a dozen in all, were silenced and whatever lights they'd held were extinguished or buried under the hell coming his way.

When they came for him, they came quickly, crawling up the narrow tunnel, impossible arms gripping at any handholds, even the ones that could not be seen. Hernandez aimed, fired, hit one of the things in the throat and sent it careening backward. It did not fall far before other demons were grabbing for it, pulling it close as if holding a lover, and then tearing away meat and blood. He did not celebrate his quick victory, but instead fired again, again, hitting more of the things and knowing that whatever damage he did wouldn't be enough to stop the tide.

Up above him a man stood between him and escaping. "Get back up the passage, you damned fool!" The narrow entrance to the pyramid was filled with warm bodies, men who, like Hernandez, wanted the gold that must surely wait somewhere below. He'd heard of such structures, of their wondrous treasures, enough gold to make all of them wealthy.

Now, he'd have traded all of it for the chance to escape.

Somewhere below him a new sound came, deeper, louder, monstrous.

The things he had seen as demons came for him then, no longer seeming hungry, but instead desperate.

He understood how they felt.

✟ ♆ ✟

The hike to the top of the pyramid was longer than expected, made worse by the growing heat of the day. Crowley made no complaint and neither did Slate.

Both men were tired, but the sounds of screams drove them on. Much as Crowley refused to acknowledge how much he wanted to make others safe, he still climbed the steep, broken path of stairs, moving faster as the desperate cries from above them grew closer.

"I fear we are too late, Mister Crowley."

Crowley said nothing in return, but his lips pressed together and he scrambled faster still over the rough stairs. The gunfire and screams faded as if to cement Lucas Slate's declaration. He did so hate it when the man was right.

The statue they'd seen before was much larger than expected when up close. What had appeared merely man-sized was nearly twelve feet in height, with widespread wings, and a fearsome face.

Crowley grunted as he walked past the monstrous thing and headed for the pit descending into the vast structure.

The bats got there first. Desperation made them crazed, it seemed, for the things came into the bright light of day with no consideration of the sun or its glare. The bestial faces cringed, and the sunlight illuminated the hideous visages as more of the things climbed free from their pit.

Crowley retreated, eyes wide. He had not expected the creatures to brave the full sun of the day. They were nocturnal, after all. Mostly he couldn't fathom what might drive the things from their relative peace.

The entrance into the pyramid was a wide one, easily ten feet around, in a circle that apparently led to a ladder, or possibly even stairs, it was impossible to clearly tell beyond the darkly-furred bodies scrambling into the daylight.

Lucas Slate looked on and shook his head. Crowley was still too close to the things, though for the moment they seemed to ignore him.

"Might I suggest retreat, Mister Crowley?" Knowing that he was down to a small handful of shotgun shells he nonetheless aimed at the closest creature and then pulled at Crowley's shoulder.

Crowley shook off Slate's hand and shook his head. "There's something amiss here, Mister Slate."

"Yes, you're standing far too close to the damned things crawling from below."

"They should not be coming out yet, Mister Slate!"

"That will not stop them from killing you!"

"I beg to differ, sir." Crowley stood his ground as the bat-creatures moved away from him and into the air, flapping furiously to gain height rather than plummet downward. They were as wasted away as the previous lot but did not approach, did not attack. Slate stared on, surprised.

"This is much worse, I fear, Mister Slate."

"How do you suppose, Mister Crowley? We are alive."

"If they aren't hungry for us, then they run from something worse than their own starvation."

Slate did not have a chance to ask what that something might be before the great roaring sound burst from within the pyramid, even as more of the winged demons took flight.

Crowley backed away a step and got no further before the claws reached up from within and hooked along the stone of the pyramid's surface. The hand that led to those claws was larger than should have been possible, and as both men watched, the darkness below them bloomed into a nightmare.

First one hand and then the next reached up, finding purchase and then the great shape began to force itself through the opening that was never designed to hold such a shape. If the pyramid was meant to be home, the exit was too small for what it housed. If it was meant to be a prison, the creature within refused to be captive any longer.

Whatever the case, the dark form forced itself from below, breaking the massive stones of the structure, shoving its obscene shape into the light. It screeched its outrage at being imprisoned even as it broke free.

Both Crowley and Slate backpedaled as the thing knocked aside the very stone on which they stood. Neither man was prepared for how large the nightmare was. Or how strong.

It pushed itself up, rising higher and higher knocking aside the stone effigy to it that had rested atop the pyramid for the Lord alone knew how many years. The carved icon collapsed and bounced its way down to the far distant ground.

Dust and debris fell away from the vast, thickly furred obscenity, and the great beast raised its wings above its body, stretched those wings toward the heavens and screeched into the air, even as it squinted against the glare of the sun.

"Well, that's damned big." Crowley spoke as softly as his companion in that moment. The beast heard him just the same and turned its head toward him.

Jonathan Crowley froze in place, his eyes locked on the fathomless depths of eyes as old as time. Throughout his years he had encountered many creatures, many beings of vast power and age and here was one of the oldest he had ever crossed paths with. In seconds, his mind was filled with the beast's thoughts.

Camazotz

His mind locked on the thing towering over him, reeled at the depth of its memories, of the endless, gnawing hunger that filled it with dark, murderous rage. How many crawling centuries had it lived? How long ago had it been forced into the ground, driven into Mictlan by the enemy, Mictlantecuhtli? Its followers driven into the underworld, forced into servitude? How had the great, skull-faced god of the dead defeated him so quickly?

Crowley did not move, his mind overwhelmed by the fury of the dark beast.

The creature continued to stare at him, to force its mind into his, hungry, outraged, boiling over with the need to—

Crowley grunted as he was shoved aside. Lucas Slate pushed the smaller man to his left, roughly, and then aimed his shotgun at the scarred and ancient face of the bat-thing before pulling the trigger.

The membranes of the beast's snout blew back in a wave of blood and meat. The left eye of Camazotz exploded. The great head of the beast reared back and then snapped forward. Teeth as large as swords came down and clashed together, tearing Lucas Slate's face, peeling away most of his nose and part of his mouth, despite his efforts to dodge the attack.

Slate fell back, howling in pain as the god-bat lunged for him again.

Jonathan Crowley's eyes were bleeding. The god had pushed into his mind, made itself at home inside his skull after forcing its way into him through his eyes. The end result was not pretty. The pain had started at his eyes and bored into him as surely as Slate's buckshot had torn into the monster.

"That's enough out of you." Crowley attacked. He used the same method that had been used against him and forced his will into the beast, locking minds with a creature that sought either to defeat him or communicate, he did not care which. As was always the case when he dealt with the supernatural, the itching sensation started where he was wounded. His eyes watered furiously.

Neither Hunter nor Godling moved. Both grew as still as the stone upon which they stood. Both bled. Blood spilled from eyes and ears as they fought. The hunger and fury of Camazotz sought to overwhelm the cold rage of Jonathan Crowley and failed.

Lucas Slate, wounded and in deep pain, did not rest while this occurred. His face burned, but his wounds were not fatal. Much as it pained him, he rose to his feet and looked at the man he wanted to call a friend, and at the creature that had very nearly killed him. Since he had met Crowley, the man had offered a strange blend of companionship, nightmares, and wisdom.

The bat-like thing had tried to eat his face.

Slate lifted his shotgun again, pumped another round in place, and shot the ugly bastard thing in its other eye.

Blinded to the sun and full of hatred, Camazotz snapped at Slate again. This time he got out of its way and fell on his ass before it could sink those massive fangs into any part of him.

Crowley stared at the thing and felt his rage grow. Twice it had invaded his mind, defiled the one place where he was normally safe from the world. "That's enough out of you."

Blinded, it still sought out Lucas Slate. The great body forced itself the rest of the way from the stone prison and crawled along the top of the pyramid, determined to kill the thing that blinded it.

Slate was just as determined not to die and retreated, pumped his shotgun, pulled the trigger and sighed when nothing happened. His eyes narrowed even more than usual, and his hands held the weapon as if it were his only possible safety.

"Not a good time to run out of shells, Mister Slate." Crowley stepped back as the blinded god snapped at the sound of his voice. It did not pursue him, for which he was grateful.

"It bit my face off." Slate dug into his pockets, seeking any more shells for his shotgun. His search was fruitless, but the bat-thing came for him again.

"Hardly. You are still speaking. A little blood, sir. Bats have frightfully good hearing. Some people say they hear better than they see." The great creature lunged for Crowley again and he pulled back. "We'd do well to remember that."

Slate said nothing. Instead he set down his shotgun and closed his eyes, his lips moving softly even as they bled across his chin.

"To be fair it's mostly your nose. The rest of your face is still intact."

Slate ignored him. Crowley continued talking as the thing came for him, lunging sporadically. It might have been more intent if it weren't so badly wounded. "You were right. This is the thing being worshipped as a god. Or at least it was. I don't believe it has any more followers."

It might well be the creature understood his words, as it came closer again and seemed more determined than before. The great form lunged and snapped and flapped wings as large as schooner sails that generated a wind strong enough to stagger the Hunter.

If he expected an answer from Lucas Slate, he was disappointed. It was not the undertaker who looked at him from Slate's eyes. The pale blue color of his eyes was replaced by a deep, nearly endless black.

It was the Skinwalker.

It was the Skinwalker, speaking with Slate's voice that said, "Thou shalt have no other gods before Me."

It was the Skinwalker that struck the killing blow. Without a single step taken, the dead-white thing that shared a body with Lucas Slate lashed out. A light brighter than the noonday sun erupted from the eyes of Lucas Slate and bathed the great bat creature. It reared back one last time and shrieked in pain before freezing in place momentarily.

That hideous, white light seared flesh and burned fur. Camazotz flapped its wings harder, faster until it started to rise into the sky. The Skinwalker's gaze followed it, leaving it bathed in that same light. Crowley squinted against the obscene glare and watched on as the beast's wings split, membrane separating from bone and fluttering loosely, incinerated by the brilliance.

Camazotz rose higher still, and then turned back the way it had come arrowing down toward Lucas Slate.

The world grew so white that Crowley was blinded.

When he could see again, Lucas Slate stood surrounded by a thick fall of white ash. Large burnt bones were scattered across the top of the pyramid. That none of them had cracked either Slate or Crowley's skulls open was a bit of a miracle.

"What did you do, Lucas?"

The man looked his way. And it was Slate who stared at him. The difference in expression alone told him that.

"I assure you, Mister Crowley, I have no idea." Slate's deathly white face was marred. His nose was missing and the flesh around his lips was swollen with fresh scar tissue. Still, he was as healed as he was likely to be.

Crowley settled himself before he spoke again. It wasn't easy to do. Mostly he found himself very unsettled. Camazotz was gone, ruined by the Skinwalker.

"I do not think I like your counterpart, Mister Slate."

Slate nodded. "To be fair, he is not fond of you either, Mister Crowley."

"Are you well?"

"I am decidedly not well, sir! I have no nose."

"To be fair, there wasn't much of it left in any event, Mister Slate." It had rather withered since his transformation, a fact that Crowley had not brought up as it seemed impolite.

Slate glared at him for a moment and then, despite himself, he chuckled. "Damn you, Mister Crowley, for making me smile."

"Given a choice between smiling and scowling, I should rather smile, Mister Slate."

"Given a choice between your smile and my nose, I would rather my nose. Or lack thereof."

"Well, that's rather harsh."

"So is your smile, sir."

Crowley started down the pyramid's steep incline, careful with where he placed his feet. "Do you think they'll come back?"

"The bat creatures?" Slate looked around and finally spotted his hat far below on the descending stairs. He walked in that direction, gathering belongings as he went. "I imagine so, and I would rather not be here when they return."

"I imagine we can find ourselves closer to Mexico City before the sun sets."

"And why exactly are we going to Mexico City again?"

"I've heard a bit of how they celebrate their Dia de los Muertos."

"I do not speak Spanish, sir."

"Their Day of the Dead."

"Why exactly do we travel together, Mister Crowley?"

"I suppose you could say we've nothing better to do, Mister Slate."

"I expect I could find easier ways to spend my time."

"Why, I imagine that's true of both of us, Mister Slate, but I rather find I like your company."

"What will I do about my nose?"

"Not much to be done about it, Mister Slate. I expect you could make a new one out of wax. I've heard of several lepers managing to hide their condition in that fashion. Might take some practice, of course."

"I sometimes do not know when you are jesting, sir."

"I have often thought the same of you, sir."

"Tell me about this Day of the Dead."

"Well, it gets complicated. I'm afraid more than one god has been involved in its creation."

Mister Crowley spoke, and Mister Slate listened, and both forgot their troubles for a while.

Thanks for reading SNAFU: Last Stand.
We hope you've enjoyed it as much as we did putting it together.

Please consider leaving us a review if (and anywhere) you see fit. Any and all reviews are gratefully accepted.

If you have any questions, or want to quote from the book, please contact us at any time via our website contact page.

I would ask please, if you DO review online, send a link to Geoff via editor@cohesionpress.com or via our Facebook page messaging system. If you review for a magazine or paper, let us know and we'll buy it.

Thank you.

+ + +

Geoff Brown - Director, Cohesion Press.
Mayday Hills Lunatic Asylum
Beechworth, Australia

Amanda J Spedding - Editor-in-chief, Cohesion Press
Sydney, Australia

www.ingramcontent.com/pod-product-compliance
Lightning Source LLC
Chambersburg PA
CBHW030622250626
47154CB00006B/1885

9 7 8 1 9 2 5 6 2 3 4 2 0